I0823172

Dear Reader,

Melissa de la Cruz Studio is thrilled to introduce *The Sacred & the Divine*, a captivating new novel by Kate Christensen and Melissa Henderson that combines mystery, romance, magic, and the timeless allure of the tarot.

At the heart of this spellbinding tale are three sisters, Daisy, Morrigan, and Avery Wolfson (inspired by the real Fox sisters of history), each gifted with unique magical abilities that have been passed down through generations. Together, they face an ancient evil that threatens their community and their lives. From the turning of tarot cards to the handsome boys in their midst, they must discover what is real and true in the face of danger.

Fans of books like *The Night Circus* and *The Invisible Life of Addie LaRue* will fall head over heels for this intriguing, sexy adventure that is equal parts enchanting and thrilling. Its rich atmosphere and fast-paced plot make it an ideal recommendation for readers looking for a deeply immersive and emotionally charged read.

A co-creation by two talented writers making their YA debut—Kate Christensen, one of my favorite authors ever, and the amazing Melissa Henderson—*The Sacred & the Divine* is sure to become a must-read for anyone who loves a touch of magic with their historical romance. I could not be prouder to publish it!

Melissa de la Cruz

THE *Sacred* & THE *Divine*

XVII
THE STAR

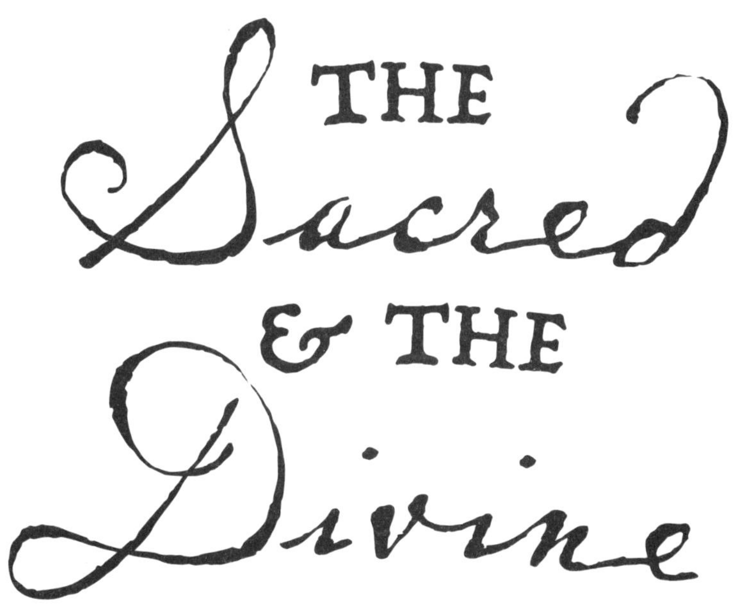

The Sacred & the Divine

KATE CHRISTENSEN AND
MELISSA HENDERSON

HYPERION
Los Angeles New York

Interior illustrations by Megan Laude

First Edition, October 2025
10 9 8 7 6 5 4 3 2 1
FAC-004510-25205

Printed in the United States of America

This book is set in Caslon Antique, Cochin/Monotype
and P22 Dearest, P22 Operina/Font Spring
Designed by Marci Senders

Library of Congress Control Number: 2024945687
ISBN 978-1-368-09943-1
Reinforced binding

The authorized representative in the EU for product safety and compliance is Disney Trading B.V., Asterweg 15S, 1031 HL, Amsterdam, The Netherlands
email: DCP.DL-EU.bookscontact@disney.com

Visit www.HyperionTeens.com

Logo Applies to Text Stock Only

FOR PIXIE

KNOWLEDGE
XIX
THE SUN

The Game of Tarot is a rhapsody of the most bizarre figures, the most extravagant. It is the World. I cast my eyes, and I recognize immediately the Allegory. Leave their Game and come see the wonderful Cards, where each one shows another. This is not the game of our imagination, but the relationship of everything we know. A discovery and a gift of this nature has escaped the barbarism, the ravages of time, fires both accidental and voluntary, to ignorance, which is even more disastrous.

–ANTOINE COURT DE GÉBELIN,
Monde Primitif (Livre VIII)

I declare
That later on,
Even in an age unlike our own,
Someone will remember who we are.

–SAPPHO,
Stung with Love: Poems and Fragments

Learn from everything, see everything, and above all feel everything! Find eyes within, look for the door into the unknown country.

–PAMELA "PIXIE" COLMAN SMITH,
On Reading the Cards

PROLOGUE

August 29, 1848, Redcliffe, Massachusetts. Shortly before dawn.

A young woman runs out of the forest, almost tripping but catching herself just in time, twin crimson points staining her pale, anxious face. Gasping, she peers into the darkness barely leavened by the milky haze of approaching dawn, sunrise not quite cusping the horizon, and beckons to her two sisters. Together, they hurry toward town, a fisherman's lantern casting a circle of muted light through the early morning gloom, wick low and flickering.

They hastily pull dresses and capes over their muslin chemises as they walk, relieved to find the sleepy streets deserted, no villagers in sight, though there's little chance of being seen. At this hour, proper citizens are tucked away in their beds.

But the Wolfson sisters aren't concerned with propriety. Or bedtime.

According to the Farmer's Almanac, this is the best time to catch the shadowed old moon nestled in a sliver of the new moon's arms.

The almanac failed to mention other, darker things their clifftop ritual might catch.

As the sisters creep into the yard of their small cottage on a rustic lane, far from the grand seaside houses of Redcliffe, the first rays of sunshine flicker through the marine layer, bathing the flower-strewn trellis in the palest pink.

In their haste, they don't notice the spectral flash at the edge of the garden, where tendrils of fog curl into shaded recesses of the trees.

They also do not see the thing that has followed them home.

CHAPTER O

THE FOOL

"The fool doth think he is wise, but the wise man knows himself to be a fool."

—WILLIAM SHAKESPEARE, *As You Like It*

Daisy was alone when the summons came. The out-of-breath delivery boy waited impatiently while she read: *My dear Misses Wolfson: My daughter Lizzie is unwell. Dr. Wellington cannot help. I would be so grateful if you could pay a visit at your earliest convenience. Yours, Mrs. Anne Cuttle.*

It was two days after the botched new moon ritual, but Daisy was still berating herself. How could she have been so careless? Kicking a foot through the protective salt circle! Morrigan and Avery had been horrified. And then the bonfire had gone out so suddenly. And all the torches!

Still, it was probably just the wind up there on the cliffs.

Morrigan, Daisy's fraternal twin, tended to worry. And Avery—at almost eighteen, a very important year and a half older than Daisy and Morrigan—took her role as the wise, level-headed one seriously. But Daisy also knew neither of them had been as enthusiastic as she had about performing the ritual from Kathryn's book. They'd insisted they weren't ready, but she'd pressed the matter, and they'd reluctantly given in.

Now Daisy found herself doubting every potential decision, terrified of making another foolish mistake. She reread the urgent note from Mrs. Cuttle, unsure what to do. Everyone was out. Their mother, Bernadette, had gone off first thing that morning to give piano lessons, and Morrigan and Avery had left on a mysterious errand after breakfast. Daisy normally wouldn't do a consultation on her own, particularly with her confidence at such a low. She hesitated.

The boy cleared his throat. "Sorry, miss, it's just..."

"Right," she said, making up her mind. "I'll come with you."

She threw on her cape and collected her reticule, the bag in which she kept her tarot cards and crystals, and hurried with him down the lane, failing to notice the slight disruption in the air just behind her, as if a small maelstrom were generated by something unseen, unknown, quivering darkly in her wake.

At the side entrance to Cuttle's Bakery on High Street, a slight, straw-haired girl whose pale face was drawn with worry flung open the door. Limping somewhat as she led Daisy up the stairs to the living quarters, she talked over her shoulder, her voice tight. "Mother's taken my two little brothers to school, and Lizzie's been so poorly. Oh, sorry, I'm Emily, Lizzie's sister. It's so good of you to come, Miss Wolfson!"

Daisy grinned at being addressed so formally. If she remembered correctly, Emily was twelve, only four years younger than her, but the girl was still outwardly a child, while Daisy had the curves and height of a young woman.

"Please call me Daisy," she said. "Have you injured your foot?"

"It's nothing," Emily said. "I missed a step and turned my ankle when I was hurrying downstairs. My own fault for being careless."

"Nonsense," Daisy said, "accidents happen."

She impulsively knelt down and encased Emily's ankle in her hands. Her palms warmed as she channeled quick bursts of healing energy into the injury.

"Goodness," Emily said. "They were right about you. I feel *much* better!"

Daisy had experienced this sort of reaction before, but she wasn't yet immune to a blush of pride when her healing touch worked.

That past spring, the night before Daisy and Morrigan turned sixteen, they had each been visited by strange dreams. Morrigan dreamed of the past, where she'd spoken to ghosts; Daisy's dreams had been of the future, conversations with people not yet born.

When Daisy and Morrigan told Avery, they were stunned to learn she'd had a similar experience. It turned out that, since her own sixteenth birthday, Avery had been able to see into the deepest parts of people's souls, almost reading their minds against her own will. Worried it was some sort of disturbance or mental aberration, she'd kept it to herself, hoping it would go away. But once their secret had been shared and divided in three, the sisters had emerged together into a collective awareness that they had a responsibility to honor these strange gifts.

As the months went by, word in Redcliffe had spread about the

Wolfson sisters and their unusual talents. They never knew when they'd come across a person in need of these curative abilities that seemed to be growing more powerful in all three of them. They'd taken to packing the tarot decks, crystals, and botanicals whenever they went out to save the trouble of having to go home and get them every time someone asked for a reading or healing . . . which happened more and more frequently.

In the front parlor, Lizzie lay very still on the fainting couch, eyes closed, breathing labored, her normally milky skin ashen. Daisy knew her only slightly; she was eighteen, a hardworking, shy girl who helped her mother look after her four younger siblings and assisted her father in the bakery below.

Daisy took the chair by Lizzie and sat quietly for a moment, eyes closed, gathering her first impressions before attempting treatment. In an instant, she saw an image so vivid it made her gasp: *black tentacles squeezing Lizzie's life force from her chest.*

"What is it?" Emily hovered. "Will she be all right?"

"Of course," Daisy replied automatically, though her heart beat furiously as she ran a finger down the inside of Lizzie's outflung arm. It was ice-cold, despite the fire burning in the parlor's hearth. From her pouch of crystals, she took out the rose quartz. She held it an inch or so directly above Lizzie's breastbone, allowing the crystal to connect just as Kathryn had taught her, explaining that healing crystals had been used for centuries by many cultures throughout history. Rose quartz regulated love, compassion, healing, and proper functioning of the circulatory system. In essence, the heart.

Lizzie suddenly gave a low moan and clutched Daisy's other hand. Her lips were dry and white. She seemed to be trying to speak. Then she let go and fell back again.

Daisy touched Lizzie's forehead. As cold as her hands. "She has no fever."

"That's good, isn't it, Miss Wol—I mean Daisy?"

"It is," Daisy soothed. Inside, however, she panicked about those black tentacles in Lizzie's chest. That she and her sisters saw the past, present, and future was all very well when they were together. But alone, all Daisy had was a blurry glimpse of something ominous happening at some unspecified time.

She felt a flash of anxious impatience, wishing her sisters were here to calm her and help discern what this Vision meant: Morrigan, to look into the past with her dreamy Piscean intuition and see whatever had caused the dark thing to take up residence in Lizzie Cuttle's rib cage, and Avery, ever the coolly analytical Libra, to analyze its intention in this moment.

An Aries by the skin of her teeth, Daisy had been born on March 21, in the first hour of the first sign in the zodiac's wheel, right after Morrigan, who had emerged in the final hour of the last sign of the circular year on March 20, still under the influence of Pisces. The two of them were so different that Daisy sometimes wondered how they could be twins, let alone related. Morrigan was thoughtful, watery-deep, and emotionally hidden, where Daisy was frank, quick to action, and full of fire.

Daisy settled the crystal directly atop Lizzie's starched navy shirtwaist to better allow it to connect with her heart and work its powerful magic. Then she reached into the pocket of her coat to pull out the hand-painted tarot deck she'd inked herself. Stilling her thoughts, she shuffled, cut the deck, and drew a card, placing it image-side down on the table next to the chaise. But before she could turn it over to reveal its message, a sudden gust of air blew it to the carpet, where it landed face up. She bit back a curse. "Is there a window open?"

Emily rushed to shut it, pulling the drapes closed. "I thought the fresh air might help."

Daisy forced a shaky smile. The girl was nervous enough.

The card had landed upright, but had it been upright when first pulled, or had it flipped when it fell? This was an important distinction. And now, the stakes felt unusually high.

Lizzie cried out. No time to dither. Daisy picked up the card and considered it closely.

The Fool: *A young woman dances at the edge of a cliff, sunlight refracted off her shining face. She balances a dogwood branch over her left shoulder, snowy blossoms swirling in her windswept curls. Hovering above the open palm of her right hand, a hummingbird dazzles in a blur of color.*

The Fool—or Card Zero—was the first card of the tarot, though some considered the Magician—titled Card One—to be the first of the twenty-two cards that comprised the Major Arcana of the tarot deck. But, as Kathryn explained, "It's the Fool who launches us into the journey through the deck; zero always comes before one."

This card came up so often for her, both upright and reversed, that Daisy had begun to think of it as her very own talisman. Headlong, daring, brash, foolishly brave, it also suggested a certain kind of divine protection from decisions others might consider, well, foolish.

"What does that card mean?" Emily's eyes widened. "It looks good. Is it?"

Upright, the Fool represented connections and synchronicity, the importance of trusting one's instincts and following essential desires regardless of the consequences. Reversed, however, the Fool was cautionary and foretold the potential of a nasty fall, a terrible mistake caused by foolhardy indiscretion.

Which was it?

"It means," Daisy said, the words pouring out as she impulsively chose to proceed as if the card had been upright all along, "that your sister is being kept from something she very badly wants."

"What can that be?"

"I don't know." But an image was forming, a new one: *Lizzie Cuttle passionately entwined in a mysterious stranger's arms.* Was this Vision a potential future or something that would definitely happen?

"I know Lizzie wants a new dress, but Father says we can't afford one this year," Emily was saying. "Is it that?"

Daisy regarded Emily sympathetically. The girl was already burdened by responsibility. Daisy had a sudden flash of the woman she would be decades from now: a content, unmarried college professor and doting aunt, delighting in her freedom from domesticity and motherhood. *How interesting!*

"When your sister wakes up," she told Emily, "tell her that I was here and said that the only cure is for her to follow her heart."

Emily nodded, alarmed but obedient.

With an uneasy feeling in the pit of her stomach, Daisy left the girl sitting by her heartsick sister.

Downstairs, she ducked into the bakery. While the counterboy selected a dozen fresh sugar-dusted doughnuts and packed them into a box for her, she watched Mr. Cuttle at work over a drum of bubbling fat. His pleasant round face glowed with heat.

When Daisy tried to pay, he shook his head, gesturing to put her money away. "Consider it a token for your services," he said in his gruff, shy way. "The doctor couldn't help her. I don't generally hold with such mumbo jumbo, no offense. But I'm so worried about my Lizzie, I'll try anything."

"Thank you, Mr. Cuttle. None taken. And I'm not sure I helped her either. But I did try."

Daisy walked along High Street in the fresh, brisk morning, inhaling briny sea air. The trees were already beginning to blaze yellow and orange, fall coming early this year even though it was only the last day of August. It was as though the seasons had changed overnight.

Just then, the wind kicked up a pile of dried leaves in a sudden violent gust, and Daisy shivered. She heard footsteps behind her, but when she turned, no one was there. The street was strangely empty for midmorning on a weekday.

Where had everyone gone? A muscle in her cheek twitched.

She was acting like a pigeon-livered child! It was a perfectly delightful day.

Nevertheless, she quickened her pace, anxious to get home. Well, she supposed it made sense after the stressful morning she'd had. And that awful—

Hands suddenly clamped down hard on her shoulders, a low voice in her ear. "Gotcha!"

Daisy whirled round to see a grinning face with a forelock of brown hair perpetually falling into puppy-dog eyes, spectacles askew as always, freckles ablaze in ruddy cheeks. "What are you doing sneaking up on me like that?" she snapped, almost dropping the doughnuts in her agitation.

"Nice to see you, too." Henry Graves snatched the bakery box from her and opened it. "Dearest Daisy, you shouldn't have."

"Those aren't for you!" She tried to wrest the box back, but he danced it out of her reach. She didn't mind; she was grateful for any distraction from her mortifying overreaction to one of Henry's typical pranks.

He was the ward of Daisy and her sisters' aunt Mary Blackwell—their late father Augustus Wolfson's widowed sister. After his parents had died in a house fire, Aunt Mary had taken him in. Having more money than she knew what to do with and no children of her own, Aunt Mary had always treated her orphaned nephew-by-marriage as an overindulged son, even naming him her heir. They'd all grown up together, wealthy Henry and the far less affluent Wolfson sisters, as close as family despite not being blood related. And in that moment, Henry was every inch the extremely irritating, slightly older cousin.

He stuffed a doughnut into his mouth as he fell into stride next to Daisy. "I was just on my way to your house. Hid behind some hedges to catch you up. Clever, aren't I?"

"Not nearly as clever as you think. And I thought you'd gone to Boston." Henry studied classics and philosophy at Harvard University's Divinity School in Cambridge.

"Well, I'm back. Obviously."

"I can see that. *Obviously*. But I thought you were supposed to be archiving books or something at your school's fancy library."

"Turns out archiving Aunt Mary's extensive collection of esoteric books on philosophy and language was even more interesting to my university advisor, so here I am again! And I brought a school friend of mine back with me. Jasper Fitzwilliam."

The unfamiliar name gave Daisy an odd jolt of recognition. She shook it off. She was so jumpy today!

Henry prattled on. "Poor Aunt Mary is not feeling well. I was coming to see if you'd mind looking in on her."

Not bloody likely, though Daisy knew better than to say that out loud. Her mother was always clucking about her "unseemly" language.

But she sensed two sickbed visits in one day would tax her fledgling powers. And if she were being entirely honest, she didn't much like Aunt Mary. She was a dry old stick and had drawn first blood with gimlet-eyed disapproval of Bernadette, and by extension her three daughters. It was one thing to be somewhat aloof. To treat her hard-working if humble family like tawdry poor relations? Unforgivable.

However, though Henry might have been spoiled and a little clueless, he himself was not a snob; there was something vulnerable about him, something a little off-kilter, like his eyeglasses. He never seemed fully present, as if his gangly body and mind were heading off in different directions. It made Daisy want to shake him and hug him simultaneously.

So she kept her heated thoughts to herself, instead saying mildly, "I'm not sure she'd appreciate my methods."

"Whatever works," said Henry. Also endearingly, he had never been dismissive of the three sisters' abilities, even after he'd become a student at an august, intellectual university. In fact, he was genuinely interested in their "research," as he called it.

Daisy was about to tell him about the exciting if unnerving cliff-top ritual the other night when he gave a shout and waved at an approaching figure, a tall, dark-haired young man striding along the road.

"I was just talking about you, Fitz!" Henry called. "This is my cousin Daisy. Be nice to her, she has doughnuts."

"I don't like doughnuts," said Jasper Fitzwilliam.

He and Daisy stared at each other for an instant, something sparking. A prickle went up the back of her neck. "Good," she said, "because they're not for you."

They exchanged another look, hostile, with something else.

Perhaps surprise that two ostensible strangers could take such an instant dislike to each other.

"I thought you were working in the library today," Henry was saying to his friend. "He's writing a book," he explained to Daisy. "A compilation of his mentor's lectures."

"I'm on my way to the apothecary for some tonic for your poor aunt." Jasper had a clipped way of speaking, precise and low, an elocution Daisy associated with wealthy young men who had their futures all laid out for them. "She's feeling unwell," he said, glancing at her.

"I'm not unaware," she shot back. Who was this officious prat? Mary Blackwell was her aunt, not his.

"I've just asked Daisy to pay her a visit," Henry hastened to add. "She has a way with healing."

Jasper raked an impatient hand through inky hair that contrasted starkly with his light-skinned, patrician features and regarded Daisy coolly from his rangy height. She was positive she saw him flare a nostril, just slightly. And his lip curled, just a little. "As I said," he told Henry, "I'm fetching a tonic. A medically approved curative, not some—" He stopped himself. "It was a pleasure to meet you, Miss . . ."

"Wolfson," Daisy said, matching his curt tone. "Have a good day, Mr. Fitzwilliam."

"Isn't he something?" Henry burbled as his friend strode off.

"He most certainly is," she muttered darkly, stalking past him as they crossed High Street. But in the middle of the road, she stumbled on the cobblestones where they met the sidewalk and dropped her reticule, spilling its contents everywhere. "Blast it!"

Laughing good-humoredly, Henry knelt beside her to help collect the scattered items, then whooped, "Look! It's your sisters!"

Glancing up, Daisy saw Avery and Morrigan standing over her.

"We found Mrs. Cuttle's note and came as soon as we could," said Avery, hitching her skirt and crouching down to help. Morrigan joined her, and soon they had everything, and themselves, safely on the sidewalk and out of the way of the carriages and horses.

Then they all saw it: a small box of phosphorous matches.

"You had matches?" Morrigan exclaimed. "That whole time?"

"We had a ritual the other night," Avery was saying to Henry. "There was . . . an incident with the flint and steel. Daisy may have mentioned."

"She did not!" Henry said, his eyes lighting up.

"An incident that nearly took my hand off," Morrigan said. She extended her palm.

"It's barely a scratch," Daisy said, kicking a pebble, to Avery's great amusement.

"It hurt quite a bit! Still does," Morrigan insisted.

"Your poor little hand," Henry murmured, bringing Morrigan's palm to his lips. "Shall I kiss it better?"

Morrigan's ivory cheeks pinkened, and she snatched her hand back. "Don't be ridiculous," she huffed primly, absently patting at her shiny dark hair, though her bun was smooth as always.

Daisy and Avery smirked at each other.

"Anyway, if we'd known you had matches, we wouldn't have had to use the flint and steel," Morrigan said.

"They were a safeguard!" Daisy protested.

"But not actually so safe," said Avery. "Think of Fossy."

"Fossy" was the unkind nickname the town had coined for the local woman who had lost the lower half of her jaw in an accident at the match factory when the phosphorous exploded onto her face.

Avery tucked a stray chestnut curl behind an ear. "There's a reason they're called Lucifer matches."

"Well, the devil's in the details." Henry murmured.

They all chuckled at that, including Daisy, even if it was at her expense. On the upside, at least they'd been distracted from the topic of the botched ritual, and her error in breaking the salt circle, which was the last thing she wanted to talk about.

Curses! She'd spotted Jasper rounding the corner at the end of the street. Thankfully, he paused to step into another shop along the way, and she took the opportunity to get things moving. She had no intention of waiting around for another run-in with Henry's pompous friend.

"You mentioned Aunt Mary was ailing?" Daisy reminded Henry. "Let's go see her!"

"But you said—"

Daisy cut him off with a breezy wave. "We're always happy to look in on our favorite aunt." She avoided her sisters' shocked expressions. "Morrigan, Avery, it's good you're here. Aunt Mary may need our services." She didn't add that she was also concerned about her own potentially disastrous diagnosis of poor Lizzie Cuttle. There'd be time enough to address that tangled ball of wax later.

CHAPTER I

THE MAGICIAN

"Magick is the science and art of causing change to occur in conformity with Will."

—ALEISTER CROWLEY, *Magick in Theory and Practice*

The old fishing village of Redcliffe was situated on the jutting outer elbow in the long, bent arm of Cape Cod. The town was laid out like a scallop's shell, its fan of intersecting streets curving in widening arcs from Codfish Cove, where the narrow harbor was filled with boats. At dawn, Redcliffe's fleet of fishermen rowed out to ply the steely blue waves for groundfish, amassing their daily hauls of slippery cod and haddock. At night, the town's two new lighthouses shone their warnings to any sailor still out at sea.

The stately Blackwell House presided over Shore Road, otherwise known as Society Row. As the sisters were pulled along in Henry's wake, Daisy marveled at the opulence of the exclusive district. Aunt Mary's late husband, a shipping magnate, had commissioned one of the grandest of the mansions overlooking the ocean, the oldest of which had been built by sea captains coming back from the southern hemisphere with sperm oil. These sprawling manors were all topped with filigreed walkways that captains' wives were expected to pace in all weather, publicly yearning for their husbands' return. But Daisy and her sisters had heard stories of the pleasurable mischief some wives got up to in their husbands' long absences before scrambling up to their widow's walks to preserve propriety at the first sight of a returning ship.

Beyond the town's outer borders was the deep, wild forest the girls had explored since childhood, gathering herbs and flowers, playing fairy games in the glades, flinging themselves onto mossy knolls for picnics with Henry. Thronged with birdsong, fragrant with needles and sap, dappled with the changing coastal light, these woods were every bit as magical as Redcliffe's long, sandy beaches. And though she yearned to travel someday, Daisy knew she'd always return home to Redcliffe, the most beautiful place on earth.

As they rounded the final corner and Blackwell House came into sight, Daisy felt a cold pressure on the back of her neck, just briefly, and then it was gone. A brief memory of chaotic, terrible dreams rushed into her mind, and then they, too, were gone. Perhaps that's what was wrong with her today. She certainly hadn't slept well the night before, or the one before that.

Henry escorted Daisy and her sisters up the granite steps through the heavy oaken door with its iron knob. They followed him into the dim hall past a startled Mr. Miggs, Aunt Mary's long-suffering manservant, a tall, slightly stooped man with weathered brown skin. Mr. Miggs's attempts to take their outer garments were ignored as Henry swept his cousins up the curved staircase to the second-floor landing and into the grande dame's sitting room.

Not one to languish in bed with a tea tray, Aunt Mary sat ramrod-straight in an armchair by the window, a book in her lap, and glared at the intrusion with her usual disapproving air. Instantly, Daisy was aware that her own hair was windblown, her cheeks still flushed, her simple dress a far cry from the fussy fashions of the elite. Avery and Morrigan seemed to be taking similar stock of themselves.

"You brought the girls," the elderly woman observed, speaking only to Henry, as if Daisy and her sisters had attached themselves to the poor boy like stowaway remoras.

"I found Daisy buying doughnuts on High Street, then came Morrigan and Avery. They heard you were feeling poorly."

"Doughnuts. How quaint. Well, girls, you've saved me having to write a letter to your mother, at least. I'm having a dinner party for our houseguest, and it might do him good to have the diversion of you three. And your mother, too, of course. I'll expect you all at seven o'clock, sharp, on Friday evening. I'll send a carriage."

"Oh" was all Daisy could muster.

Avery rose to the occasion. "We'd be delighted."

"Truly," Morrigan added.

"I should think so." Aunt Mary sniffed. "You hardly get out into polite society much, do you."

Instead of rising to the bait, Daisy made a discreet assessment of the unwilling patient. Aunt Mary looked normal enough, not that that was saying much. She was far too thin, as usual. But the sharp planes of her cheekbones had a hectic rouge that looked like fever. And a dark rash shadowed the thin parchment skin around her eyes and nose like a strange mask.

"Are you more tired than usual?" Daisy asked, her intuition prickling. "Do your joints ache?"

Aunt Mary's nostrils twitched as she regarded her upstart of a niece, the youngest daughter of the French Catholic Acadian orphan her younger brother had insisted on marrying. Redcliffe's upper crust still saw Bernadette LeBlanc Wolfson this way, even though she had converted to Protestantism and was the most devout churchgoer in town. Ever since she'd been widowed, Bernadette hadn't had anyone to protect her from the chatter of this small town's society women, the most judgmental species known to humankind. And Aunt Mary was the queen bee of them all.

"Why, yes." Aunt Mary narrowed her eyes. "How did you know?"

Daisy reached into her reticule and hefted her small pouch of crystals, the stones inside tumbling with a satisfying *clack* in the silk pouch.

But before she could select one, Aunt Mary's face lit up. "Jasper," she said, her voice suddenly honeyed.

"I've brought you this from the apothecary," said Jasper Fitzwilliam at the doorway, striding in to offer a small brown glass bottle with a stoppered lid.

"I am so grateful to you, dear."

Daisy stifled a snort. Aunt Mary was practically purring. It was as if this Jasper person had her under a spell. Avery and Morrigan caught Daisy's eye, and they all had to look away quickly to avoid laughing.

"It's laudanum," Jasper said with a quick glance at Daisy. "The best thing for your symptoms, two drops in water every hour."

"Don't take that," Daisy snapped. "It'll make you stupid and sleepy, and you'll become dependent if you use it for too long."

"Daisy!" Aunt Mary gasped.

"My sister is not wrong, Aunt Mary," said Avery, her innate knowledge of plants prodigious.

"It's the juice of the poppy." Jasper shot another censorious look at Daisy. For a brief flash, she saw herself through his eyes: a silly girl with a wild tangle of red hair and a disrespectful attitude, green eyes blazing far too bright for this proper room with its brocade wallpaper and heavy furniture. "A *plant*! Surely you can't disapprove of that."

"Plants can be dangerous in the wrong hands." Daisy slid her bag of crystals back into her coat pocket. "I'd think someone of your education, Harvard and all, would know that."

The room went silent, Daisy's sisters too astonished by her outburst to speak, even twitchy Aunt Mary lost for words. Though Daisy could feel her sisters' silent agreement, she knew they were far too tactful to fan the flames of the argument.

"We haven't been properly introduced," said Jasper to Avery, correctly guessing her to be the one in charge. "I'm Jasper Fitzwilliam."

Avery nodded. "I'm Avery Wolfson, and these are my sisters, Morrigan and Daisy, though it appears you've already met Daisy." She glanced speculatively from him to her youngest sister.

"I have indeed." With a pointed flick of a glance at Daisy, Jasper bowed slightly to Avery and Morrigan. "I am pleased to meet you both."

Daisy's face was flaming. "My sisters and I bid you all good day," she said, mentally willing Avery and Morrigan toward the door.

"Don't forget to tell your mother," Aunt Mary called. "Friday night!"

Outside, Daisy lifted her face to the sun, welcoming its warmth, swinging her *quaint* box of doughnuts with insouciance. She was glad to get out of that stifling place and away from that horrible man. The arrogance!

"What was all that about?" said Avery as they walked toward Main Street.

"If I didn't know better, I would say you and Mr. Fitzwilliam had a long-standing feud," said Morrigan.

"Have you ever taken an instant dislike to someone?" Daisy asked. Then she frowned. "Where were you two this morning?"

"We went to see Kathryn," said Avery, pausing ever so slightly. "We didn't want to alarm you. We consulted her about . . . the break in the circle."

Daisy stopped in her tracks. When she and her sisters had become aware of their shared gifts, they had naturally sought out Kathryn, the town's foremost herbalist and soothsayer. Since then, Kathryn had been guiding the sisters in their developing powers, sharing her ancient book of spells, explaining its meanings and uses, and educating them in tarot, crystals, and herbalism.

Daisy and her sisters hadn't mentioned their budding clairvoyance to their mother, but Bernadette was no fool. Though she hadn't said anything about Kathryn's teachings and hadn't outright forbidden them to consult her, they also knew perfectly well that she didn't like it.

Bernadette was tightlipped about her past, but it was obvious that there was some deep rift between her and Kathryn. They had been raised together as girls at the convent in Falmouth after both were orphaned at a young age. It was rumored they had once been inseparable best friends, as close as sisters, but now, they no longer spoke, and Daisy and her sisters had no idea why. Neither Kathryn nor their mother cared to discuss it.

After her sisters, Kathryn was Daisy's most trusted confidant, but her heart sank to think she knew of her gaffe the other night.

"You told her I smudged the—"

"We didn't," Avery said. "That's why we went first, so we could share the blame."

"You're both so loyal," Daisy said, chastened.

"Just go see her." Morrigan put a steadying arm around her shoulders.

The sisters parted at the crossing of High Street and Forest Road, and Daisy hastened toward the forest, where Kathryn's cottage was tucked away in a small orchard of apple and pear trees. She found Kathryn in her garden.

"There you are," Kathryn said, though she had her back to Daisy and couldn't have heard her silent footsteps on the grassy path. "Come and help me tie up these squash vines."

Kathryn Herlihy was small and sturdy, with silver-threaded auburn hair she wore in a simple braid. Though she was more than twice Daisy's age, her creamy skin was mostly unlined, with freckles and a snub nose set into a wide face that exuded clarity and purpose. Daisy trusted her wholly because she was always honest, even when it was painful.

"Kathryn, I might have made a dreadful mistake." The words came tumbling out as Daisy held the vines against the stakes so Kathryn could tie them up. "Lizzie Cuttle—she's unwell. I'm worried I misread the cards. The Fool was upright at first but flipped itself in a breeze. I think she's in the grip of an infatuation she's denying, maybe because she was taught to marry for money, not love? I gave her sister instructions to tell her to follow her heart. But what if I was wrong? What if the Fool was reversed all along, and that's a dangerous path? And then we visited Aunt Mary, who's ailing, but

I couldn't help her either, all because of Jasper, that pigheaded..." Daisy ran out of steam.

Kathryn said nothing as they moved along the garden's rows, just handed Daisy a basket and began pulling herbs and piling them into it. Daisy caught a small uplift of the corner of her mouth. They worked in silence for a few moments.

"What can I do?" Daisy burst out finally.

Kathryn shot her a look, not unsympathetic. "What you can do is quiet yourself and practice breathing deeply to still your mind."

Daisy blushed. Impatience was her worst flaw. After temper. And impulsiveness. And...oh, how would she ever overcome the overwhelming list of her shortcomings if she couldn't even organize them in her own mind?

"Your fire sparks your gift," Kathryn said. "But it can burn you up. Now what's this about...Jasper, was it?"

"Oh, him! He's nobody. I just let him get under my skin is all. He's just a..." She flailed for words.

"Pighead?"

"He doesn't even merit discussion!"

"Clearly. So let's see what they say."

Daisy glanced down and was startled to see she'd pulled the tarot deck out of her reticule, having shifted the basket to the crook of her elbow without realizing.

Kathryn nodded. "The cards always know when they need to be read."

Daisy quickly ruffled the deck, cut it, and slid out the Magician card. *Strange.* The Magician was the next Major Arcana card in the deck after the Fool. But she was certain she'd shuffled the deck.

Kathryn regarded Daisy's rendering of the card: *A figure with a head of black curls stands in a cave of magic treasures, one hand bearing a wand aloft, the other holding a thick leather-bound book. His ivy-belted monk's robe is decorated with golden symbols of cups, coins, and swords. His sidelong, dark gaze is merry but commanding. A green parrot sits in the rowan tree behind him.*

"Well, that's interesting," Kathryn said, tilting her head. Her eyes sparkled, looking into Daisy's. "It's too early to know for sure, and I've only seen it happen once—"

"Seen what happen?" Daisy interrupted excitedly.

"This! The Fool's Journey, which is when you pull the Major Arcana cards one after another, in order. It's very rare."

"But I didn't pull the last card for myself. It was—"

"Makes no difference. You're part of the reading, no matter your role," Kathryn said. "It's also called the Hero's Journey, though in your case, perhaps we should call it the Heroine's Journey."

"You mean I'm . . ." Daisy couldn't finish the sentence. The sheer audacity of it.

"So it appears. You have to let it unfold. If your next card ends up being the High Priestess, we'll know for certain," Kathryn said as Daisy rewrapped the cards in their protective cloth.

A shadow passed over Kathryn's face. "Meanwhile, about your moon ritual the other night." She said it lightly, but her eyes were sharp.

"I know my sisters told you *we* stepped through the salt and broke the circle, but it was me. It was my fault." Daisy sighed.

"Breaking the salt circle is serious enough, but I'm more worried about the timing of the ritual."

"What, the new moon?"

"The new moon is just beginning now."

"But I consulted the almanac carefully," Daisy insisted, her face growing hot again. "It was the very first day of the new moon."

"This is what I worried about when you rushed off with that book. You've been careless, Daisy. The astronomical new moon is when the moon lacks all illumination in the days leading into the transition toward the waxing crescent."

"Yes but—"

"Which is not," Kathryn cut her off, "the same lunar phase we use for rituals. What the astronomers call new, we consider dark, or dead. These practices predate astronomy. I don't suppose you read the next chapter about dark moons, also called dead moons?"

A tingle ran down Daisy's spine. "A . . . dead moon?"

"Yes." Kathryn sighed. "This lunar phase is an extremely powerful time for casting out negative energies and unwanted entities, habits, or diseases. Because of its great potency, it's all too easy to fall prey to any malevolence it might attract."

"But the book—"

"What the book means by *new moon* is the true waxing of the crescent moon a few days after the dark moon, when the crescent is fully visible in the sky." The older woman's tone was the more foreboding for its evenness.

"Oh no," Daisy breathed. She felt near tears.

Kathryn pulled Daisy into her arms. "Hush," she murmured. "You know now. Just promise you'll take more care in the future."

Daisy was grateful for the warmth of Kathryn's embrace. "I'll never be foolhardy again!"

"Is that a promise?"

It felt good to laugh.

Later, as Daisy made her way home through the forest, she imagined she was already forging her own path. She trailed her fingers along the vines that twined around the trunks of the trees, reminded of the ivy belt the Magician wore. Was Kathryn right about this being the start of her own Heroine's Journey? Daisy was eager to find out.

Coiled around the base of a tree, close enough to fang an unsuspecting ankle, a formless savagery of venom shimmered in the underbrush, seething in Daisy's direction, furious at being dragged from its quiet if unwitting prison.

You don't even notice me, do you? Would you startle if you did? Poor Lizzie couldn't.

If Daisy's newfound ability to envision aspects of the future had developed further, she might have foreseen that the Magician's belt would one day be drawn as the ouroboros, a ravenous snake devouring its own tail endlessly throughout time.

This snake was also hungry. And it would feed.

You'll soon hang yourself with that rope of ivy. But skip along for now, little fool.

Daisy was right about one thing. This journey would change her life.

And then the hellish entity she'd invoked would take what was left of it.

CHAPTER II

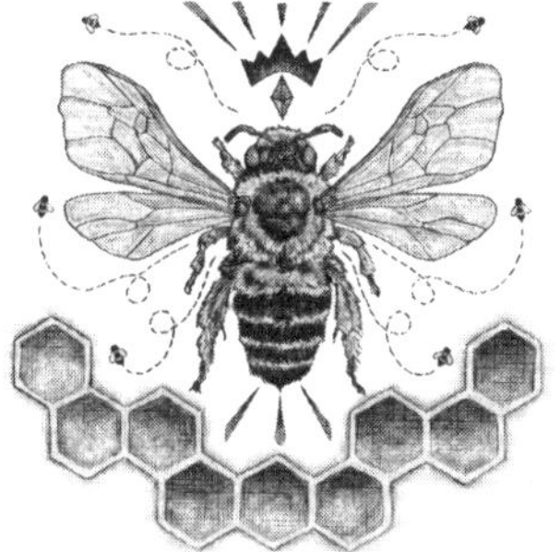

The High Priestess

> "Lady of all powers,
> in whom light appears,
> Radiant one
> Beloved of Heaven and Earth,
> Tiara-crowned Priestess of the Highest God,
> My Lady, you are the guardian
> Of all greatness."
>
> —Enheduanna, "The Hymn to Inanna"

"No, I've got it." Daisy waved Morrigan off, trying to sew herself into her bodice.

The question of what to wear to Aunt Mary's party had been occupying the sisters all week. Daisy had redesigned one of Avery's cast-off gowns by taking up the hem two inches and letting it out on the top. It had a tight waist and flared bell skirt and was a shade of bottle green that nicely set off her hair. She'd thought herself very clever until her impatient fingers fumbled and she stabbed herself with the needle.

An angry bead of blood welled. "Putain!"

"Daisy! You know Mother doesn't like us speaking French," Morrigan said. "Not to mention cursing."

"It's not a curse if it's not about God," Daisy mumbled, sucking on her wound. Embarrassed, she let Morrigan take the needle.

Avery plucked a linen hankie from her bodice and gave it to her youngest sister. "When Morrigan's got you all tucked in, come do something with my ridiculous hair. Assuming you haven't lost too much blood from your injury."

"Funny." Daisy rolled her eyes. Avery's barbs were always unerringly well aimed. It was one of her most annoying qualities, and also one of her best.

While Morrigan stitched, Daisy unwrapped her tarot deck from its embroidered cloth and instinctively plucked a card. She flinched when she saw the High Priestess, card number two: *A woman draped in a shimmering mantle of bees reclines in a golden hive. In her lap, she cradles a scroll stamped with crescent moons and hexagons. Her open palm holds out an orchid, her eyes filled with the secrets of the universe.*

Daisy slid the card back into the deck, wondering what the High Priestess would say about the no-doubt stultifying evening ahead.

"It's the third step of your journey," Avery said excitedly.

After Daisy had filled her sisters in on everything that happened with Lizzie, she'd also given them a full accounting of what Kathryn had told her about the dead moon and how that may have affected their new moon ritual, as well as Daisy's own Fool's—or Heroine's—Journey.

Morrigan was staring into space with a peculiar expression. "And Daisy's not the first to take it!"

Avery gave her a look. "What do you see, Morrigan?"

"That's it," Morrigan said, her eyes coming back into focus. "That's all I know."

Avery and Daisy knew that pressing Morrigan would lead to nothing. It was the same with all three of them. The Visions couldn't be forced. Still, Daisy was disappointed.

Morrigan cut the thread with her sewing scissors and stuck her needle back into the pincushion. "You're ready!"

"Morrigan!" Daisy marveled, twirling in the looking glass. The dress now fit as if it had been made for her. "You're a brilliant seamstress."

"I know," Morrigan agreed. Then she ducked her head at this uncharacteristic display of pride.

"It's not a sin to feel good about being good at something." Avery arched her neck to let her hair fall into Daisy's hands. Daisy began to braid brightly colored beads and flowers into the tawny waves to create a delicate crown. The Wolfson girls didn't own any jewels, precious or not, so they had to get creative. The flower crown accentuated Avery's rosy cheeks and mossy hazel eyes and added a touch of color to her pale blue dress and white lace shawl. With her bow-like mouth, high forehead, and proud blade of a nose that wouldn't be out of place on a Grecian coin, she almost seemed of a different era. Daisy loved looking at her.

"According to the Sisters," Daisy said, "pride is the queen of sins."

"True, but what they don't know won't hurt them," Avery answered. "Anyway, we're Protestants. We only have to obey their rules when Mother takes us to visit the convent."

Morrigan didn't look convinced but dropped the topic, knowing she was outvoted. She parted her thick, dark-brown hair and coiled the entire length into a high waterfall chignon. She wore a simple, high-waisted gown whose warm tones set off her violet eyes and snowy skin. She'd made it herself out of the remainder of a bolt of muslin she'd been given in exchange for a particularly insightful reading for one of the town's wealthy matrons, and this was her first chance to wear it.

"As long as we don't end up like Mr. Blue." Daisy shuddered.

"Oh, what a ghastly story," Morrigan said. "That poor man."

They fell silent for a moment, chastened by the reminder of the beaten and half-drowned clairvoyant left to perish simply because someone didn't like a fortune he'd told. The strangest thing about the tragedy of Mr. Blue was that he didn't actually exist. At least, not yet. Daisy had seen him in one of her Visions. He was an elderly deaf-mute man from England somewhere in the future, a fortune-teller dressed all in blue, who'd been descended upon by a mob of witch-hunters. Daisy never learned his location, nor his true name. *Dummy* was the cruel slur given him by the ignorant villagers of his time. Daisy had told her sisters about her Vision, of course, but they had agreed not to perpetuate such shameful bigotry and instead called him Mr. Blue.

"Girls, the carriage is due to arrive shortly," Mrs. Wolfson's voice floated into the room.

The girls paused before the looking glass for a last glance: They were like three flowers in a vase. Morrigan was a warm buttercup, Daisy a fluffy titian peony, and Avery the bluebell, an introverted bloom, deceptively demure but with a strength that went steely when tested.

"See how beautiful we manage to pretend to look," said Morrigan.

"Aunt Mary will choke on her soup," Daisy crowed.

"I'd rather stay home in the comfort of my breeches," said Avery, who'd several years ago unearthed Augustus's clothes from the attic and had Morrigan take them in for her. To Daisy's eye, she seemed most herself in them. "But I do have to admit that we look grand. Poor relations, indeed!"

They traipsed downstairs to join their mother in the parlor. Bernadette LeBlanc Wolfson was tall and fine-boned, her Acadian heritage evident in her olive skin, dark deep-set eyes, and thick salt-and-pepper hair. Tonight, she looked elegantly understated, her hair in a simple twist, wearing her one good brown dress. She inspected her daughters. "My dears," she said. "You are all young ladies now. Not my little girls anymore. Whatever will I do with you?"

"Don't marry us off to the butcher's sons," said Morrigan.

"Or anyone," said Avery.

Their mother shook her head. "That is not what worries me."

The sisters knew their mother was not unaware of their tarot readings and healing consultations, if only because the donations people gave them had been augmenting Augustus's modest military pension and her small salary from teaching piano lessons. But while she tacitly accepted these goings-on, if she had known about their deeper practices—especially the new moon ritual—she might have put a stop to all of it.

"The other night," said their mother with uncanny timing, "you were out until dawn. . . ." She paused strategically, waiting.

"We went to the forest, Mother," said Morrigan.

"It was such a beautiful evening," Daisy chimed in. "We couldn't resist the pull of the midnight sky. The moon, the sea, it was—"

"Be careful," their mother interrupted. "You cannot possibly know how powerful vengeful spirits can be. And I do not refer only to the devil. He has many minions."

Just then, there was a clatter of hooves outside, so the conversation ended as quickly as it had begun, at least for the moment.

Everyone climbed into Aunt Mary's promised carriage and was deposited at Blackwell House at just after seven o'clock. Mr. Miggs had set up a coatrack in the foyer. But none of the Wolfsons had worn coats, as the evening was warm enough to go without, so they left him empty-handed and proceeded into the grand parlor.

The large, high-ceilinged room was already thronged with guests, a chatter of voices rising above the music of the string quartet Aunt Mary had hired. Daisy could imagine her dismay at the expense, even though she was rich as Croesus. She attributed this uncharacteristic lavishness to her aunt's baffling adoration of the horrible Jasper. Well, the two of them deserved each other.

And there he was, lurking by the window, talking to Henry and a young woman Daisy didn't recognize. Shining flaxen hair, pearly complexion, radiant in cream and lace. Daisy inadvertently caught Jasper's eye and felt a quick flare of antipathy as their gazes tangled. They both quickly looked away, but the back of Daisy's neck had gone hot and prickly again.

Head high, she charged in through the arched doorway, Avery flanking her like an aide-de-camp, while Morrigan took their mother's arm at the rear. They marched up to Aunt Mary, who held court on a sofa between two other society matrons, her closest cronies, Mrs. Stockbridge and Mrs. Godwin.

"Dear Bernadette," said Aunt Mary, raking Bernadette's simple dress with her beady eyes, a magpie collecting bits of future gossip. "How good of you to come. I know how much you dislike formal company."

Daisy noticed that the rash on her aunt's face was still there and wondered if she had begun taking laudanum. If so, it wasn't making her any nicer.

"Thank you for inviting us, dear sister Blackwell," said Bernadette, who was neither cowed nor impressed by her late husband's sister's rank and money. Bernadette prized plain speech and hard work and devoutness, not a scrap of which Aunt Mary exhibited. She moved away from their hostess, obligatory politesse discharged. Morrigan, as always, stayed by their mother's side. Daisy watched them greet Henry and join his little group, aware that Morrigan, by virtue of her ability to see the past, knew things about their mother's life that she couldn't or wouldn't articulate. Maybe that was why she was always Bernadette's defender and shield, her staunch, obedient ally.

"Hello," said a young man standing nearby. He gave Daisy and Avery an easy smile. "I'm Nathaniel Winthrop, a school friend of Henry and an utter newcomer to this town. I hope you'll rescue me from making a fool of myself in front of the hoity-toity types." He gave a self-deprecating half bow.

Momentarily tongue-tied, Daisy was grateful when Avery gracefully handled the introductions. Nathaniel was possibly the handsomest boy she'd ever met. His hair sprang in copious waves from a clear brow, his skin golden from the sun, eyes the translucent blue of ocean surf. And she couldn't help noticing how well-made he was, with a wide chest and strong arms that filled out his cutaway coat.

He was also charming, especially compared to Jasper Fitzwilliam, whose churlish dark eyes met Daisy's once again in an unwelcome frisson.

"Ah," said Nathanial, "the famous Wolfson sisters! Henry says you're gifted in the spiritual arts." Nathaniel nodded at Avery, gesturing in Morrigan's direction and including Daisy in his twinkling gaze. "I'd greatly enjoy a tarot reading sometime. I'm curious about my own future."

"And what do you hope this future holds?" asked Avery.

Nathaniel inclined his head as he considered her question. "That's a bit of a mystery at the moment. I was at Harvard, but I lost my scholarship. Bit of bad luck," he said, flicking a glance in Jasper's direction. "Hullo, Fitzwilliam."

"Winthrop," Jasper said tightly. "I didn't know you'd be here."

Nathaniel laughed. "You didn't see the notice in the *Barnstable Patriot*?"

Jasper frowned and looked away.

So they know each other, Daisy thought. *How intriguing!*

"Now I work for a living," Nathaniel continued. "Henry was kind enough to find me a position with one of the top cabinetmakers on the Cape."

"He's a natural," Henry enthused, joining their group. "He makes the most marvelous objets d'art with only a piece of wood and a chisel!"

"Well, those were just toys for the children I met in the hospital, when I was still studying medicine. Seemed to help more than all that doctoring did. And I like making things people can use, the honest labor of working with my hands."

Daisy was torn between curiosity about Nathaniel's past and the urge to simply gaze at those magnificent hands, strong and capable. "Am I to understand you live in Redcliffe now, Mr. Winthrop?"

"I'm here for the duration of my apprenticeship, living above Mr. Bell's shop," he said. "And please call me Nate, Miss Wolfson. Both of you."

"Then you shall call us Daisy and Avery," Avery said.

"A bargain." His voice rumbled with warmth.

"And we would be delighted to give you a reading, whenever you like," Daisy added. "Please do call on us." Was she a little breathless?

Avery shot her a piercing look.

Recalling the essence of the High Priestess's feminine power, Daisy could barely resist the strong temptation to move closer to Nate and inhale his scent.

Fortunately for her reputation, Mr. Miggs chose that moment to ring the bell for dinner.

They all filed in pairs into the formal dining room, Nate offering Daisy his arm, Henry escorting Morrigan, Avery on the arm of another young man, and Jasper escorting the blond girl. The long table was beautifully laid for sixteen. Two footmen, hired for the occasion, stood at attention by the sideboard, where many bottles of wine, claret, and port stood open, as well as a fragrant soup steaming in a silver urn.

The young people were arranged around Henry, who sat at the head of the table. Their elders had been placed near Aunt Mary, who sat at the foot. Bernadette, stuck between Mr. Stockbridge and Mr. Godwin—the papery whaling-magnate husbands of Aunt Mary's cronies, whose bloodless, chalky skin had clearly not been exposed to the sea in many years—appeared resigned to making the best of things with a glass of wine, the one indulgence she allowed herself. It was the blood of Christ, after all, and she would always remain Catholic in her heart. Aunt Mary had seated herself between widowed Pastor Stewart and perennially single Dr. Wellington, the two most eligible older bachelors in town.

As for Daisy, she was delighted to find herself next to Nate, with Henry on her left.

"Who are they?" she quietly asked Henry, gesturing to the young woman Jasper was still talking to and the dour-faced fellow next to her.

"You don't mean Annabelle and Phineas Stewart?" he replied, not at all discreetly. "I know they've been off at school for the past few years, but you can't possibly have forgotten them!"

Daisy was too stunned to be embarrassed that they were both now staring at her, along with the rest of the table. They had all played together as children. How had that moody dumpling of a little girl transformed into such a vision of loveliness? And could that be her brother?!

"My word, Finny," Daisy exclaimed. "I barely recognize you without chocolate smeared all over your face!" She called to her sisters, "This is Finny Stewart! Remember when we'd catch him stealing treats from the pantry?"

"It's Phineas now," he said, shifting in his seat.

So Finny Stewart hadn't changed; he'd always been a self-serious little prig. Daisy and her sisters avoided one another's eyes to forestall the attack of giggles bubbling in their throats.

Daisy suddenly shivered, and the fine hairs on her forearm stood on end, goosebumps rippling across her skin. A peculiar chill had snaked its way through the dining room. Trust Aunt Mary to stint on the heating. Oddly, no one else at the table seemed to notice the draft. And then it was gone, and Daisy was distracted by something teasing the back of her mind, some memory or recognition having to do with Finny. She couldn't place it. It was like a familiar taste or melody out of context, somehow known but impossible to identify in the moment.

Henry leaned forward. "I've been negligent in performing my hostly duties. You must all learn one another's names."

In the hubbub of introductions that followed, Daisy was aware of Jasper's silent scrutiny across the table. When she caught his eye, he held her gaze and said with low intensity, under cover of the general conversation, "Your aunt is doing so much better since I brought her the tonic. She is herself again. You can't deny it."

"Her rash is unchanged," Daisy said, dipping her spoon into her soup and sipping delicately.

"Her spirits are improved."

"That, I attribute to laudanum's narcotic effect and the gaiety of a party."

"It is *medicine*," he said. "Its healing power cannot be disputed."

While Jasper demanded Daisy's attention, Nate had turned to Avery on his other side and was now engrossed in discussion with her and Finny Stewart. Daisy would have given anything to join them, whatever the topic. Instead, she addressed Jasper with all the level calm she could muster. "Nonetheless, I dispute it."

"What are you two arguing about?" Morrigan asked, and Henry chimed in, "Let us be the arbiters. What's the case?"

"Medical methodology and science," said Jasper. He narrowed his eyes at Daisy. "Versus herbalism and spiritualism."

"You doctors are always so sure you're right," said Annabelle, her dewy skin glistening, neatly parted hair like two smooth, shining golden wings. "I'm sure the Misses Wolfson will agree with me that your discipline isn't infallible. It's as much of an intuitive practice as it is a science."

"Do call me Daisy, please, Annabelle. We're old friends, even if it's been ages," Daisy said gaily. "And here's one juror on my side." She gleamed at Jasper. "Henry, what do you say?"

"You know I'm sympathetic to my friends' talents," said Henry. "But I'd like to hear from Nate where he stands on the question. He's gone sour on medicine, that much I know."

Nate turned to Daisy with a grin that made her breath catch. "I've already asked for a reading," he told Henry, keeping his eyes on Daisy, "so I can't pretend disinterest in the spiritual arts."

"And you shall have a reading," Daisy told him. "Whenever you like."

Morrigan twinkled at her from across the table, and she could hear Avery coughing into her hankie but pretended not to notice.

"This leaves my brother," said Annabelle. "The rest of us have come down on the side of at least an interest in or sympathy for spirituality. Phineas, what do you say? Will you bolster our new friend Mr. Fitzwilliam and rescue him from his solitary dissent?"

Finny gave his sister a long, serious look, and then he nodded at Jasper. "I will indeed," he said. "All this trickery has a whiff of blasphemy and subversion. It is at best a harmless diversion for the fairer sex, at worst a source of troublemaking damage."

At once, it was clear. Daisy almost gasped aloud: Finny was the shadowy figure in the Vision she'd had of Lizzie Cuttle. The embrace she'd seen in that quick moment had been real; she suddenly knew it beyond a doubt. He was the source of the heartache that was tormenting that sweet, quiet girl, not a thwarted love match. But that meant her advice had been so terribly wrong!

"He has to take this stance," his sister was saying. "He's becoming a clergyman like our father."

Hypocrite, Daisy thought darkly.

This meant her carelessness with the reading and encouraging Lizzie to follow her heart now made her uncomfortably complicit. She'd need to make things right for poor Lizzie. She resolved to send a note first thing in the morning. At least she and Finny hadn't yet run off together, so thankfully there was still time.

"I take this stance," said Finny, "because I am on the side of rational and civilized discourse."

"Hear, hear," said Jasper. "I'd rather have one reasonable ally than a crowd of misguided sentimentalists."

How perfectly fitting that Finny Stewart and Jasper Fitzwilliam would find themselves in alignment. *Supercilious snake, meet condescending reactionary.*

"Pompous ass," Nate muttered, echoing her thoughts.

Daisy turned to look at him, not sure she'd heard correctly.

He caught her eye, glowering. "No love lost between that man and me," he told her under his breath.

"We have that in common," she breathed back, and they shared a quick, clandestine smile.

Jasper meanwhile had turned to Annabelle, murmuring something that caused her to dimple at him.

"I have an idea," Henry said to Daisy and her sisters. "The famous Dr. Franklyn, who happens to be Fitz's mentor, is giving a lecture on the latest medical discoveries and methods at Harvard Medical School. You three could join us in Boston! This might be the perfect opportunity for you to settle your opposing stances on spiritualism versus modern science, perhaps even learn from one another."

"What an intriguing proposition," said Avery, glancing with merry adventurousness at her sisters. She was never one to back down from a challenge. "Thank you for thinking of us, Henry."

As the footmen cleared the soup plates and served the next course, Daisy lost herself in the attentions of her charming neighbor. The meal was sumptuous: cod baked in cream with green beans, curried lobster with rice, chicken croquettes with broccoli, saddle of mutton with Yorkshire pudding, vanilla blancmange and Boston cream pie. But Daisy hardly tasted a thing, so taken was she with Nate and their engaging conversation.

Still, she could feel the tension between Jasper and her tightening. A thin wire stretched between them, vibrating with a true argument that was only suspended and not at all resolved.

And she couldn't shake the unease she'd felt the first time she heard his name. That, too, was only intensifying.

Later, after the meal had concluded and the guests gathered in the foyer, Daisy raced back into the dining hall to search frantically beneath the tables. In the distraction of the evening, she'd somehow left her reticule behind, with her precious tarot cards. Suddenly, she paused, her bare arms once again blossoming in goosebumps. She faintly perceived a hissing, faraway and barely audible, as if the air currents themselves had animated with electricity. She scanned the room, barely daring to breathe.

Finally, she looked up.

Do you still not see me? I'm beginning to feel unwanted! And to think I'm here at your invitation.

"Will that be all, Miss Wolfson?" a figure asked, melting out of the shadows.

"Mr. Miggs!" Daisy exclaimed, her hand over her chest. "I didn't notice you there!"

"Terribly sorry, miss," Mr. Miggs said, looking pained.

"No, it's me," she said, "I shouldn't, I was just— Oh, there it is!" She bent down to retrieve her bag. "Sorry, I won't keep you," she murmured, hurrying toward the hall, not seeing the brief flare of fluorescence high above.

CHAPTER III

THE EMPRESS

"You philosophers are lucky men. You write on paper, and paper is patient. Unfortunate Empress that I am, I write on the susceptible skins of living beings."

—CATHERINE THE GREAT

A hearty knock resounded on the door at precisely nine a.m. Nate stood on the flagstones, his abundant waves of hair catching the morning sun, his posture slightly slouched, looking at ease in his own skin.

"Good morning, Nate." Daisy's voice was breathless and high. She tried to lower her tone and calm her pulse. "I've set the table up in the parlor. Can I offer you some refreshment?"

"I just ate an entire pig for breakfast with a dozen eggs and a loaf of bread." Nate laughed. "And a whole apple *cake*. Mr. Bell's wife is a brilliant cook."

His broad frame filled the cramped little cottage, unaccustomed to a masculine presence. Shedding sunlight and fresh sea air and the smell of autumn leaves, he loomed through the narrow parlor doorway and fell into the chair Daisy had set out for him. It creaked under his weight, and his shoulders dwarfed the narrow back. She poured him some tea she'd set out earlier.

As she sat across from Nate and unwrapped her tarot deck from its silk covering, swiftly separating the twenty-two Major Arcana cards from the rest into a pile, Daisy realized that she had never before in her life felt so aware of her own person. Her body and surroundings suddenly felt alien. What must he think of their simple home after the opulence of Aunt Mary's?

Nate leapt up and paced around the room. "Who's the chess player?" he asked, catching sight of the board and pieces carved out of local woods, black walnut and pale oak.

"That's Morrigan's," Daisy told him. "Our father carved it and taught her to play when she was a very little girl. She has a gift for it."

Nate picked up a king and held it up to the light, admiring the artistry but also, it seemed, stalling. Daisy sensed her mother's listening presence in the dining room.

"So what do I need to do to prepare for this reading?" Nate asked. His voice cracked a little. Was he nervous, too?

Daisy handed him the stack of Major Arcana cards, face down.

"Think of a question," she told him. "Focus on it as you shuffle, and rearrange the cards until you feel ready."

"Ready for what?"

"For your answer."

He met her eyes, his expression unreadable. Clearing her throat, Daisy continued, "For this reading, we'll be doing a five-card cross spread, using only the Major Arcana cards. Each one signifies an archetype, a particular character in your story."

"And how does that work?"

"I'm going to lay four cards out in a cross—north, south, east, and west—and then a fifth one in the middle. I'll tell you what each one signifies. The arrangement will answer your question in a way you may not expect. The ultimate interpretation is up to you. I'm just the messenger."

He hefted the deck from hand to hand as if he were reluctant to delve into it.

"Shuffle," Daisy said. "The deck needs your energy."

He looked at Daisy, head tilted. She shrugged off a powerful urge to touch his cheek, to grasp his forearm and pull him to her. Now that she was actively working with the cards, she was back in her element.

"You talk about this deck of yours as if it were alive," he said.

"To me, it *is* alive, in a way. It's a conduit to the truth, a means of understanding what we can't see or touch, the answer to all questions, even the ones we don't know we have."

"I do have a question," he said.

Daisy heard her mother turn over a leaf of paper in the dining room, the *skritch* of her pen.

Taking a deep breath, Daisy concentrated on Nate. "Ask the cards, silently, while you shuffle."

"When do I tell it to you?"

"You don't have to tell me."

"What if I want to?"

Was he teasing her? He was clearly far more versed in the art of flirtation than she was. Daisy composed her face, willing it not to crack into a smile. "When the cards are in place."

Nate nodded and began to shuffle the deck, concentrating with a small furrow between his brows. Daisy took this opportunity to study him closely. She found herself entranced with his nose. It was such a sweet nose, with a short, straight bridge. And a grin lurked just behind the corners of his mouth, his intoxicatingly beautiful mouth, his—

"Is this enough?" Nate asked mildly, interrupting her reverie.

"The deck will tell you if you listen," she forced herself to reply in her most professional manner. Distractingly handsome boy notwithstanding, this was in fact serious business.

As Nate wordlessly handed Daisy the deck, their fingers brushed. Ignoring a definite spark of electricity, she lay the cards out in the shape of the cross: left, right, top, bottom, flipping each one as she placed it.

"Think of this arrangement as a court of law," she told him. "This card on your left, Justice, is your defense, everything weighing in your favor in this matter. On the right, Temperance, is your opposition, the perils you face, the arguments against you. The card in the north position, the Empress, is the judge who presides and pronounces a verdict." She'd felt herself tremble slightly as she pulled the Empress, that powerful card of nature and power. Last night, she'd had a dream about her mother as the Empress, reclining on a bed of crimson flowers under a pomegranate tree by a brook. Empress Bernadette picked up a ripe fallen pomegranate, cracked it open with her hands, and threw a handful of seeds into her mouth, the juice running down her chin. She proffered the other half to Daisy, smiling with generous invitation, and Daisy reached her hand out eagerly. But before she could taste it or even reach it, she woke up to early morning sunlight streaming through the window. If dreams counted, there was the next card in her journey, right on schedule.

Now, startled by the Empress's appearance in real life, she forced herself to carry on as though everything were perfectly normal. "The south card, the Hanged Man, is the outcome and result of the trial. Think of it as your verdict."

"The Hanged Man?" Nate looked at her askance. "That doesn't sound very promising."

"That card isn't always what it seems." Daisy held the deck still. "It's not terrible in itself. It all depends on the cards it's with, the company it keeps."

"Interesting." He leaned in, peering closely at the cards. "I've seen tarot decks before but never one like yours. Where did you get it?"

It had been a revelation when Daisy had been visited by a Vision shortly after her sixteenth birthday. She'd seen a striking woman in some future place painting her own deck of tarot, daring to re-create them in her personal Vision of an exceptionally inventive, beautiful deck. Daisy had been electrified with the realization that she could do the same thing. Thus inspired, Daisy had allowed her own imagination to run wild and created bespoke decks for herself and each of her sisters, taking cues from her new muse.

But how could she explain to him that she had seen future tarot decks that didn't exist yet? That she had rendered her version of them, with no idea how she knew what she knew?

She couldn't, especially not with her mother listening to every word.

With a quick glance at the doorway to the dining room, Daisy said simply, "I painted it myself."

"That's impressive! You must have inherited this artistic gift from your father."

"As well as my mother," Daisy said. "She's a fine musician."

"And how did you learn to interpret the tarot cards?"

"I practiced it," she said carefully. "And . . . I also already knew it."

A silence hung in the air. Nate waited for Daisy to say more. Bernadette presumably absorbed what she'd said. Daisy cast about for a way to turn everyone's attention back to the reading.

Just then, to her simultaneous relief and disappointment, there was a commotion at the front door: laughter in the vestibule, the rustle of coats being hung. Her two sisters burst into the parlor, both talking at once.

"Sorry to interrupt!" Morrigan said. "Tabitha took ill and sent us home."

"Hello, Nate!" Avery took a quick glance at the spread and flung herself onto the wingback chair. "Looks like Daisy's got you in quite a fine stew."

Morrigan hurried over to peer at the cards Daisy had laid out.

"What's the center card, Daisy?" Avery asked without looking up from the apple she was polishing on her shirtwaist.

"I haven't done the math yet." Daisy narrowed her eyes at them, trying to telegraph *go away* as clearly as she could.

But they ignored her. "Don't let us stop you," said Avery. She took a loud, crackling bite.

Bernadette appeared in the doorway, holding her neat sheaf of papers, a rogue ink stain on her right forefinger. Her hair was smooth in its bun, her expression serious and distracted. It was impossible to reconcile this reserved, formidable person with the bountiful Empress of Daisy's dream.

"I'll be upstairs," she said. "I trust your guest has everything he requires?"

"Yes, thank you, Mrs. Wolfson," said Nate. Even he, in all his confidence, seemed cowed by the matriarch.

Listening to her light tread on the narrow staircase, Daisy and her sisters waited for the telltale creak of their mother's chair overhead.

Daisy looked at her sisters. Their expressions were brimming with mischief and curiosity as they looked from her to Nate, and back to her again.

"Tabitha took ill, did you say?" she asked them.

"Suddenly," said Avery. "It came over her, a fit of ague. She was shaking with chills. She called for her coachman and went home. I'm sure Dr. Wellington is at her bedside right now."

Daisy glanced sharply at Morrigan. Had her sisters fabricated an excuse to leave the church and come flocking home to spy on her meeting with Nate? She might have done the same in their shoes. She could read every twitch in her twin's face. She'd know instantly if Morrigan were fibbing.

But Morrigan nodded in all earnestness. "It was strange. She was perfectly well when we arrived, and then one minute later, it was as if she'd been struck with influenza."

"It's only September," Daisy said. "Too early for influenza."

Nate drummed his fingers on the table.

Avery tossed her apple core into the fireplace and joined them at the table. She and Morrigan studied the four cards again closely along with Daisy, all focusing on the story they were telling: the Empress to the north in the Judge's spot, Justice as the defense, Temperance the prosecutor, and the Hanged Man the verdict. There was still one card left to determine.

"The center card," Daisy said. "That will be the heart of the matter. I just need to tally the numbers to see which card goes in the center."

"We call this draw the Full Heart," said Avery. "It involves some fairly intricate calculations using theosophic reduction, whereby all digits are reduced to their essence by adding double-and-above digits until they pare down to—"

"I didn't realize there was so much math involved in telling someone's fortune," Nate interrupted merrily.

"Well, it's not that much math but—" Daisy paused to scribble briefly in her notebook.

"Were you good at it in school?"

"I wouldn't—"

"You must have been. Teacher's pet, right?"

"Oh. You're teasing me."

"I wouldn't dare." But his eyes were definitely twinkling.

Daisy's face grew hot, and she dipped her head, pretending to be absorbed in her calculations, even though she already had the final count.

Then she felt something against her throat, a soft squeeze, as gossamer as silk, and for a moment it was all she could do to breathe.

CHAPTER IV

THE EMPEROR

"Let men see, let them know a real man, who lives as he was meant to live."

—MARCUS AURELIUS

The frightening sensation of soft choking around Daisy's throat like a spiderweb vanished as quickly as it had come on. How strange! She hoped she wasn't coming down with the same flu that afflicted Tabitha. Thankfully, Nate was focused once again on the cards and hadn't seemed to notice.

Daisy took a sip of tea and placed the Tower, number sixteen of the Major Arcana, at the center of the spread. When she looked at the cross, she saw quite a dramatic courtroom scene playing itself out. She was very curious to learn how the spread related to Nate's personal circumstances.

"Now that all the cards have been revealed, this would be a good time to tell me your question, if you still want to," she told Nate.

"Happy to," Nate said. "I want to know if I should exact revenge on a person who has wronged me."

The three sisters exchanged startled glances.

"Let's see," Daisy said. She was dying to know who had wronged him and could feel her sisters' keen interest. Frankly, she was already on Nate's side, even though she didn't know a thing. But the cards were more powerful than her own opinions, and they were the arbiters. "We'll start by looking at the center card, the heart of your question. This is the Tower, and it's very powerful. It signifies crisis, as well as change. A disruption that can feel life-threatening."

"That's what this cur did to me," said Nate. "He threatened my life."

Morrigan gasped. "How shocking!"

"So is this a bad card for me, or a positive one?"

"Both. A terrible wrong has been done to you, the card clearly indicates that. But the positive aspect is that you can emerge stronger. You're asking your question in the wake of turbulence, but the card itself gives perspective."

"What does that mean, exactly?"

"In time, you can find calm waters, a safe harbor."

"By exacting revenge?"

"Maybe not." Morrigan looked anxious.

"But on the other hand," Daisy said, "the heart of the matter is the act that's been committed against you. The verdict as to your course of action remains to be seen. Let's go now to your defense: Justice." She tapped the card to his left. "Look: The Judge holds a scale for balance and a sword for retribution, possibly through force."

"That's exactly what I want." Nate leaned forward like a hunting dog getting a whiff of rabbit. "The use of force. And retribution."

"There's something to consider, Nate." His name tasted sweet in her mouth. "This card advocates for objectivity and isn't swayed by raw emotion."

Avery nodded. "An accounting of actions and restoration of balance."

"An accounting of the actions of my enemy," Nate said, pleased. "Yes, that's exactly what I'm gunning for. I want to make him pay the price."

"But now let's look at your prosecution, Temperance," Daisy told him. "This is the argument against taking revenge."

"I already don't like this card."

"This is a card of balance, too. Taking the middle road."

"Well, that's good at least." Nate grinned in that charming way of his. "Not the high road!"

Daisy couldn't help smiling. "It's arguing for a different approach. It invites you to keep a cool head."

"Wait," Avery said, peering at Nate curiously, clearly getting a flash about him. "When is your birthday?"

"April seventh."

"I'm March twenty-first!" Daisy said. "We're the same sun sign, Aries. Ruled by fire, we're impetuous and seldom look before we leap." Her sisters chuckled, but Daisy ignored them. "So given that, this card"—she tapped Temperance slowly—"urges you to exercise restraint."

"What about this charming creature up here? I like the look of her. What does *she* say about all this?"

"The Empress is presiding over your trial."

"And what does she think about my question?"

"She understands your need to hurt the man who wronged you."

"Good!"

"But she urges temperance," Daisy added. "She argues for the prosecution. She heeds the Tower's warning and promise: Trust in the power of time."

"She misreads me, then," said Nate.

"Maybe you misread her." Daisy forced herself to take a breath. Nate didn't know the Empress was Bernadette.

"What about this last card, down here?" Nate gestured at the card with a grimace.

Daisy contemplated the upside-down figure, suspended from a wood frame by a rope tied around one ankle. Most people interpreted the card's name literally, but the man wasn't hanged by his neck, and his expression was unperturbed. "The Hanged Man is your verdict, the outcome of your question. You have to make a sacrifice, or else you'll stay stuck in midair, upside down."

"What sacrifice? Who *is* this character?" Nate seemed rattled.

"There are interpretations of the Hanged Man as a traitor," Avery piped in, "someone who has betrayed something or someone."

"I was betrayed by a former friend!" Nate said. "This must be him."

"Well, not necessarily . . ." Daisy said.

"That's perfect! I'm going to hang Fitzwilliam upside down by the ankle and leave him to rot!"

Daisy gasped. *His enemy was Jasper Fitzwilliam!* Of course, she'd sensed their mutual animosity at Aunt Mary's dinner party, and she'd wondered what the cause was.

"That's a literal interpretation," Daisy said, trying to keep her own dislike of Jasper out of her voice. "But if you do that, you'll have to contend with the judgment of the Empress, the powerful mother of all living things."

"My own mother is dead," he said, "so I don't fear her judgment."

Daisy looked up. "Oh, I'm so sorry."

"Both my parents died when I was a child," he said, his eyes shadowed.

"Might I ask what Jasper Fitzwilliam did to you?"

He spoke without hesitation. "His parents took me in and raised me alongside Jasper. He and I were the closest of friends, like brothers, or so I thought."

"And he threatened your life?" Daisy asked. She already knew Jasper was rude, but that he was also violent was chilling.

"Well, my livelihood," Nate allowed. "We were at medical school together. To complete my studies, I was apprenticed to a great man, that professor mentioned at your aunt's dinner party, Dr. Edward Franklyn, who took an interest in me. Jealous, Jasper told falsehoods about me, which led to me losing my apprenticeship and my place at Harvard. If it weren't for the generosity of Henry Graves, finding a place for me in Mr. Bell's cabinet shop here in Redcliffe, I'd be destitute." Nate's voice was filled with grief and regret.

"Oh, that's awful!" she cried. "What a terrible man!"

"I'm sorry if you and he are friendly but—"

"Oh no," Daisy said staunchly. "I think you already know he's no friend of mine."

"Good," he said. "But I truly hope *we'll* be friends." He held her gaze for a moment, and then they both looked away.

Daisy blushed, unsure what to say.

Avery stepped in to break the tension. "I propose a final quick reading. I think that there is one more answer to be had concerning this question of revenge."

"Avery has a special understanding about unseen things in the present moment," Daisy impulsively explained, grateful for her eldest sister's tact. "The same way I know what's coming, the same way Morrigan knows what's already been."

Morrigan coughed gently into her hand, reminding Daisy of their mother's finely tuned hearing, directly upstairs. Daisy stared at the ceiling as though it might turn to glass.

Nate regarded the sisters with admiration. "How extraordinary you all are," he said.

Daisy glowed as she swept up the Major Arcana cards and reunited them with her deck. She shuffled it three times and handed it to Avery, who promptly handed it to Nate.

"Cut the cards," Avery told him. "Wherever it feels right."

Unhesitatingly, he lifted the top half of the deck as Avery wandered back to the other side of the room to sprawl once more in their father's chair. She waved at Daisy to continue. Daisy lifted the top card he'd revealed and turned it over.

"The Emperor," Morrigan said with a quick intake of breath.

Daisy hadn't expected the next card on her journey so soon. Startled, she looked at her eldest sister. "Avery, it's your card to read."

Avery leaned forward in the chair, elbows on her knees, tapping her right cheekbone the way she always did when she was thinking. "The Emperor," said Avery, "indicates living to your own demands and no one else's. You take charge of your own life."

"Now that's my kind of card!" cried Nate.

"It means you can chart your own path," Daisy added. "And you'll be rewarded with what you most desire."

"Through hard work and self-control," Morrigan added. "Not rash action. You must show discipline and measured fortitude, like our father."

"Your father? What does he have to do with anything?"

"He's staring right at you," Avery said.

"What, where?" Nate leapt up.

Daisy hastened to clarify. "I modeled this card after our late father. That's his image. He's the Emperor."

They studied the card together: *A noble but battle-worn soldier commands a throne of brass-studded leather and heavy oak in a study filled with books. In one hand, he holds a scepter ending in a globe of the earth topped with the Egyptian ankh, in the other, a chess piece, the white king. He has neat mutton chops and a full head of chestnut hair beneath a crown carved with rams' heads, the symbol of Aries.*

Peering at the card more closely, Nate asked, "Did you draw this king after the one in the chess set on the table there?"

"Yes," Daisy said with a glance at Morrigan. "Chess was our father's favorite pastime."

Nate suddenly pulled his pocket watch from his vest, then his wallet. "This has been a very interesting morning, and I wish I could enjoy your company for much longer, all three of you, but—" He pressed some bills into Daisy's hands. "Will that be enough?"

"Yes, of course," she said, leaping to her feet and walking him to the vestibule and out of her sisters' immediate line of sight. Handing him his coat, she opened the door for him, and he stepped outside.

"It was a—" Daisy began.

"I need to see you again," Nate said urgently.

"I would like that," Daisy replied, feeling the heat rise to her face again. "We can discuss your reading whenever you like."

"And other things," he added with a courtly bow, kissing her hand. It was a gentlemanly gesture, but there was nothing gentlemanly in the way he did it. And then he was gone, pulling the door closed behind him.

Daisy heard a faint cough behind her. It took everything she had to not jump at the sight of her mother.

"Thank you so much for allowing me to have this meeting, Mother," she managed.

"I hope I wasn't mistaken to do so." She fixed her youngest with a sharp look. "I must be off to give Annabelle Stewart her piano lesson. It's her last before she leaves for her grand tour of Europe."

"Oh, lucky girl!"

"There are more important things than wealth," Bernadette said crisply.

Daisy held her tongue. That wasn't what she had meant at all. It was hard to believe her mother had ever been young and passionate. Hadn't she yearned to travel the world? Had she never felt a flash of delicious heat when a boy kissed her hand?

After Bernadette left, Daisy swayed into the parlor and fell onto the fainting couch. Her sisters sighed dramatically, mocking her breathless state.

"Stop it, you two!"

"My dear youngest sister," said Avery, immediately contrite. "I know your feelings are strong. But I must counsel you to heed the cards, even if he can't."

Daisy frowned. "What did I miss? What am I not seeing?"

"I'm mistrustful of Nate's interpretation of the Emperor. I'm afraid he thinks he now has license to act in any way he wants. But I think the card was really telling him to listen to his higher nature."

"But Jasper betrayed him!"

"Then it's settled," Avery laughed. "Pistols at dawn. Or do we just hang Jasper right now?"

"No," Morrigan said. "I think . . . poison. Yes, let's poison his tea cakes!"

"Tea cakes? That man never met a sweet thing he liked," Daisy spat.

"Oooh," said Morrigan. "I bet there are some of Avery's apple muffins left over from that breakfast you were too nervous to eat this morning."

"Come on, little one," Avery said, pulling her off the couch and leading her to the kitchen. "There's time to kill your young Master Fitzwilliam tomorrow."

"He's not my—"

Just then Daisy's disloyal stomach rumbled thunderously. Her sisters cackled.

Muffins it was.

But tomorrow? Revenge.

CHAPTER V

THE HIEROPHANT

"Religion is regarded by the common people as true, by the wise as false, and by the rulers as useful."

–SENECA

Late that night, Daisy lay still with a pounding heart and a dry mouth. She had been trapped in a void, a lightless cavern somewhere deep inside a mountain.

It took a moment to realize she was safe in bed. Her sisters' soft breathing nearby steadied her own.

She sent her mind inward as Kathryn had trained her to do. As she meditated, she became aware that she wasn't the one stuck in that void, someone else was. But that person was connected to her. She felt an urgent responsibility to help.

Daisy lit the candle on the bedside table, reached for her tarot cards, and shuffled the deck languidly, still in that liminal space between waking and dreams.

She cut the deck and pulled the first card from the top of the pile. With a thud of irksome inevitability, she beheld the Hierophant, the fifth card in her Heroine's Journey. Although she always leapt at the possibility of adventure, the inevitability of this path tugged at her nerves. Who or what was steering this?

She peered at the card in the flickering candlelight: A figure cloaked in three layers of robes—white, blue, and luxurious red. Sporting a golden triple crown, he looms over two tonsured acolytes on a throne flanked by twin pillars, crossed keys at his feet. His right hand is raised in a blessing, the other bearing a triple cross.

Upright, the card symbolized the full weight of authoritative spiritual wisdom and power, conformity to traditional values and institutions. But this card was reversed, indicating rebellion against those very ideas. It was a reading of subversion at its most elemental.

With a sigh, Daisy tucked the cards back into their silk pouch, snuffed out the candle, and tumbled back to sleep. She fell almost immediately into another dream: The Fool card spun madly in a strong wind and glowed, lit from within by a strange light. The faint echo of eerie laughter taunted her.

And then the card winked out of sight. Tumbling deeper into unconsciousness, Daisy's mind emptied at last.

Some hours later, Morrigan jostled Daisy awake, propelling her into the day along with the bright morning light. It was Sunday, the day they cleaned the house and planned out the week's meals. There was a family meeting with their mother at breakfast, to be missed at one's own peril.

Daisy tumbled down the narrow staircase and slid into her place at the table. Because of her nightmare and the hours spent tossing and turning, she was rubbing her eyes. Avery thrust a cup of tea under her nose. Daisy buttered a piece of bread and dunked it in the milky beverage.

"You look like death warmed over," Avery said.

"Thanks," Daisy muttered. Then she glanced at her mother and fell silent, cracking the top off the soft-boiled egg in the eggcup, dipping her bread in the warm, runny yolk.

Bernadette sat worrying a piece of paper with a stub of a pencil. "Don't forget, girls," she said, "Mother Superior is coming for supper. I want to offer her a nice cut of meat, something special for dessert. We can skimp the rest of the week."

"Well, there's plenty of rye and wheat flour and cornmeal," said Avery. "To go with the molasses bread, a pot of hearty soup. We have a big jar of dried split peas in the larder, as well as onions and carrots. I just need some salt pork, and that's cheap. That's supper for the next few nights. So we can afford a feast tonight."

Just then, there was a timid knock at the door. They looked at one another, and Daisy got up.

She was surprised to see Lizzie Cuttle standing outside. Her hair was windblown. Her face looked drawn, dark circles under her eyes.

At the first sight of her, Daisy felt relief that she was well enough to be up and about. But the girl's careworn expression made her heart lurch.

"I'm so sorry to call so early, miss," Lizzie said, "but I couldn't sleep."

"Come in, Lizzie," Daisy said. "Let me take your coat."

In the parlor, Daisy indicated the chair across from her. Lizzie sank into it gratefully.

"What can I do for you?"

"Miss Wolfson," she whispered, "I'm in such trouble, I hardly know where to turn." Her eyes were wild, her lips cracked with dryness.

"Whatever it is, I will do whatever I can to help you. And please, call me Daisy."

"Oh, thank you." Lizzie was whispering urgently, looking around as she spoke to make sure no one else could hear.

"My family is all in the breakfast room. I promise, I'm the only one within earshot. And your secret, whatever it may be, is absolutely safe with me."

"I came because Emily gave me your counsel to follow my heart," Lizzie began.

"Did you not receive the note I sent?" Daisy interrupted anxiously.

"Yes, but I knew you'd just sent that to cover your tracks," Lizzie said. "You couldn't be seen to encourage me in my illicit love affair."

"Well, no, Lizzie, that wasn't quite—"

But Lizzie buried her face in her hands and wept.

Inwardly reeling at this appalling development, Daisy forced herself to remain calm and handed the girl the handkerchief she kept tucked in her sleeve.

Illicit affair?

Oh, of course! She was the one trapped in the dream void. It was Lizzie she had to save because she had sent her there with her inept reading.

Out it came, haltingly but clearly: Because of Daisy's advice, Lizzie had gone to Finny Stewart to tell him she loved him, and that she was with child, and he was the father. "It was the only proper course of action," she said. "You were right. But..."

Daisy's heart sank. It was even worse than she'd feared. "What did he say?" she asked, seeing the answer in Lizzie's face.

"He sent me away." Lizzie's voice was bleak. "He told me it couldn't possibly be his child. Daisy, there is no one else! There has *never* been anyone else. I've loved him since I was a girl."

"I am so sorry." Daisy took poor Lizzie's cold hand in her two warm ones.

"I don't know where to turn," Lizzie said. "I won't bring this shame on my parents."

"Lizzie, will you allow me to tell my sisters? We work better together, and they're trustworthy in any matter."

Lizzie said through slow, leaking tears, "If you think it best. Just please send word. As soon as you can."

After Lizzie left, Daisy's stomach felt leaden. It would be hours before she and her sisters would be alone. As the morning crawled by, she swept the floors and dusted, stripped the beds, and washed the sheets in a tub of hot water and hung them to dry on the line, her mind replaying Lizzie's words over and over.

At least she now knew she couldn't have prevented Lizzie's predicament even if she'd read the Fool correctly. If Lizzie was pregnant with Finny's child, this had clearly been going on for some time. Still, that was scant comfort, all things considered.

Finally, when the house was clean, and the beds crackled with fresh linen, Daisy and her sisters put on their bonnets and coats and went out with baskets to buy food for Mother Superior.

"What did Lizzie Cuttle want?" Avery asked, coming straight to the point.

"I have to swear you to strict secrecy. . . ."

When Daisy told them, her sisters lurched to a stop in the middle of the road. A horse and cart swerved around them, the alarmed driver shouting imprecations in Portuguese.

The sisters scrambled to the safety of the sidewalk, waving their apologies at the man.

"I assume she'd rather not see Dr. Wellington for an emmenagogue," Daisy said, "Given her unmarried state. He's such a gossip. But we could ask Kathryn to make her a tincture."

"Yes," said Avery. "If that's what she wants."

"Lower your voices," said Morrigan, looking around us at the public street.

Daisy had a sudden brief but powerful Vision: a young woman crying in a courtroom, on trial. She had no idea what it meant, but the sense of foreboding hit her hard.

"There is another course she could take," Morrigan was saying. "We could urge her to tell her parents. The Cuttles and Pastor Stewart could come to some agreement." These matters were often settled by the parents when the mother-to-be was so young.

Just then, a Concord stagecoach swinging down the road and close to the sidewalk engulfed them in a cloud of dust. Coughing, they brushed themselves off.

"I think," Morrigan went on carefully, "that we should call on her now and talk all of this through with her. The threat of public shame is the worst of it. Poor thing, she must be in such agony."

As they hastened to High Street, the bakery sent smells of warm cinnamon and butter out onto the sidewalk. When Daisy knocked on the door, Lizzie answered almost at once. "Thank goodness you're here," she said. "My mother is at home, so I'm not free to ask you upstairs."

"We have a safe place where we can all talk freely," said Avery warmly.

The walk to Kathryn's had never felt longer. The sisters' empty baskets bumped against their hips. There would be time to buy supplies later.

As they turned onto Forest Road, Daisy thought she glimpsed Jasper Fitzwilliam in the distance—tall, imperious figure striding along, head held at an arrogant angle. Just the sight of someone who resembled him was enough to give her an unpleasant start. Everything Nate had told her rushed back to fill her mind with antipathy for Jasper. That snake!

The memory of Nate's tale of betrayal, combined with this new knowledge of Finny Stewart's dastardly behavior, blurred her perception of Redcliffe, a town she'd always, perhaps naively, considered safe and wholesome. The quiet streets now struck her as sinister, and the cloud-dimmed faces of the cottages along Forest Road looked blank and hostile. The sky was overcast; a wind off the ocean sent fallen leaves scudding along the tips of the brown grasses. She sensed a coldness at the heart of the town, a simmering danger for anyone who breached convention, especially and always women. Only a hundred and fifty years ago, young women like Daisy and her sisters were persecuted, strangled, drowned, and burned, suspected not only of casting dark spells or using devilish charms but also of using the most innocuous of plant remedies as poison, when all they'd done was try to help. In most cases, they'd not even been herbal practitioners but had just made an unfortunate enemy of a spiteful neighbor. Merely not fitting in with the herd was so often the most unforgiveable of crimes. And it seemed that dark time would come again in another form. Daisy's brief Vision had chilled her with foreknowledge.

Kathryn was in her garden, as usual. She wore white gloves and was cutting great blowsy blooms from her chrysanthemum bush with a pair of scissors. "Come in," she said, "all of you. I'll put the kettle on."

They sat together at her wooden table while Kathryn prepared a chamomile tisane and poured it out. Once everyone held a small ceramic mug, she joined them at the head. "It must be something important to bring you all here like this on a Sunday."

In a rush, the four of them took turns telling her what had happened. Her gaze on Lizzie's anguished face, Kathryn said, "I am of course so sorry, my dear girl. But you must know that all is not lost. You have several choices. You can determine the course your life will take."

"But how?" the poor girl wailed. "He won't marry me. He will scarcely speak to me anymore or tolerate my presence. I am nothing but a baker's daughter, and he is to be a clergyman, graduated from Harvard University. He has higher hopes for himself and the kind of wife he will marry. He has made that perfectly clear."

"His feelings in this matter don't concern me at the moment," said Kathryn crisply. "We must focus only on a solution."

"Tell me, please," Lizzie implored.

"If you like, I can prepare you a tea not so different from the one you're drinking now," she said. "It's a common practice, often used."

"And then there would be no baby?" Like all young women, Lizzie had heard of this method.

"Exactly," said Kathryn. "Though I assure you there is no baby yet even now, not until the quickening. Until you feel the baby move in your womb, all that exists is the potential for one to develop. This herbal infusion removes that possibility and restores you to normalcy. Dr. Wellington would tell you the same thing."

Lizzie nodded. "I've heard of such things. But I always thought they were . . ." She hesitated. "Dangerous. And painful."

"There is little danger," said Kathryn. "The herbs themselves are relatively safe, though it is not without discomfort."

"I see." Lizzie looked faint.

Daisy took her limp hand and squeezed it gently. Lizzie gave her a bleak half smile.

"You may want to think on it some more," Kathryn said.

"I don't need to think on it," said Lizzie. Something stubborn crept into her face, her lips compressing into a thin line. "I want this child. I want to marry Phineas. I love him so much I fear I will die without him. It's just that I cannot bear the way he is treating me. I want him to change back to how he was with me before. Is there not a spell for that?"

"These aren't spells, Lizzie," Avery said. "We're talking about medicine."

"But can't you—"

"It doesn't work like that," Kathryn said.

"So there's nothing else to be done?"

"You could tell your parents," Morrigan said softly. "They could speak to his father. Together, the adults could help Phineas see reason, urge him to take responsibility."

"Impossible," said Lizzie faintly.

"It's been done in this very town, countless times," Kathryn said.

"It has? When?" Lizzie was startled out of her despair.

Morrigan went rigid. Daisy stared at her twin, certain she'd just had a Vision. Daisy suddenly wasn't certain she wanted to hear.

Kathryn, on the other hand, did not hesitate. "What is it telling you?" she said, leaning forward. "Can you still see it?"

Morrigan shook her head. "It's gone now. But it showed me a glimpse of our mother and father at the altar at the church here in Redcliffe. I think . . . they were getting married."

"What else?" asked Kathryn.

Morrigan looked a little startled by the intensity of Kathryn's questioning, but she remained calm, thinking hard. "Something strange about their wedding. I don't know what it was. And there was very strong feeling between them." She swayed in her chair as she looked inward, trying to make sense of whatever she'd seen. "Happiness!" She smiled. "And love."

Daisy felt herself unclench somewhat.

"Of course they loved each other," Kathryn said impatiently. "Was there anything more?"

"I saw empty pews behind them," said Morrigan after a moment. "No witnesses but Reverend Potter and . . . I think his housekeeper? And the church was dark, as if they were there at night."

"Is there something you're not telling us, Kathryn?" Avery asked.

"It's not my place to say," said Kathryn.

Daisy's insides tightened once again. *This day!* "Kathryn," she said, "did our parents elope?"

Kathryn's silence confirmed it.

Lizzie Cuttle broke the moment with sudden laughter, high and giddy, almost like sobs. "What a beautiful story! Forgive me, I don't mean to wish that on your mother, to have been in my wretched predicament. But even if she was, he married her! And they were happy together, I know they were. I recall seeing them as they walked about town when I was just a child. Oh, this is immensely comforting!"

"Morrigan said nothing of the kind!" Avery burst in. "Lizzie, you're reading into things, seeking a story that casts your own in a happier light."

Unlike her twin, Daisy could see nothing of the past, and she only understood the present as anyone did. All she could see was the future, but she didn't need her gift to know that what awaited Lizzie was an overwhelming sense of futility and loneliness. A husband who did not respect or honor her, who treated her with impatient contempt. A sense of entrapment, unending. She would be buried alive in the black void, just like in that awful dream.

"Lizzie," Daisy said carefully, trying to defend her mother without giving offense, "there's no guarantee that marriage to Finny Stewart will give you the joy our mother found with our father. Whatever the circumstances that propelled their marriage"—she stayed Avery's interruption with a look—"he never showed any sign of regretting them. But I urge you to think carefully about what it would be like to marry a man who treats you this way now, who is forced into a union he neither wants nor is ready for."

"I love him." Lizzie's face was hard and set. "That's all that matters. In time he will come to love me, too. We are fated to be together. You saw it, Daisy, in the cards."

"Oh—" Daisy flailed for words, unsure how, or even whether, to explain her mistake with the Fool card.

Lizzie was caught up in her own conviction. "That's all that saved me from dying of heartsickness. You told me I had to live, and have this child, and that Phineas would marry me, and it would all be all right."

"Well, I didn't say quite all that. . . ."

"You must give me a magic spell. I will see Phineas at the Apple Ball in a few day's time, and I'll give it to him then. He can't refuse me if I ask him to dance, it's the rule of the ball. But I need a spell!"

"I think what's needed here is some careful consideration," said Avery.

Lizzie waved this off, now looking so much surer of herself, almost calm. She directed her appeal to Kathryn. "Please give me a charm, an amulet."

Kathryn shook her head firmly. "Interfering with matters of the heart is dangerous and unreliable."

Lizzie pleaded, but Kathryn stayed firm, and nothing was resolved. Daisy and her sisters walked Lizzie back to High Street, all of them in the same restless, solemn mood as they parted ways. By tacit agreement, the sisters skirted the topic of their mother's past. Instead, they rushed through the errands, racing home to cook supper in time for their guest, having lost so much time to Lizzie's predicament, and now their own. But it was certain they would return to this explosive news.

Mother Superior arrived at six o'clock, regal in her black habit.

Bernadette gave her childhood protector and guide a kiss on each waxen cheek and led her into the parlor, where a fire was lit in the grate. After they'd settled themselves by the hearth, Daisy poured small cups of wine for them both. Avery was in the kitchen cooking, and Morrigan was arranging the table.

Daisy perched awkwardly at the edge of the sofa and smiled politely at the venerable mother, this person who had always loomed large in all their lives. Years ago, she had sheltered orphaned three-year-old Bernadette at the convent after both her parents, refugees from French Acadia, were killed in a house fire along with her baby brother.

Daisy now wondered what Mother Superior had felt about her mother's wedding to a man not of the Catholic faith. If Morrigan's Vision was right, is that why they'd eloped? What else didn't she know about her own mother? Her entire sense of the world was in an uproar. And if the slamming she could hear from the kitchen was any indication, Avery wasn't having an easy time of it either. That out-of-wedlock pregnancy had likely been her.

Daisy and her sisters had only the vaguest notion of Bernadette's childhood. All they'd known before today was what they'd been told, and that wasn't much. Just that the Sisters had raised both Bernadette and Kathryn—also orphaned. They'd educated, clothed, and fed them. Then Bernadette had met Augustus Wolfson and converted to Protestantism to marry him here in the church in Redcliffe. His family was very wealthy, but Augustus and Bernadette had had little money, which had always struck Daisy as odd. Given that pervasive chill between Aunt Mary—her father's only sibling—and Bernadette, Daisy now wondered if he'd been disowned for marrying beneath his station. Was *that* why they'd married at night in an empty church?

As Daisy listened to the reverend mother tell her former ward about the goings-on at the convent, the usual tensions with the Vatican, financial worries, and petty day-to-day gossip, she could not stop goggling inwardly at the idea that Bernadette LeBlanc and Augustus Wolfson had been married in secret! Here was incontrovertible evidence that her mother really had been young and passionate and madly in love. Even downright rebellious.

"Dinner is served," announced Avery from the doorway, her face unreadable, and they took their places at the table. Avery had cooked a roast with carrots and onions, along with succotash, baked squash, and mashed potatoes with pepper-flecked gravy. Everyone collectively turned their attention to eating. Forks clinked against plates, sips of wine followed bites of meat, and napkins were delicately lifted to swab at chins gleaming with the rich gravy.

Bernadette, always so dignified and self-composed, seemed a little wary and cowed in the presence of her erstwhile benefactress, as if she weren't exactly comfortable but knew she owed her a great debt. Mother Superior was in Redcliffe fairly frequently on convent business, raising funds for the orphanage, meeting with the prominent

Catholics in town to apprise them of the charity work of her order. She was a distinguished personage, somehow made superhuman by her habit, with neither womanly form nor human needs. Her voice was even and low, her gestures minimal, and she rarely looked anyone directly in the eye, preferring instead to cast her eyes upward to the heavens, as if that were the only place that mattered.

As Daisy stared at the reverend mother, the image she had drawn of the Hierophant in her tarot deck superimposed itself upon the older woman's face. With an inward jolt, Daisy realized that she had been the unconscious model, even though the Hierophant was meant to be a male figure, a pontiff bridging deity and humanity. Like the Hierophant's robe and headpiece, Mother Superior's wimple framed her large, soft face, and her habit gave her an aura of power and solidity. All she was missing was a golden key and a staff topped with a triple cross.

Daisy shivered as something brushed the back of her neck.

Morrigan glanced at her, concerned.

Oh, some strands had come loose from her braid. She was so antsy these days! She tucked them back in, smiling at Morrigan as much to reassure herself as her twin.

"More wine, Mother? . . . And Mother?" As Daisy sloshed wine into cups before they could nod their assent, Bernadette shot her a sharp look.

"Are you listening, child?" Mother Superior said huffily.

"Yes, Mother," Bernadette murmured, quickly rearranging her features into a mask of deference.

It occurred to Daisy that this reunion was perhaps not as warm as it had at first seemed, that this seemingly devoted relationship might actually be fraught underneath the veneer of politesse. Was the reverend mother merely deigning to dine at the home of her former ward? Was Bernadette not the lucky orphan who'd created a happy family life for herself, but instead an infidel who had been ousted from the church under dubious circumstances? The Hierophant card Daisy had pulled earlier had been inverted. Something about her mother's secretive marriage, as well as her subsequent conversion to Protestantism, signified a total rejection of her past and upbringing. Had Bernadette rebelled against her guardian's teachings? Daisy had no idea how much Mother Superior knew of the reasons for her parents' hasty marriage, but it seemed likely she hadn't been uninvolved. Now that Daisy truly thought about it, she couldn't imagine the stern woman approving of it in any way.

After the iced currant cake had been eaten down to the last crumb and all the claret drunk, Daisy and Morrigan excused themselves to the kitchen to wash the dishes. As Morrigan polished the meat platter with a dishtowel, she whispered, "I saw something else, at dinner. It wasn't a Vision, more of a 'knowing.' About our parents."

Morrigan then confirmed everything Daisy had been suspecting during dinner. There had been great opposition to the union from everyone. The entire convent was against their father. And his family was against their mother, all the Wolfsons. But their parents had defied them all.

Morrigan continued, "I saw a huge force of negativity surrounding their union. I couldn't tell why. And then I saw their wedding, this time more clearly. It's like you said: They eloped in secret! Here in Redcliffe, at the chapel. And Daisy, Kathryn wasn't there."

"Could you see who was?"

"They were married by Reverend Potter, with one witness. I can't see who it is. I first thought it might be the reverend's housekeeper, but that doesn't seem right somehow. Anyway, when I look at our parents at the altar all I see is a shining cloud of joy emanating from them both."

"What else?" Daisy commanded her twin. "We need to know why Kathryn wasn't there. And why all the opposition if they loved each other so?"

"We'll have to ask Kathryn," said Morrigan.

Daisy handed her a dripping bowl. "Don't bet on it. She's as tight-lipped as an oyster."

Morrigan laughed, then turned serious again. "What do you think will become of Lizzie? Will Finny ever marry her?"

"Nothing good will come of her marrying Finny, assuming he can be coerced into it. And what if he won't?"

They looked at one another. There was no need to spell out the horror of this for the poor girl.

"Poor Lizzie," Daisy sighed. She thought of the fluttery feeling she'd had after Nate had kissed her hand, the unexpected and powerful yearning that had been awakened. She could almost understand what might have led Lizzie to give herself to Finny Stewart if she felt that way about him. And this gave Daisy a spike of actual fear. The strict, chaste, judgmental presence of Mother Superior in their house girded her like a cautionary stay. Whatever happened, no matter how high her feelings ran, she couldn't give in to these strange new urges. She knew too well what happened to poor women who bore children unmarried. They were scorned, shamed, branded seductresses... and worse.

Daisy shivered again, her spine tingling with a foreboding sense of unease. Impulsively, she rushed to the kitchen window, flung it open, and peered outside.

But she saw nothing untoward.

"What is it?" Morrigan said, her delicate brow creasing with alarm.

"Oh, I just..." Daisy hesitated, using all her senses to scan the garden beyond the natural boundaries of sight and sound.

But all was silent and still.

"It's nothing," she said. "I'm jumping at shadows these days."

"In all the excitement, that makes perfect sense," Morrigan said.

With a sigh, Daisy pulled the curtains shut and rejoined her twin at the sink.

Perhaps if she'd trusted her instincts and stayed just a moment longer, she might have caught the earthly scent of petrichor at odds with the rainless evening or noticed how the dense fog seemed to undulate and coil in the moonlight.

Because hidden in the unseasonable early gloom lurked a malevolent presence that transcended the physical realm, an otherworldly energy that illuminated the darkened garden with an unholy glow, casting uncanny shadows that writhed and slithered in a macabre dance upon the umbrous trees.

You'll see, my young beauty, you'll feel those burning fires, just you wait. They'll warm you right up. And not one of these mothers, superior though they may be, can protect you from the havoc I'll wreak.

CHAPTER VI

THE LOVERS

"Being deeply loved by someone gives you strength, while loving someone deeply gives you courage."

—Lao Tzu

Daisy and Morrigan were finally old enough to attend the annual Apple Ball. Held in the town's Grange Hall, all of Redcliffe was invited, and the tradition was that the women asked the men to dance. Eve had offered Adam the apple, after all. There was applejack and apple brandy, hot cider mulled with cinnamon and cloves, apple cake, and apple-and-cheese savory pies. The dance always went on until the early hours of the morning, and then long tables were brought out and a big breakfast was served, after which everyone went yawning home to bed.

"Before we go," Bernadette said, on her way to the kitchen, "I'll brew a tea to protect against colds. All that dancing in a crowd."

Avery was perched on her favorite armchair in the parlor,

grinning at her sisters sitting carefully on the sofa in their frocks. "Quick, Daisy, do a reading before Mother gets back."

"My cards are all the way upstairs."

"Use mine." Morrigan tossed Daisy her own deck, folded in plain paper and tied with twine.

Daisy had based the bespoke tarot decks she'd created for herself and her sisters on a blend of those currently in fashion and her Vision, adding further customizations for each of them. Her own deck was deeply influenced by the exhilarating world of the tarot artist she'd Visioned in the future. For Morrigan, she'd created a historical deck steeped in the mythology of ancient civilizations. And for Avery, given her affinity for science and the natural world, she had added illustrations of plants, animals, and celestial bodies.

Daisy unwrapped Morrigan's cards, getting the distinct feeling of them warming in her hands.

"Let's have an open-ended one-card pull for the evening," suggested Avery.

Daisy gave the cards a thorough shuffle and had Morrigan cut the deck, then gave it to Avery to cut again, doing the final split herself. She lifted the top card from the deck and flipped it over to set the Lovers card down on the tea table.

"Of course," said Avery.

Daisy stared at Morrigan's card, the Lovers, which she'd drawn as the Garden of Eden: *A man and woman clothed only in leaves join hands around a shiny red apple. Twelve rays of a glorious sun blaze through the wings of an angel beaming down at their union. In the background, a serpent twines up a tree heavy with ripe fruit.*

"So, the garden of earthly delights," Bernadette said, sliding back into the room on those little cat feet of hers. "The Lovers, a fitting card for the Apple Ball."

As her mother and sisters laughed, Daisy felt a flash of delight at the mischievous girl she'd suddenly glimpsed in her mother. But was that really a surprise now in the face of what she and her sisters had learned about their parents' secret marriage? It was becoming evident to Daisy that she'd vastly underestimated her mother's depths.

Bernadette plucked up the Lovers card to examine it more closely, placing a tray one-handedly on the table with unerring accuracy, spilling not a single drop. "Daisy, your inkwork is exquisite. Drink up, girls." And with that, she disappeared upstairs to fetch her shawl and sheet music.

"What was that?" Daisy hissed at her sisters, agog at the playfulness, the lack of censure . . . the compliment!

Avery and Morrigan shrugged and reached for their mugs in tandem, gesturing at Daisy to do the same.

They were all impatient to get to the Grange Hall. Bernadette was the pianist for the dance, and it had become Avery's favorite social occasion of the year. She wasn't shy with boys, enjoying their company and never seeming to worry about what they thought of her. She assured her younger sisters that it was a magical night.

Once there, Daisy found she lacked Avery's confidence and huddled on the outskirts of the dance floor with Morrigan, Annabelle Stewart, Lizzie Cuttle, and a few other girls, watching couples twirl around the vast wood expanse of the Grange. It had been swept clean, the huge rolling doors thrown open to moonlight and the fresh night air. Village dogs wandered in and out, weaving between the dancers' legs and begging for scraps of apple cake. Like other yearly festivals in Redcliffe, the ball was a celebratory occasion that brought the entire village together. Daisy spotted the pastor's housekeeper dancing alongside the eldest Baird girl, from one of the largest Wampanoag farming families. Snatches of Portuguese and Creole drifted over from clusters of recent Cape Verdean immigrants, and Aunt Mary's dashing young footman spun a surprisingly agile church matron around the dance floor. Bernadette was transformed at the piano, so vivacious and lively in her playing Daisy hardly recognized her. The dance floor filled with men dressed in their finest breeches and tails, their female partners attired in pretty frocks in autumnal shades, high-waisted and easy to move about in.

Daisy smoothed her own russet dress, another hand-me-down from Avery that Morrigan had tailored just this morning. Morrigan's was a pale apple green, and Avery was draped in rich gold muslin.

"There's Nate," Morrigan said, nudging her twin. "I dare you to go ask him for the next dance. You know he's just waiting for you to ask."

Indeed, Nate was smiling at Daisy, hovering just outside the girls' circle.

Another factor provoking Daisy's shyness, aside from her feelings for this one particular handsome boy, was that this year the town council had approved a new form of dance. Traditionally, it was all group dances, everyone lining up in rows, men handing women along and women twirling from partner to partner. But in recent years, a bold craze had swept New England, and it had finally reached Redcliffe. Couples, dancing!

Daisy asking Nate to dance meant asking him to take her in his arms and hold her close and guide her by pressing his hand against hers, his other hand at her waist, the two of them engaging in a deliriously close interlude. Daisy had never danced with a boy before, and she found she feared it as much as she longed for it. The stern figure of the Hierophant had stayed with her as a warning, along with the example of Lizzie Cuttle, who at this moment nervously clutched Daisy's hand, her own damp and hot.

Daisy had no magic spell for Finny, but she hoped a conversation with the two of them in close proximity would help the cause, so she took it upon herself to intervene. "Lizzie," Daisy said, "I'll ask Nate if you ask Finny."

"Do you truly think he'll say yes?" Lizzie asked. "He's been avoiding me all night."

"He has to," Daisy said. "As you said the other day, those are the rules of the Apple Ball."

"All right, then." Lizzie took a deep breath.

Bernadette began playing the opening chords to a lilting air in 3/4 time, so Daisy and Lizzie disengaged their hands and walked off in opposite directions to claim their respective partners.

Nate greeted Daisy eagerly. "I thought you would never ask."

Daisy smiled back so hard she feared her face would crack open. "Shall we essay a waltz?"

Nate took Daisy's hand and led her onto the dance floor. After a bit of fumbling, because the dance was new and they were all still learning it, she and Nate fell into a rhythmic and joyful swirl, wafting by other partners as they circled the floor, beaming into each other's eyes.

"You're good!" he exclaimed.

"I have to confess, I've only ever waltzed with my sisters at home."

"This is your first year at the Apple Ball?" he asked. "I'm so glad you're here. I was secretly hoping you were sixteen already."

"Since last spring," Daisy said. "How old are you? How many have you been to?"

"I am eighteen," he said, "but I was raised in Sandwich, and we have no Apple Ball there, so this is my first one, too. I'm very happy to spend it with you!"

The rest of the dance was so giddy and euphoric, Daisy became dizzy with breathlessness. She was glad of the strong, bracing arms that held her as close as they could without breaching etiquette. When it was over, Nate led her back to her group of friends and gave her his courtly-but-cheeky bow. "I hope you will ask me again," he said, and strode away.

"I will," Daisy breathed in his wake, clutching Morrigan for support.

Lizzie rushed up to them. "He said no. He said no, outright. In front of Jasper Fitzwilliam and Colin Hynes, he said no."

Daisy put her arm around Lizzie and gave her a quick, hard hug. "I'll have a word."

Morrigan gave Daisy a quick glance. "Are you sure that's a good idea?"

"I only want to encourage him to make it right." Daisy made a beeline for Finny. He stood in a small group with Jasper and Colin Hynes, the cobbler.

"Hello, Miss Wolfson," said Jasper, managing to infuse both disapproval and skepticism into what on the surface was a perfectly polite greeting.

"Please, call me Daisy," she forced herself to say, not to be outdone by his faux politesse.

"I hear you told Nate quite the fortune the other day, *Daisy*."

"Tarot reading. Where did you hear that?"

"From Henry. Nate told him it was quite provocative. What the devil did you tell him?"

Ignoring Jasper, Daisy turned to Finny Stewart. "Finny, may I have the honor of this dance?" She dropped her voice to a slightly deeper register, her tone playfully courtly.

Finny bowed with a smile. "It's Phineas now. And of course, Daisy, it's good to see my old playmate looking so well." *The rat.* And with the mother of his child-to-be weeping into her hankie, mere feet away. Daisy realized she needed to take control of her face, or her plan to help Lizzie would come to nothing before it had even started.

She was provided a welcome distraction when Finny's sister, Annabelle, chose that moment to waft into their circle, luminous in an apple-red dress. Annabelle approached Jasper, and he bowed deeply and swept her off with a flourish. How had such a kind and seemingly intelligent girl as Annabelle fallen for horrible Jasper's questionable charms?

Finny cleared his throat, looking a little pouty. "Would you rather stare at Jasper, or did you want that dance?"

"Not hardly!" Seeing his stricken expression, Daisy hastened to explain. "I mean, yes, let's!"

Finny took Daisy's hand and led her onto the floor. Bernadette was playing a polka. Finny was proficient, but nowhere near as good a dancer as Nate. Or Jasper, she was forced to admit, who twirled Annabelle with effortless grace. Daisy forced her attention back to her own partner, whose hold was limp and clammy, not firm and warm like Nate's. It was hard to talk with all the hopping and leaping about, but she was determined to complete her mission.

"Finny," Daisy panted, "I asked you to dance because I have something I want to say."

"Phineas, *please*," he said, looking pained.

"I apologize," Daisy said.

"I forgive you, dear Daisy. And please, unburden yourself to me."

"It concerns Lizzie Cuttle."

Abruptly, he stopped dancing to glare at her. "You must not interfere," he snapped imperiously, as though scolding a small child.

Daisy was rendered temporarily speechless by the force of the rebuttal and the condescension with which it was delivered. Finny took the opportunity to drag her once more around the room, as though the matter had been settled. *How typical,* she fumed, as they moved with half the finesse of their fellow dancers. In contrast, when Avery and Henry danced past, so companionable did they look that it was impossible to tell who was leading the other, both so agile and elegant.

Daisy forced her attention back to the important matter at hand. "And yet I must interfere," she told Finny without apology. "If only out of sympathy for my dear friend."

"You of all people, Daisy, are the last person I would want to know of this matter and to speak to me of it."

"Why is that? Surely we can speak frankly. We were friends as children, and I hope that continues now, and onward into adulthood." Though to be honest, Daisy found she didn't much care. Still, whatever helped.

"Because," said Finny, his face red, his eyes boring into hers, "because, Daisy, I will confess that I have an interest in you that goes... beyond friendship. I dared to hope that you might feel the same way."

This was an entirely unexpected and unwelcome development. "I assure you, *Phineas,* my opinion of you is of no consequence. What matters to me is Lizzie, the girl you've wronged by refusing to acknowledge your responsibility for her... condition."

He gasped, as if Daisy had slapped him. "I must say, it strikes me as out of line for a young woman of your respectable social standing to speak with such impudent frankness. Perhaps the Apple Ball tradition has loosened your tongue."

"I do beg your pardon," Daisy retorted, "but I don't see how addressing a topic directly is out of line. If I were a man, you wouldn't think twice about it."

"But you're decidedly not a man," he said with a tight, teeth-baring smile, "and thank goodness for that! You are of the fairer sex, one to be trusted to observe decorum and speak with respect and tact."

"I *respectfully* and *tactfully* disagree." The tips of Daisy's ears blazed red. "It doesn't surprise me that you have treated poor Lizzie with such contempt, given how you speak to me. But understand this: Others know what you've done. And we're all hoping you quickly see the error of your present ways and take pains to make it right."

"Daisy," he said hotly into her ear, "let me also speak frankly, since that is what you wish. This sort of fire is precisely the sort of thing I want in a wife—but only in the bedroom." His hand on her back gripped so tightly, Daisy thought he might break one of her ribs.

For once, she had no quick comeback.

"And all I have to say about Lizzie Cuttle," Finny went on, "is that if she has spoiled my chances with you, then I am doubly turned against her. I disavow any responsibility for whatever distasteful predicament she finds herself in. We shall speak no more of this."

"Unhand me at once, *Finny*."

With a grunt of frustration, he let Daisy go. She stalked over to the table that held the drinks. She considered a glass of cider, then poured herself a neat dram of applejack and tossed it back. Then she had another. She felt heady and powerful with the righteousness of her anger.

"What did he say?" Lizzie asked anxiously when Daisy rejoined her.

"He's a dastardly lying scoundrel," Daisy said, her brain deliciously loosened.

"Oh, Daisy," Lizzie sighed. "My heart is breaking inside my chest. He denies our connection?"

"He does," Daisy confessed, "although I hope I've given him some things to think about."

"Daisy, you have to make a charm that will bring Phineas back to me." Lizzie's face was naked with yearning desperation. "I swear to you, he loved me once. He only needs something to help him remember. I'm begging."

"Lizzie, it's too dangerous. There's always another—"

"Dance partner? Here I am."

Daisy glanced up to see Nate, grinning flirtatiously.

"Oh, Nate! I'm sorry, but Lizzie and I were—" Seeing Lizzie's horrified face, Daisy stopped herself just in time. "I would love to dance, but I can't right now."

"There's nothing I can do to tempt you?" Nate said. "Perhaps I could remind you of your social duty in seeking another dance partner. I wouldn't want you to get in trouble with the authorities."

With Lizzie clutching her arm, Daisy found herself unable to rise to Nate's warm banter. Wordlessly, she shook her head.

Nate caught sight of Morrigan, who was approaching their small group. "Perhaps this fair lady will oblige me, then," he said playfully. "Miss Morrigan, may I induce you to ask me for the next dance?"

"You may," she said with a quick glance at Daisy, "although I understand it's highly improper for men to try to provoke women to invite them to dance."

"I accept!" he crowed, in high spirits, and swept Morrigan onto the dance floor as she gazed back at Daisy in mute apology.

For a moment, all Daisy could do was stare after them, her heart sinking. There was no denying that Morrigan and Nate made a handsome couple. Her lovely sister with her luminous skin and raven hair shone in the arms of her broad-shouldered partner. Daisy felt the pang of a new emotion: envy, that monster, of her very own twin sister, her most trusted confidant, with whom she had been entwined since before they were born. It was ugly, it felt terrible, and she needed to vanquish it as quickly as it had arisen.

Daisy looked from Morrigan and Nate over to Avery, who was now dancing with Colin Hynes, of all people. How had he inveigled her into asking him to dance? He was fox-faced, with wispy blond hair. There was a canny, trickster look about him, as if he were always looking for a better angle on life. Daisy knew that his young wife was bedridden, in the final stages of a difficult pregnancy with their second child. What business did he have dancing with an unmarried girl?

As Avery and Colin waltzed past the piano, Daisy's gaze went to her mother. Her color was high, and she was clearly in her element, casting a spell with her music.

Lizzie was still clutching Daisy's elbow in a silent plea when someone jostled her other elbow. Like a bad penny, Jasper Fitzwilliam had returned, his brows knit together.

"On the topic of the . . . *reading* you gave Nate," he said. "I have a personal reason for wanting to know, and Henry won't tell me."

Daisy itched to silence Jasper any way she could, short of outright rudeness. As Bernadette swung from a waltz to an up-tempo mazurka, a nice bouncy tune that would soon have all the dancers too breathless to talk, Daisy pounced. "Will you give me the pleasure of this dance?"

Surprised but clearly bent on continuing his interrogation, Jasper offered his arm and led Daisy onto the dance floor. He was an astonishingly good dancer, particularly after the clumsy ferocity of Finny Stewart. Wordlessly avoiding eye contact, Daisy gave herself over to following his lead, their feet moving through the pattern together in controlled leaps.

"It might not be clear from my silence," Jasper said to the top of Daisy's head after they had made a turn of the floor, "but I assure you, I am avidly awaiting your answer."

"I have none," Daisy said to the air just below his right ear. "Readings are confidential. Nate is welcome to tell you anything he chooses. But I'm not at liberty."

He scoffed. "You can't tell me this claptrap has professional standards!"

"If Nate's reading was claptrap, why are you so curious?"

"Because I sense it had to do with me, and that I should be wary of your advice to him."

"You should ask Nate, then," Daisy said. "I only read the cards."

Daisy and Jasper flew along the floorboards, conversation at a stalemate, their bodies in an easy synchronized sway and pace. Even as their minds were at loggerheads, their joined hands were pressed together, Jasper's other hand on Daisy's waist, strong and assured, hers resting lightly along his shoulder, their legs interweaving as they rose and fell to the pounding beat.

Daisy became increasingly aware of Jasper's warmth; the sweet, clean, heady smell of him; his very particular physicality, lean and coiled as a cat. *Oh, blazes!* Her body betrayed her with its primal response to his, no matter how vehemently her mind reminded itself that this man was not to be trusted. The mazurka built to a rousing peak, the increase of tempo inevitably bringing them closer together in the centripetal swirl, and she felt them melt together so that even the slightest pressure from his fingers against hers told her where to put her feet, the most subtle arch of her back informing him which way to send her spinning. She had no idea where Nate or Finny or Lizzie or even her sisters were, forgot that it was her mother at the piano. She knew only an intoxicating physical clarity of movement, a concentrated whirl of sensation.

The music ended, and Jasper released Daisy. Cool air rushed between them, dispelling the kinetic heat they'd created. Daisy could barely meet his eyes, and when she did, she saw a similarly baffled expression on his face. For an instant, they locked gazes. And then they parted without a word. She bumped into Morrigan, who was leaving the floor with Henry, the two of them laughing, their arms entwined. "Impossible," Henry was saying, "kick, hop, what? I'm like a windblown duck in a thunderstorm!"

"You almost had it!" said Morrigan, and then, "Hello, Daisy! How did you and Jasper manage that impossible dance? You looked awfully good!"

Daisy was grateful when the town dance master saved her from replying by announcing a brief pause. "To allow our most brilliant pianist to have a well-deserved refreshment." The man gestured at Bernadette, who rose smiling from her bench, bowing her head to acknowledge the applause. Daisy drifted with her twin and Henry over to Avery. "You acquitted yourselves pretty well out there," Avery said to them all. "The steps are the devil's work."

"Daisy and Jasper did," said Morrigan. "Henry and I made up our own steps!"

"We had more fun than anyone, I'd wager," said Henry.

Daisy noticed that their arms were still linked, and Morrigan was leaning against Henry, smiling up at him. Morrigan and Henry had always been particular favorites, their mutual fondness going back to childhood, but this was an interesting twist.

Their match was a plausible one, though not without its complications despite there being no blood relation. Daisy foresaw Aunt Mary standing firmly in the way of her beloved ward's love for a penniless daughter of Bernadette, that orphaned Catholic who'd been so unworthy of her adored younger brother. For Aunt Mary, it would no doubt feel like history repeating itself. And Daisy suspected Henry would be deeply loath to cross his guardian, to whom he owed so much. If and when they decided to pledge their troth, Morrigan and Henry would have a battle ahead of them. They were both so accommodating, Daisy feared they might cede defeat before it had even begun. Daisy's earlier attack of jealousy dissolved into a pang of compassion for her twin, to have the likes of Aunt Mary standing in the way of marrying her true love.

The next two sets of dances were as lively and vigorous as the previous, and Nate and Daisy gave up all pretense of looking elsewhere and danced all of them together. By the early hours of the morning, they were flushed and laughing, and their steps were less precise than enthusiastic. Damp strands of hair were pasted against Daisy's cheeks and the back of her neck. The ball ended with an old-fashioned group dance: men facing women, taking turns stepping hand in hand through the corridor of bodies and whirling down the shifting lines to do it again.

Unexpectedly, Daisy found herself face-to-face with Jasper. She hesitated as their eyes met, but he reached for her and deftly spun her through the arches of hands overhead, searing her with a brief glance before handing her off to her next partner, who turned out to be Nate. The two men visibly recoiled from each other, and then Daisy was off, head spinning as wildly as her skirts. Nate released her to Henry for the next round and danced off in another direction, then she was passed to Finny for a brief, deeply uncomfortable circuit, then to a village lad she knew only slightly, and she once again gave herself over to the exuberance of the dance.

After the reel ended, everyone collapsed on rough wooden benches at long tables and fell ravenously on platters of apple fritters, pork sausages, baked beans, and slabs of ham with pickles and preserves. After breakfast, as the sky began to lighten, the Grange Hall emptied as the townsfolk drifted homeward to sleep off the night's joy and excesses.

The sisters burst through their cottage door with their mother in their wake. There was clearly no need to interpret the Lovers card Daisy had pulled at the beginning of the night. They'd all felt the energy of temptation, innocence, youth, love, passion, and even despair that had infused the Apple Ball.

But what to make of it all? What would become of Lizzie and her doomed love for Finny? And how to explain Daisy's uncanny physical response to Jasper, when she knew she already had feelings for Nate?

Unanswered and unanswerable for the moment, these questions buzzed in the air just beyond Daisy's reach.

A wistful figure lingered at the edge of the forest, drawn inexorably toward the spectral form of a serpent swirling in the shadows, its essence more felt than seen. A heady scent glided through the early dawn's mist, the air dusted with desire.

The apparition was cloaked in a shimmering light and undulated within a sheath that pulsed in shifting hues of iridescent blues and eerie greens. It seemed to breathe, expanding and contracting with a sinuous rhythm that was both mesmerizing and unsettling.

Come to me, my sweetness . . .

Overcome by a longing so potent it eclipsed all reason, the serpent's victim shuffled forward in a trancelike state through the almost-darkness, helpless against the pull of certain doom.

CHAPTER VII

THE CHARIOT

"Adventure is not outside man; it is within."

—GEORGE ELIOT

After a few hours of sleep, Daisy flung off the damp bedclothes and hurled herself into the morning, shocked to see she was alone. She could hear her sisters discussing the day's agenda with Bernadette.

Daisy cast about for something to fling on so she could rush downstairs, her absence assuredly already noticed, but she caught a whiff of a . . . ripeness emanating from her person. Not entirely surprising, given last night's strenuous if exhilarating dancing. She tipped some water from the pitcher into the basin on the washstand, dipped a sponge into it, and scrubbed her face and body.

Morrigan and Avery popped into the room and gawped.

"She lives!" Avery shrieked.

Blushing, Daisy flung a towel over herself, unaccountably shy. "What happened to the courtesy of knocking?"

"It's almost noontime, sleepyhead," Morrigan said.

"What, no!" Forcing herself to shrug off the strange new modesty, Daisy toweled herself off and slipped into her underclothing. "How did this happen?!"

Morrigan came to stand behind Daisy, finger-combing the knots from her mass of coiled curls. Avery plucked Daisy's weekday dress from its hook in the armoire and tossed it to her. Daisy hastily pulled it over her head.

"Well, you see, Daisy, when the sun shifts in the sky..." Avery buttoned her up in back as Morrigan cackled.

"Oh hush, both of you!"

"We decided you needed some extra sleep," Avery said. "After all your... excitement last night."

Daisy's scalp tingled. She felt the evening's apple wine pounding in her head, which whirled with unwelcome memories of her dance with Jasper. Her mouth went dry. How could she have responded so viscerally to that supercilious person?

"Did I really dance with Jasper?" Daisy asked her sisters. "Please tell me it was just a bad dream."

Morrigan pulled Daisy's now-tamed hair back into a knot at the nape. "I wonder what Nate made of that dance. Who knew the mazurka could be so..."

"Sensual?" Avery finished to Morrigan's great delight.

"It was *not—*" Face burning, Daisy absorbed the implications of what Morrigan had just said. "Tell me honestly, do you think Nate was displeased?"

"Doubtlessly," Avery said, now sprawled in the hard-backed chair in the corner of their little room. Daisy threw her an agonized look. "Oh, don't fret, we're just teasing you."

"I find myself at a loss this morning," Daisy confessed to her sisters. "I can't explain what I feel or even think."

"Let's do a quick reading for you before we go down," Avery said. "To settle your nerves."

Morrigan nodded. "She's right, Daisy."

Daisy felt an odd prickling of disappointment that she already knew what card would come up. When had reading tarot become so . . . predictable?

"Thinking the card isn't the same as experiencing it," Avery noted, as if Daisy had said this aloud.

Daisy sighed, deciding to get it over with. Cards in her hands, she strove to empty herself of all thought as she shuffled her deck. Feeling energy dance in her fingers, she contemplated the necessity of clarity, along with its sister, insight. She'd always liked that word, the marriage of *in* and *sight*, the mental act of looking inward and seeing what lay there. She and her sisters had been endowed with the ability to see beneath the surface, to find unspoken ailments and pains, silent regrets and yearnings and hopes, things people often weren't fully aware of themselves.

But why had they been granted these powers? Daisy only knew that their abilities were a great responsibility, an onus even, as much as they were a gift. It was mutually understood that they had to use them for good, to help people, offer solace, not attempt to control or manipulate. It would have been so easy to allow dark, self-interested impulses to override their nobler aims. They weren't angels or paragons; they were young and very human. Daisy didn't like to admit it, but she was aware that their mother's warnings often stood the three of them in good stead, her cautionary, admonishing voice strong in all their inner ears.

"It's time, Daisy," Avery commanded.

Daisy handed her the deck, and Avery drew a finger lightly down its spine.

"Stop," Daisy said.

Avery flipped the card with a flourish. "Your chariot awaits!"

Despite knowing that this would be the card, Daisy had still had the faint hope that it might be something different, the comforting Six of Pentacles maybe, or the lovely Sun.

"Daisy, what's wrong?" Morrigan embraced her sister. "Surely you're not surprised."

"I *want* to be surprised," Daisy said irritably. "It all feels predetermined."

"But it's not," Avery said. "Look at the card."

"I know what the card looks like, I painted it," Daisy muttered.

"Look again," Avery urged.

Daisy peered down at the card. She knew every line of it as well as her own hand, but she willed herself to see the Chariot with fresh eyes: *A young man crowned by a gleaming mane of stars and carrying an onyx-and-pearl scepter straddles two winged horses, one white and one black. Behind him unfold the arches and spires of twin towns.*

"This seems to be about your inner situation," Avery said, tapping her right cheekbone thoughtfully. "The Herox's Journey is both inner and outer."

Morrigan clapped her hands excitedly. *"Herox!"* she said. "Both hero and heroine at the same time, how perfect."

Avery watched, waiting.

A Vision tugged at the periphery of Daisy's senses, one she felt as much as saw: a scroll of parchment paper, the impression of fluidity, a man and woman blending together prismatically in a kaleidoscope of colors. It was as though time itself were unspooling.

"I'm in charge of my own journey." Daisy was speaking slowly for once, feeling her way forward in words. "But I don't lose anything by choosing one route over another. There is no single path, there are many all woven together. Those seemingly opposed horses on the card are really twins, aspects of the same line, expanding in all directions, each one leading toward its own equilibrium."

"Blazes," Avery said with a low whistle of approval.

Where had this uncharacteristic willingness to explore without knowing the end point come from? "I don't understand—"

"But you do," Morrigan interrupted. "That's what Avery's been getting at. You've always known. It's more about . . ."

"Remembering," Daisy said suddenly.

They all nodded at one another, comprehending together this thing that couldn't be explained with simple words. Everything existed all at once: past, present, future, all the infinite possibilities and choices that created a life. For a brief, shining moment, the three of them saw the Vision together: *the chariot of time, the great wheels that turned in all directions at once.*

"Girls!" Bernadette's voice came from downstairs, piercing the moment with an urgency that could not be ignored. Something was wrong.

Avery leapt to the door and raced downstairs, Morrigan on her heels. Daisy hastily slid her stockinged feet into shoes and brought up the rear. Bernadette stood at the vestibule with a young boy not more than eight or nine years old, his tweed cap askew.

"He's come from the Godwins'." Bernadette's voice was steady but her face tight. "It appears Tabitha has taken a turn."

So Tabitha Godwin really *had* fallen suddenly ill when Morrigan and Avery had gone to help her with her charity work at the church. They hadn't fabricated the excuse to interrupt Daisy's reading with Nate. And Tabitha hadn't been at the Apple Ball, Daisy realized belatedly.

"She's calling for you," said Bernadette. "All three of you. Isn't that right? What's your name, young sir?"

"It's Lucas, ma'am, and yes, ma'am," said the boy in a gruff little voice. "That what Mrs. Pippin said: Miss Godwin's awful poorly and the doctor's been and nothing's helping."

Briskly, the sisters put on their cloaks and fetched their reticules from the basket by the door. Daisy felt Bernadette's hand slide something into her pocket, but she couldn't tell what it was.

An eerie laughter suddenly punctuated the air, reverberating inside Daisy's skull.

"Do you hear that?" Daisy whispered.

"Hear what?" Bernadette frowned at her.

As quickly as it had come, the laughter ceased, leaving behind a silence that was even more unsettling. Had she imagined it? Daisy shuddered involuntarily.

She glanced into the garden. Avery stood right outside the door, waiting with Morrigan. Just beyond the gate, Lucas was standing by a rustic buckboard, an unsprung cart pulled by a single horse. Birds chirped and leaves rustled in the light breeze, but amid these familiar sounds, the atmosphere felt thick with unspoken tension.

Bernadette held the door open. "Daisy. Run."

CHAPTER VIII

STRENGTH

"There is nothing so strong as gentleness and nothing so gentle as real strength."

—ST. FRANCIS DE SALES

Daisy was so caught up in the feverish haste to get to Tabitha that she scarcely noticed sudden, gloomy changes to the town they raced through, the overcast skies a disconcerting purplish color.

Straddling a narrow wooden box, Lucas drove the sturdy workhorse as fast as he could through back lanes and alleys, taking shortcuts known only to him. In the back of the cart, sharing limited space with tarpaulin-covered hay bales, the sisters clung to leather straps bolted to the sides of the rickety vehicle, bouncing at every turn.

Lucas shouted another apology over the racket of the wheels on the cobblestones, steering around an impediment. Daisy caught a brief but disturbing glimpse of an empty perambulator crumpled in the street. They careened around a corner, and then it was gone, almost as if she'd imagined it.

They lurched to a halt before the front entrance to the Godwin estate on Society Row, and Lucas leapt down to drag open the imposing iron gate, leading the horse by its halter and pulling the cart and his passengers past the heavy gray limestone walls. After pushing the gate closed behind them, he clambered back onto his box and drove up the grand boulevard flanked by tall sycamores that opened to the broad lawn surrounding the mansion itself.

"We're here," he announced. Daisy gazed up at the turrets casting long shadows into the courtyard. On the balustrade at either side of the wide staircase leading up to the main entrance, two stone lions glared from newel posts.

The giant wooden double doors at the top of the stairs were thrown open with a thud. A tall, stout woman clad in the formal black and white of a housekeeper's uniform came rushing down with a nimbleness impressive for a person of her age. This must be Mrs. Pippin.

"You're here at last!" She gestured for Daisy and her sisters to follow her up the wide stone steps.

Mrs. Pippin ushered them into an enormous room, larger than the entire floor plan of their cottage. Gilt-framed paintings hung on silk-papered walls, heavy velvet drapes pulled tight across the tall windows, the only light coming from flickering amber sconces. In the center of the room hulked a giant four-poster bedstead cloaked in embroidered canopies. Tabitha was barely visible beneath the luxurious pile of quilts and coverlets.

Awake and in possession of her powers, Tabitha Godwin was a somewhat intimidating young woman of twenty-three, the Godwins' youngest child and the last living here in her childhood home. Village gossips maintained, on the whole admiringly, that instead of a husband, she was married to her charity work. She was beloved by the poorest souls of Redcliffe.

Now, Tabitha seemed to be in a deep yet troubled sleep. Under her nightcap, her skin was mottled with raised pink hives that extended up her cheeks and along her forehead. Daisy's own scalp prickled in response. She'd seen something like this before, but when, and with whom?

"How long has she been in this state?" Daisy asked, digging through her reticule.

"For days, and she worsened this morning after her parents departed for Boston." Mrs. Pippin was clenching and unclenching her hands. "The doctor's already been, but he said she was just tired from the ball, though I told him she hadn't gone, she was already too unwell. But he didn't have time for this information." She looked close to tears.

"Doctors," Avery huffed.

Morrigan and Avery helped Daisy push aside the heaviest of the bedclothing. How did rich people sleep, smothered by so many layers?

"I told him she's been like this for days, only rarely awake! And I know what's normal and what's not, especially when it comes to my mistress." Mrs. Pippin was chattering, helpless to stop. "But he was no help at all. Then I remembered you girls are known for your healing, though it's not something Mr. Godwin would approve of, him not being much for this newfangled spiritualism, no offense, misses."

Daisy rested the tips of her fingers on the inside of Tabitha's wrist. The pulse was faint and sluggish.

"It's all right," Morrigan consoled her. "You did the right thing in calling for us."

"And it's not newfangled," Avery said. "Our methods go back centuries."

"We'll do our best, Mrs. Pippin," Daisy said, selecting a few crystals from the pouch and tucking them into the folds of Tabitha's skirts, "but I can't guarantee miracles, particularly since we don't know what exactly is ailing Tabitha."

Daisy unbuttoned her patient's flannel night jacket and placed her hands palms-down directly on Tabitha's nightgown, feeling the heat from her body burn through the linen fabric. She centered one hand on the older girl's chest, above her breast, the other upon her belly, which was hard and unnaturally distended.

"Gracious!" Mrs. Pippin exclaimed. "She looks with child."

Daisy glanced at her sisters, hoping they'd hear her silent plea to distract the distraught woman.

Morrigan put a comforting hand on Mrs. Pippin's arm. "Perhaps some tea?"

"Oh of course, how rude of me not to offer!"

Avery took a cloth pouch from her reticule. "These medicinal herbs may help Tabitha. Echinacea and rose hips, some elderberry."

Mrs. Pippin looked dubious.

"And while we're downstairs brewing the tea, Daisy," Avery continued smoothly, "here's the new elixir I've been working on: belladonna, apis mellifica, and arsenicum. Under her tongue, no more than three drops. Kathryn said it's aces for a fever and hives." Avery set the small green glass vial on the bedside table.

Now the older woman looked even more doubtful.

"It's quite all right, Mrs. Pippin," Avery said soothingly, edging her away from the bed, Morrigan at her other side, taking her arm. "These herbs have been used as medicine for centuries. But I for one could murder a cup of strong black tea. Shall we all go down together?"

Relieved by the mention of a curative she understood, Mrs. Pippin allowed herself to be swept out of the room.

Daisy used the welcome silence to focus her full attention on Tabitha's physical being, listening to her speak through touch. Often, when Daisy dropped deep into a meditative state, bodies had much to say. But Tabitha's was silent. It was as if she weren't even there, her body an empty casing she'd taken leave of.

Daisy scooped the crystals from her lap and let them warm in her hands briefly, transferring some of her own energy to the stones before placing them on Tabitha: orange carnelian on the lower belly to fortify the immune system and enhance vitality; moss agate in the hollow between throat and collarbone to reduce swelling and fever; and green fluorite in the dip of the solar plexus just below the breastbone to clear infection and boost the strength of the other crystals.

Then Daisy poured some cool water from the pitcher on the bedside table into its basin, dipped the washcloth and wrung it out, and tapped out a few drops of a cooling, soothing tincture of lavender Avery had made. She laid the lavender-infused damp cloth on Tabitha's rash-darkened forehead and gently tipped her chin to open her mouth slightly, easing the dropper of Avery's new elixir under her tongue, administering three drops exactly. Finally, Daisy reached for her cards, shuffled them, and peeled the top card from the deck, placing it image-side down above Tabitha's heart.

When Daisy had painted her first deck, she'd swapped the numbers of the Strength and Justice cards, taking the lead of the woman from her future Vision, not bothered with why, just knowing it felt right. She hoped this reading would benefit from that departure from tradition. Above all, Tabitha needed strength.

And when that card revealed itself, Daisy mentally gave thanks to the architect of her future inspiration. She laid the Strength card across Tabitha's chest: *A young woman in shining armor kneels before the open jaws of a lion. She extends her bare hands to gently cradle its immense head, and it gazes placidly at her with undisguised adoration, making no effort to escape the chain of flowers that yoke the two together.*

The card's significance of contemplation and self-control fortified Daisy. Having done everything she could for the moment, she sat back on her heels and waited, closing her eyes and urging herself inward. She concentrated on Tabitha with waves of healing thoughts.

Daisy had no idea how much time had elapsed when she felt a gentle tap on her shoulder. "What's happening?" she cried, horrified to find she had fallen asleep.

Morrigan shook her head sadly. Behind her, Daisy saw Avery, her own face wracked, comforting Mrs. Pippin, who wept at the foot of the bed.

"No!" Daisy leapt to her feet, already knowing.

Tabitha Godwin, her skin leaden, was gone. No breath, no pulse, no color, even. Her rash had vanished, taking with it her life.

"How did this happen?" Daisy was shaken to her very core by the loss of this young woman she'd barely known, and now never would.

"We were too late." Avery's voice was gentle. "We couldn't save her. Sometimes this is just what happens."

"But I drew Strength and laid it across her breast! Look at it! It's there!" Daisy reached over the bed and picked the card up from Tabitha's still body, flipping it to show them the image. Avery's eyes went wide, and Morrigan's hand flew to her mouth.

"Daisy," Avery said carefully. "Turn it toward you."

With a deep dread, Daisy did as told. The card had been reversed. Inverted, it didn't signify strength and triumph over adversity; it represented anger, fear, depletion . . . failure.

And then Daisy remembered Bernadette slipping something into her pocket before they'd left the house. She pulled out a strange dark stone covered in unreadable scratchings. She'd seen Bernadette worry this object between her fingers when she thought no one was looking. Could this amulet have helped? Was it yet another tool she had misused, if only through neglect?

The pity in Morrigan's and Avery's eyes was more than she could bear.

"She was very ill." Avery's voice was a comforting caress. "You did everything you could." Daisy knew Avery meant to soothe and absolve, but she took no comfort. She had never lost a patient before. She was almost insensate with shock. All her healing methods had failed. She had forgotten her mother's amulet. And, once again, she had foxed the card, just as she had Lizzie's Fool.

The moments that followed were hazy, but Daisy's sisters somehow got her down the endless staircases, through the labyrinth of hallways, and down the front steps, where Lucas waited solemnly by the buckboard. They climbed into the cart, and Daisy stared bleakly up at storm clouds, heavy and angry in the sky. Lucas pressed a safety leash into one of Daisy's hands and with a soft clicking sound at the horse took them on their bumpy way back through town. Daisy felt the leather strap trail limply through her fingers and found it hard to care if she was tossed from the cart. It was the least of what she deserved for not preventing Tabitha's demise.

Suddenly, Avery gave a shout. "Stop the cart!"

Lucas jerked the horse to a halt.

Avery pointed at the sky. "Do you see that?"

Startled momentarily out of her fugue, Daisy stared upward. "Storm clouds?"

"Not that," Avery repeated. "Look! It's right there!"

"I just see the clouds." Morrigan's voice was small and afraid.

"It's a shadow come down upon the earth." Avery's voice had gone flat and toneless in that way it did when she was Visioning. "The town is dissolving. The Bleakness is upon us. It may be too late. . . ." She drifted off, sounding far away.

Daisy was abruptly lost to a horrifying Vision of her own: *buildings catch fire, helpless shrieks fill the charred sky; people fall to their knees and weep; a figure plummets from a tower to shatter on the stones; the tide turns red and recedes, leaving behind death-blackened bodies to thrash violently on the shore and crumble to dust.*

Morrigan screamed.

And then everything finally, mercifully, went dark.

CHAPTER IX

THE HERMIT

"Listen to silence. It has so much to say."

—RUMI

Daisy's body was lifted, carried. She was aware of but could not parse the voices that rose and fell around her. It was as though she had sunk to the bottom of a sea and could merely glimpse flickers of light high above at the surface. Time passed in invisible sheets. She lay still.

She would have been content to remain buried by grief within the shadowy deep, but the pungent scent of lavender mixed with elderflower and sage pierced the fug of her mind.

The first thing she saw was Morrigan's face, forehead creased with worry. "She's awake!"

"Oh thank goodness!" said Bernadette, all trace of her usual sternness erased from her voice. "It's been almost a full day."

When Bernadette leaned over Daisy, the amulet she'd given her swung from her neck on an antique chain. Bernadette tucked it back into her bosom and tipped a dropper of something liquid into Daisy's mouth, feeding her like a baby bird. An unexpected thirst took hold of Daisy, and she grasped weakly at the vial for more.

"No, you'll make yourself sick," Bernadette soothed, handing it to Avery, who stoppered it and bent to place it on the occasional table, revealing Kathryn, standing behind her with a steaming mug. Daisy's mother and sisters helped her sit upright to allow her to sip at the hot tea, fragrant with herbs that warmed her from the inside out. She was on the sofa in the parlor. A fire crackled in the grate.

"Dear, sweet Kathryn," Daisy croaked, "you always make the best..." She stopped. What was Kathryn doing here? Was she still dreaming? Her mouth gaped open.

"You'll catch flies," Bernadette observed drily. "Finish your tea, you've had a shock."

"Your mother's right," Kathryn said, righting the mug as it almost fell from Daisy's boneless hands, guiding it back up to her mouth. "There's a good girl."

"Kathryn, a moment?" Bernadette swept up the stairs. With a quick kiss on the top of Daisy's head, Kathryn followed.

Above, Daisy could hear doors opening and closing, two pairs of footsteps rapidly moving from one room to the next.

Never in all Daisy's life had Kathryn stepped foot inside their home. Nothing was making sense.

"You'll never believe it," Morrigan said, rushing over to sit beside Daisy on the sofa. "When we got home, Kathryn was already here! Mother had sent for her after hearing from someone at the Godwin residence about, well, everything."

"But how did they get word to her so quickly?"

"The domestics' telegraph is not to be underestimated," Avery chuckled, wedging onto the sofa on Daisy's other side, and then quickly composed her features into a scowl. "But never mind all that, you gave us a scare!"

"I gave *you* a scare?" Daisy exclaimed, Avery's eerie pronouncements rushing back. "That portent of doom of yours, my god."

"And yet it paled alongside the things you were saying," Morrigan murmured.

The disturbing elements of Daisy's own Vision also came back to her, her insides coiling in as she remembered. "But wait, how did you—"

"You spoke them aloud," Avery interrupted.

"But I never do that!"

"We know," she said. "And Morrigan saw the past, where . . . Well, you tell her."

Daisy listened attentively as Morrigan sketched the scenes of past horrors she'd seen, devastation and hopelessness on a biblical scale. "I can't say where or even when it was, just that it was from the before times, and then, as now, it was called the Great Bleakness, exactly as Avery said."

"I didn't say *great*," Avery muttered. "That's a lovely development."

"So, wait," Daisy said. "Is that what this is? Are we in . . ." She hesitated.

"The Great Bleakness," Bernadette said, reappearing with Kathryn, both laden with bolts of fabric and bundles of candles and other items Daisy couldn't identify.

"Or at least *a* Bleakness," Kathryn corrected, ignoring what Daisy recognized as a dangerous twitch in Bernadette's jaw. "Well, we can't know for certain, can we, Bernadette?" She met the other woman's steely gaze with one of her own.

"I frankly find the details less important than the fact that you involved my daughters in this dreadful business in the first place, Kathryn."

"Perhaps if you'd taught them yourself, they wouldn't have been forced to come to me," Kathryn retorted.

"It's not Mother's fault!" Morrigan cried. "We didn't want to worry you, Mother, so we—"

"You hid nothing from me," Bernadette snapped. "You're my daughters. Did you really think I didn't know?"

Even Avery blanched.

Kathryn rolled her eyes. "Can you imagine her missing a thing like that? Not the Bernadette I know!"

"Knew," came the terse reply.

"You're just as irritating as I recall." Kathryn not-so-gently elbowed Bernadette in the ribs.

To Daisy and her sisters' astonishment, their mother tittered. She actually tittered. And then she elbowed Kathryn back, even harder. "You'd know," Bernadette rejoined flintily. "You wrote the book on irritating."

"If I wrote it, you revised it, edited it, and bound it in leather!" Kathryn shot back.

At which point the two women dissolved into a fit of giggles.

"This is weird, right?" Daisy said to no one in particular.

"It is so weird," Morrigan replied.

"Words fail," said Avery.

"And yet you're still talking," Kathryn observed. Bernadette guffawed and Kathryn clutched her sides, both laughing so hard tears ran down their faces.

The girls were transfixed.

But then the tears became sobs, and Bernadette just stood

weeping, arms still full of her mysterious supplies. Kathryn immediately took the bundle, handed it off to Morrigan, and pulled Bernadette into her arms. "It's okay, Bernie," she cooed, rocking her like a small child. For a moment, Bernadette let her, but then she collected herself and extricated herself from the embrace.

"You don't know that, Kit," she said, wiping her eyes with hard fists. "Just like you didn't know what would happen when we..." She trailed off.

"When you what?" Avery pounced.

"What happened?" Daisy chimed in.

As though just realizing the girls were all still in the room with them, the women stepped apart and shuttered their faces. "Nothing," Bernadette said, abruptly taking her basket back from a stunned Morrigan.

"But—" This time it was Morrigan who pressed.

"Mind your mother, girls." Kathryn picked up her basket.

"I've made a big batch of tea using the strengthening elixir we gave Daisy as a base," said Bernadette, placing her own basket on the living room table. "It's a revitalizing mix of herbs and blessings that should keep the Bleakness at bay. The trick will be getting it out to the rest of the townspeople. If anyone has ideas, now is the time."

"Easy," Avery said. "It's very nearly influenza season. We can take it to market tomorrow and give it out as an autumnal fortification cider."

Bernadette briefly smiled at Avery's ingenuity and continued: "Next: These are supplies for poppets, which we will now teach you to make."

Poppets, it turned out, were personal charms of a sort, individualized for the wearers, which in this case would be Daisy and her sisters. They were put to work cutting strips of felt to create triple-sided pouches: black to banish the dark, white to draw in the light, and purple to invoke the spirit world. They filled them with protection herbs Kathryn and Bernadette had selected: sage to banish negativity and evil spirits; comfrey for strength; and mugwort, which Kathryn said increased the potency of the other herbs.

Daisy felt a tug on her scalp and then heard the snip of scissors. Bernadette handed her a lock of reddish-gold hair, indicating with a gesture that she was to put it in her pouch. "Really, Mother?"

"Really, daughter," she said, moving on to Morrigan and Avery, cutting small locks of hair from their heads.

"Hands, please," said Bernadette, and she trimmed their fingernails with a small pair of scissors, catching the tiny piles of clippings in her palm and tipping them into the poppets.

This was all so . . . well, utterly unlike Bernadette. Daisy loved it.

The last step was to thread buttons on the pouches for eyes and affix colored yarn to the top in an approximation of each girl's hair color.

Avery regarded her tan-colored length of yarn skeptically. "This looks nothing like my hair."

"It doesn't have to be perfect," Kathryn said from atop a stool, spritzing the windows and door frames with lemon and clove–infused water. "The idea is to get close and, most importantly, imbue it with a sense of your inner self's spirit."

Daisy and Morrigan shrugged at Avery, sewing on their orange and black yarn, respectively.

"Now we create a pentacle for the healing and protection circle," Kathryn said, "as there's clearly a malevolence hard at work in our little town."

Sobered by the reminder of yesterday's horrors—which felt simultaneously a million miles away and urgently inescapable—Daisy helped her sisters push the furniture to the far edges of the room. Kathryn knelt on the floor and, beginning with the top angle pointed northward, drew the five points of a pentagram, which she explained became a pentacle when enclosed within a circle. She then handed Daisy the bag of salt and tactfully looked away.

Daisy blushed at the reminder of her gaffe at the new moon ritual and poured a thick line, curving it into a wide circle and closing it off with particular attention, looking up to see Kathryn placing purple-tinted candles at each point of the star to "call down the five elements: earth, air, fire, water, and spirit." The top represented spirit; the upper right, water; the bottom right, fire; the bottom left, earth; and the upper left, air.

"And one goes in the middle, to bind us all together," she said, setting a sixth purple candle at the epicenter of the pentacle. She pulled a box of matches from her voluminous skirts and lit the candles.

"Don't we need rowan for spellcasting?" Avery asked, never failing to impress Daisy with her breadth of knowledge.

"What do you think we used to dye the felt black?" asked Bernadette, coming in from the garden with something that looked to Daisy suspiciously like a wand. "It *is* a wand," she said, reading Daisy's thoughts precisely the way Avery always did. She even winked. Bernadette never winked. "And don't forget to tie your poppets in the highest branches of the rowan tree after the ritual. Not the willow. Willow is good for wands and casting, but rowan's better for protection."

Kathryn cocked her head. "You made sure to bless the tree before—"

Bernadette wilted her with a look. "The book, please."

Kathryn handed her the ancient tome she'd loaned the girls all those months ago.

Daisy was stunned at the sight of a spell book in her mother's hands. "Oh, that's our—"

"Is it, though?" Bernadette ruffled the pages as one would a cherished pet, thumbing to a section with easy familiarity.

Kathryn waved the girls over. "Step back inside the circle and place your poppets beside the candles as follows: Avery, as a Libra you represent air, so you'll go behind the candle at the top left. Good. Now, Morrigan, you're a Pisces, so you can go across from her at the top right for water. Excellent. And finally, Daisy. You're our Aries, so you can put your poppet at the bottom right for fire. Stand behind your poppets in line with the direction of the pentacle point you've been assigned. Very good!"

The sisters stepped inside the circle and positioned their poppets as directed.

"But that's only three elements," Avery said.

"Then I suppose it's a good thing your mother and I are here." Kathryn smiled, pulling two more pouches from her satchel—one long and thin, the other slightly smaller and rounder—and placing them at the topmost and lower-left points.

When had they made their poppets? Daisy peered closer. The little dolls were worn, even a bit ragged. Kathryn watched as understanding dawned. "You've had these for a while," Daisy said, feeling a little numb from all the surprises.

The two women glanced at each other, communicating something complicated and textured. Clearly, the sisters would have much to discuss.

Bernadette stepped inside the circle at the top point, spirit.

"But you're a Taurus," Daisy said, chinning at the lower-left position.

"As am I," said Kathryn, stepping into the circle at the earth point. "We were born on the same day, your mother and I, zodiacal twins."

"So how do you decide who goes where?" Daisy asked, filing that other juicy detail for later.

Avery got it first. "Mother is the spellcaster."

"Exactly," Kathryn said. "And as such represents the very spirit of this entire enterprise."

Daisy's rational-minded, antispiritualist mother—who had from the very get-go been dead set against her and her sisters' attempts to work with their gifts—was the spellcaster?

"Just let it be," Morrigan whispered to her right.

"We're in good hands, Daisy," Kathryn murmured, to her left.

Bernadette frowned. "Enough," she said. "It's time to begin. Daisy, pull a card."

"Oh!" Daisy said, startled, casting about for her reticule.

"Your left pocket," Bernadette said.

Daisy patted her skirts and, sure enough, there was the soft silken bag. She shook her head, releasing her hold on everything about the day.

"Let the silence be your teacher," Kathryn told her.

As Daisy shuffled the cards, Bernadette began tracing shapes in the air, chanting words in a language Daisy didn't recognize. Daisy wondered if she was supposed to wait until Bernadette finished, but then she closed her eyes and gave herself over. After all, she was standing inside a sacred circle around a pentacle with her four favorite people in the entire world, her own mother at the top of the circle as the spellcaster calling upon the element of spirit to guide them.

Daisy was jolted at the sight of the upright Hermit, which, in the turmoil of the day, she'd almost forgotten was the next card on her journey: *A white-robed figure peers into the darkness, a golden staff in one hand, a lantern in the other, the lustrous glow illuminating a small patch of the path ahead.*

"Just as the lighthouse is a beacon for ships traversing dangerous shoals, the Hermit's beacon guides the seeker to the enlightenment of the Divine Mysteries," Kathryn said. "Notice how the lantern only reveals the next step?"

"Because one mustn't rush into the unknown without first taking time to know oneself," Daisy said. "But when will I know?" She worried she wasn't ready, that she wouldn't be strong enough or wise enough to chart her own path.

But as though from inside her own mind, she heard the answer: *Look around. You won't be alone.*

At the top of the pentacle, Bernadette continued to swirl the air with her wand, weaving the molecules of their very beings into communion.

"So mote it be," Bernadette intoned, bringing her palms together and holding the wand at rest between them.

"So mote it be," they all repeated. Daisy couldn't say how long they stood like that, meditating together silently. She sensed she'd never forget the profound beauty and power of the moment.

Bernadette stepped away abruptly, as if she had woken from a trance. "Well," she said. "Well."

"Goodness," Morrigan murmured, pride shimmering in her eyes.

"That was wonderful, Mother," Daisy said on a rush of warmth.

"Truly," said Avery.

Bernadette silenced them with a sharp glance. Her face closed and chilly, she snapped the willow wand in half and swung toward Kathryn, who took a quick step back. "We did what needed doing, but now we're done. Girls, we shall never speak of this again. And

Kathryn, if I ever catch you sharing these dangerous teachings with my daughters again, I shall come for you. We're finished here."

Bernadette marched over to the hearth and tossed the bits of wand and the book of spells on the coals, shooing Daisy back when she tried to stop her.

They all watched, horrified, as the book and wand immediately sparked into flames and quickly burned to ash. Even Bernadette seemed surprised by the rapid and uncanny immolation, as if the broken wand and spell book possessed their own self-destructive powers. And then the light of each candle within the pentagram snuffed itself out.

Bernadette swirled back toward the top point of the pentacle and reached down to snatch her poppet. She swept her boot roughly through the salt, breaking the circle, and stalked from the room, slamming the kitchen door behind her.

They all stared after her, too stunned to speak. A long moment later, her face drawn, Kathryn gathered her things and slipped silently out of the cottage.

CHAPTER X

THE WHEEL OF FORTUNE

"Fortune, good night: smile once more; turn thy wheel!"

—SHAKESPEARE, *King Lear*

There was no time to dwell. Shortly after the front door closed behind Kathryn, Daisy heard a pounding on it.

"Misses Wolfson!" came a man's voice. "You must come quickly! It's your aunt Mary!"

Henry had sent a closed carriage. Daisy and her sisters lurched back toward Society Row, staring out the windows at the hushed air outside, which seemed darkened with soot or ash, tinged with sepia, heavy with a whiff of something acidic.

As they raced through their almost unrecognizable town, Daisy wondered at how familiar, how *right* that book of spells had looked in her mother's hands. And she had been so magnificent in her role as spellcaster! Except now the precious book and willow wand were gone, reduced to embers. Daisy's own heart felt snapped and burnt along with them.

Tabitha Godwin's death still resounded through her bones like a wave of earthquake aftershocks. No one voiced the shared fear, that they might once again be too late, that their aunt would suffer the same fate. Daisy gritted her teeth and willed the horses to run faster. She gripped Avery's and Morrigan's hands so hard she could almost feel their bones crunching, but her sisters didn't protest, instead holding Daisy's hands with the same force.

Under the porte cochere, Daisy and her sisters tumbled from the carriage and clattered up the broad granite steps, flinging open the double doors to the front hall before Mr. Miggs could let them in. They slipped past his outstretched hands, not stopping to hand over their cloaks, in whose pockets were the things they needed, instead racing toward Henry, who whisked them through the arched doorway that led through a long hallway into the back of the house.

"She's in the solarium," Henry said.

"Is Dr. Wellington here?" Avery asked.

"Yes, and Jasper Fitzwilliam. But something tells me you're the ones she needs."

Aunt Mary lay on a fainting couch at the far end of the glassed-in room. She wore a bed jacket and nightcap and was swaddled in a quilt, her eyes open but unfocused. Watery, dim sunlight fell through the glass panes of the ceiling onto her jaundiced skin. Around her were leafy trees and ferns, flowers tumbling in bright cascades from hanging pots, vines draping a treillage by the wrought-iron doors that led out to the stone terrace overlooking the sea. This formidable lady, always in command with a sharp remark or glance from her beady eyes, was now a shrunken bird, plucked and flightless in her verdant indoor jungle.

The sisters went straight to Aunt Mary's side. Daisy's treacherous gaze flashed briefly toward Jasper, but as soon as their eyes met, they both looked away.

Aunt Mary had clearly been treated with all the most advanced techniques of modern scientific medicine, as well as some of the older ones. A pan of congealing blood stood on a table, along with a bowl of writhing leeches and an array of stoppered vials and powder boxes that contained what Daisy could only surmise were cocaine, mineral poisons, morphine, and emetic and laxative purgatives.

From the pocket of her cloak, Avery drew the packet of Bernadette's herbs. Despite their mother's vehement rejection of all things "magical"—doubly astonishing in the wake of her earlier spell-caster performance—she would never have denied treatment to anyone, not even her haughty sister-in-law. And though not overjoyed that her daughters continued to practice healing with crystals and herbs and tarot cards, she still hadn't outright forbidden it.

"Add this to boiling water and bring me the teapot right away with a cup," Avery quietly commanded a housemaid who stood cowering near a potted tree.

"Yes, miss." The girl bobbed her head and disappeared. Dr. Wellington followed, hot on her heels, doubtlessly to ensure the sisters weren't trying to poison his wealthy patient with their strange potions. Good riddance as far as Daisy was concerned.

Henry motioned to the chair to the right of the daybed, and Daisy hitched it closer to better examine her aunt, who peered back as though from a vast distance. Her forehead was clammy, her lips were cracked, and the skin surrounding her eyes and nose was shrouded in the same dark rash Daisy had noticed on her last visit. *Just like Tabitha Godwin,* Daisy realized. Except these hives had progressed to small, pustulant lesions.

Taking a deep breath, Daisy drew out her silk bag and picked through the stones, selecting a few and letting them warm up in the palm of her left hand, the one connected most closely to the heart. She'd chosen the same crystals she'd used on Tabitha, forcing herself to trust in her abilities. That they hadn't worked before was no fault of the stones. And unlike Tabitha—whose spirit had already been lost to the world, even before her body died—Aunt Mary was still with them. They had a chance.

Jasper made a scornful sound in the back of his throat. When Daisy glared at him, he shook his head. "You know full well what I think of this hocus-pocus."

"Come now," Henry murmured. "She's just—"

"So do not affect outrage," Jasper continued, addressing Daisy alone. "I only stand by because the wishes of Mrs. Blackwell's ward, my dear friend Henry, supersede medical authority."

Henry shrugged helplessly, imploring Daisy with his eyes to not make a scene.

Well, he was about to be disappointed.

With her free hand, Daisy held up the bag of crystals. "These have power," she told Jasper hotly. "They've been used for healing for thousands of years by many people, including your own Irish ancestors. All of them knew that these stones give a sick body the ability to use its own wisdom to heal itself alongside the wonders of medicine, ancient and modern. It's our faith in their power that creates the magic."

Jasper had no answer to this, or else didn't deign to give one. No matter. Daisy put the bag of crystals on the bedside table. She had work to do.

After Morrigan and Avery moved the quilt from Aunt Mary's chest and eased open her bed jacket, Daisy bent down to listen to her breathing, a shallow rasp. She gently pressed the first two fingers of her right hand to the inside of Aunt Mary's left wrist to find a weak pulse. Daisy dotted the brilliant little stones along Aunt Mary's nightdress: moss agate in her throat's hollow, fluorite on her solar plexus, carnelian on her abdomen.

Then Daisy hovered her right palm above the lesions staining her aunt's forehead and her left palm over her heart, keeping a small cushion of space between them. She closed her eyes and with each inhalation focused her mind's eye on the image of a cord drawing healing energy from the core of the earth up through the very foundation of the house—past the wooden floorboards and the plush carpets and even the soles of her shoes—through her feet, along her legs, and into her heart. With each exhalation, Daisy channeled that same healing energy out along her arms and down through her palms into Aunt Mary.

Her eyes still closed, Daisy breathed circularly, directing the flow of the earth's sacred fire toward her aunt. She could sense the stones shimmer in response, feeling heat pulse between her hands and the older woman's body, as though there were an invisible coil of light and vitality passing between them.

With a final exhalation, Daisy pushed the healing spiral deeper into Aunt Mary's system, and then, on a fast, sharp inhalation, flipped her hands palms up, whisking the soiled energy up and away from her aunt's body, blowing it back out into the universe.

Daisy opened her eyes to find everyone staring.

"I never get tired of watching you do that," Morrigan said softly.

Avery handed Daisy the cool glass of water she knew she needed. Daisy emptied the vessel in a few deep swallows, using the water to ground back into herself.

"I'm not sure what I just saw," Jasper said, startling her.

In her focused state, Daisy had forgotten he was there. "I understand," she told him. It was impossible to feel petty human grievances when connecting with the compassion-state necessary for this work.

Just then, the housemaid came running in with the tea tray, Dr. Wellington scowling behind her. Avery took the pot and cup and set both on the table to let the herbs steep. The flower-painted porcelain looked incongruously homey alongside the vials of chemics and dishes of leeches and blood.

"What's in that?" asked Dr. Wellington, stroking his large walrus mustache. Daisy suspected he'd grown and maintained it to distract from his small stature and smaller imagination.

"Nothing that can hurt her," said Avery. "Henry, you were wise to take every possible measure."

Henry sat in a chair by his guardian's other side, holding her limp hand. "I trust you, dear Wolfsons," he said. "Just look at her face, Dr. Wellington. The hives, they've already begun to diminish."

Dr. Wellington frowned. "Clearly, the bloodletting has begun to take effect."

Aunt Mary was showing some signs of enhanced vibrancy, her eyes darting around the room. The next step was up to Avery. They just had to distract everyone. Daisy placed her fingertips again on the inside of Aunt Mary's wrist and nodded discreetly at Morrigan, who held her own tarot deck loosely in her hands while she shuffled, moving cards over and under each other with a soft shushing sound.

"Card games, is it?" Dr. Wellington said with a dismissive snicker. "I suppose that can't hurt either." He patted his waistcoat for his pipe and wandered out to the terrace.

Avery poured out some tea and held the steaming cup to Aunt

Mary's lips, holding her head up, urging her to drink, a kerchief at her chin to catch any dribbles. Aunt Mary took a few tentative swallows, and Daisy felt her pulse strengthen, though she didn't dare get her hopes up yet. Another otherwise healthy woman had just succumbed to the same plague, and Tabitha had been so much younger. What possible reason could they have to think this time would be different, even with the improvement they'd seen so far?

But Daisy could almost see the blood seep back into Aunt Mary's face as Avery cradled her head and poured tiny sips into her mouth, veins and capillaries slowly flushing with renewed life. As her aunt swallowed the rest of the cup, Daisy heard Avery whisper something. She repeated her words twice, and then the tea was gone.

Aunt Mary's whole frame seemed galvanized.

"It's working," Avery said. "We're weakening its hold on her."

Daisy's heart pounded with the dreadful suspicion that they were contending with a dark entity, perhaps something that had been drawn to that bedeviled new moon ritual she'd hastened her sisters into doing before they were ready. She was uncomfortably reminded of Bernadette's worries about vengeful spirits and Kathryn's cautions of the dangers of practicing magic during a dead moon. She'd been wondering about it ever since those sinister Visions she'd shared with her sisters. It would explain what was happening to the town, the eerie silence, why the air had gone dark and smoky, Tabitha Godwin's sudden death, maybe even Finny Stewart's behavior.

The Bleakness, Kathryn and Bernadette had called it. Was the entire town of Redcliffe in its grip? If so, she had been the fool who ushered it in, she realized remorsefully. The sheer magnitude of her astounding carelessness threatened to crush her with remorse.

Aunt Mary shot upright in her bed and frowned at Daisy with

baleful clarity. "My stars." Her voice was a dry croak. "Whatever are you doing, girl?"

Daisy's heart sank. Did her own aunt not know her? Had the Bleakness done damage that couldn't be reversed? "It's Daisy."

"Of course I know who you are, Daisy Wolfson. But why are you staring at me like that? And what is this awful brew, Avery? Why are these horrid little rocks all over me?"

As Daisy hastily collected her crystals and returned them to their bag, Aunt Mary struggled to pull the blankets back onto herself, clutching her bed jacket to cover her exposed breastbone.

Henry shook his head. "They healed you, Mother, when leeches and bloodletting failed. We all feared we would lose you until your nieces came."

"Well, here I am, not dead yet." Her sharp eyes took in Daisy and her sisters, each of them in turn. She pulled a handkerchief from the sleeve of her bed jacket and coughed. "What wretched tea. Just dreadful."

"Oh thanks be," said Henry. "You are yourself again."

"We'll be going," said Avery briskly. "We will leave you in the care of the physician and the medical student." She emphasized the word *student* in a way that made Daisy want to laugh out loud.

"I have completed my studies," said Jasper. "And I believe," he went on darkly to Aunt Mary, "that our treatment had a delayed effect and was the reason for your recovery, madam."

"Maybe so," said Aunt Mary, taking in the sinister medical accoutrements on the tray with a look of horror. "You may all go. I am quite well now."

Dr. Wellington leapt forward and began packing up his bag as swiftly as he could, slipping handfuls of vials and boxes into its depths. He left the dish of blood on the little table for the housemaid to dispose of and tipped the leeches into a jar, which he sealed with a stopper. "I am heartened by your recovery, Mrs. Blackwell," he said.

Aunt Mary's pulse was stronger, it was true, but Daisy still felt it fluttering, could see a whiteness coating her tongue. Though markedly improved, she was not fully cured.

As Aunt Mary disengaged her wrist from Daisy's probing fingers, Morrigan plucked a card from her deck, smiled to herself, and held it up: the Wheel of Fortune. Of course. For Morrigan's deck, Daisy had spun the card's symbolism through the Greek myth of Jason's odyssey to retrieve the Golden Fleece—the winged ram with wool of gold—stolen from him through betrayal and violence.

She'd reimagined the ship *Argo*'s tiller as a great wheel that was simultaneously a clock and a compass, guiding him on his journey: *Jason grasps the wheel one-handedly, his other arm bearing a shield to stave off giant birds of prey. Behind him, the goddess Hera stares down powerful waves entwined with venomous snakes that batter the ship, while above, the* Argo*'s sail, emblazoned with the head of the golden ram, snaps at the clouds of an approaching storm. But in the top-left corner, the rays of the sun beam out a message of hope.*

Daisy had painted Hera after the queens her father had carved in Morrigan's chess set, the proud angular face modeled on his own muse, Bernadette, whose eyes seemed to flash a warning up through the card. The Wheel of Fortune was the most complicated of the tarot deck, representing the cycle of human life. It was a card that symbolized destiny, karma, unseen forces of good and evil, and one's course, ever-changing in response to the circumstances surrounding the journey.

Just then, in burst Nate. "Fitzwilliam," he said to Jasper, his tone low and intense, "it is time for your reckoning."

"Hell's teeth," muttered Avery.

Daisy was stunned at the unexpected sight of Nate, who remained as deucedly handsome as always. But he didn't even glance her way, his eyes pinpoints on Jasper's wary face. And what could Nate have been thinking, barging into what was essentially a sickroom? This was hardly the time or place for a confrontation, no matter how important his reasons.

"What the devil are you doing here, Winthrop?" Jasper asked haughtily.

"I have been installing a writing desk in Mrs. Blackwell's library, not that it's any of your business. What is, however, is the unfinished matter between you and I."

"I think you'll find you mean to say 'between you and *me*,'" Jasper said with supercilious condescension.

"I think you'll find I don't give a damn."

"Impertinence!" Aunt Mary clapped her hands. "I insist you leave us in peace, young men."

"This is a sickroom," said Jasper. "In case you haven't noticed, we are attending a patient. You have no place here."

"Then stop hiding behind women and come outside, Fitzwilliam." Nate's fists were clenched. "It's time to repay you for your villainy."

"*My* villainy?" Jasper gave a mirthless laugh.

"You ruined my life."

"You ruined your own life!"

"Out!" Aunt Mary made a shooing gesture with both hands.

Nate swept through the door onto the terrace, Jasper hot on his heels. Henry hurried along behind them. The doctor had slipped away toward the front of the house, the craven worm, but Daisy and her sisters rushed outside, where Nate and Jasper were locked like angry rams, shouting at each other as they grappled and exchanged blows. Henry was yelling at them to stop, barely dodging flying elbows and boots. Beyond the wall at the end of the terrace, the sea was a dark, roiling mass under charcoal clouds shot through with intermittent sun rays, eerily matching the scene painted on the tarot card.

"What's happened?" Daisy demanded of Henry.

"They've lost their heads." He was panting. "Stand down, I say! Come inside and talk like civilized men."

Just then, Jasper jerked Nate down and over his shoulder hard enough to send him crashing into the terrace wall. As Jasper bent over to catch his breath, Nate lay where he had been flung, a thin line of blood snaking down from his scalp.

Jasper sprang to his feet, a dangerous glint in his eye, but Henry pulled him back.

"That's quite enough, gentlemen—and you're forcing me to use the term loosely," Henry said, his usually amiable expression nowhere in sight. "Nate, I must ask you to leave. And Jasper, step back or you'll be next."

Nate pulled himself up with a low groan and made his unsteady way to the stairs leading down to the garden. Without a word, he was gone, across the lawn and through the wrought-iron gate, which clanked shut behind him.

Jasper, lip split and bleeding, a bruise purpling near one eye, seemed not to even feel his wounds. He glowered after Nate, and then whirled to look at Daisy. "And this is what comes of those cursed card games you insist on playing."

"How dare you speak to my sister like that!" Avery snapped. "This was not her fault, you thick-skulled ape."

"And tarot is no mere game, cursed or otherwise," Morrigan chimed in.

Heartened by her sisters' defense, Daisy took a deep breath. "You're not entirely wrong," she told him.

"I'm not?" Jasper looked as taken aback as everyone else.

"Which isn't to say that I don't agree with Nate's complaint," Daisy hastened to add, though privately she was shocked at Nate's recklessness. "But the card Nate pulled in our reading did indicate revenge and—"

Jasper's voice was keen as a knife. "You must stop this superstitious, humbug meddling at once."

Daisy stared at him. *"Humbug?"*

"Meddling?" Avery sputtered.

"That you mock us is clear, Mr. Fitzwilliam," said Morrigan, her voice like ice. "Do you accuse us as well?"

"Well, no, I wouldn't..." Jasper was at a loss for once, the question having been put so directly by someone whose manners were as unimpeachable as gentle Morrigan's.

"You said tarot was superstitious hocus-pocus." Daisy scowled at Jasper.

"Well, it is," he grumbled.

"I have the solution," Henry said quickly, his tense face suddenly lighting up. "The medical lecture in Boston I mentioned the other night at our dinner party? I think you should all attend. We can settle this debate once and for all!"

"Never," Daisy said, though she could feel Avery's interest prickle.

"Afraid to see the truth?" Jasper muttered.

"Absolutely not," Daisy rejoined. "Though you should be."

"That'll be the day," Jasper scoffed.

"There's only one way to find out," Henry said. "Please, Daisy... all of you! Come as my guests. Jasper and I will stay at the university, and you three can stay with my mother's friends, the Copeland family in Beacon Hill. They would be delighted to receive you; their two daughters are just a bit younger than you."

Jasper was clearly against the idea on principle, and Daisy had no desire to be condescended to by some boring old man. But Henry looked so happy at the idea of this scheme, so patently eager to make things right again, to smooth the rough waters between his friends. And after what he'd just been through, almost losing his guardian and adoptive mother, no one had the heart to deny him.

"Perfect," Henry said, blithely ignoring the lack of collective enthusiasm, his excitement enough for everyone. "We'll all go up to Boston together on the train. I'll procure the tickets."

And so it was settled.

INTERLUDE

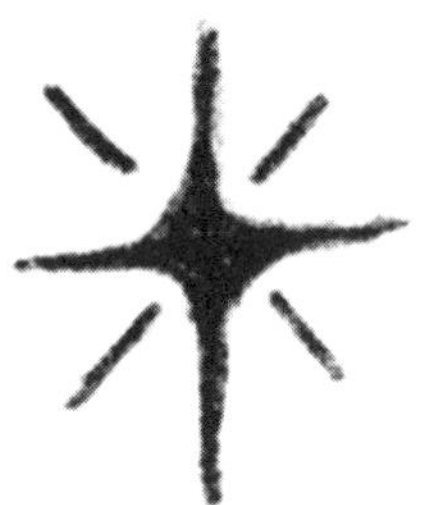

THE PASSAGE

"The only journey is the one within."

—RAINER MARIA RILKE

Of course, they could have gone to Boston by the packet ship that sailed around the end of the Cape and across the bay. But the novelty of the train, while a longer journey, promised too much excitement to pass up. The railroad extending from Boston to Sandwich had only been completed in May, and the sisters were thrilled at the chance of a ride.

With Bernadette's reluctant blessing, and special instructions from Kathryn, the girls departed two days after Nate and Jasper's dramatic brawl at Blackwell House. They traveled to Sandwich in Aunt Mary's carriage, a journey of thirty miles, while Jasper and Henry galloped ahead on horseback to arrange lodgings and tickets for the journey, and to send word to the Copeland family.

The carriage ride from Chatham to Sandwich took the better part of the day, but as it was fine, brisk weather, the horses could go at a good steady trot. Out on the high road that ran along the spine of the Cape, the air was full of birdsong and blowing leaves. They traversed vast cranberry bogs, seagulls shrieking overhead, past Wequaquet Lake, through the forests and gentle rolling farmland up to Sandwich.

Daisy couldn't deny that it was also a great relief to have a respite from the Bleakness. Daisy wondered if, in their absence, things might return to normal. If her suspicions were correct, and the Bleakness had been created by her mistake at the new moon ritual, she feared her presence in Redcliffe might also be sustaining it. Could it have brought the trouble between Nate and Jasper to a head? She hoped that leaving for a few days might cause it to lift.

Daisy was also gripped by the puzzle of her mother's erratic behavior. The book of spells had looked so at home in her hands, which she had only ever seen ruffle the pages of a hymnal or Bible or sheet music or a letter to the convent. And there had been a strong hint of something, some answer to the question of her parents' marriage, and the mysterious reason for the rupture of her mother's old and apparently very close friendship with Kathryn, which had come back to life with such tantalizing briefness.

Mind-boggling, all of it.

"Do we know our mother at all?" Avery burst out, reading Daisy's thoughts as usual. "I find myself doubting everything I've been told about her. All our lives, we've known her to be against spiritualism in all its forms."

"And now we learn she's a spellcaster!" said Morrigan. "An expert one. Who taught her?"

"And when?" said Avery. "As far as we know, she grew up in the convent, and then she married Father."

"And why did she give it up?" Daisy chimed in. "Who or what turned her against the practice?"

"And what happened to make 'Kit' and 'Bernie' near enemies?" Avery asked.

"I can't see any of it," said Morrigan, "no matter how hard I try. It's hidden in a fog."

"Avery," Daisy said, "what was our mother thinking when she burned the wand and book? Could you sense anything at all? What have your impressions of her been since then?"

"I try as hard as I can to read her, believe me," said Avery. "But I'm blocked. It's like she's put up a curtain around her heart and mind. Or maybe it's me, maybe I can't see beyond my own feelings, the way something gets blurry when it's too near your eyes."

"I just realized, this is our first trip away from Mother," said Morrigan.

"I hope she's not too lonely without us," Daisy said.

They all grinned, imagining Bernadette's relief to have the house to herself, basking in quiet and solitude.

When they arrived at the Stagecoach Inn, Henry and Jasper were in the low tavern, sprawled at a table with foamy tankards. Their merry greeting shouted across the noisy room suggested this wasn't their first beer of the day. After Daisy, Morrigan, and Avery had settled into their room upstairs, washed their faces, and shed their traveling cloaks, they joined the men for a simple supper and a mug of beer by a roaring fire.

Sipping her beer, Daisy could feel her spirits rising. Jasper said little, but there was a high color in his cheeks, and he downed his tankard and signaled to the barmaid for another before the sisters had finished their first. He seemed unusually agitated, which at first Daisy attributed to the fight with Nate the other day. He kept glancing around, clearly uncomfortable. Was he expecting trouble?

Then Daisy overheard the barmaid greet him by name, and Jasper hastened to explain that the woman was his family's former cook's daughter.

"You're from Sandwich?" Avery asked, making no bones about her curiosity, which was a relief because Daisy was dying to know more.

"Born and raised," said the barmaid, whose name they soon learned was Lucy. "Just like me! And his mum and dad. He's a Sandwich man, our Jasper. The whole town's missed him ever since—"

"Yes, it's been a long time," Jasper said tightly, cutting her off.

Lucy blushed, adding only, "I'm happy to see you looking so well," giving him a sympathetic look and moving to the other end of the bar to take another order.

Daisy was full of questions, not the least of which was how Nate had come to live with Jasper's family in the first place. She could tell Avery and Morrigan were curious as well, but Henry gave them a meaningful look and suggested everyone get some rest for the long journey the next day.

As the sisters went upstairs to their shared room, Daisy said, "But if Jasper is from here, why wouldn't he stay at his family's home?"

"There's a story here, I'm certain of it," Avery agreed. "Morrigan, you'll have to get it out of Henry. He'll tell you anything."

"Or perhaps we should let it be," Morrigan said. "I know you and Jasper have your differences, Daisy, but even he deserves his privacy."

Abashed, Avery and Daisy made faces at each other, but they couldn't deny Morrigan's point.

The sisters were kept awake by the noise down in the stable yard of men talking, tobacco smoke drifting up through their window. And even after the inn fell silent, they continued to toss and turn, pressed close together in their hard, lumpy bed, keeping each other awake with mutual restlessness.

"As Mother always says when we can't sleep, just rest your bones," said Avery finally.

"And let your thoughts drift like smoke," said Morrigan, yawning.

"And give your spirits a moon bath," Daisy murmured, and the next thing she knew, it was dawn.

They leapt out of bed, washed and dressed, had a quick breakfast downstairs, and set off for the train station with Henry and Jasper. They all stood together in the crowd on the platform as the arriving train pulled into the station with a great shrill of its whistle and a coughing plume of black smoke.

It was a behemoth, chuffing and roaring with flames, made up of one oblong wheeled iron coach after another. Instead of hay, this beast of burden ate coal. Instead of blowing steamy air out its nostrils, it belched black smoke from a chimney on its head. There was something gentle and almost comical in its grandiosity, but it was a dignified and powerful thing. In a mad rush, Daisy fell in love with it.

Porters in caps and uniforms rushed up and down the platform as passengers climbed aboard. Leading the way, Daisy entered a long car full of wooden seats padded with thin green velvet cushions and found two benches facing each other with a table in between. Morrigan and Avery sat on either side of Henry, leaving Daisy next to Jasper, the hamper of food between them. He looked pale and distant after his restless agitation the night before.

A whistle blew and with a shuddering start, the train chugged out of the station. At first it didn't go much faster than a stagecoach, to Daisy's dismay, but then it picked up, racing along so quickly that just looking out the window at the city streaking by made her dizzy.

"You'll get used to it," said Henry, laughing at Daisy's expression.

"Amazing," Daisy said. It felt like the future, like the beginning of the modern era she had glimpsed in her Visions, where everything was fast, and new, and exciting. She soon fell into the rhythm of the wheels on the track, the lulling clacking noises and occasional deafening bursts from the whistle.

At lunchtime, the five of them ate and drank from the hamper Avery had packed: bread, cheese, apples, and ginger cakes, along with one flask of cider and another of water. The day had grown warm, and other passengers opened windows to let the fresh air stream in. Along with the breeze came the smell of coal smoke and motes of soot from the engine.

Jasper bit into an apple, and its white flesh came away tinged with blood. Forgetting their enmity for a moment, Daisy peered at his split lip. "You're still bleeding," she said, instinctively reaching for her kerchief. "Does it hurt? I have some salve in my reticule if you'll permit me to apply it. It's nothing too hocus-pocus," she added tartly when she saw him flinch, "just a little arnica and chamomile."

He gingerly touched his lip and brought his finger away to see a drop of blood. "Oh," he said, disconcerted. "Thank you."

Daisy took out the ointment and leaned in to dab a fingerful on his lip. Their faces were so close together, she could feel his breath on her mouth and her exhalations intermingling with his. Instantly, there was that disturbing zing she had felt when they danced at the Apple Ball. She drew back sharply, looking away from his steady gaze.

"Afraid I'll bite?" Now it was his turn to be forward.

Ignoring this, Daisy smoothed the salve on his lip, dabbing with her handkerchief to catch the blood that welled up. She forced herself to meet his gaze and was surprised to see the glint of laughter in his eyes.

"You're teasing me," she said.

"It is surprising," he said, "how much it delights me to do so. You are a worthy adversary."

Daisy glinted back at him. "I suppose I should take that as a compliment, the alternative being tedious offense and lack of humor."

He gave her a swift but dazzling smile. The train lurched, and Jasper and Daisy were flung together just for an instant, their mouths perilously close to touching. Against her will, Daisy breathed in his damnably intoxicating scent as her arms braced themselves against his chest. Then they sprang apart, looking at each other dazedly out of the corners of their eyes.

Daisy put the salve back into her reticule and snapped it shut, handing Jasper her bloodied kerchief.

"Keep it," she said coolly. "You'll need it to stanch the bleeding."

"It's stopped, I think," he said.

"I meant later, at the lecture," she said, and abruptly leapt up. "I'm going to take a walk."

Daisy paced down the center aisle of the car before he could get in a rejoinder. Her face aflame, she forced herself to look out through the back window, take in the glimpses of scenery, listen to the rhythmic rumble of the train that she could barely hear over the roaring in her ears.

"You'll learn the pleasures of this feeling in due time, my dear" came a woman's voice near her elbow, the tone eerie, penetrating. "It won't always scare you to feel this way."

But when Daisy looked down at the person sitting alone on the last bench, she was surprised to behold a man. Even seated, she could tell he was tall. He was garbed in a brown monk's robe and had a headful of glossy black curls, milky skin, dark eyes under arched brows, and a flared beak of a nose in a soft, ageless face. He observed her disconcertment with fond amusement, almost familiar.

"Do I know you?"

"No, but I know *you*, my dear. Now you must go and sit down again."

"Wait, I have—"

"Yes, questions. I know, dear girl. Worry not, we shall see each other again sooner than you might think."

A dense cloud of coal smoke poured through the open window, obscuring everything. When it cleared enough for Daisy to see again, the stranger was gone.

Baffled, she swayed with the motion of the train back up the car to rejoin the others.

"Where were you?" Morrigan asked.

"The strangest thing just happened," Daisy said, speaking softly under cover of Avery's jocular banter with Henry and Jasper, leaning across the table to look her twin in the eye. "I was talking to someone. A man, I think. But at first, I thought... and then he vanished. Maybe it was the coal smoke."

"Was it a Vision?" she whispered.

"I don't think so," Daisy whispered back. "But I'm starting to question whether I can ever know anything for sure."

The train ran through farmland and small villages, salt marshes and forests, until they reached the outskirts of Boston, and soon the rails had plunged them straight into the city itself. They pulled into the station with a great belching of smoke and a long, shrill whistle to dock like a great ship coming into port.

"Stay close," said Henry, "don't get lost in the crowd."

Carrying the hamper between them, Jasper and Henry disembarked first; then, one by one, the conductor handing the girls down from the high carriage onto the platform. Daisy and her sisters waited while Jasper collected the luggage and Henry procured a hansom cab to take them to the Copelands'.

As the driver helped them into the carriage, they said goodbye to Henry and Jasper, who awaited Dr. Franklyn's personal barouche to take them to the university faculty houses. As they set off, they looked at one another, grinning broadly at the sheer adventure of it all.

"That was awfully nice of you to play battlefield nurse to the wounded soldier from the enemy side," Avery laughed.

Daisy blushed. "Well, his lip *was* bleeding. . . ."

"Yes, yes, of course," Morrigan said.

The cab rumbled through thronged, noisy streets up to the leafy quiet of Beacon Hill and stopped in front of an imposing grand brick townhouse. They were ushered inside and welcomed by a butler. Seconds after he rang a little bell, a housemaid appeared to show them to their room.

It was all so efficient and orchestrated, Daisy felt a brief pang of envy for the girls who lived here, to be attended to so solicitously by such a staff, to live in an exciting city in this beautiful house. As the maid led them up the tall staircase that curved around to the second-story landing, Daisy couldn't help gawking at the brass sconces festooned with candles, the ornate plasterwork, the ceiling medallions and intricate moldings. And the large bedchamber they were given to share was so plush and ornate, Daisy went silent. Her twin stared. Even self-contained Avery was impressed. Two large casement windows, each inset with deep, cushioned window seats, looked down into a deep garden in the back. The wallpaper was hand-painted with a bucolic country scene, willows drooping by a brook. There was one enormous bed and one smaller one against the far wall, and a fire was lit in the grate, around which were ranged three plush chairs on a soft rug. And instead of a washstand in the corner, there was an actual *sink*!

"Running water," Daisy breathed.

"It's all so... *deluxe*," Morrigan whispered.

"It ain't bad a-tall," said Avery, flinging herself onto the smaller bed to appreciate its softness. "Ahhhh... I don't think I ever want to leave."

They burst into laughter at themselves, three little country-mouse bumpkins all agape at the big-city finery. But their laughter was tinged with an odd mania, the sense they shared that though they might be miles away from the Bleakness, it remained ever present. Daisy had a flash of memory of Tabitha's drained face, the crumpled, empty perambulator in the road, and she shuddered.

A polite rap came at the door. It was the housemaid again, bobbing her head. "Tea is served in the dining room. I'll be outside in the passage to take you down as soon as you are refreshed."

"How does one *refresh* oneself?" Daisy whispered.

"Splash cold water on our faces?" said Avery.

Morrigan grimaced at her image in the mirror. "And maybe we should arrange our hair; we look like scarecrows."

A few moments later, their appearances somewhat improved, the girls followed the maid downstairs and were ushered into a grand dining room, where the Copelands awaited them at an elegant table laden with a feast. Daisy faltered a little, and felt her sisters do the same.

Back in the Wolfson sisters' room, the crackling fire flashed out, replaced by an eerie light that charged with an otherworldly energy. The formerly warm and inviting room was now filled with a chilly luminescence that seemed to pulse with a life of its own. The silence was broken only by the occasional hiss and pop of the dying embers.

Don't worry, little ones. I haven't forgotten about you. Or your precious town.

But run along. I'll be waiting for you when you return—if there's anything left.

The fire in the grate sputtered back to life, casting its glow around the room once again, as if nothing had happened.

CHAPTER XI

JUSTICE

"The golden eye of justice sees, and requites the unjust man."

—SOPHOCLES

As it turned out, there was no need for shyness. Almost instantly, they were folded into the warmth of this welcoming family: Susan and Jane, two sweet girls of twelve and fourteen, and their smiling parents. Mr. Copeland disarmed Daisy immediately with a jocularity at odds with what she'd pictured when Henry had said he was the president of one of Boston's largest financial institutions. And Mrs. Copeland, though every inch the wealthy society matron, was kind and gracious, giving no indication that the Wolfsons weren't her equals in social standing. What a welcome change from Redcliffe's snooty Society Row matrons.

The table was draped with a snow-white cloth that would have made Aunt Mary swoon, festooned with fresh-cut autumn foliage and flowers, and lit overhead by not one but two crystal chandeliers powered by actual gas. When Daisy admired them, Mrs. Copeland explained that the chandeliers were in fact called gasoliers. Daisy found this portmanteau as delightful as the enormous, elegant four-branch gaslit chandeliers, connected by long, involved pipes, adorned with a gilt-painted morning-glory vine and an agate lion-head medallion in the center of their glowing frost-glass globes.

The repast that followed in no way fit with Daisy's concept of "tea." Though it was just the seven of them, the multiple-course meal seemed more suited to a fancy dinner party: oysters on the half shell followed by creamy asparagus soup; a delicately flaked salmon in hollandaise sauce; and roast chicken with peas, potatoes, and carrots. Then came the sweets: stewed gooseberries folded into chilled whipped cream, lady fingers, mousse au chocolat, and lemon sherbet.

Daisy didn't think she could eat another morsel, but next came something called a savory course: ham timbales, custard tartlets that Mrs. Copeland apologetically explained were "just leftovers from weekday dinners." By the time the cheese and fruit plate arrived, the sisters were stuffed.

At his wife's nod, Mr. Copeland bade them all good evening and retired to the library for cigars and port, the ladies left with their Lapsang souchong tea and cinnamon-dusted cookies. It was a relief when Mrs. Copeland observed the sisters' heavy lids and stifled yawns. She packed them off to bed, where they immediately collapsed into a deep sleep on their luxurious feather mattresses.

The next morning, they woke up refreshed and unaccountably ravenous.

"We've developed an appetite, it seems," Avery observed, as they raced down for breakfast, which was a sumptuous affair with Susan and Jane, whose parents were nowhere to be seen.

"We breakfast on our own," confided Susan, the elder of the two.

"Breakfast as a verb," Avery mused.

Susan blushed charmingly. "Oh, I didn't mean—"

"She's just teasing," Daisy reassured her.

The long table was laid out with platters of mixed sausages, thick slices of bacon, three kinds of eggs—scrambled, coddled, and poached—soft, fragrant bread rolls, a dizzying collection of preserves, and the most gloriously creamy butter.

Finally, bellies bursting once again from the feast they'd barely dented, the Wolfsons admitted defeat and sipped English breakfast tea to settle their digestions.

"Will you tell us about the tarot?" Jane asked shyly.

"Jane!" Susan scolded, very much the older sister. "We mustn't bother our guests with foolish questions."

"I'm so sorry," murmured Jane, her cheeks matching her deep auburn ringlets. "It's just that Henry said—"

"It's no bother," Daisy hastened to reassure her. "And when it comes to tarot, there's nothing wrong with being *foolish*."

Avery and Morrigan chuckled at Daisy's pun, explaining it to the girls and then joining her in teaching them the basics of tarot, each taking turns talking about the Fool's Journey through the Major Arcana.

"And that's not even getting into the Minor Arcana, the four suits," Avery said.

"Like suits of armor?" Susan asked.

"Well, in a sense," Avery replied. "The suits are the categories of the fifty-six Minor Arcana cards—which isn't to say the Minor Arcana are minor. They relate to the elements of daily life, as opposed to the Major Arcana, which have more to do with bigger life goals and... Let me start over! So, the Minor Arcana cards—also called the Pips—are divided into four suits, or categories, of fourteen cards each: wands, cups, swords, and pentacles. And each suit has ten numbered cards, ace through ten, as well as five—"

"What our sister is trying to say is yes, sometimes the cards have people wearing suits of armor on them," Morrigan interrupted with a wry smile.

"Sorry, I get carried away!" Avery laughed.

"Henry says you ladies are very well-known for your expertise," Susan said carefully. "And we were just wondering . . ."

"We'd be honored!" said Morrigan. "Whose deck shall we use?"

"You have more than one deck?" Jane breathed.

"Indeed we do," Avery said. "Not only is our baby sister a brilliant tarot reader, she's also a gifted artist. She designed one for each of us."

"You *made* your own tarot cards?" Susan exclaimed.

"Easy now, it'll go to her head." Avery winked at her youngest sister.

"I just really like to draw," Daisy said.

"Oh, I'm the same," said Jane. "Art is my favorite subject. I love painting . . . well, everything! Here, I could show you if you like. . . ."

"Jane!" Susan hissed. "They don't want to—"

"I'd love to see your artwork, Jane," Daisy said, already having bonded with Jane as a fellow younger sister. She also warmed to her unbridled enthusiasm and utter lack of social finesse. "But I'm afraid my sisters and I have errands this morning. What about a quick reading for now, and then later, if you're not too busy, perhaps a viewing of your work?"

"A splendid idea," Jane said with grave dignity.

"I love it when a plan comes together," Avery said. "And now I have a suggestion. Let's use all the decks!" She glanced at Daisy and Morrigan, raising her eyebrows as if to say *why not?*

Why not, indeed! And how had they never thought of this before? What a grand suggestion, perfect for so many sisters together in one room.

Daisy, Morrigan, and Avery got out their respective decks and walked Jane and Susan through the basics of centering with the breath and setting an intention for the spread, shuffling slowly, asking the girls to tell them when to stop and pick a card.

Susan pointed at Avery and said, "Now."

Avery smiled, relating to this older-sister bossiness as only a fellow firstborn could. She cut the deck and restacked it, selecting the top card and placing it on the table face down.

"Aaaaaand... Stop!" Jane shrieked at Daisy. They all giggled as she placed her own card.

"Who picks the next one?" Susan asked.

"Good question," Morrigan said, still shuffling. "May I?"

"Oh yes, please do," Susan allowed. Morrigan cut, restacked, selected, and placed her card. The three cards were now lined up face down, one in front of each Wolfson.

"Why don't we do a classic mind, body, spirit reading?" Morrigan suggested to the girls, who nodded sagely. "Eldest to youngest."

Avery turned over her Justice card.

At this point, Daisy wasn't really surprised, but it still gave her a giddy frisson to get more tangible confirmation of her Herox Journey.

Then Morrigan turned over her card: Justice again.

Daisy and her sisters gasped.

"Did you do that on purpose?" Susan asked, narrowing her eyes.

"No," Daisy said, reeling.

"Trust the cards," Avery said evenly, though Daisy could tell she wasn't unmoved by the synchronicity.

Unaccountably nervous to turn over her own card, Daisy

nevertheless took a deep breath and flipped it over, though she found she couldn't bring herself to look.

"Justice!" Jane shrieked.

"This seems very strange!" Susan said. "Is it strange?"

"A little . . ." Daisy allowed, her heart fluttering. Morrigan glanced over, biting her lip.

"Strictly scientifically," Avery said, "the permutations of . . ."

"It's certainly unusual," Morrigan began, "but it is within the realm of possibility."

"And it's not a trick?" Jane asked. "I do love card tricks. I have a special deck upstairs that I could—"

"Not a trick," Daisy said faintly, still processing the uncanniness of their each having pulled the exact same card, from three separate, well-shuffled decks, and that card being Justice, the next in her journey.

"Tell me, Jane, what do you see?" prompted Avery.

"A man on a throne with a sword," said Jane.

"No," Susan corrected. "That's a woman. Isn't it?"

Daisy tilted her head, distracted from her inner turmoil by the question. She'd never thought too deeply about the sex of the various personages on the cards. Some were male, some were female. And it differed in each of their decks, no two cards quite the same. She'd let herself be guided by instinct, which wasn't given to predictable outcomes. But this one card was somewhat indeterminate in gender in all three decks, something she'd never noticed before. The knowing face of the stranger from the train appeared in her mind's eye.

"Why don't we call them 'the person'?" Morrigan suggested.

Everyone nodded, regarding the figure on the throne, a double-edged sword balancing a set of scales on its tip in one hand and a heavy gavel in the other.

"And the person is wearing a crown." chimed in Jane. "With an *X* and a capital *I* in the middle. Is that for . . . eleven? Wait, I saw a tarot deck once, and I thought this was supposed to be card number eight!"

"Very astute," Morrigan said, smiling at Jane's precociousness. "Our clever sister switched it with the Strength card."

"But why?"

As Daisy wondered how to explain her future Visions to the girls, she found herself pulled abruptly into a brief trance, eyes unseeing, and murmured, "Astrologically, Virgo comes after Leo, the lion."

And just as quickly, she was back in the room.

"But can you just do that, change the cards?" Susan's brow furrowed.

"Not only can we," said Avery, "it is our duty always to question."

While Susan pondered that for a moment, Jane chimed in again. "One bare foot is sticking out. And the dress . . . or robe . . . is quite fancy. Like a queen. Or a king?"

"Or a judge," Morrigan offered.

"So what does it all mean, the card?" Susan asked.

Everyone looked at Daisy. "It means truth . . . and consequences."

"*And* intuition *and* compassion," Morrigan added. "Exploring the truth that is in alignment with your highest principles and trusting in the answer, even if it challenges your beliefs."

Just then Mrs. Copeland wandered in and remarked at the late hour. "Girls, you really must give our guests a moment to breathe!"

The sisters gathered up their cards as the butler brought in their cloaks. They tumbled down the stone stairs to the narrow sidewalk, where a coach awaited, clearly having been arranged in advance by their generous hosts. Daisy's head was whirling with everything that had happened these past few days, but then she thought of Kathryn's advice about the Hermit card, how the beacon would illuminate the next step when it was time.

"As long as we're together, everything will be all right," Avery reminded her. Impulsively, Daisy hugged both her sisters close, feeling their unstinting loyalty buoy her spirits.

"Now, who wants to go look at books?" Avery asked, eyes twinkling.

The carriage rumbled over the cobblestones from Beacon Hill down to a street near the waterfront. "Your establishment is over there, misses," said the coachman, tipping his hat when Avery gave him a few extra cents for his pains.

The sisters set off toward a row of shops in a small, crooked lane, all with signs swinging from rods over their front doors. Past a bakery, a fishmonger, a tailor, and a cobbler, they found the Brothers' Bookshop—the shop Kathryn had bade them visit. A bell jingled when the door opened, and they stooped slightly to enter the low-beamed room crowded with bookshelves, sparkling dust dancing in the morning sunlight. The air smelled of paper, and the small shop was empty aside from a wizened old man who sat at a table in the back.

"May I help you?" came his quavering voice.

"We're looking for something called"—Avery unfolded Kathryn's paper—"*The Book of Hidden Doors.*"

His face rose suddenly over the stacks like a moon as he peered closely at each of their faces in turn. "We don't have it in stock here..." He paused, clearly waiting for them to say more.

Avery checked the paper again. She cleared her throat and read aloud, "When the moon is full..."

The old man's eyes lit up with recognition, and he responded almost instinctively, "The shadows reveal their secrets." Evidently, they had passed some sort of test. Then his face shuttered, and he pressed a button in the wall, the bookshelves swinging open to reveal a narrow staircase leading three steps down to a hallway. "Knock twice on the door at the end," he said, dismissing them with a brisk nod.

They filed down the stairs into the dimness. The wall of books slid shut behind them. A candle set into a recess in the wall cast a flickering light.

Daisy and Morrigan followed Avery to the door. Avery rapped twice, and it swung open.

And there was the mysterious disappearing person from the train, still dressed in a monk's robe.

"You," Daisy breathed.

"Come in, my dears," he said, as though he'd expected them.

They entered a glowing underground treasure palace, lit by many candles and lamps, the air warm and alive with amazing smells, herbal and mineral, musky and sweet. A parrot leapt from a golden cage onto the monk's shoulder.

"Think in the morning! Act in the noon!" the bird yelled. "Eat in the evening! Sleep in the night!"

"Hush, William," said the monk. "He's the reincarnation of William Blake. At least that's what he tells me. It seems rude to pry."

Daisy gaped at the amazing chamber. Shelves were neatly ranged with brass pentacles and bells; glass chalices and copper offering bowls; herbs in jars; fossilized stones, animal skulls, and crystal spheres; painted horseshoes and crystals and geodes; tarot boxes; wands, pendulums, brooms, and athames with carved ivory handles; candles, pendants, and jars of tinctures and elixirs; and piles of leather-bound books.

"Who are you?" she demanded of the monk, turning to face him.

"A fellow seeker. And you're right. I have been expecting you.... since before you were born." The stranger said this offhandedly, as though casually throwing breadcrumbs to pigeons. His black curls gently writhed in the dim light. His eyes were likewise gleaming, and his skin looked soft as velvet. His mouth curved, merry and confident, as he looked at Daisy and her sisters.

"Careful you don't catch flies. And yourselves on fire," he said, gently moving them away from the candelabra.

"Tyger, tyger, burning bright!" yelled his parrot with rusty fervor.

"Sorry, Brother..." Daisy stepped to the side. "Or... I mean..."

"Either, or. I am that I am." The monk shrugged with easy good humor.

Avery nodded. "What would you like us to call you?"

"Currently, I go by Terrence, as in Brother," he said, indicating his robes with a slight dip of the chin. He knelt with ease and from the depths of a large trunk drew out an enormous book. "And meanwhile, my dears, you've come for this."

Daisy held out her arms, and Brother Terrence deposited into them an age-darkened leather-bound book, sealed shut with a sapphire-studded clasp, its binding a leather strap. Engraved into the leather was a single word: *knowledge*.

"The road of excess leads to the palace of wisdom!" shouted William Blake the parrot in his creaky, uncanny voice.

"This is the original," Brother Terrence said. "Kathryn and Bernadette have a copy. So be very careful with it. And Godspeed on your journey."

"How do you know our mother and Kathryn?" gasped Morrigan.

"I've known them both since they were babies."

Avery peered at him more closely. "Did you live near the convent in Falmouth?"

"We have been acquainted, yes."

"How old are you?" Daisy asked before she could stop herself.

"Ah," he said with a finger held aloft, "that could be considered an impertinent question of your elder. *Much* elder." And he shooed them to the door. "Off you go, my dear Wolfsons. We shall meet again. When you least expect, I'd wager."

"What does that mean?" demanded Daisy.

He fixed her with an unreadable look. "You have set something in motion that cannot be stopped."

"The Bleakness," said Morrigan.

Brother Terrence neither confirmed nor denied. "There will be a time very soon when all seems lost. You will meet me again in your darkest hour." They waited for him to elucidate this warning, but he shook his head, his curls bouncing slightly, his expression puckish. "Off you go," he said. "For now, our business is finished."

As his parrot squawked, "Exuberance is beauty!" the sisters tumbled out through the tunnel and into the bookshop again, the secret wall sliding open as they approached it.

"Did you find what you came for?" asked the shopkeeper. They glanced at each other before answering, but when they looked up again, he had vanished.

Just like that, they were back out on the street. People hurried past as they stood still among the hustle and bustle of the neighborhood, strangely disoriented by the familiar scream of seagulls wheeling overhead, the redolent smell of brine and sea air.

CHAPTER XII

The Hanged Man

"Men, my brothers who live after us,
have your hearts not hardened against us.
For, if on poor us you take pity,
God will sooner show you mercy."
—Francois Villon, "The Ballad of the Hanged Men"

In the carriage on the way to Harvard Medical School's lecture hall, Daisy sensed something was troubling Morrigan. So while Avery made conversation with Mr. Copeland, she turned to her twin. "You've been brooding. Is it poor Tabitha? You're not alone in that sorrow, if so."

"Yes, I know," Morrigan said. "But please don't continue to blame yourself, no matter what anyone says."

"Why do you say that, have people—"

"Oh, Daisy," she sighed, "I meant nothing by it. I merely sought to reassure you."

"Thank you," Daisy replied evenly, though Morrigan's uncharacteristic dismissal stung a little. She took a quiet breath and pressed on. "Tell me, please. I know here's something you're not saying."

Morrigan shook her head. "It's nothing."

Daisy pulled her tarot deck from her pocket and ruffled the cards, waiting.

"If you must know, I'm deeply uncomfortable about this lecture," Morrigan burst out. "I worry it's a trap and will expose us to ridicule."

"Nonsense," Daisy said. "This is a challenge, not a trap. Henry knows we're up to the task."

"But it's not a true challenge, Daisy! We're just meant to attend the lecture, not actually participate in some sort of debate. I know you have an affinity for the spotlight—"

"Affinity!" Daisy took a deep breath, stung.

"But I'd much rather go about my own business and allow others to attend to theirs. Let these doctors practice medicine as they will, think what they want, as long as they leave us alone."

"Yes, but they won't, will they?" Daisy was shuffling her tarot deck over and over, pouring her agitation into the cards. "Personally, I'm grateful of the chance to prove my mettle."

Morrigan seared her twin with a rare flash of annoyance. "Of course you would say that. You're burning to show up Jasper. You two have a feud that has nothing to do with the rest of us. I don't want to be a pawn in your game."

Avery raised an eyebrow, and with another sigh Morrigan folded herself into the window. Daisy turned her burning face to the deck and plucked a card. Unsurprisingly, it was the Hanged Man, which put her in mind of Nate. She hadn't seen him since the fracas with Jasper at Aunt Mary's. She hoped he was all right. She knew it was childish to take things personally, but she couldn't help remembering he hadn't even glanced at her, though she'd been standing right there. She wondered what if anything it boded for their burgeoning romance.

She shook him out of her head and forced herself to concentrate on the next card of her journey: *Suspended upside down by an ankle, the Hanged Man hooks his free foot jauntily around his bound leg, arms clasped behind his head. He hangs from a leafless branch, but its twisted trunk is green with new growth.*

Earlier interpretations of the card considered the Hanged Man a traitor. Was Daisy the traitor here? That was certainly how it seemed Morrigan saw her. As she'd done with Nate, Daisy forced herself to remember that the Hanged Man card wasn't as dark as it seemed. The setting sun's halo around his head signified illumination of thought and surrender to new perspectives. And he was hanging from a living tree and was himself alive, after all.

Intuiting Daisy's thoughts, Morrigan reached over and placed a hand on hers. "Perhaps we could both heed the card's message and remain open to fresh viewpoints."

"Then you're not against this lecture and . . . me?"

"You, never! The lecture? Well, I don't love it, but the card says we must let go. All I can promise is that I will try. Perhaps you could, too?"

Daisy wanted to press her for more reassurance, but she knew she had to surrender to what Morrigan needed: time, reflection, space. So she nodded and took a deep breath, doing her best to model the Hanged Man's serenity.

Still, as the carriage pulled up in front of the medical school building on North Grove Street, Daisy couldn't help but say, "Just this last thing: I promise you're not a pawn; I promise this is important. And who knows, we might even have fun."

Morrigan looked away, biting her lip.

Henry and Jasper waited in the vestibule of the lecture hall and had saved them seats in the front row, with Mr. Copeland somewhere back in the gallery. Their genial host had told them he was greatly looking forward to the lecture, as he had an amateur interest in all things medical.

Daisy could feel her twin retreat into herself, swim deep into her Piscean depths, while Avery was curious and engaged but neutral. It seemed there was nothing personal in this for her. Perhaps Morrigan was right, and this was Daisy's battle.

As the room filled with medical students, Daisy noticed with interest three Black men among them. And one white woman, who so resembled Avery she could have been another Wolfson sister! Along with feeling a pang of envy at the good fortune of the lone female, Daisy couldn't help but notice that many of the young male students were handsome and well-built, broad shoulders filling out smart coats, hair pressed and parted neatly. What was the source of her increasing fascination with the opposite sex of late? Even the ones she despised, she thought ruefully, glancing at Jasper, whose tension she could sense even from a few seats away.

For an anxious moment, Daisy thought she glimpsed Nate, but it was only another young man who resembled him. The disappointment and then sympathy she felt, remembering that he'd been sent away from this very place because of Jasper not long ago, was followed by confusion. Though she'd understood his reasons, his fury had been unsettling. When she pictured his face, a knot of worry hardened in the pit of her stomach.

The medical students were opening notebooks, setting their inkwells close at hand on the desktops in front of them. Daisy felt a flash of that same envy she'd felt when she first entered the Copelands' house, an intimation of some other, parallel life she might have led. But this time she didn't ache to be wealthy; she yearned to sit so easily among her fellows, in a hall of learning, with the sure knowledge that the information she gleaned here would lead her to a respectable and useful career, healing the sick.

This was the most famous medical school in the country, and here she sat, a small-town girl from Cape Cod. Although they were all prodigious readers, she and her sisters had been forced to relinquish their formal schooling after eighth grade, like most girls. Daisy was keenly aware of her own ignorance and the sheltered provincial nature of her upbringing.

When Dr. Franklyn appeared onstage, there was a burst of applause. He made his way to the lectern, limping very slightly, favoring his right foot. He flexed his fingers before he picked up his notes and launched into his lecture, beginning with a recapitulation of the lesson from the week before. Daisy sneaked another glimpse at Jasper. His profile was aglow with rapt concentration. Several times, he nodded as he scribbled notes. All around, fountain pens were similarly busy.

Dr. Franklyn swiftly laid out the current medical methodology of the treatment of chronic infectious disease. Daisy found herself quite interested in all he had to say. Many of the treatments he described—blistering, leeches, bloodletting, and quinine and arsenic poultices—seemed quite barbaric, dangerous, and invasive, disruptive to the healing process. As he spoke, a fantastical Vision arose in her mind's eye of a future hospital, with ingenious devices that could see inside a body, surgical theaters where diseased organs were replaced with healthy ones, medicines that extended lives by decades.

But this would all be due to centuries of hard work and research done by earlier doctors, including Dr. Franklyn, all of whom practiced medicine to the best of their ability and limited knowledge.

Dr. Franklyn expounded for close to an hour, regaling the medical students with case study upon case study of contagion and other atrocities. From the cries of horror that sprang from the room, the good doctor spared not one single gory detail. At least, Daisy assumed so. She didn't understand most of what he said, so highly specialized was the terminology.

Dr. Franklyn paused to take a sip of water. "I'd like to remind you that much of what is now accepted as fact was once considered outrageous and even heretical. If you may recall, it was commonly believed that the world was flat, and yet no one has sailed off the edge, excepting poor Galileo, condemned for his heresy. And to think! Smallpox was held to be a punishment from the gods. Or a curse by a demon!"

The gallery erupted into laughter at such ridiculous superstition. Daisy avoided eye contact with her sisters, who knew as well as she did that a malevolent entity might at this very moment be destroying their beloved town.

"As I hope you recall from last week's lecture, particularly if you're planning to pass the winter exams"—Dr. Franklyn paused for the obligatory groans from his students—"the smallpox vaccine was championed and first tested in the United States over fifty years ago by a professor at this very school, the late Dr. Benjamin Waterhouse, who postulated that miasmas of animalcular life in our very blood are what cause illness and disease. This was at a time when anyone who proposed such an outrageous idea was ridiculed, and still is." Dr. Franklyn paused for effect. "But gentlemen . . . and ladies"—he acknowledged the Wolfson sisters and the lone female student with a small bow of his head—"the question I bring to you now is this: If you can't see something with your eyes, can it indeed be there?"

This got Daisy's attention. Such a line of thinking was downright exhilarating. A doctor who believed in the power of the unseen?

There was a general silence in the room, and then a few low murmurs. No one seemed to understand what the great doctor was getting at. But Daisy was bursting with ideas that surged hotly on the wings of her distress about Tabitha's death. She had died of something unseen, something to do with the Bleakness. Daisy had felt it. Although she hadn't known what it meant, hadn't known how to prevent it from killing her patient, and she wasn't sure what to call it, Daisy knew, as much as she knew the chair she sat in existed, that so many things invisible to the naked human senses were real. All they needed were the instruments, courage, and belief to find and name them. Daisy felt the words forming on her lips, her hand itching to fly upward.

To Daisy's great irritation, Jasper stood up, blocking her with his stupid, gigantic shoulders. When Dr. Franklyn nodded at him, Jasper said, "Ignaz Semmelweis thought so."

"The Hungarian physician and scientist that some of you may want to research," said Dr. Franklyn mildly. From the sound of the scritch of pen nibs on paper in the quiet gallery, this was clearly not a suggestion.

"He recently proposed that the rampant cases of childbed fever killing women in maternity wards was caused by doctors not washing their hands after performing autopsies," Jasper said. "And though Semmelweis was subsequently denounced, a few forward-thinking members in the medical community did believe him, adopting his method of antiseptic procedures. One of those doctors is our own

Dr. Franklyn." Jasper clapped for his mentor, prompting a roar of applause from his cronies, all clearly angling for high marks in this course.

Dr. Franklyn smiled. "Yes, I thought his thesis had much merit. Damn shame." He took another sip of water, nodding approvingly at his protégé, who sat back down. "And so, in conclusion, I will answer my own question. There are many hitherto undiscovered and unseen elements in medicine, and we are on the forefront of discovering what those are. I submit to you all that these 'germs' do exist. They live among us invisibly, in our air and water, causing contagion and illness, and they are as real as this lectern I stand before."

At this, Daisy's hand shot up.

The great doctor peered at her through his lenses with an indulgent smile. "The young lady wishes to speak?"

"Thank you, sir," Daisy burst out. "I am very keenly in agreement with your conclusion." She stopped, realizing how audacious she sounded.

Instead of taking offense, the doctor gave a guffaw of pleasure. "Well, that is a compliment indeed, Miss—"

"Wolfson," Daisy said, ignoring Jasper's horrified stare. "Daisy Wolfson."

"And what leads you to agree so keenly with my no-doubt controversial conclusion, Miss Wolfson?"

"I propose that in addition to illness being caused by the existence of *germs*, the sick can also be healed through methods based on invisible forces we can neither see nor explain."

"I see," he said, stroking his beard. "Are you by any chance . . . a spiritualist?"

At this the gallery erupted into hoots of laughter, though

interestingly none from Jasper, who just stared straight ahead, his face shuttered. Daisy's own face was aflame.

"I take no offense at the term," Daisy said clearly. "My sisters and I heal the sick through ancient methods, including using herbs, of course, which, as we all know, are widely accepted in medical practice. But I also use crystals and the energy of the earth's healing power channeled by my own two hands. These methods have been used for thousands of years, all over the world, by many different races and religions."

Dr. Franklyn pushed his spectacles back up his nose. He was a kind man, Daisy was starting to realize. She could tell he did not want to make a fool of her. But she had put herself forward so importunately. She dared not look at Jasper or even her sisters, fearing their reproach would hobble her, stop her from completing her mission. Meanwhile, Dr. Franklyn pressed on. "The . . . energy of your hands, did you say?"

To gasps and astonished laughter, Daisy rose from her seat and stepped up onto the stage. "If I may, Dr. Franklyn." She reached for his hand, which he resisted at first. "Don't worry, I've washed my hands," she said to much laughter, "and it's been at least a day since I attended an autopsy," and there was more laughter, happily no longer aimed directly *at* her. She could feel the crowd enjoying this deviation from the usual academic formality of the lecture hall.

Sensing the curiosity of their audience, and clearly not wanting to be impolite, Dr. Franklyn reluctantly allowed Daisy to take his hand.

"Dr. Franklyn," she said sweetly, "if I may ask: What ails you?"

He hesitated. Daisy imagined him wondering who this slip of a girl thought she was, playing doctor to the great man. "I have a touch of gout, which, I might add," he said as he turned to his students, "a remarkable new study by the British doctor Alfred Garrod suggests may be due to the presence of uric acid in the blood, cured with lithium."

From his limping entrance and the gingerly way he'd flexed his fingers before he began speaking, Daisy had already guessed about the gout in his big toe, plus arthritic pain in the joints of his hands. While he talked, she concentrated her entire presence on his hand in both of hers, settling her gaze softly on a point just beyond them on the floor, not wanting to appear any more outrageously newfangled by closing her eyes. Drawing healing energy from the core of the earth once again, Daisy allowed it to channel up through the wood and steel and brick of the building into her very body, coalesce in her heart center, and radiate out through her hands into his. She felt nature's power gather within her being as her own hands became hot, and she propelled that flow of vitality steadily into Dr. Franklyn's hand.

Dr. Franklyn went silent, his eyes wide on Daisy's face. He looked alarmed and amazed. As Daisy's hands continued to surge fiery energy through her and into him, she heard him gasp. He patted her hand and tried to take his own back, but she hung on, cranking up her internal energetic thermostat to deliver the most powerful charge she could.

Dr. Franklyn snatched his hand away.

"Well," he said then, "it's not entirely astonishing that a robust young woman such as yourself would have warm little hands." He inclined his head slightly in acknowledgment of the wave of laughter at his joke.

Daisy was well aware that her curative method was not deemed "scientific," nor was it sanctioned. She couldn't explain it, and neither could Dr. Franklyn, the acknowledged foremost medical mind in America. All she knew was that it had worked. She had felt it, and so had he. He couldn't deny what he had experienced. Well, he could, but she was counting on his commitment to scientific logic and the truth.

"Let me ask you, Doctor: How is your pain now?"

He looked as though he wanted to dissemble, but he was an honorable man, and it wasn't in his nature to lie. Daisy knew this as well as she knew her own character, such had been the strength of the connection they'd just now forged. "It is almost completely gone," he said simply. "I cannot say why."

Daisy nodded. "I understand, Dr. Franklyn. It's hard to accept what we cannot see. And yet is that not the very foundation of science, as you yourself so eloquently explained to us a few moments ago? To explore what can only be initially put forth as theory?"

"Well, yes, but—"

"Even a country girl like me recognizes that you are a learned man of science, renowned throughout the medical community for your open-mindedness to the most far-fetched ideas in the relentless pursuit of healing modern disease."

"Well, science is a process of—"

"And that's all I ask, for your consideration of phenomena we may not yet be able to fully explain. I appeal to your rigorous wisdom."

Dr. Franklyn said with kindly befuddlement, blinking in the aftermath of Daisy's relief of his ailment, "In the spirit of scientific rigor, I pledge to remain open-minded."

"I accept!" Daisy hopped down from the stage and took her seat again, her cheeks burning with a triumph she could do little to mask. Many in the audience jumped to their feet, laughing, applauding, and hooting. Daisy sensed that they were probably more amused by her brashness than impressed with her abilities, but she dared to hope they might in the future question their assumptions.

Daisy did not look at either of her sisters, certain they were scandalized by her untoward display, already dreading their censure. But Avery chucked her on the shoulder, saying, "Brilliant!" Then Morrigan smiled and said, "Well done, you." Daisy almost wept with relief.

In the hubbub after the lecture, Henry and Morrigan sat intently talking, their heads together as always, and Avery jumped feetfirst into a heated argument with an opinionated antispiritualist. Daisy heard her say, "Healing with plants is spurious? Is not morphine from poppies, cocaine from the coca plant? Like any powerful intervention, it can be dangerous in the hands of a careless practitioner."

Daisy suddenly found herself surrounded by young men, all of them anxious to ply her with questions: What had she done, exactly? How did she know how to do it? Could she teach them to do it?

Dr. Franklyn parted the small crowd and beelined for Daisy, a very reluctant-looking Jasper in tow. "Miss Wolfson, thank you for a most entertaining display."

"I hope your gout will improve, Doctor," Daisy replied.

"Fitzwilliam," he said jocularly to Jasper, "your girl has quite a head on her shoulders. We should have her over to the charity wards."

"She's not . . . my girl," Jasper muttered, flustered.

Dr. Franklyn raised an eyebrow, smiling broadly. "In that case, allow me to suggest you do something about that before some other young fellow snatches her out from under you." He gestured to the gaggle of young men.

Now both Daisy and Jasper blushed furiously. "I would be most honored to visit the charity wards," she told Jasper, just to break the tension.

"The charity wards," said someone, a tall blond fellow with a neat mustache. "Wasn't that where—"

Jasper gave the man a quick look. "Not now, Felix."

"It was," said someone else. "Gave our medical school a bad name."

"What happened?" Daisy asked, instantly curious.

Jasper put up a hand. "It was an unfortunate incident is all. A former student made a fatal mistake with a patient."

"A poor woman with no one and nothing in the world," insisted Felix. "The Sisters protested it would harm her, but he swore he knew best, and he gave her too much arsenic for a simple fever, and she died a dreadful death. All she needed was a good bowl of soup, if you ask me."

Daisy wondered whether Jasper was being noble and protecting the identity of the irresponsible student, or protecting the good name of his school and, by extension, himself. Mr. Copeland appeared before Daisy could ask any more questions. "Now, young ladies, let's get ourselves home to tea. And, Miss Wolfson, I suspect my own gout would benefit from your ministrations. Good day, gentlemen, and many thanks for a most illuminating lecture, Dr. Franklyn!"

As the sisters were swept under the wing of their host and escorted to the waiting carriage, Daisy felt a strange longing to remain at the medical school.

Instead, as instructed by the Hanged Man card she'd drawn earlier, she let go, surrendering herself to the future. Remembering Brother Terrence's warning that there would be dangers waiting back in Redcliffe, all she could do was to trust in the just and balanced nature of the universe to guide her.

CHAPTER XIII

DEATH

"Everyone thinks of changing humanity, but no one thinks of changing himself."

–LEO TOLSTOY

Leaving Henry to get up to whatever post-lecture mischief he had planned with Jasper and their Harvard cronies, the sisters accompanied Mr. Copeland back to Beacon Hill. After another meal of gut-busting proportions, Daisy and Morrigan retired to their room to refresh themselves with cold water from the marvelous sink.

Avery stayed downstairs, ensconced before a roaring fire with the Copelands, regaling the girls with highlights of Daisy's performance at the lecture. Daisy was itching to go down and join them all.

Morrigan flung herself onto a window seat and stared broodingly at the darkened garden and her own reflection.

"What is it?" Daisy asked, with a surge of impatience. "I thought you said I did well. Was that not true?"

"I told no lie, Daisy. I *am* very proud of you!" Morrigan assured her. "But I cannot deny that I am also worried."

Daisy couldn't help but feel unfairly attacked. "Is this about the spotlight again?"

"If you must know . . . a little! Though impressive, your performance today has called so much attention to us. Henry was saying that he expected all of Boston will soon be asking us to read their tarot and heal their aches and pains. And frankly, it feels dangerous to stick our necks out so far. Remember Tabitha and the Bleakness."

"As though I could forget," Daisy muttered.

"Henry also said he's heard—"

"Good grief, not more about Henry. It's always Henry this, Henry that. One would think *he* was your twin, not me!"

"Oh, Daisy, don't be ridiculous." Morrigan looked supremely exhausted.

"And in case you've forgotten, your Henry isn't so perfect! In fact, he was the one who led us into the mouth of the lion like little sacrificial lambs in the first place!"

"He did no such a thing!" Morrigan exclaimed. "He was merely creating a diversion from your ceaseless squabbling with Jasper at Blackwell House. He most certainly did not suggest this public display, no matter how well done."

"I heard it differently," Daisy said tightly.

"You heard what you wanted. It's as though you crave conflict, Daisy! But Henry isn't like that. He's gentle and thoughtful, more concerned with the happiness of others—"

"Yes, yes," Daisy said hotly, "I know quite how *highly* you think of our aunt's ward. If you love him so much, why don't you just marry him!"

Even without Avery's barely audible intake of breath at the open doorway to their room, Daisy knew she'd gone too far. Morrigan's face slammed shut. Daisy desperately wanted to explain, to apologize, but she also knew that to directly address the topic of Morrigan's unspoken feelings would only make it worse.

"All right, enough!" Avery said. "We're wanted downstairs, and you're behaving like children."

"Then go," Morrigan snapped. "We don't need you chivvying us along."

"Exactly right," Daisy chimed in, automatically siding with Morrigan against Avery's big-sister bossiness. "You're barely two years older than us, in case you've forgotten."

"I haven't," Avery said with a maddening smirk.

"Good, then!"

"Great!" Avery snapped back.

For a moment, they just stared at one another, breathing hard. Then they all burst out laughing. Within seconds, they were clutching their bellies, gasping for breath.

"Why are we fighting?" Morrigan gasped.

"I don't know!" Daisy cried.

"God's nails, I'm going to wet myself," Avery shouted.

Daisy managed to say, "There's a water closet, just along the hallway!"

"Do not speak of liquids!" Avery raced to the chamber pot on its stand in one corner, hitching up her skirts and opening her bloomers. "I'd like to kiss the person who invented this merciful undergarment."

Daisy pulled Morrigan out of the window seat into a tight embrace. "I'm sorry," she whispered, heartened when Morrigan hugged her back.

"I suspect we're all a bit overexcited from our adventures," Avery observed, as she stepped into the hug, encircling her younger sisters in her long arms. And for the first time since they'd arrived in Boston, Daisy felt calm and almost cheery.

"There she is!" cried Mr. Copeland. "The girl with the magic hands!" He beamed hopefully at Daisy, reminding her that she'd promised to help him with his own gout.

One of the maids entered the parlor with an astonishing contraption to light the lamp on the table next to Mr. Copeland's armchair. Holding it firmly by the wooden handle, she used a flange at the end of a brass tube to twist the gas line's knob open, then dipped a wick into one of the sconces, carefully guiding the flame back to a small opening in the pipe to spark the gas. The subsequent illumination gleamed out through the lamp's silk shade.

"That's so lovely," Daisy marveled.

" 'Twas an anniversary gift from my dear wife," Mr. Copeland said, "who I must say is looking radiant this evening."

The maid crossed the room to repeat the lamp-lighting procedure with the twin of the first lamp on a small table next to Mrs. Copeland, who twinkled briefly at her husband over her needlepoint. "On our last trip to the continent, the most amazing find!" she said conspiratorially.

On our last trip to the continent, indeed. Their spat all but forgotten, Morrigan and Avery goggled at her from the sofa, where they were curled up with Susan and Jane.

"She was very clear on that point, that it was not to be left behind," Mr. Copeland said, a grin creasing his plump face as he beheld his wife. How heartwarming, Daisy thought. And after two almost-grown girls, both of whom tittered and rolled their eyes. "Now to my aching toes. I beg of you, Daisy, please help an old man."

"You are hardly old, Mr. Copeland," Daisy said, laughing. "Will you allow me to place my hands on your feet?"

"Indeed." He kicked off his slippers as his wife and daughters laughed.

Daisy knelt on the floor and took his feet in her hands, keeping a loose hold on the soles and ankles and letting his feet naturally wing out and rest along the insides of her forearms.

"Just blast them, little lady!" Mr. Copeland implored theatrically.

Daisy winced at Mr. Copeland's enthusiasm, which, though flattering, was somewhat misinformed. That was her own fault, she realized, and Morrigan hadn't been entirely wrong. She needed to set things straight before people got the wrong idea.

"It doesn't quite work like that." Keeping her focus on her breath, Daisy gestured with her gaze toward the gas lamp on Mr. Copeland's side table. "It's like the pipe that brings gas to this amazing lamp. The pipe isn't the gas, it's a conduit for it to travel from its source to where it's needed. I'm like that gas pipe. I simply provide a path from the earth's vital energy core to your feet."

"How fascinating," Mr. Copeland said. "So what's the trick, then? The light doesn't come until we light it with the torch and key."

"An excellent question," Daisy said, feeling the tingle in her hands indicating the connection had been made. She visualized a golden halo of healing encompassing Mr. Copeland's feet. "I suppose you could say I'm the lamplighter. I open the line and draw the gas, or in this case the earth's vibrations, by focusing my entire being on visualizing and connecting with it and then sparking it into illumination.

Then I shine that light upon you through the palms of my hands, making you the lamp. It's a meditation of sorts."

"Marvelous technique!" he said, wonder in his voice. "Meditation can be quite powerful. We do that in church sometimes. Never would have thought this kind of magic had any crossover with the church!"

"Few do," Daisy said, shifting her attention to Mr. Copeland's big toes, visualizing the tiny crystals of uric acid from Dr. Franklyn's lecture dissolving back into the universe. "But it's not magic, even though it certainly feels that way at times. If you think about it, what is prayer but forging a connection with a higher power?"

"And that's the great bottom fact! So when am I going to get that big blast you gave the doctor?"

Across the room, Daisy's sisters laughed.

"You're getting it this very moment," Daisy said, looking up at him, able to open her eyes now that the lines were open, and the healing light was in free flow. "What I did in the lecture hall was for effect, cranking up the thermostat in my own body and sending it through my hands to make a point. Generally, it's a much subtler experience. Can you feel anything?"

"In fact, I do!" He stared with amazement. "I feel like I'm toasting my toes at the grate of a nice winter fire."

"And the pain? Has it decreased, increased, stayed the same? If you're not sure, try directing your attention down to your extremities and noticing what sensations you're feeling."

He took a moment to answer. "I feel . . . warmth, warm as spiced apple pie! But my feet won't smell like cinnamon, I'll promise you that," he chuckled. "And by Jove, the pain . . . it's almost gone! You're a miracle worker."

"Well, I wouldn't go quite that far. . . ."

"I would, and I will: You've done what no doctor has been able to.

I've been plagued by it for months." Daisy didn't doubt it, considering the Copeland's extravagant meals. "And now you've cured me!"

"As much as I'd like to take credit for that, I must defer all credit to Mother Nature," Daisy told him, nevertheless pleased by the compliment. "But it's not gone completely, I'm afraid. This is merely a temporary reprieve."

"From the gallows of gout!" he chortled.

"And we should now talk about diet, though I imagine you may not want to hear it," Daisy said. Mr. Copeland's sigh made it clear just how much he didn't. Daisy smiled sympathetically and continued. "Gout has also been called 'the disease of kings' because it's often caused and aggravated by rich foods such as red wine, cheese, fatty meats—"

"So all the good things, then?" he said ruefully. "You sound like my wife."

"You know what the doctor told you, Ellwood," Mrs. Copeland said softly, not looking up from her work but clearly pleased to have her viewpoints reinforced.

"Yes, yes, my love," he said to her, grimacing at Daisy. "And now you're also telling me I have to quit living the high life?"

"Not entirely," Daisy said, "but if you could perhaps moderate those foods and possibly also increase your water intake, eating more whole grains and fruits and—"

"Vegetables!" he exclaimed with mock fury. "My mortal enemies!"

"I know, I know." Daisy laughed. "But maybe they could become, if not friends, perhaps amicable social acquaintances, at least occasionally?"

"A détente, then," he said with an amiable grumble. "But I promise nothing!"

"Fair enough." Daisy whisked away the invisible remnants of diseased energy from Mr. Copeland's feet and blew them back into the universe where they would be reabsorbed and cleansed.

Over the next several days, the Wolfson sisters were whirled into a melee of social attention, exactly as Morrigan had feared. To meet the demand for their services, they returned to Brother Terrence's backroom shop to purchase sachets of herbs for Avery, an array of new crystals for Daisy, and a small ceramic traveling chess set for Morrigan.

Armed with their new tools, the Wolfsons became a mobile production line of esoteric healing. Morrigan capitulated to the adventure, if only because she felt bound to help.

But at one point in the carriage, going from one house to the next, she said direly, "We're just like the circus, come to town with our contortionists and fire-eaters, a mere curiosity."

She wasn't entirely wrong. The wealthy blue bloods and barons of Beacon Hill and Back Bay flocked to the Copelands' parlor or sent carriages to deliver the sisters to their own grand houses. They extended the visit nearly an entire week to meet the demand that swelled around them. Henry and Jasper had also delayed their return to Redcliffe, but the sisters did not see them, as everyone's schedules were equally packed.

During the days that followed, Daisy and her sisters were treated to intimate views of the insides of more lavish homes than they had ever dreamed existed in the world. At times, Daisy felt almost drunk with opulence.

Along with the splendor of the houses they visited, the sisters were given a window into the lives therein, which turned out to be as fraught with worry and anxiety and pain as any humble cottage. They called on a nervous pregnant wife, who suffered from a severe backache. Daisy's hands eased her pain, along with one of Avery's herbal tinctures. The woman's much-older husband almost wept with gratitude, wringing Daisy's hand in his as he saw the sisters to the door of his enormous mansion, back to the Copelands' waiting carriage. His bride was the light of his life, he said, and this was to be his first, long-yearned-for child. "You are brilliant," he breathed, stuffing a wad of cash into Avery's reticule. "Simply a miracle."

Daisy and Morrigan read tarot for a middle-aged businessman who was afraid that he had squandered his children's inheritance on a fly-by-night scheme. In a Knowing, Avery examined the forces currently affecting his money and encouraged him to be patient, allowing events to unfold. A day later, the stocks he'd invested in soared abruptly, tripling in value overnight. The man had an envelope of money delivered to them with a note of thanks, telling them that their counsel had prevented him from selling his stocks in a panic and losing everything.

Morrigan looked into the past of a fretful unmarried woman of thirty who lived with her elderly father and uncovered a rejected marriage proposal. After Morrigan relayed her Vision of the unsavory truth about her erstwhile suitor, the woman finally felt at peace about her refusal. "You've given me unexpected solace," she said as she pressed money into Morrigan's hand. "In fact, I now realize I'm much happier going my own way!"

The only hitch in their steady stream of successes occurred during a reading for a society widow, Mrs. Vandermark, who'd been plagued by disturbing dreams since her husband's recent death. As Avery read their client's tarot, Daisy saw to Master Mopsey, Mrs.

Vandermark's fluffy Pekingese, using energy work to calm the wild puppy energy. As she whispered discreetly to the woman's maid about the need to have him walked more frequently, Daisy was startled by a piercing shriek.

"Ah me, I am slain!" Mrs. Vandermark cried at the card Avery had flipped over. "I knew these heart palpitations were more than nerves. Frederick wants to pull me into the afterlife with him!"

Daisy rushed over to peer at the Death card: *Contained within a spiral of spring flowers and tender young shoots, an armored skeleton rides a phoenix toward snowy clouds, ash trailing in their wake.*

"It's not what you think," Morrigan entreated the woman, who was clearly not unacquainted with the theater.

"He's lost without me, but I'm not ready to go," wailed Mrs. Vandermark.

"If I may..." Avery murmured. "This card can be eerie, but it doesn't always signify physical death. As you can see from the growing crocuses and the phoenix, it can indicate rebirth, transitions, new beginnings. And an increased sense of self-awareness."

Revived by the smelling salts her maid waved beneath her nose, Mrs. Vandermark allowed herself to be assisted back upright.

Just then, Daisy was overcome by a sudden future Vision: an older man consulting with a young woman dressed in multihued scarves and skirts. She held a palette in one hand as she leaned in and daubed her version of the Death card with paint. Daisy recognized her as the artist who'd inspired her to create her own and her sisters' tarot decks. Now she saw more of the artist's futuristic garret, with strange lighting that seemed to come from modern appurtenances she barely recognized. But as quickly as it came on, the Vision was gone.

Daisy repeated aloud the words she'd heard the man say in that strange room from a faraway future: "The veil of life is perpetuated in change, transformation, and passage from lower to higher."

"I'm quite sure I don't understand," said Mrs. Vandermark, taken aback.

Daisy attempted to explain in her own words: "Change can *feel* like death because it's the end of something. But it's also the beginning of something else. And that's the definition of life, when it's lived to the fullest."

"That's certainly less alarming." Mrs. Vandermark settled herself into her settee. "But what does it mean for me?"

"Well," Daisy said, choosing her words carefully, "you have lost your husband recently."

"Yes," Mrs. Vandermark sighed, her eyes watering almost immediately.

Daisy pressed on: "And that puts you in the new position of being in charge of the rest of your life. So what I believe this card indicates is that you are about to launch your next great adventure." She glanced at her sisters for reinforcement.

"Is there anything you've always wanted to do but never had the chance to explore?" Morrigan chimed in.

"Well," the woman said. "Do you know, I've always wanted to travel! But Frederick never liked leaving the comfort of his own home. And if I may say, I always found that more than a little disappointing."

"And why wouldn't you?" Avery offered the client a cup of valerian root tea, one of her more calming tinctures. "We women so often live at the pleasure of our menfolk, which I find quite restrictive."

"I suppose it is!" said Mrs. Vandermark.

"Perhaps now," Daisy said, "is the time for your own exploration and metamorphosis."

"What a novel idea!" said Mrs. Vandermark, eyes agleam.

Just then, the puppy sent a stream of urine onto the salon carpet, putting a quick end to the visit. The offending creature wrapped in a towel and tucked under an arm, the maid escorted the sisters out, slipping a fat envelope into Morrigan's coat at the last moment. The girls looked at one another in amazement.

On the last night before the sisters returned to Redcliffe, Henry was invited to the Copelands' for their goodbye supper. Daisy was careful to treat him with every courtesy, desperate to earn back Morrigan's trust. The truth was she *did* like Henry. He was their biggest champion. In fact, when Daisy had started designing her own tarot decks, Henry had liberated a pot of gold paint from Aunt Mary's private collection of treasures gathered abroad so she could paint the cards with what looked like actual gilt. Henry had explained it was really only powdered brass, despite being called Bessemer's gold, but to Daisy it was priceless.

Henry reported that he had been avidly following the sisters' progress through Boston society, gleefully informing them that, as he had predicted, they'd become famous overnight. Daisy worried that this news would unsettle Morrigan. Indeed, she seemed almost uncommonly restrained around Henry. Daisy sensed that he was discomfited by Morrigan's coolness but didn't know how to broach the topic.

Not that it would have mattered. He could scarcely get a word in edgewise, so excited were the young Copeland hostesses to tell him all about the Wolfsons' exploits.

"It was something to behold," crowed Susan to Henry, her face alight with vicarious pride. "You wouldn't have believed it! I've had my tarot read three times, and now I know more about my past and present and future than you would think possible."

"As do I!" Jane cried. "Did you know that I will have success as an authoress? Daisy said so. And Avery cautioned me against putting too much stock in beauty, urging me to concentrate on higher pursuits. And Morrigan assured me that the ghost of my great-grandfather is my guardian angel! And he was a writer! I plan to begin writing my first novel tomorrow."

"As for me," said Susan happily, "Daisy said I am going to marry a clergyman and live abroad and have all sorts of adventures!"

"I didn't *exactly* say that." But it was no use. Susan and Jane had taken the plain meat of the tarot readings and spiced them with the strong seasoning of their own private hopes and aspirations. Daisy and her sisters had merely given the girls permission to admit to themselves the things they most wanted in life. And how could that be a bad thing?

Henry, looking dazed at this barrage, turned to Morrigan.

"And you, Morrigan?" His tone was unusually cautious and formal. "Have you enjoyed yourself here in Boston?" Normally, he and Morrigan practically spoke in code together, interrupting each other and laughing, but their manner was now stilted and painful to watch.

"It will be good to get home to Mother." She hardly met his eyes.

"I will be back in Redcliffe within the next week," he offered hopefully.

"Aunt Mary will be glad of your return," Morrigan said coolly. "I do hope you will find her health much improved."

Henry looked consternated, and would have said more, but Mrs. Copeland chimed in. "All of my friends are convinced that these girls are the eighth wonder of the world. We have decided to form a spiritualist society here on Beacon Hill! We will take lessons in tarot and the ways of herbal healing. Did you know, there is a monk in the back of a dusty little bookshop near Faneuil Hall who sells all manner of curiosities of the occult arts?"

"Brother Terrence!" Daisy burst out, deeply disappointed that he wasn't their own secret. But they'd had to know a password to go back there, hadn't they? Or had she imagined it? How could that shop be known to the general public, when it was so well hidden?

The next morning, the girls bade the Copeland family a fond farewell, promising to see them again in the future. The Copelands swore to visit Aunt Mary sometime in the coming year. Susan and Jane looked bereft as the carriage pulled away from the curb.

Then off the Wolfsons went, down to the wharf at the east end of Water Street, thrilled with their big city adventures but equally excited to return home for some peace and quiet.

But neither peace nor quiet awaited the sisters back in Redcliffe, where the townspeople had been dreaming of black forebodings, whispered into their minds as they slept. The entity spun the Bleakness, trussing the town in sticky, toxic gossamer.

To relieve their nightmares, the townsfolk spread the Bleakness in daylight, passing along gossip dipped in venom, one person to another. Now the little community was ablaze with whispers, poison-tipped anger raging through the people like a fever that wouldn't stop until everything had been reduced to ash.

My own black thoughts, broadcast to the dull-eyed trucklers, one and all. Aren't I the cleverest, my darlings? Come back soon. I've missed you.

CHAPTER XIV

TEMPERANCE

"It is circumstances and proper measure that give an action its character and make it either good or bad."

—PLUTARCH

Daisy's spirits always rose at the prospect of travel, even if the packet ship wasn't nearly as thrilling as the train. The morning was windy and clear, sunlight glinting on gently rolling waves, promising a smooth voyage on the *Fortunata* under full sail. They claimed a bench on the starboard side, watching the deckhands stow all the luggage belowdecks, followed by crate after crate of dry goods and provisions for the shops and homes of Cape Cod. The ship was crowded with familiar faces: Daisy recognized Mr. Bain, a dairy farmer, with his two young sons, and creepy Colin Hynes the cobbler, as well as Mr. and Mrs. Stockbridge from Society Row. She saw Pastor Stewart in an aft cabin, traveling alone, reading his Bible. As the low skyline of Boston gave way to open ocean, she heard people nearby discussing the recent discovery of gold in the American River in California; others discussed the failure of the European Revolutions. Mr. Bain's two young sons began a raucous game of checkers.

"What a time that was," Daisy said to Avery and Morrigan under the thrum of the steam engine, the gentle luffing of the sails. "It will be odd to be home again. I feel as if we'd gone to the moon and are returning back to earth completely changed."

"Will Mother disapprove of where all this money came from?" Morrigan asked.

"How can she, now that we've learned that she has powers of her own?" Daisy said.

"She'll find a way," Avery said wryly.

A figure loomed above them.

"Mrs. Stockbridge," said Avery carefully. "How pleasant to see you."

She was a severe-looking woman of forty-odd years with piercing blue eyes, a narrow nose, and a thin line of a mouth. Her sour-faced husband was the only son and sole heir of a whaling magnate and one of the richest men in Redcliffe. The woman nodded. "I trust you had an agreeable sojourn in Boston?"

"We did, thank you," said Avery. "And I trust that you and Mr. Stockbridge enjoyed your time there as well?"

Mrs. Stockbridge gave them a skeptical, judgmental half smile. "We were there only for two nights," she said. "Though we did attend a dinner party at a home on Beacon Hill, and the conversation was quite provocative."

Daisy smiled politely. "We were in Beacon Hill as well, staying with the Copeland family."

"I have heard," said Mrs. Stockbridge, "quite a lot of news of your doings of late. There's been a great deal of gossip about you three at home, of course, and now, most disconcertingly, in Boston."

"What are they saying about us at home?" Morrigan asked, worry clouding her face.

"That you attended our dear Tabitha Godwin on her deathbed." Her eyes flashed. "There has been talk—"

"Miss Godwin's death was tragic and unavoidable," said Avery. "She was beyond human intervention."

"We have felt great anguish about it," Morrigan added.

Daisy kept silent but sat up very straight, trying to mirror the composure of the figure on the Temperance card.

"My dearest friend in Boston, Mrs. Cornelia Beaton, told me how you soothed her chronic joint pains with your bare hands. I could scarcely believe you'd have the audacity to claim expertise in medical matters." Mrs. Stockbridge looked scandalized. "And then Mrs. Beaton's younger brother Nicholas told us of that spectacle you made of yourselves at the medical school, a lecture interrupted by one of you who gave *quite* the demonstration—"

"Me," Daisy burst out. "That was me."

"Of course it was," Mrs. Stockbridge said.

"We were there, too," Morrigan piped in, staunchly loyal. Daisy could have kissed her.

Mrs. Stockbridge sniffed. "Well, let me tell you, I stared at poor Nicholas until he wondered if he'd sprouted a second head. 'That young girl!' I told him. 'She's all of sixteen and has only the most basic village-school education!' But he assured me it was true, that you had shown the illustrious Dr. Franklyn a manner of treatment that he had never seen before. This bare-handed *energetic* . . . transfer of *heat*?"

"That's right," Daisy said, doing her best not to sound defensive.

"I'd be careful if I were you, dear girls," Mrs. Stockbridge said with a small shake of her head. Her luck in encountering the notorious Wolfson sisters on the homeward journey would be a feather in her social cap. She could return with fresh gossip. "You may find that public sentiment toward you at home is not nearly as warm as the reception you've found in Boston society."

"Do you refer again to the terrible death of Tabitha Godwin, or is there more?" Morrigan asked.

"I suppose my loyalty to your aunt compels me to give you fair warning." Mrs. Stockbridge heaved a stagey sigh. "Young Phineas Stewart has been suggesting that you practice black-sorcery spells and enchantments. And that you hold rituals at night and conjure evil spirits! Some hold that you are charlatans; others, that you are witches. Both camps agree that you are bringing bad spirits to our town."

Daisy and Morrigan stared up at her, alarmed.

"Thank you, Mrs. Stockbridge," said Avery with curt finality.

"Allow me to bid you good day, Misses Wolfson." She gave her head an imperious little shake and marched away in full sail.

"I'm sorry," Daisy said in a rush to Morrigan. "You were right, I was careless and—"

"Hush," Morrigan said, grasping Daisy's hand. "Mrs. Stockbridge doesn't need a reason to insult us and spread baseless rumors. It's what she lives for. Hateful woman."

Those were harsh words from Daisy's normally restrained twin.

"Agreed," Avery said, scowling after Mrs. Stockbridge's retreating form.

Daisy gasped. "That damned Finny Stewart! I told him at the Apple Ball that I knew he was responsible for Lizzie's condition. This must be his retribution! He's trying to protect himself against whatever we may say. And it can't have helped that I also spurned his tawdry advances."

"Keep your voice down," hissed Morrigan, glancing over at the nearby cabin where Pastor Stewart sat reading his Bible. "His father is right over there."

"Well, I don't care if he knows about his son's atrocious behavior," Daisy said, but she lowered her voice all the same.

They fell into a thoughtful silence. Daisy felt for her tarot deck in her cloak pocket and pulled it out. It tingled with information, almost buzzing with so much recent use. She knew it needed recharging, but she began shuffling it anyway. *Help me understand my mother,* she implored the cards silently, cutting them and selecting one.

Temperance emerged upright from the tarot deck: *A child with an old face and great feathered wings stands with one foot in shallow water, one on the stream bank, serenely pouring liquid between gold chalices, diluting wine with water.*

"It's the next card in my journey." Daisy couldn't keep the disappointment out of her voice.

"Patience, harmony." Avery grinned. "Moderation and inner calm."

"I'm happy to see that card," said Morrigan.

"Not the card I was seeking, though."

Avery looked at Daisy. "But maybe it is. Maybe it's exactly the card you need right now."

"A clear head," said Morrigan.

"We all need to clear our heads," said Avery. "And that's the perfect card for a calm sea voyage on a clear day."

Daisy relented. "Fair enough! I'm just glad it's upright." She looked at the Temperance card again: *Patience, balance, calm? Blast it!*

A melody floated to Daisy's ears on a gust of wind then, a sweet, high voice singing a plaintive tune, an air in a minor key, in a language she didn't know. She saw a boy standing at the railing, singing to the waves, his face turned to the wind and salt spray. He wore a green linen tunic over rough breeches. On his feet were well-worn brown leather boots that laced up almost to his knees.

Just then, a tremendous gust blew the boy's hat from his head, unleashing a pile of curly black hair that whipped around his face in the wind. The tweed cap flew down the deck, but Avery stuck out a leg and stopped it with her foot, reaching down to pick it up.

"Your hat, my . . . lady?" Avery stood up to give a half bow, her eyes glinting with merriment as she returned the cap to its owner, who'd run after the wayward item.

"Avery, you're mistaken—" And then Daisy realized her sister and the boy were laughing, that the boy was in fact not a boy but instead a young woman about their own age.

"Ah, the jig is up, I see." She spoke with a lilt. Her skin was brown and her eyes a startling, vivid bright green. She wore a beaten-silver pendant on a chain around her neck, a Celtic cross, intricately ornate and inset with a green stone, peridot from the look of it. She stuffed her hair back into the cap. "Kept me safe on the journey from Ireland."

"If I could get away with it, I'd do the same," said Avery, and the two girls exchanged a look full of unspoken understanding. "I'm Avery Wolfson, and these are my sisters, Daisy and Morrigan."

"Pleased, I'm sure," Daisy said, popping up with a little curtsy, as Avery regarded her with banked amusement.

Morrigan laughed and stood to introduce herself as well.

"Frances Morrison's my name," the girl said, beaming at each of them in turn. "Though I go by Frankie. Much more suited to me, and being a boy kept me safe on the cross-Atlantic passage from Ireland.

I'll be working soon, and I'd rather do it outside than in. Better to pass as a boy."

"Sound plan," Avery agreed.

"And is that Temperance you've pulled?" Frankie turned her attention to the card still in Daisy's hand.

"Oh, yes," Daisy said, "we were just pulling a card for the journey."

"Considering the tarot's a journey in itself"—Frankie grinned—"that makes perfect sense." Daisy handed Frankie the card so she could examine it more closely. "That's terrifically pretty. Never seen anything like it!"

"Are you familiar with tarot?" Morrigan asked.

"Sure, my whole entire life," Frankie said. "I learned it from my family as a child, but before I mastered it, I was distracted by the glorious art of astrology taught by this old woman in the village, and now I'm mad about the stars and heavens!"

"How could you not be?" enthused Avery. "They're so . . ."

"Otherworldly," Frankie finished for her.

As Daisy watched Avery and Frankie beam and chatter at each other, it was like observing two lifelong friends reuniting after a long separation, though they'd only just that moment met. Daisy was reminded of how she and her sisters so often finished one another's sentences. Or how Morrigan and Henry quietly delighted in each other's company.

And then Daisy was unaccountably put in mind of her first encounter with Nate, that unexpected thrill she'd not until that moment known she'd longed to feel—before it all went sour. She shook that memory out of her head, not wanting to spoil the afternoon. And anyway, Frankie was nothing like Nate. It occurred to Daisy that this was a good thing. Though Nate's aggressive outburst at Aunt Mary's had been shocking—how he'd just stormed into the solarium and demanded Jasper fistfight him, like they were drunks in a tavern—it also . . . hadn't been. Had she always suspected he contained the potential for sudden violence but hadn't been able to see past the attention he'd lavished on her? She felt a tiny hitch in her breast, like something had broken away, never to be repaired.

"If it weren't so windy out here, I'd do a reading for you all right now," Frankie said, distracting Daisy from her unsettling reverie.

"Well, we can do a reading for you instead!" Avery exclaimed.

"Before we do anything, we must eat," Morrigan insisted. "Frankie, will you join us for lunch?"

"Yes, you must," Avery enthused.

Daisy noted how sharp Frankie's cheekbones were, the hollows in her eyes, her wrists as thin as birds' bones. "We have plenty!"

"Well, I haven't eaten in . . . a few days," Frankie allowed ruefully. "And I can't recall the last time I had a proper bath or even changed my clothing." She laughed, pretending to sniff her own underarms and then making a horrified face, so frank and self-deprecatingly charming the sisters had to laugh with her. "Have you really got enough, then?"

Morrigan gestured at the big picnic hamper, saying, "We'll never finish it on our own!"

"Sit by me," Avery said, hooking an arm through Frankie's and pulling her down to the bench, while Daisy uncorked the wine and Morrigan laid out linen napkins. The Copelands' housekeeper had packed them a generous lunch of cold roast chicken, ham-and-tomato pies, sweet pickles, fresh-baked rolls with cheese, and jam tarts and candied oranges.

As they ate, Frankie regaled the sisters with stories of Ireland.

She was eighteen, the only girl in a large family, with seven little brothers she'd left behind on the family farm in County Clare.

"What was that song you were singing?" Daisy asked.

"It's called Dulaman. It's about seaweed! Silly, I know, but singing it helps the homesickness. And it's in Gaelic, from home."

"My sisters and I are traveling back to Redcliffe," Avery interjected. "Is that where you're going to stop?"

"It is," Frankie said. "And this is my first time in America." She flung her arms out. "The new world!" Her joy was infectious. "Don't mistake me, I miss my homeland, but the poverty of our land cannot support the feeding of us all and Ireland's too small for the likes of me. I need this big wild country to stretch out in."

Noticing the hesitant curiosity in her new acquaintances' eyes, Frankie didn't miss a beat. "My father's parents were enslaved Africans in Dublin," she said patiently, clearly used to having to explain things even if she seemed somewhat tired by the topic. "My father is a freeman, my mother an Irishwoman. In Ireland, marriages like theirs aren't too uncommon."

"I wish that were true here of such marriages," said Avery, meeting the matter head-on with her usual candor. "Though slavery was abolished here in Massachusetts over sixty years ago and people of all nationalities trade together—"

"So, you mingle with other non-whites?" Frankie asked directly, clearly cut from the same cloth as Daisy's plain-speaking eldest sister.

"Yes, of course," Morrigan said, then paused. "Although to be fair, it's mostly at festivals or on market days. . . ."

"With slave catchers profiting off the chattel slavery still booming in the southern and western states," Avery continued, warming to her subject, "I'm afraid we can't hope for true equality of all people until the abhorrent institution is abolished across the entire country and—"

"It's abolished in Britain, but that doesn't mean folks mix overmuch back home either," Frankie interrupted, sighing. "I told you marriages like my parents' aren't uncommon in Ireland, but that doesn't mean our family's had it easy by any stretch of the imagination."

As Frankie and Avery dove into a discussion about the sociological differences and similarities between the two countries, Daisy pondered Morrigan's earlier response, realizing that for all the times they'd bought goods from the Black and Portuguese and Native sellers at the market or danced together at the Apple Ball, the interactions, though courteous and kind, had been the extent of her dealings with people of other races, excepting servants, and that was its own segregation. She thought of Mr. Miggs, her aunt Mary's butler. Though he, too, was a freeman, the unstated boundary of class had always been clear, like there was an invisible line she wasn't supposed to cross, as though it might be rude, even, to travel from her community into another's, an imposition into a world in which she didn't belong. But it made no sense to Daisy that a person's skin color or the language they spoke should be the basis of a division between fellow humans. Could it be that things might change?

Reading her mind as always, Avery paused. "Daisy, have you had any Visions about any of this?"

"Not as yet," she said carefully, startled that Avery had spoken so freely of her gift in front of a relative stranger. Still, her older sister clearly sensed that Frankie could be trusted. And Daisy got that impression herself. "But perhaps I haven't been looking in the right places."

Frankie and Avery smiled at each other, seeming to assess something in Daisy she'd only just that moment begun to discover herself.

As the *Fortunata* docked at Redcliffe Harbor, the Wolfsons gave Frankie their address, all making fervent promises to meet again soon to exchange readings, and perhaps even collaborate with their complementary skills. But first the sisters needed to rush home to see their mother, and Frankie was anxious to seek work that very afternoon on the boats—as a boy, since women weren't allowed to be sailors. "Though I've been on the sea my whole life!"

"You're going to work on a whaling ship?" Morrigan marveled.

"Well, I don't know about that," Frankie chuckled. "But on the ship, I overhead some travelers mention the cod fishing fleets run by immigrants from Cape Verde. Can't be so different from the cod we have back home." Frankie nodded, making up her mind.

"You might want to cut that hair of yours," Avery noted.

"It's in the way, isn't it?" Frankie agreed. "I'm also wanting to track down my mother's cousins. They left before I was born, in search of a better life. All we know is they settled hereabouts, and then the letters stopped, but it'd mean so much to my mam. I'm not sure where to start."

The sisters assured Frankie they'd do all in their power to help her find her cousins. "It's a small town," Daisy assured her.

She was only just beginning to realize quite how small.

CHAPTER XV

THE DEVIL

"The mind is its own place, and in itself can make a heaven of hell, a hell of heaven."

—JOHN MILTON, *Paradise Lost, Book I*

Daisy stood at the railing, waiting with the other passengers to disembark, looking down at the line of waiting carriages and wagons. The crew unloaded supplies and luggage from the hold as people streamed down the gangway. When Daisy and her sisters reached the rough planks of the dock, Mrs. Stockbridge swept past without a word. At the same instant, they were almost bowled over by a housemaid in an apron and cap who was rushing in the opposite direction.

"Someone's in a hurry," Morrigan said as she was jostled in the ruckus.

They turned to watch as the girl dashed straight for Pastor Stewart, a few people behind in the line. Whatever the maid had to say had the effect of causing the pastor to hasten, his servant trotting behind to keep up. His black-clad figure parted the milling crowd and vanished in the direction of the church.

"I have a terrible feeling," Daisy said.

"We should not tarry," Avery agreed.

Thankfully, Aunt Mary's buggy awaited at the dock, Henry having sent word ahead. Daisy turned to ask Frankie if she needed a lift, but she had vanished into the throng.

When the buggy pulled up at their garden gate, the sisters traipsed into their cottage. The footman kindly carried their heavy trunk up to their bedroom, then took his leave.

The cottage, spotless and orderly, had a chilly air of desertion. No fire was lit. A deep silence rang in their ears.

"She must be off giving lessons," Morrigan said.

"Or on errands," Daisy said.

Upstairs in their room, they quickly freshened up with the old familiar pitcher and basin on the washstand. They left their smaller bags and the trunk where they were. There would be time to unpack later.

The one thing they had to do right away, before attending to anything else, was to bury their tarot decks. Suffusing them in the light of the full moon would have been the ideal way to cleanse them, but the cards badly needed even a quick recharging after their constant use in Boston, and Kathryn had taught that wrapping them in rags and interring them for a time in the soil worked almost as well as a moon bath.

Then they would see to the matter of Finny Stewart.

The Redcliffe township Presbyterian church sat atop the hill above Main Street, its spire dwarfing all the other buildings in town. Daisy and her sisters were out of breath as they dashed up the long flight of steps to the heavy wooden door of the manse. Taking the lead, Daisy let the brass knocker resound a few times.

The door opened to the strained face of the same young housemaid they'd seen at the docks. "Yes, misses?" she said in a whisper, reaching out a hand to cover the knocker, should Daisy be tempted to pound on it any further.

"We've come to see Finny." Daisy took one of those deep breaths Kathryn had taught. "Please tell him it's Daisy Wolfson calling."

"And sisters," added Avery tersely.

"Both Master and Pastor Stewart are engaged at the moment," the girl said, bobbing her head, neat in its white ruched cap, preparing to close the door. Impulsively, Daisy stuck the toe of a boot in the doorway, daring the maid to close it all the way.

"It's a matter of utmost urgency," Morrigan said softly.

"As I said, this isn't the best—"

"We'll wait in the hall," Avery interrupted, sidestepping around her into the foyer, Daisy and Morrigan close on her heels.

The girl fluttered around for a moment. Daisy could see her wondering whether she could physically throw them out. Finally, she flung up her hands and disappeared into the depths of the narrow stone house.

They could hear raised voices from within the main house. The maid had failed to pull the door to the parlor fully shut behind her and the words were so heated that much of the conversation filtered through. It didn't take much imagination to know that the voice demanding that "your son do the right thing!" was Lizzie's father, Mr. Cuttle, nor to recognize the other angry male voice insisting he'd not had "anything to do with that strumpet's miserable condition" as that of Finny.

As Mr. Cuttle and Finny began shouting over each other, an older woman's voice that Daisy assumed belonged to Mrs. Cuttle cried, "Please make peace, I beg of you both!"

"But you do love me, you said you did!" The owner of that voice was obvious.

Oh, Lizzie, thought Daisy. *You poor, misguided girl!*

The only voice Daisy didn't hear was Pastor Stewart's. He was a kind man, but he often struck her as somewhat bewildered, as though he was unsure what he was doing at the pulpit, occasionally losing track of his thoughts mid-sentence or forgetting the names of parishioners he had known for decades. She imagined him standing in a daze, his head in a muddle about what, exactly, was going on here.

"I fear we're too late," Morrigan murmured.

"You're right," Avery agreed. "Should we just go away and leave them to it?"

"No!" Daisy cried.

Finny smashed open the parlor door just then, crashing out into the vestibule and catching sight of the sisters.

"You!" he cried, pointing a stubby index finger so close to Daisy's face she could smell the onion he'd had for his lunch. "*You* did this! You put ideas into that pathetic creature's head! Why, you're lower than—"

"I wouldn't finish that sentence if I were you," Avery said quietly, stepping in front of Daisy.

A sour expression came over Finny's face as he edged sideways toward the front door. "You're witches," he spat. "All three of you. I've known it since the very beginning! I can smell it on you." He wrinkled his pug nose.

"Did you know it when you practically asked for my hand in

marriage at the Apple Ball?" Daisy snapped. "Seems odd. Unless you like that sort of thing." And then Daisy impulsively hissed at him like a cat. It gave her a peculiar thrill when he jumped.

"She's teasing you, Finny," said Morrigan, "though I can't say you don't deserve it. Your behavior is shocking."

"Don't think this is the end of it!" he fumed.

"The end of what?" Daisy challenged.

But by then he'd thrown the door open and flung himself out, slamming it behind him with a thud that rattled the doorframe.

In his wake, the parlor door flew open again, and Lizzie staggered into the foyer. "Where is he? What have you done with him?"

"Done with him?" Daisy gasped. "We were here to—"

"I heard what you said, that he'd practically asked to marry you!" she said with teary accusation. "Is that why you wouldn't give me a love spell? Because you wanted him for yourself?"

Daisy stood with her mouth agape.

"Lizzie, how could you suggest such a thing?" said Morrigan. "Daisy is your friend! As are we! We've done nothing but—"

"This is why he fights the marriage," she cried. "You never cared about my fate; you only pretended you wanted me to be happy. But *why*, Daisy?" Her voice was hoarse. "You don't even seem to like him. Is it because he's wealthy? Are the proceeds from your *witchery* not enough to help your mother with her bills?"

The girl's eyes sparked with cold glints. In spite of herself, Daisy was impressed by Lizzie's sudden show of gumption.

"I think that's quite enough, Lizzie," Avery said, her voice still soft and dangerous. "You're not thinking clearly, you're distraught. I suggest you—"

"I came to you for help, and you refused. Well, my love and I will be married, no thanks to you!"

"Are you sure of that, Lizzie?" Daisy asked cautiously. "There's still time to change your mind...."

"You'd like that, wouldn't you?" Her voice was pitched low, like the growl of something inhuman. "You wanted me to kill the tiny spark of life that binds me to Phineas. I won't listen to any more of this hatefulness. And if you try to interfere again, you'll be sorry!"

She dashed out the side door that led to the churchyard.

Just then came a measured murmur of adult voices, speaking more calmly now that both their children had fled the scene. A moment later, Mr. and Mrs. Cuttle emerged from the parlor. At the sight of Daisy and her sisters, their expressions hardened.

"She was a perfectly sensible girl until she took up with the likes of you," said Mrs. Cuttle. "And see where that got her, listening to your big talk of following her heart."

Mr. Cuttle shook his head. "That's all well and good for you society types, but she's the daughter of a simple baker!"

"Mr. and Mrs. Cuttle," Daisy entreated them, hot tears of distress springing to her eyes, "we're not society anything; you've known us all our lives! That wasn't what... I was only trying to help!"

"I think this town's had quite enough of your help," Mrs. Cuttle said quietly.

"Come now, Sally," her husband said, handing his wife her coat.

The two of them hurried down the steps together, their heads lowered with the shame of their daughter's predicament.

"I think it's time for everyone to go home," said Pastor Stewart, appearing in the parlor doorway, leaning against the jamb for support. "Janet," he called into the depths of the house for the housekeeper.

"No need," Avery told him. "We'll let ourselves out."

Daisy tumbled with her sisters down the manse steps to the path, hearing the latch click behind them. The autumn air came as a welcome shock, bracing and crisp, goading her to action.

"I'll be right back," she said to her sisters. Then she hurried into the chapel, where daylight filtered through one stained-glass window. Daisy peered into the glow cast by the sconces at the altar.

"Lizzie?" Daisy whispered. "Are you here?"

A tall figure in a brown robe emerged from the underwater gloom, materializing before her like a ghost.

Daisy jumped. "Brother Terrence! Where did you come from? What are you doing in Redcliffe? Don't you live in Boston?" Her voice sounded breathless and high in her own ears.

"If you mean do I have a mailing address in Boston, the answer is no. Nor do I subscribe to such pedantic concerns, which I could have sworn we'd already established." He slunk down the aisle, his eyes alight. "More to the point, dear girl: Is that any way to greet an old friend?"

"I'm sorry," Daisy faltered, head swirling. "You're right, of course. I just..." She sank into the nearest pew. "Have you seen a young woman in here? About so tall, upset?"

"You mean besides yourself?" he said, laughing. "Come now, I'm just teasing. She was here, but now she's gone."

"You saw Lizzie? What did she say?"

"She explained her unfortunate circumstances, poor child. So I helped her." He looked pleased with himself.

"Wait, what?" Daisy gasped. "How precisely did you help her?"

"How precisely do you think I helped her?"

"You gave her a love spell? But that's so dangerous—"

"Only for mere dabblers, my dear. The way I see it, it would be far more dangerous for the poor girl to be unwed and unprotected in her condition. As for the baby's father, when has a boy ever known what he wanted until it was forced on him?"

"But Kathryn told us—"

He said with a fond smile, "Kathryn has always been cautious. Not like your mother. Now there's a force to behold!"

Her mother? What was he talking about?

"As for me, I have never been one to step in the way of a person's true desires. To quote my namesake, Publius Terentius Afer, 'Let nothing human be foreign to me.'"

Daisy covered her face with her palms, attempting to rub the confusion out of herself, if only through her eyeballs.

"You're very unsettled, Daisy," he said with a strange gentleness. "Perhaps a reading might help?"

"I don't have my... Wait, you're distracting me. I want—"

"Answers, yes, I know," he said, producing something from within his robes. "I believe you'll recognize the design."

Daisy gaped. It was her deck, the one she'd left beneath the willow tree!

"I thought it might be comforting," he soothed. "Worry not, yours is safe at home where you buried it, such a quaint tradition."

"Are you a—witch?"

Brother Terrence's laugh rippled through the church as he shuffled the deck lightly and extended it to her to cut, ignoring her question.

Curious despite herself, Daisy indicated a point along the spine of the deck.

"An excellent choice," he said, flipping over the Devil card.

Of course Daisy had no business being surprised anymore by the inevitability of the Major Arcana, but that Brother Terrence was now presenting the very next card in her journey, from what looked to be a duplicate of her own hand-painted deck, was dizzying.

"I suggest you let go of your thinking brain and give yourself over to the wisdom of the card," he said, reading her as keenly as Avery or Kathryn.

With another sigh, Daisy regarded the imagery she'd painted, the flipped coin of the Lovers card: *A man and woman stand naked beneath the towering gaze of a horned and winged creature. They're loosely draped in unlocked chains that also loop around the altar upon which the apparition looms.*

"And?" he prompted impatiently.

"Seek to avoid the entrapment of desire and materialism, leading inevitably to emptiness and lack of fulfillment," Daisy intoned, like a student reciting lessons by rote.

"How dull," Brother Terrence said. "Why not allow yourself the adventure of exploring your wildest, darkest fantasies?"

"There you are!" cried Morrigan as a brilliant splash of sunlight poured through the door of the church. She and Avery rushed down the aisle toward Daisy.

"We were worried," scolded Avery.

"I'm all right, I promise," Daisy assured them. "I was just getting a reading from . . ." She gestured toward Brother Terrence.

But he was gone.

CHAPTER XVI

THE TOWER

"Invention, it must be humbly admitted, does not consist in creating out of void, but out of chaos."

—MARY SHELLEY, *Frankenstein; or, The Modern Prometheus*

As she and her sisters walked home together, Daisy noticed that their little town seemed to have grown more wretched in the ten days they'd been gone. The houses and shops they passed looked worn and weather-beaten, colors faded and windows dimmed, and the familiar streets were emptied of life. The sky was clouded, casting a dull light over everything, and the eerie silence was broken only by the occasional creak of a sign swinging in the wind.

To distract herself as much as to keep them apprised of the latest events, Daisy told her sisters the news about Brother Terrence giving Lizzie a love spell for Finny Stewart.

"You'd think that someone with his experience and training would know better!" Avery fumed.

"What experience, though?" Morrigan mused. "None of us knows anything substantial about Brother Terrence's background or training."

"Precisely!" Daisy said, nodding at her twin in agreement. "And in what? By whom?" A chill crept along her arms. "He had a tarot deck exactly like mine. Where did he get it?"

At this, her sisters were silent. It struck all of them at once how easily they had simply accepted the story he'd told.

"Just that he'd known us since before we were born," Avery said.

"No, that's not quite right," Morrigan said. "That he'd been *expecting* us."

The three went silent, digesting that subtlety of language. "Expecting us," Daisy repeated. "Does that mean he has Visions, too?"

"Well . . . it stands to reason, if he has prescience, right?" Morrigan chewed her thumb thoughtfully, almost tripping on an exposed root along the path. "Ugh, what an awful day."

"At least we can fortify ourselves with a good supper now that we're home," Avery said.

Daisy followed her sisters in through the wrought-iron gate. As they made their way along the flagstone path beneath the willow and rowan trees, she stopped to dig up the tarot decks. Sure enough, her own was next to her sisters', right where she'd left it.

They found a basket on their doorstep containing packets of herbs and a note. "Kathryn's sent the ingredients and recipe for an elixir to combat the Bleakness," Avery said. "I'll brew it tonight."

Inside, the sisters shed cloaks and cards, reticules and boots, and slid sore feet into house slippers. "Mother," Morrigan called, but the house was still empty.

Avery and Morrigan headed into the kitchen, and Daisy fetched the bowls from the sideboard, giving the spoons and butter knife a quick polish with a rag. As she added earthenware mugs to each place setting, filling them with well water from the jug, Daisy admired the way the last rays of late-afternoon sun danced in the low-ceilinged room. Their humble cottage was so different from the Copelands' mansion—the plain candles and kerosene lamps, the well outside, the rustic outhouse. But simple though it was, it was theirs, their place of belonging.

Avery came into the dining room with a basket of freshly baked biscuits, Morrigan with a pot of vegetable soup. With the briefest grace ever spoken, they tucked into the plain but hearty meal. After supper, all of them wondering where their mother could be at such a late hour, Daisy and Morrigan washed the dishes while Avery brewed a large pot of apple cider with several handfuls of the dried herbs Kathryn had left. Morrigan and Daisy helped her pour the elixir into stoppered bottles and packed them into baskets, ready to distribute at the Harvest Festival the next day.

"I hope this works," said Morrigan.

"The Bleakness hasn't lessened in our absence," said Daisy.

"It's grown worse than ever, I fear," said Avery.

Early the next morning, as they approached the village green, Daisy heard a familiar voice saying her name. Before she could turn around, Nate reached out with his large, warm hands, pulling her into the intoxicating orbit of his physical charisma.

"I'm so glad you're back," he said, capturing both her hands in his large, callused ones.

Daisy was suddenly warm all over, as if he were a hot fire whose glow she was suffused by. But then she remembered his strange actions at Aunt Mary's, and his unsettling diffidence toward her.

"Hello, Nate," she said cautiously, as Avery and Morrigan tactfully paused a few feet ahead.

"You're upset," he said, stepping back. "Sorry about Blackwell House. I guess I was out of line."

"I shouldn't have encouraged revenge at the reading," Daisy said. Despite his boorishness, Jasper's accusations about her role in unwittingly helping to aim Nate's grudge hadn't been entirely misplaced.

Nate gave her a helpless grin that made his sun-kissed face look boyish. "He roundly deserved it, but I didn't mean to upset you. I was so mortified, I could barely look you in the eye."

Daisy gazed at him, confused by his renewed affection but wanting to forgive. "Perhaps Jasper deserved that rage."

Nate narrowed his eyes, indicating she'd struck a nerve. Then, just as quickly, his expression shifted again to a beaming smile. "I should have known you'd take my side, Daisy. You're one girl in a million."

He brought his face close to Daisy's, so close their lips almost touched. Daisy realized that he intended to kiss her full on the mouth, right there, in broad daylight. Swayed by the power of his nearness, she couldn't help lifting her mouth closer to his.

"Watch yourself, Winthrop," Avery said, flanked by an anxious Morrigan. "And you too, little sister."

Unkissed, Daisy glared at her bossy older sister. Avery ignored Daisy and spiked Nate with a steely expression.

Nate glanced at Avery with quick, defensive alarm, dropping Daisy's hands and taking a step backward. "Whatever Fitzwilliam said to you about me, it's not true, I swear it. And haven't we all been unfairly accused? Daisy, surely you understand, look what happened with the Godwin girl."

"That wasn't my fault," Daisy said faintly, her heart pounding. "Please believe me."

He looked stricken. "Of course it wasn't! I only meant that I know what it's like to be wrongly accused."

"Nate, I'm sorry, I—"

"Drink this," Avery interrupted, placing a bottle of the elixir into Nate's hand. "It's a powerful influenza prevention."

"I'll come find you later," Nate told Daisy, taking the bottle without looking at it. With a last searching look at her, he plunged back into the crowd.

"Have you lost all sense, Daisy?" Avery's forehead was creased with worry.

Daisy's cheeks burned, though whether it was with embarrassment or excitement, she couldn't have said.

"Well, at least we helped one person today," Morrigan said, ever the peacemaker.

But this gave Daisy small comfort as they pressed onward. Exactly as Mrs. Stockbridge had warned, some people seemed skittish of the sisters, others almost afraid of them, and few would accept the bottles of herbed cider they attempted to press into their hands. They approached a group of girls and boys a little younger than themselves, listening to the fiddler on the village green. The youngsters looked at them with suspicion. When offered the cider, they shrieked and scattered.

"It's as though they think we're offering them rat poison," said Avery as the sisters walked away.

The Harvest Festival was usually a daylong celebration of autumnal abundance, a chance for people to visit over mugs of ale, to toss pennies to jugglers, to buy heaps of the apples, cheeses, cured meats, and herbs local farmers had worked so hard to provide. Now, the air was as sour and clotted as curdled milk.

The sisters passed by the green again. It was thronged with all of Redcliffe, all its stations from heiress to beggar, every age from the most ancient elders to the smallest babies, a panoply of accents and ethnicities. But Daisy noticed that the usual calm atmosphere had soured with palpable discord. The fiddler had stopped playing and was packing up his instrument. Several girls sat in a heap together on the ground, wailing. Two housewives jostled each other, muttering imprecations, and turned away without apology. Then Daisy saw a young boy run headlong into a group of men and go sprawling in the dirt. Instead of helping him up, the men roughly shoved him to his feet and boxed his ears. Crying, he lurched on his way past a married couple Daisy recognized from church. They stood locked in a bitter argument, hissing and spitting at each other, while their baby wailed and their small tearful daughter tugged again and again at her mother's skirts. Without looking down at her, her mother shoved her hands away, slapped her face.

A few men sat at the edge of the green playing cards. Daisy and her sisters recognized them all, local shopkeepers who knew their names, their family. "Be off with you," said Mr. Thomason, shooing the girls away.

"Oh no," said a farmer a moment later, standing by his big baskets of root vegetables, potatoes and onions, beets and turnips and rutabagas, all of which he resembled. "We've heard of your doings with the Cuttle family."

"Tabitha Godwin was a treasure to this town," said their former schoolteacher, Miss Abigail Grover, a twitchy woman who'd never liked the Wolfsons to begin with. "I hear you three were involved with her demise."

"This is terrible," Daisy said, almost in tears.

"We're outcasts," Morrigan sighed.

Daisy echoed her sigh. "But we're innocent, and we can help them all."

"Not if they won't drink our elixir," Avery snapped.

"Has Brother Terrence bewitched the entire town?" Daisy wondered aloud. "Was he here all along, invisible to us, working black magic?"

"Look," said Morrigan.

Finny Stewart and Lizzie Cuttle came strolling on the edge of the green, hand in hand. She leaned into him, smiling up at him. Finny's gaze was glassy and unfocused. He seemed to lurch along like a marionette with an incompetent puppeteer.

"Hello," called Lizzie. Her eyes glittered as she showed the sisters her prize. "We're to be married this afternoon, by Pastor Stewart. It's all arranged. No thanks to any of you."

"Congratulations," Daisy said skeptically.

Morrigan looked from Lizzie to Finny. "Is this true, Phineas? It's all settled?"

"All settled," Finny intoned. His face looked as if it were melting, his hand in Lizzie's grip limp as a fish in a net. "All arranged."

"He loves me so," said Lizzie in a treacly voice. "Don't you, my darling?"

"I love Lizzie," said Finny. "I love her!" he shouted with an angry half smile, his head cocked at a strange angle.

"You're clearly under a spell," said Avery, "but we will try to undo it."

"You touch him, and you'll rue the day," Lizzie hissed.

Finny shouted, "These sisters are witches! They killed Tabitha Godwin!"

Avery went pale. Her hand flew to her cheek. "I can see it, hear it," she said in a hushed tone to her sisters. "Whisperings, right now, all over town, about us: *mixing their diabolical potions, their bodies covered in warts beneath their dresses. She was just a child, and they killed her! They drank her Spirit for a pleasure!*"

Morrigan gasped. "They mean us?"

"Who is saying this?" Daisy demanded.

"I can't tell," said Avery. "I can only feel the planting of the ideas, the bloodlust: *Catch the witches! Bind them and beat them! Douse the witches! Find them and drown them! Kill the witches! Stack them and burn them!*" Then Avery's eyes shuttered, and she swayed precariously.

"Avery!" Daisy cried, supporting her with Morrigan's help. "Come back to us." Impulsively, Daisy gave Avery a quick, hard slap, and, with a lurch, Avery shook her head, opened her eyes, and stood upright again, shaken. Daisy and Morrigan hugged her in relief.

"Sorceresses!" Finny yelled.

Mr. Godwin emerged through the gathering crowd to stand at Finny's side. "They killed my daughter," cried Mr. Godwin as the growing crowd surrounded them. "My dearest, only daughter!"

"Their treatments go against medical science," said Dr. Wellington, glowering with barely banked animosity. "These charlatans only cause harm."

"Abominations against God," Finny shouted, moving closer. Lizzie clutched at his arm to bring his attention back to her, but he was not to be deterred. "If we are aware of such immoral practices underway in our community yet remain silent, we are guilty." He turned to look at his fellow citizens, his arms raised to the heavens. "The Lord sayeth, 'Thou shalt not suffer a witch to live,' and I shall not! Who among you stands with me?"

"I do!" came a rough shout from the back of the crowd, followed by several more calls of "Aye!" and "To the death!"

There was a hubbub of voices, male and female, old and young.

"Let's go home," said Morrigan.

"We have to defend our name," said Avery.

"She's right. We can't run away," Daisy said, fixing Finny with a glare. "Finny Stewart, you know as well as I do that you're lying! Why are you doing this?"

Finny sidestepped Daisy and shouted to the crowd, "A witch always denies she's a witch!"

Daisy could feel the press and surge of bodies all around them. A sharp rock hit the side of her arm hard, tearing her sleeve. Her hand came away bloodied. Before Daisy could put her handkerchief over the wound, she felt a rough hand pulling at her shoulder, another shoving her back.

"We must run," Morrigan cried. "Now!"

But the sisters were surrounded on all sides. The sheer size and madness of the mob had given it a mind of its own, a hunger for blood that couldn't be reasoned with.

"Let me through!" came a clear, commanding voice. There was Bernadette, holding a small bag, parting the crowd with sheer force of will. And something else. As she came closer, Daisy could see her reaching into her bag and pulling out a powder that she blew with all the force of her lungs over the crowd, letting it sprinkle down on everyone's head.

Daisy and her sisters watched, amazed, as their mother spread this glittering dust, speaking strange words, moving slowly, deliberately, calmly, bringing her own calm with her. Bernadette was utterly magnificent. And whatever that powder was, it had the effect of stunning the townspeople into muted silence and dispersing their rage.

People shook their heads as if waking up from a dream. In clumps, they wandered off, moving sullenly, in confusion and bewilderment.

Finny subsided into torpid silence. Lizzie clutched his arm and drew him away.

"What was that?" Avery wanted to know, but Bernadette only murmured some words under her breath, flicking her fingers in a subtle motion.

"This is merely a temporary measure," she said in a low voice. "We need to get away, and fast. Leave your baskets. Maybe someone will have the courage to drink the protection."

Beside themselves with relief to be reunited with their mother again at last, the sisters followed Bernadette through the strange, silent streets. Enfolded in the safety of their cottage, they sat huddled together by the fire. While Bernadette bandaged Daisy's arm, Avery stoked the blaze until it crackled.

"Mother," Daisy burst out, "where have you been?"

Bernadette's narrow face looked drawn. There were dark circles under her eyes. "I've been working all through the night with Kathryn to understand the Bleakness. Despite my misgivings, it was clear something had to be done. But we had little luck, I fear. We must learn what it is, what's causing it, in order to counteract it." She gave the three of them a sharp look. "What happened to poor Phineas?"

"Finny took the love spell Lizzie gave him," said Avery, adding quickly, "She didn't get it from us, I swear. We'd never have done something so foolhardy, Kathryn made sure of it."

"But that doesn't explain his rage," Morrigan said. "A love spell should have only caused him to do what Lizzie wanted, made him docile as a lamb. Something else got to him."

"But where did she get the charm in the first place?" Bernadette demanded.

Daisy wondered how they were going to explain this one. Thankfully, Morrigan changed the subject, exclaiming suddenly, "Mother, you're spellcasting again!"

Bernadette looked weary. "Sometimes you have to use the danger you know to protect yourself against a greater one."

"But you burned the . . ." Daisy started, confused.

"You mean this?" From the side table, Bernadette hefted *The Book of Hidden Doors*, the replacement book of spells they'd been given by Brother Terrence in Boston. "You didn't hide it very well; it was at the top of your trunk." She regarded the cover, taking in the new title. "A spell book by any other name still carries danger."

"I'm sorry, Mother," Daisy said, "it's just that Brother Terrence said—" She clapped a horrified hand to her mouth.

"I was wondering when I'd hear that name again," Bernadette said. "The maddening marplot."

"So you *do* know him!" Morrigan exclaimed, excited. "Do you think he's involved in the Bleakness? He's the one that gave Lizzie that love potion."

"Yes, of course he gave her the potion. I'm well acquainted with his ways," Bernadette said. "But I don't think . . ." She looked doubtful.

"Is Brother Terrence a demon?" Daisy demanded.

"No," Bernadette said with finality. "Brother Terrence can be meddlesome and unpredictable, but he's no demon."

"How exactly *are* you acquainted with him, Mother?" Avery pounced.

"Now's not the time." Bernadette stood abruptly.

Avery clearly wanted to push it, but Morrigan jumped in. "Is it Finny who's orchestrating the Bleakness?"

"What if it's Jasper Fitzwilliam?" Daisy blurted in a rush. "I knew something was off as soon as we met. Maybe he's the source of the Bleakness. After all, he came to town exactly when this all started!"

"So did Nate," Avery said with an apologetic glance at Daisy. "You also felt strongly about him. And before you say it, I know you like Nate and loathe Jasper. But such strong and immediate reactions are often opposing sides of the same coin."

Though Daisy hated the idea, she knew it had to be considered. She'd felt pulled to them both, despite herself. And how well did she know Nate anyway? Could it be she only preferred him because he hadn't insulted her pride? "Fair enough," she conceded, pained. "Could it be Nate, then?" Morrigan squeezed Daisy's arm in support.

Bernadette shrugged. "There are many suspects to consider. If something has indeed taken possession of someone human, their identity won't be obvious. Sleight of hand is part of the game. For now, I'm going to make a pot of tea. Concentration requires sustenance." Bernadette went to the kitchen.

"Let's consult the guides," suggested Morrigan, handing out their decks.

As always, the solidity of her cards steadied Daisy. She closed her eyes as the room filled with the soft sound of shuffling.

The sisters opened their eyes at the same instant, each pulling a card from her deck, just as they had in Boston, somehow having decided simultaneously to do another three-way reading. As one, they held their cards facing outward.

"The Tower," they all said in unison.

"Daisy's is reversed," said Morrigan.

Daisy turned her card to look at it. *A crumbling tower is struck by lightning, a shrouded figure leaping from it headlong, arms outstretched in the plummet to the stones below.*

"It does feel like we've been hit by a destructive force," she said.

"Morrigan's and my cards are upright," said Avery. "For us, this is a time of external chaos, forces from without causing destruction."

"But the reversed Tower means that the lightning is within me," Daisy said. "It's some kind of revelation, an awakening I'm meant to have in my journey."

"We're in this together," Morrigan reminded Daisy. "And now we have Mother with us, too."

CHAPTER XVII

THE STAR

"Dwell on the beauty of life. Watch the stars, and see yourself running with them."

—MARCUS AURELIUS, *Meditations*

The Bleakness was deepening. It sifted ever more thickly down upon Redcliffe like a steady rain of charred ash, piling higher and higher around the Wolfsons' little cottage. For the next ten days, they all stayed inside. There was no sense in going out and inviting more controversy and invective. Judging by what had happened at the Harvest Festival, their presence seemed only to inflame the townspeople.

The worst part was not knowing what exactly was causing the Bleakness, never mind how they were supposed to overcome it. How did one best a demon? What even *was* a demon? Was it possessing the townspeople, or one person, or merely fomenting discord against the sisters? And why?

Bernadette told the girls what she could, but even she was forced to admit she didn't entirely understand what was happening. "Certainly, I've read of dark entities," she allowed one evening, "but I've never encountered one, I don't know anything beyond what is written in the book."

Avery and Morrigan nodded, thrilled to even be discussing any of this with the normally reserved Bernadette. But that wasn't enough for Daisy. She wanted to find answers, go to Kathryn, or consult Brother Terrence.

But Bernadette wouldn't hear of her leaving. She insisted it wasn't safe. Said they needed to wait until the coming new moon, which would shore up their defenses and enhance their powers; Daisy just had to be patient.

"But how can I be patient," Daisy cried, "when I'm the one who's done this to us?"

"You made a mistake. You didn't drive the town mad," Avery said, grabbing Daisy by the hands and guiding her back into her chair. "This thing, whatever it is, was already out there. It just found a door in."

"Which I opened!" Daisy wept bitter tears of self-recrimination.

"Not necessarily," Morrigan said. "I told you I also saw the Bleakness in my Vision. It's been here before. This time, you just happened to be the conduit."

"She's right," Bernadette said. "That's one thing I do know: Malevolence exists unto itself. Even I'm forced to admit that had you taken all the precautions that night it likely still would have found its path to us. But that's neither here nor there. What we need to do is stay safe so we can fight it when the time is right."

Daisy was pacing, agitated. "Fight it *how*, though?"

Bernadette said with calm assurance, "The answers are already within us. We need to wait until we have the wisdom to receive them."

And so Daisy waited, willing herself to call on the patience she knew she had to use. She had to be ready to receive the Tower's bolt of revelation, whatever it ended up being. Still, her mind felt dark.

And so did the town. They could hear scuffles in the lane in front of the house, heated arguments, and even fighting nearby. Someone threw a rock at the front door in plain daylight. Late one night, Daisy thought she heard someone at the bedroom window, but it turned out to be just a bare tree branch creaking in the wind.

Their elderly next-door neighbor, the widow Mrs. Rockwell, came to bring them eggs from her chickens one afternoon. She and her family had drunk Avery's mulled cider elixir, and it had evidently helped her ward off the Bleakness.

"There was a bonfire on the green last night." Mrs. Rockwell's soft, wrinkled face trembled. She coughed deeply, then went on. "Men gathering, not for any good purpose. My dears, your names were on their lips! I heard it from my son. We're so very worried about you."

"Let me give you some apple jam in exchange for the eggs," said Bernadette. "And some licorice root tea for that cough."

After Mrs. Rockwell had gone home, the Wolfsons ate their bowls of root vegetable soup, ladled every suppertime from the simmering pot that had been getting thinner by the day. The evening sun lit up the small dining room, making the glass glow with reflected fire.

A knock came on the front door. Avery rushed to unlatch it and returned with Henry.

"I can't stay," he said as they all burst out with joyful greetings. They'd been cooped up so long, it was exciting to see anyone new. "Aunt Mary is worse. She has sent me to fetch Daisy. We can get back quickly on my horse."

Daisy knit her brows. "Are you sure she meant me?"

"Quite sure," he said. "She said you were the one who pulled her out of it last time, not Dr. Wellington. She won't have him. And she's very poorly."

Bewildered, Daisy tried not to feel even a little bit flattered. She didn't deserve it.

"Henry, you must drink this," said Morrigan, handing him a bottle. "Avery made it. I'll send enough with Daisy for your entire household. It's protective."

"Of course," he said at once, catching her hand as he took the bottle. He quaffed the elixir down to the last drop.

Morrigan gave a start. "I see a wolf, with our aunt." But she didn't remove her hand from Henry's, caught in her Vision.

"From the past?" asked Avery.

"Yes, although I have no idea why. It's a great shaggy wolf. It's almost as if she's... wearing it. How odd." Blinking back into the room, she finally noticed Henry still held her hand and looked up at him, unguarded and open after her Vision, almost surprised to see her small fingers in his. He gently released her, but not without something private passing between them.

Bernadette pushed back her chair loudly and stood up, arms crossed, breaking the mood. "I'm not one to get in the way of caring for our relatives, but it's not safe for Daisy to—"

"It's dark, and I'll wear a hood," Daisy told her sisters and mother, seeing Henry waiting with barely restrained impatience, "so the big bad wolf can't find me. I won't be alone. And you know I have to go."

At Bernadette's reluctant nod, Daisy threw on her cloak and fetched her reticule, making sure it contained her crystals and tarot deck. She took the basket Avery gave her, filled with bottles of elixir.

Daisy followed Henry out through the garden gate and swung up behind him onto a majestic bay stallion with a blazing white star on his forehead. They rode toward Society Row at a gallop. At Blackwell

House, Henry left the horse with a stable boy and raced up the stairs to catapult himself inside, not even slowing down to hand his cloak to Mr. Miggs, who stood with his usual air of dignified watchfulness. Racing to keep up, Daisy tumbled behind Henry, shooting Mr. Miggs a look of apology as she pressed the basket into his hands, saying quickly, "Please give one of these bottles of protective medicine to each of your staff, and drink one yourself as soon as possible."

He took the basket reluctantly. "What's in them, miss?"

"Only cider and herbs, but it's a powerful mixture."

He hesitated.

"Forgive me," Daisy hastened to add, "I don't have time to explain. I must go and help your mistress. I'm so sorry she's ill; the household must be in a state."

Something twisted in Mr. Miggs's face, some complex feeling.

"Or not," Daisy said. Aunt Mary must not be a picnic to work for, and the man had a difficult, demanding job. "I understand, I think."

Daisy ran up the stairs and along the landing to Aunt Mary's bedroom. For the first few seconds, she couldn't find her in the murky depths of the room. The setting sun sent a weak shaft of light through the closed velvet curtains.

Daisy had never been in this room before and hardly knew where to look until Henry led her over to an enormous four-poster bed hung with brocade curtains and canopy. In its depths, ensconced amid numerous cushions and down comforters, was her sickly aunt, her face scarcely visible under the sachet that covered her eyes.

Henry took a chair close by the bedside, giving Daisy room to work, and Daisy felt her hands grow warm in anticipation. But then she faltered, wondering who she was to think she had the power to help anyone. With a flash of sudden shame, she remembered leaping onstage in the medical school lecture hall, so cocksure. Dr. Franklyn had been in real pain, she had seen it plainly, but she'd just wanted to show off. When she'd asked him, "What ails you?" it hadn't been out of genuine concern, it had been because she'd wanted to prove to him, and Jasper, and all of them, what she could do.

Whatever healing she had done in Boston, Daisy realized that she had done it only for herself.

But now Redcliffe was against her family, in the grip of ire and bloodlust and frenzy. And no matter what anyone said, Daisy remained convinced it was because of her foolish actions that her once-safe world was now fraught, dangerous, and sad.

Daisy regarded her aunt, reduced to this limp pile of bones and flesh. It struck her for the first time that Aunt Mary was an indomitable woman. Daisy was accustomed to only thinking of her as Henry's unbearable guardian and her family's cross to bear, but she couldn't deny that Aunt Mary was a steely force in a world designed by and for powerful men, left to fend for herself after the death of all her protectors. How hard that must have been. And she was the sister of Daisy's beloved father, after all, the closest person to him in blood still living. Daisy didn't want her aunt to suffer, let alone die.

"My dear aunt Mary," Daisy said. "What ails you?" This time, she meant it. She truly wanted to be of service.

Her aunt's lips moved slightly with a weak, hoarse rattle on an exhalation.

"Please tell me," Daisy said. "I'll do anything I can to help you."

A voice came from the corner. "Earlier she said she felt as if her very joints had a fever."

Daisy peered into the gloom of the edge of the bedchamber.

"Jasper Fitzwilliam," she said. "What are you doing here?"

Jasper emerged out of the dimness to join Daisy at the bedside.

He looked very tired, his usual imperiousness nowhere to be found. In contrast to the bruised-looking circles beneath them, his eyes were clear and direct.

"Dr. Franklyn sent me back to Redcliffe to study your methods of healing," he said.

Daisy was unexpectedly speechless.

"And I'll admit that, despite some initial hesitation, I wanted to come," he added. "I'm as curious as Dr. Franklyn to know how you do . . . whatever it is you do."

"I'm afraid most folks here would not agree at the moment."

"Henry told me everything," said Jasper. "And I frankly don't understand it. The surge of public opinion against you and your sisters feels dangerously irrational."

"Dangerous," Daisy echoed in a rush of relief. "Exactly."

"Well, you can count me among your family's allies."

She blinked at him, oddly touched. "We haven't got very many right now. Thank you."

"I would like to consult with you, Daisy, on the matter of your aunt's condition. I thought maybe we could attempt to formulate a plan of treatment together."

"And I heartily agreed with this," said Henry. "I was relieved when Fitz asked."

"It wasn't my aunt who sent for me, then?"

"Well, it was my idea," said Jasper. "Her ailment is mysterious to me. I thought you—you might have some insight."

Just then, Aunt Mary groaned softly. The maid was lighting the candles and lamps, and even with the sachet over her eyes, it was clearly bothering her.

As one, Jasper and Daisy turned to their patient.

"What other symptoms are troubling her?" Daisy asked him. "In addition to the fever in her joints."

"The rash on her face is worse, and very painful. She's too tired to eat or raise her head. Sunlight intensifies her symptoms, so we moved her from the solarium."

Remembering that Morrigan had mentioned a wolf, that she had said it was as if Aunt Mary were *wearing* the animal, Daisy gently lifted the sachet. The rash on her aunt's face was in the shape of an angry red butterfly around her eyes and brow. Then she understood. "The mask of the wolf. I've read about this! Lupus, the Latin word for wolf, because the rash was thought to be like that of a wolf's bite. Except it's her body that is attacking itself."

Jasper nodded with a mixture of surprise and excitement. "That was exactly my thought! Cazenave was the first to describe the facial lesions as *erythema centrifugum*, though it was Ferdinand von Hebra who noted the butterfly shape a couple years ago. That *mask of the wolf* you just described so perfectly. It's scientifically proven!"

"Though, to be fair," Daisy told him, tamping down her own natural inclination to bristle at Jasper's need for her diagnosis to be backed by science, realizing suddenly that they shared this proud stubbornness, "the disease was known and treated going as far back as the Middle Ages."

"True," he allowed. "Though the treatments then weren't as effective as now, I think you'll admit. At least, I hope you will."

So. He was open to working with her, but he didn't entirely trust her. Fair enough. Daisy didn't entirely trust herself. "I will," she said. "I'm curious to learn more about these modern treatments. What do you propose?"

"Quinine can be an effective remedy. I have some with me; it's the obvious first line of treatment." He said this with his old peremptory high-handedness, then, catching himself, added, "If you agree, that is."

Daisy smiled inwardly. "Absolutely," she said, "and I can augment that with crystals." She pulled out her pouch, placing stones on the bedside table, under Aunt Mary's pillow, some tucked into the palms of her hands. Daisy had selected the new ones she'd brought back from Boston: bloodstone and smoky quartz to cleanse the circulatory system, aquamarine and amber to both treat the root of the disease and stimulate the body's natural healing abilities, and jade to release toxic blockages. Jade also promoted self-compassion, which felt oddly fitting for her prickly aunt.

Meanwhile, Jasper was telling Henry that Aunt Mary must eat as much fish as possible, which caused Daisy and Henry to look at each other with a flash of guilty amusement. Aunt Mary famously loathed fish, taking great delight in quoting King Philip of Spain at her dinners, describing the sole meunière as "but element congealed!" Daisy and her sisters were convinced she put it on her menus specifically for that purpose.

"A jelly of water," Henry said under his breath. Daisy shot him a quick grin, glad for this bit of humor in an otherwise grim situation.

Jasper was administering the quinine tincture with a remarkable gentleness, easing the dropper through a corner of Aunt Mary's mouth and aiming it under her tongue, where so many other doctors would have just forced her mouth open and drowned her in the stuff. "Along with fresh fruits and vegetables," he continued, "absolutely no meat, and very little butter. And she must stay out of the sunlight."

"She should drink a lot of water all through the day as well, with a splash of apple cider vinegar in it," Daisy added, noting Jasper's keen interest as she spoke, strangely gratified by his attention. "And plenty of tea brewed with turmeric root and wild ginger. I'll bring a basketful to her as soon as I can. And she should be given this as well." She set a bottle of Avery's herbal cider elixir on the bedside table. "Henry, you'll instruct her to drink it all?"

"I promise," he said.

"The question is," said Jasper under his breath, "*will* she do these things? I imagine she'll chafe against every single thing we tell her to do."

"Once she's awake again," Daisy agreed, matching his tone, "she will be the world's most difficult patient."

"We must both stay vigilant, then."

"Without rest." They smiled at each other.

Henry looked at them with gratitude. "Thank you both," he said. "I'll tell the cook to modify her diet."

"I'd better be getting back," Daisy said. "I don't want to be in the streets too much after dark."

"I'll prepare the horse," said Henry.

"No need," said Jasper. "I'll walk Daisy home, Henry. I promise to keep her safe."

Henry merely nodded his agreement and led them back down to the front entrance. He acted as though Jasper escorting Daisy home was the most natural thing in the world, but just before he closed the door, he flashed her a discreet grin. Blushing, she pretended not to see.

Once again hooded in her cloak, Daisy felt securely invisible to the eyes of the very few people abroad at this hour. The streets were almost deserted. Most of the town was likely at home by their fireplaces. Jasper took her arm—which set off not entirely unpleasant alarms in her body—and they kept a brisk pace.

Daisy was conscious of the warmth of his tall form shielding her from the wind off the ocean. "Thank you for escorting me home," she said. "In better times, I would be unafraid to walk this route alone."

"I'm glad to have a chance to speak to you in private," he said. "The Blackwell House staff hears everything, you know. And they talk in the kitchen."

"And with the servants of all the other houses, too," Daisy laughed. "There's an entire network of information. No secrets, ever." She hoped Mr. Miggs would take the elixir. She knew that if he drank it, they all would. "Speaking of which," Daisy said slowly, "I wonder if you would accept this." She pulled one of the last remaining bottles out of her cloak pocket. "It's mulled cider with herbs, and it's protective. Think of it as . . . influenza prevention."

"Can it hurt me?"

"Of course not!"

"Then I'll drink it. But first, I want to ask you a question. . . ." He hesitated, pocketing the bottle. "I ask for my own personal reasons, not out of prurient curiosity."

"Of course," Daisy said. "Ask away."

"It concerns Nate Winthrop. I wonder if you and he are . . . Has he spoken to you directly about his feelings?"

At the sound of Nate's name, Daisy was immediately anxious. The strong pull she'd felt toward him from the moment they'd first met at Aunt Mary's dinner party those many weeks ago had been dimmed somewhat by his baffling behavior of late. But there was no sense trying to explain any of this to Jasper.

"No, he hasn't."

"The two of you don't have an understanding, then?"

"Understanding?" Daisy repeated, nonplussed. "There is no . . . understanding."

"Good," he said. The relief in his voice was so strong and forceful, Daisy was taken aback.

"Why?"

"First of all, he's a bounder and a cad. And second, Daisy..." Here, he stopped, as if feeling around inside his head for the exact right words. He looked straight ahead, seemingly not comfortable meeting her gaze, unusual in someone generally so blunt as to be insulting.

Oh god, what might he be about to say?

He cleared his throat painfully and continued, his expression like that of a doctor about to break the news of an incurable disease to some poor unfortunate. "I feel I should inform you that, given the correct circumstances, and of course depending upon your own inclinations, such as they might be—not that I have any right to their contents... That is, the contents of your thoughts... Which is to say..." He paused again.

"For the love of god, Jasper," Daisy said, "just spit it out. I promise I can take it."

"Well, if you must know, I would not be displeased to learn you were free. That is, it would be of interest to learn you hadn't given any... promise... elsewhere."

Was he asking if she'd work with him again, perhaps on a more formal footing? How astounding! She couldn't deny she was flattered, but she also didn't want to seem too desperate. Privately, she was jumping with joy at the chance to get involved in true healing, with access to better resources and the support of a team. Or at least a partner. In medicine, of course.

"I don't know what promises have to do with anything, but I am quite... interested in collaborating together. On medical treatments.

For, you know, science." Daisy winced at her own strangled speech. Jasper's awkwardness was infectious.

"You mock me."

"I do not!" Daisy told him. "I take these matters very seriously, as I would hope you've seen tonight."

He stopped walking and turned Daisy to face him, giving her a gentle but forceful shake. Then he lifted the hood from her head and tipped her chin upward so he could peer into her face. In the starlight, his eyes glinted. She had to tilt her head back farther to see his face in its entirety, so disconcertingly close was it to her own.

"I tell you this as a man, not a doctor," he said, frowning in exasperation. "Now do you understand?"

"Jasper Fitzwilliam," Daisy said slowly, amazed, "are you saying you're . . . *fond* of me?"

"Something like that," he said quietly.

Before she realized what she was doing, Daisy lifted herself up onto her toes, pressing her hands against Jasper's chest for support, and brushed her lips against his cheek, as quickly and lightly as a hummingbird.

"Huh!" he said, his expression utterly dumbfounded.

Daisy's entire being caught fire in mingled horror at her impulsiveness and another sensation, something alight and tingling. But before she could react, Jasper laughed and pulled her close, pressing his forehead against hers, their faces turning toward each other, mouths close enough to touch but not, breath intermingling, his sweeter than she'd have imagined.

Daisy's heart raced enfolded in his arms, alone in this little world of their own making. She leaned ever so slightly forward—all rational thought out of reach—when they were interrupted.

Two men strolled along the street, their footsteps ringing out loud and clear against the former quiet of the night. Suddenly aware of her exposed identity, Daisy stepped back from Jasper's embrace, quickly scooping the hood of her cloak over her head once more.

But the men walked past without a glance, swiftly disappearing around a corner, her fears for naught. Jasper reached for Daisy again, but, strangely unsettled, Daisy hesitated.

Jasper put his hands up. "I'm sorry, I misunderstood."

"No!" Daisy said quickly. "I'm just— You caught me off guard."

"My apologies. Let's get you home," he said stiffly.

It was clear the conversation was closed, all tenderness from before vanished, as though Daisy had imagined it. She had no idea what she could possibly say to him to explain the terror she'd felt when she'd heard those footsteps in the dark. Mortified by her childish response and what now seemed like a ghastly error of judgment on her part—what had she been *thinking*, lunging at him like that?—Daisy stayed silent until they stood by her front gate. He paused there, stepping back to allow her to go inside without him.

"Jasper," she said, and then stopped. The words wouldn't come.

"Please, Daisy, there's no need," he said.

"But I..."

Except Jasper turned away and melted into the night. Shaken, Daisy pulled the gate closed behind her and made her way into the front garden. Had she imagined what had just transpired, made it all up in her own head? She had been the one to kiss him, after all. Suddenly, she was suffused with humiliation. He had intended a kindness, and she, so desperate for approval from a man she now realized she'd been attracted to all along... She'd thrown herself at him like an overeager puppy. How pathetic! Could she ever face him again?

So deep was Daisy in her muddled thoughts and roiling emotions as she went along the walk toward the front door that when a figure emerged from underneath the willow tree, she gasped.

"You're home, finally."

"Nate?" Daisy whispered, her insides first relaxing in relief and then almost immediately tightening back up.

In a flash, he took her in his arms. "I've been waiting for you," he said, burying his face in her neck. "Your mother and sisters said you'd gone out. I've been beside myself."

This was all too much. Daisy's nerves were in an uproar, she was shattered by the endless days of the Bleakness, not to mention Aunt Mary's sudden turn, and all she wanted to do was crawl into bed and go to sleep.

"I came to take that kiss that got snatched away from me the other day," he murmured. He leaned in, but she held him at bay. The image of the Hierophant hove into her mind's eye, that stern and churchy figure. It was a warning, and she needed it. More immediately, the thought of Mother Superior—as well as her own mother—killed the mood, dead.

With both arms, Daisy pushed Nate away. "No," she said. "I can't. This is wrong."

"How can it be wrong when we both want it?"

Nate's voice sounded disordered. From the haze of alcohol that wafted off him, he'd clearly spent some time in the public house. Maybe the Bleakness had got him in its tentacles. Daisy asked, hardly daring to hope she was wrong, "Did you drink the contents of the bottle I gave you at the Harvest Festival?"

"When? I don't remember a bottle."

"It was protective! Oh no." Daisy fumbled to pull her cloak tightly around her, and then, feeling the weight of the last bottle of protective cider bump against her hip, she pulled it out and pressed it into his hands. "Please, Nate, I beg you: Drink this as soon as possible!"

She was heartened to see him down the contents in one slug. He wiped his mouth and stared at her with barely banked heat. "I must see you again soon, Daisy," he said, reaching for her again, breathing hard, frustration thick in his voice.

"I'm sorry. It's impossible. And now you must go."

With a muttered curse, he leapt over the fence and bolted into the night.

As her gaze followed Nate's retreating back, Daisy caught a flash of movement at the gate.

"Sorry," came Jasper's pinched voice through the night's dark chill. "I didn't mean to eavesdrop. I just came back to... But I see you're otherwise engaged. My apologies for the interruption. Good night, Miss Wolfson. And good luck with Winthrop. You'll certainly need it."

"Jasper, wait..." Daisy cried out.

But then he was gone, too.

CHAPTER XVIII

THE MOON

"My barn, having burned to the ground, I can now see the moon."

—MIZUTA MASAHIDE

The next morning, the soup pot was empty and there was no flour left for bread, so over a breakfast of their neighbor's generously proffered eggs, the Wolfsons held a family meeting. "I'll go to the market," Daisy said. "I can wear my hood over my head. No one will recognize me. It worked last night."

"Until you saw Nate," said Avery under her breath. Daisy had shared the confusing events of the night before with her sisters, as well as her equally baffling feelings on the subject, upon which Avery had instantly handed Daisy her deck. She'd fumbled, and the Star had fallen out sideways, neither upright nor reversed: *A naked figure straddles land and water, pouring water from a vessel in each hand. Atop a tree in the background a bird hesitates, wings poised for flight. Above, an enormous star gleams in the night sky, surrounded by seven smaller stars.*

"That's me right now," Daisy had lamented at the sight. "Half in the water, half on dry land. Intuition or common sense? Instinct or reason? Should I trust myself? Should I let myself feel renewed hope? Inspired?"

"You can be illuminated and guided by the stars," Morrigan had suggested.

Now their mother cut in. "Oh, did you see that boy Nathaniel last night? He came looking for you, and we told him you weren't here."

"He was waiting for me in our garden," Daisy told her, feeling herself redden. "I sent him away."

"He seemed very intent on speaking to you," Bernadette said.

"Well, he spoke to me. And I bade him good night."

"I see. Well, in any case, I'll go to the shops myself." Bernadette mercifully dropped the topic.

"No!" cried Avery.

"The three of us will go," said Morrigan. "We'll set out in the late afternoon when it starts to get dark, just before closing. We can wear our hoods so they cover our faces, as Daisy said. It will take all of us to gather the provisions we need."

Reading the determination on her daughters' faces, Bernadette sighed. "But stay together," she urged. "And come home at the first sign of trouble."

And so, Daisy and her sisters ventured out in the wet amber fog of late afternoon with their baskets through the dripping, shrouded streets to the shops. They were surprisingly successful at remaining invisible to potential ill-wishers and evildoers. Inside the shops, the shopkeepers said nothing, merely filling the orders without comment.

Apparently, their money was as good as anyone else's in the world of commerce, evil charlatan witches or not.

The girls moved swiftly through High Street, darting in and out of the greengrocer's and dry goods store and butcher's, buying flour and butter, milk and tea, squash and corn and onions, pork chops, and more eggs. When their baskets were full, they set off toward home again. Up to that point, they had exchanged not one word, hadn't met one another's eyes, had just tunneled through the errands silently and efficiently, moving like a group of prey.

They were almost to the end of High Street when Avery spoke. "Who is that?"

The others looked ahead where a slumped figure limped along the sidewalk holding a handkerchief to short dark hair.

"It's Frankie!" said Avery. "From the packet ship."

"Is it really?" Daisy peered closely through the dusk at the bent, thin silhouette, remembering the gallant traveler singing at the railing of the ship, eyes alight with adventure, hair blowing in the wind. The person ahead barely resembled that free spirit.

"Something terrible must have happened," said Morrigan softly.

As one, they increased their pace and hurried to catch up.

"Frankie," said Avery softly, putting out a hand.

The young woman jumped. When she recognized the Wolfson sisters, her voice caught. "Thank God it's you three!"

Up close, she appeared even worse for wear. Her face was bruised and bloodied, and her tunic was torn wide open in the front. With one hand, she clutched it to her chest, using the other hand to dab at a wound in her scalp with a dirty handkerchief.

"I got work on a fishing boat, and they took me for a lad. I never said I wasn't, just chopped off my hair before I went, told them my name was Frankie, and they drew their own conclusions—though I'll not lie, that was my intention. Men don't tend to take well to girls working the boats, not that I've met one who can haul a net as well as I."

"Who did this to you?" Avery asked.

"The skipper caught me literally pants down, having a piss in the bucket. That was the end of my luck."

Avery reached over and took Frankie's hand. "What a backward, cowardly rat hole."

"True enough," Frankie said. "Though 'twas the crew, not him. I guess they also didn't like being fooled, and by a girl no less, and there's me among them without their knowledge, hearing their rough talk and sharing their rum right under their noses." The pride she took in her exploits was evident in her flashing eyes. "Escaped before they could chance me properly. I've had plenty of practice dealing with their type after two months on that coffin ship across the ocean. Never thought I'd miss my long hair, mind you. I could have used a hair pin today." She gave the sisters a steely smile, but there was a deep shadow of distress and pain in her eyes.

The sisters exchanged a look. Clearly, there was more to Frankie's story, more ways in which she'd had to defend herself. There was an entire world they knew nothing of.

"Where are you staying?" Daisy asked.

Frankie shrugged. "Here and there."

"You must come home with us," Avery said. "We'll get you bandaged up and give you supper and a warm bed."

Frankie tried to protest, but the sisters swept her up with them.

They were almost to their front gate when Daisy saw another, even more familiar figure, hurrying along the road, carrying her own basket of provisions.

"Kathryn," Daisy called, keeping her voice low. The street was deserted except for them, but she didn't respond until Daisy forgot caution and yelled. "Kathryn!"

She turned, startled. "My dear girls! What are you . . . Who is—"

"In due time," Avery cut in smoothly. "Will you please come for supper?"

Kathryn wavered, her eyes not leaving their new friend. "I should be getting home," she said. "This town isn't safe after dark. But here, let me give you something for—"

As they had with Frankie, the sisters bustled Kathryn into their midst and pulled her through the gate. They burst in to find Bernadette giving the fireplace a good stir with the poker. "About time!" she called over her shoulder, and then paused, seeing Kathryn.

"We brought company," Avery announced with a certain formality.

"So I see." Bernadette took her time to replace the poker and wipe her hands on her apron.

"I knew this was a bad idea," Kathryn said.

"I see you still like to nurse your grudges, Kit," Bernadette said.

"It's not me who's bearing a grudge, it's—"

"Okay, great!" Daisy interrupted. "No one's bearing any grudges! Perfect!"

Both Kathryn and Bernadette looked at Daisy as if she'd grown a second head.

"Careful how you speak to your mother, child," Kathryn clucked.

"Always such a hothead," Bernadette said to Kathryn, who just snorted.

Daisy glanced at her sisters imploringly.

Morrigan stepped forward. "Mother, this is Frankie Morrison," she said, a hand gently tugging on Frankie's elbow, as she had been hanging behind the group.

"Your friend from the packet ship?" Bernadette said. Then she spotted Frankie's state, all signs of teasing forgotten. "Oh you poor thing," she said, helping Frankie to a chair. For her part, Frankie barely resisted when Bernadette tucked her in with a blanket.

"She needs medical attention," Avery said.

"That is clear to anyone with eyes in her head," Bernadette said crisply. "Kit, do you . . . ?"

"Of course," Kathryn murmured, digging through her bag.

Bernadette took a clean cloth dipped in witch hazel that Kathryn handed to her and dabbed gently at Frankie's wounds. "Who did this to you, chérie?"

Frankie barely flinched, though Daisy knew it had to burn. "I was working on a fishing boat as a boy," she said, clearly uncomfortable with the attention. "Turns out the other fishermen didn't like being tricked. They caught me out and let me have it."

"Espèces de salopards," Bernadette said in a low voice, shocking her daughters with this descent into her native French.

Kathryn frowned, an unreadable expression on her face.

"This is a matter for the authorities," Bernadette said.

"No, I beg you," Frankie said staunchly. "That'll only make it worse. Please, just let it be."

With a glance at Kathryn, Bernadette nodded.

"Perhaps the cranberry bogs would be a better fit," Kathryn said. "Women are more accepted there."

Frankie tilted her head, considering. "I've always preferred working on the sea, but—"

"I understand," Kathryn said, giving the girl a squeeze on her shoulder. "It's frustrating to be so constrained by one's sex."

"Let's get you upstairs," Bernadette said, helping Frankie to her feet with Kathryn's assistance. "Nice and slowly, there you go, we've got you now."

Leaving Frankie in their healing care, Daisy, Avery, and Morrigan went to the kitchen to unpack the baskets.

After an efficient flurry of teamwork, supper was almost done. Daisy took Avery's quick rolls out of the oven by the fireplace. "She's pretty banged up," Daisy said to her sisters.

"I'm just glad she got away before they violated her," said Avery gruffly, stirring corn and lima beans into the crisp bacon and its rendered fat in the deep cast-iron skillet.

Morrigan gasped. "So that's what she meant."

"The bastards!" Daisy flushed at her naiveté. Of course; her mother and Kathryn had gleaned this from the beginning.

"Why do you think her tunic was torn in the front? They meant to punish her in the worst imaginable way. And not just them. The skipper doubtlessly encouraged it."

Putting a big piece of butter into an earthenware dish, Daisy thought of Nate's drunken aggressiveness the night before. At least she'd managed to make him leave her alone. And if he hadn't? Daisy would have screamed, and her mother and sisters would have rushed right out to protect her. Frankie hadn't had anyone, only herself and her wits.

Draining the greens and tossing them with vinegar, Avery paused for a moment, sensing Daisy's thoughts, then said softly, "Yes, we are lucky, and not just because we have one another. Still, some men take what they want from us, do what they want to us, and they don't much care how we feel about it."

"Always have." Morrigan's gaze was distant as she spooned some sweet pickles into a dish.

"Always will," Avery added.

"You say that as though someone has done the same to you," Daisy said carefully. She wasn't sure how to phrase the rest of the question that tugged to be asked.

"No, nothing like that, not yet at least," Avery said, hearing Daisy's meaning. "But there's a reason I only wear Father's breeches when we're at home. It's the feeling I get from the world. I can't explain it better."

But she didn't have to. Daisy understood Avery had spoken from a Knowing of the way things were now in the world when it came to men and women, just as Morrigan had seen the same thing in the past.

Avery arranged the cornmeal-fried pork cutlets, succotash, and boiled autumn greens on serving platters. "Don't misunderstand me, I don't dislike men. I often prefer their company, in fact. And I do think a man can hear reason if he's by himself. But groups of men can turn into mobs."

Daisy remembered Jasper's gentle shyness the other night when he'd dropped his guard, and then his crisp courtesy when he thought he'd interrupted her in a romantic moment with Nate. Despite his outrage, Jasper had not lost even a measure of his propriety. Regret washed over her at the memory of the sweetness of their brief embrace, the restrained strength in his arms as they'd encircled her, how safe she'd felt with him. "Some men are thoughtful and kind," she said.

"They are," Bernadette agreed, appearing at the kitchen door in her soundless way. Daisy wondered how much she'd heard. "Your father was. But enough of this cheerless talk," she said, shaking away the memories in her brusque way. "We have guests to feed." And with that, she picked up the tray of rolls and butter and sweet pickles and swept back into the dining room.

When the sisters brought out the serving dishes, they found Frankie in one of Avery's warm nightgowns, her hair damp, her forehead bandaged in clean linen like a wimple, and her face a little less pinched. Watching Bernadette pour wine, exchanging an amiable glance with Kathryn as she filled her glass, it seemed to Daisy that they took any excuse to suspend their rift. And with the current trouble afoot in their town, safety in numbers was more appealing than sustaining old resentments, no matter how bitter.

The six of them gathered around the small table with a palpable feeling of renewed strength. After the hearty meal, they sat by the fire with mugs of tea.

"Let's have a reading, Daisy," said Morrigan.

"There's so much present turmoil, I can't even think about the future," Daisy said. "Avery, you should do it. And Frankie can ask a question."

"Only if you let me do your charts," Frankie said, casting about for her satchel.

"Yes, please!" Avery said.

"Girls, Frankie is our guest," Bernadette admonished. "And I'm certain she's still shaken and tired."

"Not at all," Frankie said, "I'm feeling much revived from that fine dinner." She beamed at her hosts, impressing upon them her fitness for the reading. It was true, she did seem much stronger and in far better spirits than before.

"See, Mother?" Daisy smiled.

"I'd at least like to have a reading, if you don't mind, Mrs. Wolfson," Frankie said. "I used to read tarot with my own ma back in Ireland."

"Did you?" Kathryn asked, while Daisy's mother said, "Frankie, please, call me Bernadette."

"As you wish . . . Bernadette," Frankie allowed.

Avery handed her a freshly shuffled deck. Without hesitation, Frankie drew her finger down the spine of the deck and said, "Here, please."

Avery cut the deck and presented it to Frankie again. Frankie peeled the top card off the deck and placed it carefully on the wooden coffee table, image-side down. She paused.

"Aren't you going to turn it over?" Morrigan asked.

"I thought I'd let Avery do it."

"Me?" Avery hesitated. "Well, of course, it's your reading, but . . ."

"I insist," Frankie said, grinning at Bernadette, who shared a laugh with Kathryn.

Avery flipped the card over to reveal the Moon: *An alabaster-clawed creature climbs from the water to the bank, where a red dog and white wolf howl up at the bright moon. The outer aspect of the moon's full face is carved into a crescent. It serenely sheds petals of light.*

"This draw is one for the books," Avery said excitedly, "because Frankie pulled it upside down, but I flipped it upright. And it's the same from Daisy's perspective, which bears consideration, this being the next card on her journey. For Frankie, the Moon indicates a release of fear through a renewed trust in the subconscious, and for Daisy the message is about allowing intuition to guide through times of uncertainty and illusion, when nothing is what it seems."

"Which makes perfect sense," Morrigan chimed in, "because Daisy's design of the moon makes this card's story about duality!"

"Right, I see that now, it's two moons in one." Frankie leaned in to to get a better look. "Full and crescent. These cards are so beautiful."

"Daisy painted them," Morrigan said proudly.

"That's brilliant!" Frankie smiled at Daisy. "In the deck we had, there was a giant maiden holding up a crescent moon, so—"

"The Visconti-Sforza," Kathryn exclaimed.

"Yes!" Frankie turned to her, seeming both surprised and delighted.

"That's a very ancient deck," Kathryn said. "Few people have those anymore."

"True," Bernadette nodded. "Generally, it's the Tarot de Marseilles, although there are some who prefer Etteilla's Thothian interpretation of the cards—"

"And most decks post-Visconti feature a full moon," Kathryn interrupted.

"We had a very old one passed down through my mother's side," Frankie said.

Kathryn cocked her head at this. "Really?"

"Though my deck," Daisy jumped in, suddenly eager to explain, "is a blend of the old and the new . . . or rather, the future. I painted my moon to contain both aspects, the full and the crescent within, the fullest through to the smallest aspect of the lunar cycle."

"And to think it's a crescent moon tonight," Frankie said thoughtfully.

"Is it?" Daisy looked out the window at the thinnest slice of a waxing crescent moon caught in the branches of the willow tree.

"One week before the new moon," Kathryn noted quietly, with

a quick glance at Bernadette, who nodded back at her in that secret language they still apparently shared.

"Mother, are you planning a ritual?" Daisy asked Bernadette, who pretended not to hear, though Daisy distinctly saw her face twitch. Oh, she was so frustrating!

"And if you look at Frankie in just the right way, you can see the outline of the crescent moon in her bandage," Morrigan marveled, distracting Daisy.

"Well," Daisy hesitated, "that could just be a coincidence."

"And that little fellow you drew on the card, coming up out of the river . . ." Frankie began.

"The sea," Daisy corrected. "That lobster came to me in a . . ." She stopped before she said too much, though everyone in the room knew what she meant. Bloody hell, why was she being so careful, then? "I saw what a woman was painting in a future not too terribly far from our own. Except in her card, the lobster had red claws, and mine are white."

"Oh, do you call it a lobster? Back home, the River Clare is full of white-clawed crayfish, which is what that little fellow looks like," Frankie laughed. "I think of them as my own personal talismans, them being so close to crabs. I'm a Virgo, but I've a Cancer rising."

Daisy noticed Kathryn had grown very still, though her eldest sister barreled on. "So, perhaps not a coincidence," Avery said, her excitement palpable. "And you're a Virgo, you say?"

"Well, cusp with Libra," Frankie explained.

"That's right, you're an astrologer!" Morrigan clapped her hands. "Can you work anywhere?"

"As long as I have my books and my tools," Frankie said, patting her battered rucksack like a pet dog. "It's my favorite thing. Did you know you can chart the impact of the heavens upon events, just like with people's lives? If you like, I could do a reading for that ritual you're planning."

Bernadette seemed about to say something but stopped herself.

Frankie faltered briefly but pressed on. "That's when you map the sky at a particular time and place to get a read on the energy."

Kathryn leaned forward in her chair, her eyes glittering. "And you're from County Clare?"

"Ennis," Frankie replied. "Though it was Kinrush before we had to leave the farm."

"I knew I recognized that lilt."

Frankie paused, head tilted. "I'd say you sound like you're from the Banner County yourself."

"Not me myself, no," Kathryn said, "My parents came from there before I was born, though I suppose theirs were the first accents I heard—before they died."

"I'm sorry for your loss," Frankie said.

"And I yours," Kathryn said.

"Mine? How do you mean?"

"You wouldn't have come here otherwise," she replied. "Morrison, was it?"

Frankie nodded. "Though I'm a Herlihy on my mam's side."

"Yes, of course you are," Kathryn said, tears running freely down her face. "That deck has been in our family longer than anyone can remember."

"Wait, do you mean . . . ?" Wonder filled Frankie's face.

"I do," Kathryn said, standing up and pulling Frankie into a fierce hug.

Frankie gasped in joyful surprise, and no little pain, the hug compressing her bruised ribs. "Can it really be true?" she breathed.

"Kit, you're crushing the child," Bernadette tutted.

"Oh, my dear, I'm so sorry," Kathryn said, releasing Frankie from her embrace and fluttering around her like a mother hen. "I knew fate would bring you to me. Frankie, dear girl, we're family!"

This happy reunion was interrupted by a loud crash, followed by a wave of heat.

CHAPTER XIX

THE SUN

"Thou sun, of this great world both eye and soul."

—JOHN MILTON, *Paradise Lost, Book V*

Shouts of "Whores!" and "Charlatans!" rang in from outside. A bottle stuffed with a flaming rag had crashed through the living room window and set the curtains on fire, flames licking hungrily up the walls and igniting the rafters. The six of them froze in their chairs for several heartbeats, stunned by the explosion of flames.

There was no time to absorb Kathryn's and Frankie's revelations. The whole world was aglow with heat and light and molten smoke.

Bernadette roused them with a shout. "Outside!"

They fled the cottage as one, collecting whatever cloaks, caps, and bags they could grab along the way, tumbling through the door. Behind them, a dormer window shattered in an explosion of glass.

Smoke poured from the rain-soaked shingles of the roof to wrap the garden in a firelit haze. A shifting breeze cleared the scene slightly, revealing a crowd in the garden and the street. Many brandished torches, faces flickering and red in the refracted light of the fire.

At the very front of the throng stood Finny Stewart and Lizzie Cuttle. His face was contorted, as if he were shouting something, but Daisy couldn't make out the words. Lizzie wore a nightgown and a shawl, her eyes wild and her face glowing strangely. Under the thin cloth, Daisy saw a firm round swelling. Could she really be showing so soon? A wedding ring caught the light with a flash of gold. As Bernadette pulled them around the side of the house, away from the frenzied crowd, Daisy had a flash of understanding. So that was why Lizzie had been so desperate for the love spell, why she'd refused Kathryn's tea: She'd been with Finny much longer than Daisy had thought. This made his repudiation of her all the worse. And her pursuit and ultimate bewitchment of him even more doomed.

And now their former friend was their enemy, echoing her new husband as he urged the mob to burn Daisy and her family alive. The blur of familiar faces shouted through the roar of flames, holding their oil-soaked flaming torches aloft, pressing forward with heedless fury as they retreated through the back garden gate and melted into the thicket just behind the garden. Flames boiled into smoke, burning the damp shingles and wood. Finny Stewart's shout rang out clearly: "Thou shalt not suffer a witch to live! Thou shalt not suffer a witch to live!"

Hidden in the dark clump of trees, the women huddled together.

"They act like they want to kill us," Morrigan breathed.

"We must stay right here," said Bernadette. "Hopefully, they'll think we've fled."

"Let's get down low," said Kathryn, tugging everyone down until they sat together on the wet ground in a pile of leaves, deep in a bramble, barely daring to breathe.

The crazed mob had no such presence of mind or care; they crashed around the yard, ranting with heedless fury.

Hands thrust deep into pockets, Daisy clutched at the solidity of her bag of crystals in one and tarot deck in the other. She pulled out the deck and began to shuffle mindlessly, realizing even as her cold-stiffened fingers fumbled and dropped some that it was too dark to see. With a muffled curse, she dropped to her knees and scrabbled in the earth to gather the loose cards.

Just then, an enormous raven flapped overhead, descending into their garden hideaway and disturbing the air with a deafening beating of its wings. No, not a raven—it was Brother Terrence! He seemed to have quadrupled in girth and height, towering above their faces. "Stay here," he said, calm as ever. "I'll be right back."

He jumped back into the night sky, soaring on the wings of his cloak, which streamed behind him.

"Brother Terrence," said Kathryn, sounding both relieved and annoyed. And a glint of something else.

"Of course," said Bernadette in the exact same tone. "He couldn't stay away."

Were they *laughing*?

A vast black-winged beast descended over the flaming rooftop to perch on the chimney, silhouetted against a curtain of billowing smoke. Pinions outstretched, wingspan as wide as the house itself. A cry came from the crowd as those great wings came down around the cottage. The fire suddenly went dark in its embrace, flames smothered by this gigantic *thing* that no longer bore any resemblance to

Brother Terrence. The roiling mob stilled, voices dropped low in murmuring disbelief.

And then the cottage disappeared.

In its place there was now only a huge bank of smoke, gray in the sudden darkness, fuming across everything, a giant creature hovering above it all, blotting out the night.

Someone screamed.

A sudden strong wind came up to whip the smoke into everyone's eyes and noses. Coughing, choking, the crowd began staggering off into the darkness, fleeing this horrifying apparition.

"The witches are flying," someone else yelled.

Feet pounded along the lane as the mob dispersed, and the sound of high cackling vibrated overhead. A chill crept along Daisy's arms. Morrigan's hand clutched hers.

Gradually, silence fell.

And then it started to rain. Drops pattered on the hoods of their cloaks, the branches overhead, and strengthened into a downpour. Meanwhile, the great bird disengaged itself from the charred chimney and leapt back into the air, vanishing in a violent flap of wings.

To Daisy's great relief, the smoke receded to reveal the cottage once more, dark and solid in the rain, wounded but still standing. She yearned to rush inside to see what remained, what they'd lost. She thought of her father's hand-carved sideboard in the dining room, Morrigan's chess set, the ancient spell book.

Brother Terrence reappeared in his own form, standing on solid ground once again. "No time," he said, catching Daisy stare at what had once been her home. "We must hurry. We'll be safe at Kathryn's cottage," he said. "For now."

They ran through the rain as fast as they could, Kathryn leading the way in a near-sprint, Brother Terrence bringing up the rear. They encountered no one along the forest road, no person, not one animal. They were soaked by the time they tumbled into Kathryn's dark cottage with its faint smells of old woodsmoke and boiled herbs. While she started a fire in her enormous brick fireplace, they piled their wet cloaks on the chairs around her table.

The four girls fell onto the braided rug, sharing the blanket Kathryn had put around their shoulders, faces bathed by the light of the hearth. Morrigan's hand still clutched Daisy's, and she pressed her shoulder against Avery, who had an arm around Frankie. With her head still wrapped in its crescent bandage, Frankie looked like a war-shocked soldier dragged wounded off the battlefield by her comrade in arms.

Brother Terrence flared about, lighting candles and lamps, humming an odd little melody. Bernadette and Kathryn poured hot chamomile tea for everyone. Bernadette joined the girls on the rug. Kathryn and Brother Terrence took the two chairs flanking the fireplace, and they all warmed themselves.

"Do you think they'll come after us here?" Avery asked.

"They won't be able to think a coherent thought for hours," said Terrence. "I addled their brains into cornmeal mush. Not that it took much, they were already halfway there." Here in Kathryn's little cottage, tipping himself in her rocking chair, his cloak off, he looked like a human being again. Though there was clearly something otherworldly about him.

"How *did* you put out the fire?" Daisy asked.

Bernadette put out a cautioning hand. "It's better not to—"

"Magic," said Brother Terrence. "Couldn't you tell? Weren't you impressed?"

"Yes!" said Avery, laughing. "Extremely. You scared them all silly!"

"Scared me, too," said Morrigan. "But in a good way."

"Can you just put the cottage back together again with magic, then?" Frankie asked, eyes wide.

"It doesn't work quite that way, child," he said.

"But if you could turn yourself into a great, feathered beast and fly through the air—"

"A sight to behold," Kathryn interrupted. "And now that we're safe and warm and dry, I think we all need some rest. So! I have only the one bed but several blankets, and I can make a comfortable place for you all here by the fire."

"I will stay up and keep watch in the garden," said Brother Terrence.

"I'll join you," said Avery.

The girls helped Kathryn spread quilts and a down-filled comforter and pillows on the floor. Daisy, Morrigan, and Frankie crawled into this nest, and Bernadette and Kathryn shared her bed at the other end of the room. It was cramped but cozy. Comforted by the knowledge that Avery and Brother Terrence stood guard outside, Daisy allowed herself to be lulled by the steady, even breathing and faint snoring of the others and soon fell into a deep sleep.

A dazzling light on her eyelids woke her, the rising sun coming through the low windows. She sat up, rubbing her eyes.

Avery burst through the door in her cloak, red-cheeked from the chill. "Come see the sunrise," she called. "The sky is bloodred!"

Outside with Frankie and Morrigan, Daisy beheld the piles of sunstruck leaves like bonfires, the air filled with birdsong and the chatter of squirrels. And through the dark bulk of the forest, the sky was a clear, bright crimson.

"Red sky at night, sailor's delight..." Frankie murmured, looping an arm inside Avery's elbow.

"Red sky at morning, sailors take warning," Avery whispered back, completing the proverb.

They stood silently for a moment, digesting that foreboding verse, still not entirely awake. Inside, Daisy heard the rattle of dishes and the low voices of their mother and Kathryn, no doubt folding the quilts and blankets and setting the kettle to boil for tea, as though all were right with the world.

"I'm eighteen today," said Avery with an odd catch of a laugh.

"Happy birthday," Daisy and Morrigan said together, rushing over to Avery to throw their arms around her, Frankie awkwardly tangled up in their ungainly embrace. Daisy was unsure what was more shocking, that this was what greeted Avery on her birthday or that they'd forgotten it.

"An auspicious beginning to your nineteenth year," said Brother Terrence.

Daisy stared at him. "Which part? Our house burning down, the entire town out to kill us, or the morning dawn that looks like it's... *bleeding*?"

Brother Terrence clucked at her. "No need to be so defeatist."

"Defeatist!" Daisy cried. "You have no idea how—"

"I know," Brother Terrence cut her off, his voice low and calm, "exactly how it feels to be misunderstood, mistreated, and maligned. You couldn't possibly dream of the depredations I've encountered in my journey through this life, and all my others."

Daisy swallowed. "I'm sorry, I didn't—"

Brother Terrence continued, "I don't need your pity, because I am not, nor have I ever been, nor will I ever *be*, a victim, and I'll thank you to remember that. You're too young and coddled to understand, but I encourage you to let go of the arrogant presumption that this world owes you safety or applause or a kind word with your tea and crumpets. Don't look at me like that, I'm well aware of your family's precarious position in society. But there are those who would sell their souls to have the little you have. Think of poor Lizzie and that love spell that gave her so much comfort. You think I did that to cause, what, *mischief*? Knowing what you do about the lot of unmarried women? Close your mouth, child, you'll swallow flies."

Face burning, Daisy said nothing. She couldn't argue with the harsh truths he'd meted out. She was being a child, he was right. Who was this person, who seemed to know her so uncomfortably well?

When they returned to the cottage, Bernadette and Kathryn were sitting at the table, their heads together.

"I think it's best if we all stay inside together this morning," Bernadette said.

Everyone nodded. Though Brother Terrence had subdued the bloodthirsty mob last night, it was clear from what he'd said that it wouldn't hold for long.

Kathryn clapped her hands together once. "And now for a birthday breakfast!" she cried with forced cheer.

"But we left all of our provisions back at the cottage," said Morrigan.

Kathryn's smile was undimmed. "I have a few odds and ends. Avery, you sit tight with Frankie and your sisters for company; your mother and I will rustle up a celebration worthy of our birthday girl."

Bernadette joined Kathryn at the counter and hearth, and the girls sat quietly by the fire, Morrigan finger-combing tangles from Avery's hair. Watching her eldest sister stare into the flames, Daisy contemplated whether she was thinking about what had happened to their cottage, wondering where they would go, how they could possibly stay in Redcliffe now that the town had set out to burn them as witches. If so, she wasn't alone in those worries.

In what felt like no time, Kathryn and Bernadette reappeared with a platter stacked high with pancakes covered in sweet apple-cranberry compote as well as a basket of sweet corn and salt-pork fritters. Plates and napkins were handed around, and each found a place to sit on a chair or a stool or the floor.

"Would anyone like a tipple?" said Kathryn, pulling out a bottle of whisky and setting it on the table next to her homemade apple cider. "It'll cure all ills."

She then paused with a glance at Bernadette, who shrugged her acquiescence, and splashed whisky generously into tiny, mismatched cups. Brother Terrence clapped his hands and began humming a strange celebratory tune. Frankie dug out her pennywhistle and accompanied him.

Sipping her whisky and trying not to cough, Daisy watched a ladybug crawl along the windowsill, its black-spotted wings catching the sunlight. She wondered if the stories were true about ladybugs bringing good luck.

"We need all the talismans of good fortune we can get," Avery murmured as if Daisy had asked the question aloud.

"Speaking of talismans," Bernadette said quietly to Avery, "your birthday gift was lost in the fire, but I want to give you something. This has been with me since before you were born. It will help keep you safe." She slipped the amulet they'd all seen her carry their entire lives into Avery's hand, the same one she'd loaned to Daisy on her trip to Tabitha Godwin.

Daisy glanced quickly at Morrigan, whose surprise mirrored her own.

"Mother, no!" Avery protested. "I can't take this."

"It's time to pass it along," Bernadette insisted, and her expression made it clear the matter was settled. She turned to Daisy and Morrigan. "And you two will have tokens of your own on your eighteenth birthdays. Now let's have a splash more of that whisky, Kit."

Like Kathryn, Bernadette was doing her best, but Daisy felt the tension thrumming in the air like a faraway war drum.

Morrigan broke the silence. "A birthday tarot reading?"

Daisy dug through her coat for the deck she'd dropped the night before. "I just need to make sure I have all the—" But to her horror, her pockets were empty.

"Might you be looking for these?" Brother Terrence held up three tarot decks. Daisy leaned forward and was stunned to see they were exactly as she'd painted them. Had he rescued them—or conjured them somehow?

"The only true wisdom is in knowing you know nothing." Brother Terrence cocked an eyebrow, smiling at Daisy's confusion as he handed the decks around, matching each one with its rightful owner. "Except if, unlike Socrates, you do indeed know everything."

"I should shuffle," Daisy said, fumbling for the rest of the cards.

"No need," Brother Terrence said, "you pulled a card last night."

"I dropped the deck," Daisy explained again, "I didn't *pull* anything."

"Didn't you? I believe this is the missing card." He produced a card from thin air and handed it to her. His smile was easy on the surface, but she could sense the solemnity behind his soft lashes. "I would be careful not to argue with what the universe draws forth, my dear."

Daisy held the card aloft, recognizing the Aries symbolism she'd drawn on the back of her own deck. Without having to turn the card around, she knew it was the Sun: *A naked child dances in a paddock with a silver horse draped in a wreath of sunflowers. The sun shines brightly upon them both, illuminating four large sunflowers that grow not from soil but a crumbled stone wall.*

"This is perfect," Morrigan said. "The Sun is the most positive card you could have selected!"

"Not that I selected it."

"No, it selected you, of course," she agreed.

"The child has nothing to hide," Kathryn observed. "A symbol of innocence, she illustrates the joy of being at one with our true selves. The sunflowers represent not only defiant optimism but also the four suits of the deck, as well as the four elements. It's all coming together!"

"On the topic of children with nothing to hide," Avery said meaningfully to Bernadette, "I might as well come out with it: I know what happened with you and Father."

Daisy and Morrigan gaped at her, shocked by her boldness but also wanting so badly to know what happened.

Bernadette looked up. "Do you, now?"

"Well," Avery said. "I think I do."

"Altogether different," Brother Terrence sniffed.

"Stay out of it," Bernadette snapped at him.

"If I'd stayed out of it, Avery would not be having this birthday, or perhaps any at all."

"More whisky?" Kathryn offered, a frown creasing her forehead.

"Whisky is not the answer to everything, Kit," Bernadette said.

"It certainly sparked your beautiful family into being, back on that glorious yule of...'29, if memory serves?" Brother Terrence said.

"That's what I want to talk about," Avery said. "We know that you and Father eloped. Morrigan had Visions about it. You were married in secret, with only Reverend Potter and a maid as your witnesses. I guessed immediately that you must have been pregnant, and it can only have been me.... Right?"

There was a taut silence while Bernadette picked invisible fluff off the sleeve of her dress. "This isn't the time," she said finally.

"If not now, then when?" Brother Terrence stretched his long legs out to the fire.

Bernadette said nothing, but her face had softened a little.

"You girls are now old enough to know the truth," he continued. "I've known your mother and Kathryn since they were girls at the convent, where I lived as the resident scholar monk. After she turned sixteen, your mother was placed by the convent with the Blackwells as a domestic, which is where she met your father. They fell in love, though it was of course forbidden because as a servant she was considered so far beneath the Blackwells' social standing as to barely amount to a bit of leaf stuck beneath Augustus's own mother's shoe." He clearly relished spilling this tale to such an avid audience.

"And if you think your aunt Mary can be...prickly," Kathryn interjected, "well, you'd have quailed before your grandmother."

"Girls," Bernadette said quickly, "it's not nearly as lurid as Brother Terrence makes it sound. We didn't have some secret affaire de coeur."

"It was clear to everyone they were in love," Kathryn said.

"We could stretch this tender tale out for hours," interrupted

Brother Terrence, "but I do believe we have a demon to catch and not much time in which to do it, considering the new moon is mere days away."

Bernadette gave Brother Terrence a resigned look, all the encouragement he needed.

"Young Augustus had been pressed into an engagement to someone else," said Terrence. "It was all set, their parents had agreed on it. A highly suitable girl of his own station."

Daisy took the bait. "Who? Tell us!"

"She's Mrs. Stockbridge now," said Kathryn. "But back then, she was your aunt Mary's best friend Charlotte Godwin, and their fathers were business partners. The two families were anxious to seal this union, and Mary and Charlotte were eager to become sisters for life. But your father loved Bernadette, and she loved him. Your aunt never forgave Bernadette, the lowly housemaid who'd stolen her beloved baby brother."

"No wonder she hates us," said Avery.

"Aunt Mary?" Daisy knew her aunt wasn't terribly fond of her and her sisters. But hatred?

"Not you, me," Bernadette said.

"I meant Mrs. Stockbridge," Avery said.

Morrigan gasped. "Wait, Mrs. Stockbridge is a Godwin? That must make her . . . Tabitha's aunt!"

"Indeed," Kathryn said.

"So she doubly hates us," Daisy said.

"Her marriage has not been a good one. By all accounts, Mr. Stockbridge is a brutish man," said Kathryn sadly.

"Back to the elopement, please," Avery pressed.

"A wedding date had been set, and things looked desperate," Kathryn said. "So I . . ." She trailed off, looking down.

"Broke my confidence," Bernadette said flatly.

"As though I wasn't already aware," Brother Terrence cut in. "But when Kathryn informed me of the urgency of the young lovers' plight, it fell to me to rescue them both. I very cleverly arranged for them each to come, unbeknownst to the other, to a romantic little scene I'd prepared in a wooded glade. And . . . well, let's just say that that was the night when the magic of young love sparked and bore fruit."

"Wait, you gave our mother a love spell?" Daisy shrieked.

"Goodness no!" Brother Terrence sighed. "There was no need. I simply—"

"Set the scene," Bernadette said, sounding unusually subdued.

"You only needed the opportunity," said Kathryn.

"It wasn't for you to create one," Bernadette exclaimed. "Why couldn't you have stayed out of it?"

"Because I'm your friend," Kathryn snapped back.

"All right, enough with the squabbling, children," Brother Terrence said.

"Maybe if you weren't such a meddler!" Bernadette's ire was tinged with more than a little embarrassment. "Maybe if you'd minded your own business and allowed things to proceed at their own pace, instead of sending me headlong into a lifetime of social censure!"

Brother Terrence dismissed her with a wave. "If we hadn't given you that push, you'd still be sweeping up after your true love's sister with no family to call your own."

"It wasn't your decision to make!"

"But it resulted in me, Mother," Avery cried. "Are you saying you regret that? That you regret . . . me?"

"No, of course not! I . . ."

But Avery had already run outside, slamming the door behind her. Frankie raced to catch up with her.

Kathryn wheeled furiously on Brother Terrence. "Why do you always do this?"

"Save you, you mean?" he spat back. "You're welcome!"

And then he vanished. If Daisy hadn't seen it with her own two eyes, she wouldn't have believed it.

The door flew open again.

Bernadette whirled toward the sound. "Avery, you must listen to me—"

But it wasn't Avery.

CHAPTER XX

JUDGEMENT

"Judge a tree from its fruit, not its leaves."

—EURIPIDES

"I'm so very sorry for the interruption," Henry Graves said, his sensitive nature immediately picking up on the mood. "When I heard the news of what happened at your cottage last night, I knew I had to come directly."

"Oh, Henry," said Morrigan in a rush, "you are always so thoughtful!" And then she bit her lip, looking abashed.

He went to her side, clasping her hands in his. "I'm so glad to see that none of you have been injured, though I realize you've lost so much. Please allow me to take you home to Blackwell House. Aunt Mary has prepared rooms for you. And I have a carriage outside, just down the path."

Daisy looked at Bernadette: Would she allow her sister-in-law to come to her rescue? After that tumultuous story, Daisy couldn't be sure of anything. But they couldn't very well stay at Kathryn's forever. Daisy watched her mother deliberate.

"We accept with gratitude," Bernadette said finally.

The ride back into town was filled with a heavy silence. Avery and Bernadette gazed out their respective windows at opposite sides of the bench, the space between them full of hurt feelings. Daisy perched awkwardly on the other bench, Henry and Morrigan wedged in on either side. Kathryn had diplomatically elected to stay behind to "put her cottage in order," and Frankie stayed with her, though she promised to join them soon.

Daisy turned over the events of the past hour, trying to make sense of all that had unfolded. She kept coming back to the heart-warming confirmation of the love that had undergirded her parents' marriage. If only her mother and eldest sister could see past their wounded pride. It didn't seem as if anything truly awful had happened back then, although she could well understand her mother's frustration with Brother Terrence's blithe attitude toward things he deemed beneath his consideration, like basic human emotion.

But Avery's question was important: Wasn't Bernadette happy with how things had worked out, with her marriage and Avery and ultimately Daisy and Morrigan?

And why had Kathryn and Bernadette's friendship collapsed over what seemed to Daisy a loving impulse to help? The two orphaned girls had been each other's deepest source of comfort and safety. But Daisy knew from her own experience that the target of misdirected blame and wounded feelings often became the people one loved most.

Daisy was so lost in her thoughts that when Henry rapped on the inside of the carriage roof with his walking stick she was stunned to see they were at their cottage, which was still smoking slightly, its eaves charred.

"I thought you might want to collect whatever belongings survived the fire," Henry said as he held the carriage door open, bidding the coachman to stay behind to keep watch.

Henry went first, carefully testing the soundness of the floorboards before gesturing for the Wolfsons to follow him. They looked around in a sad daze. They didn't linger, hurrying past the puddles left by rain seeping through the charred ceiling and making their way carefully through the acrid smell of burning horsehair upstairs to their bedrooms. They gathered what clothes could be salvaged beneath burned gaps of the half-caved-in roof, then packed the food they'd bought the day before into a hamper, the kitchen somehow having mostly survived the assault. On her way out, Daisy was stunned to see the book of spells lying on the hearth, unscathed. Bernadette picked it up with the fire tongs, wrapped it in a clean cloth, and wordlessly handed it to Avery, who tucked it into her satchel. Daisy exchanged glances with her twin as she gathered up her chess set, which was also untouched.

Back in the carriage, Bernadette sighed, peering out at the still and silent town. Avery saw Daisy shuffling her deck and gave her a solemn look. "Pull another," she said softly.

"For all of us," said Morrigan.

Without ceremony, Daisy plucked Judgement from the middle of the deck: *Winged messengers trumpet in the sky. Below, bodies rise, arms outstretched in supplication, floating coffins like a sea of tiny boats.*

It was a chilling image, but Judgement struck Daisy as the promise of change, an awakening and rebirth, a dramatic ending to make way for an exciting new beginning. At least it would have meant that, had it been upright. "But it's reversed," she sighed.

"Judgement is calling for you to let go of your doubt and heed the call to action, to step into the role of the one who sees clearly and acts accordingly, no matter the sacrifice," Morrigan said.

Avery nodded. "As long as you are willing to do what it takes."

Daisy shivered, wondering what further sacrifice the universe expected of her. Had she and her family not lost enough? Would she be strong enough for the challenge? Avery squeezed her hand. Morrigan pressed a gentle kiss against her cheek.

"This town needs a change, that's certain," said Bernadette, not looking away from the window.

When the carriage pulled up in front of Blackwell House, Henry handed them down, one by one, while the coachman went off with a stable boy to haul the food hamper to the kitchen and their trunks to their quarters, wherever those might be.

Daisy was startled to see Jasper Fitzwilliam standing at the top of the granite steps. "Mrs. Wolfson, Avery, Morrigan... Daisy," he said, stumbling slightly on her name. "How are you all? How did you find the cottage?"

"A bit charred but still standing," said Henry, while Daisy ducked her head, discomfited by the sight of Jasper, freshly mortified by memories of their last encounter.

"We all are," Avery said, sticking a hand against Daisy's back to propel her forward.

"Thank you for bringing us here, Henry," said Morrigan.

With no trace of their former strain, Henry tucked Morrigan's hand into the crook of his arm and guided her up the steps. "I'm so glad you're all here. This house is too big and empty. Even with old

Fitz taking up so much space." He made a face at Jasper, who smiled weakly back.

"I've set up the card table in the solarium," Henry went on, leading them all through the front hall. "I thought we could celebrate Avery's birthday with an excellent new game called Pollack. And tea and cake and . . ." He sniffed the air around their heads and chuckled wryly. "More whisky, if you'd like."

"Spirits for the spirit," Avery said wanly. Henry regarded her with an earnest expression and glanced meaningfully at Jasper.

Jasper nodded and vanished into the depths of the house.

Daisy wondered if it was just her own heightened anxiety or if Jasper was being strange, even for him. Her insides roiled from the sudden nearness, and then absence, of his unexpected presence. She'd assumed, even hoped, he'd gone back to Boston, particularly in the wake of their disastrous encounter.

In the foyer, Daisy and her family shed their cloaks for possibly the first time ever. They were so used to resisting Mr. Miggs's futile attempts to take them, if only out of sheer bloody-mindedness, that it felt strange to finally let him.

But he was nowhere to be seen.

"Mr. Miggs has a touch of ague," said Henry.

Daisy felt a pang of worry. Had he succumbed to the Bleakness, too? Or was there a more ominous reason for his absence?

She remembered his expression when she'd tried to offer reassurance about his employer's illness. She'd had a sense that Mr. Miggs disliked Aunt Mary, not that she could blame him. But did his antipathy go deeper than that? And could it have anything to do with the Bleakness? Daisy tried to shake off her suspicions.

"Bridget is supposed to be taking his place today, but—" Henry looked around for the errant girl. "Anyway, Aunt Mary has directed me to put you all in the west wing. It overlooks the ocean. She trusts you'll be very comfortable. Please come with me."

Carrying their cloaks, they followed Henry up the stairs and down two corridors. He flung open a set of double doors with a flourish.

"Your new home, for as long as you need it," he said.

The high-ceilinged room had a spectacular view that looked straight out to sea over the cliffs. There was a fire in the grate, chairs arranged before it, a writing desk, and a breakfast table. At either end of the room, open doors revealed two bedrooms. It was all so much finer and more luxurious than the cottage, but Daisy would have given anything to be able to go back home. This place wasn't lived in, it wasn't cozy, and it wasn't theirs.

"Please thank my sister Blackwell for her generosity," Bernadette said. "The rooms are lovely."

Daisy suspected that her aunt would never let them forget this charity. "How *is* Aunt Mary? May I go and visit her?"

"I think Jasper would be glad of the chance to consult with you," said Henry with a smile.

"Why is he still here?" Daisy blurted, "I thought he'd have gone back to Boston by now . . . unless Aunt Mary has taken a turn. Has she?"

"Maybe you should go ask him yourself," Avery whispered.

"Avery!" Morrigan tried to protest, but then she ruined it by giggling.

Annoyed, Daisy flung her cloak on the bed. "I'll go right now, if you'll take me to her door. To see Aunt Mary, that is. Obviously."

"Yes, of course," Henry said, "You two healers can put your heads together in *deep consultation* while the rest of us have a little party in the solarium."

Everyone laughed, even Bernadette, while Daisy pretended not to notice. They left her at the door to Aunt Mary's bedchamber on their way downstairs.

"Aunt Mary," Daisy whispered into the darkness of her room, her heart beating fast. Was Jasper lurking in the shadows beyond the canopy bed?

"There you are, child," came a voice from the bed, a hand outstretched in the gloom, and Daisy went to her bedside. "I hear the town is in an uproar, and they burned your house down. What on earth did you do to provoke such a thing?"

"What did *we*—" Daisy started to exclaim, then remembered that this was Aunt Mary's way. She caught the canny eyes glinting at her. "Oh, the usual, Auntie. Being witches," Daisy joked, patting her aunt's hand and feeling inside her wrist for a strong if thready pulse. "More importantly, how are you feeling?"

"Better, since Jasper's ministrations. And yours, truth be told," she admitted.

"I'm very glad to hear it. You're following the regime?"

"Every bit of it." She sounded irritated, a very good sign. "The sunlight still bothers me, so I lie in the dark all day. And I never want to see another *fish* again."

Daisy's gaze darted around the room, looking for Jasper now that her eyes had adjusted. He wasn't there, she realized with a prick of disappointment. "I'm sorry about that," she said, smiling at her aunt. "But I can tell you're feeling better."

Aunt Mary adjusted her bed jacket, then rang a little bell on her side table. "It's time for my bath," she said. "Please leave me now."

"As you wish. I'll return later to give you another treatment with the crystals."

"At least I don't have to eat those."

As Daisy was descending the staircase, Jasper emerged from the solarium and crossed the foyer. When he heard footsteps on the stairs, he paused, looking up at her with an expression she could not read. "Daisy," he said. "I am glad to see you are well, despite the . . . trouble."

"Thank you," she said carefully. "I just visited our patient. She seems much improved."

"Yes, she's been eating seafood with vigorous ill humor," he said dryly.

Daisy laughed and was happy to see the hint of a small smile hovering over Jasper's mouth. "She also seems more like herself again, which is to say . . ."

"Crotchety."

Now they both laughed. "I'm so glad we could help," Daisy said in a rush, coming down the last of the stairs and hesitating before stepping into the front hall. "By working together, I mean."

"Indeed." Jasper paused, uncharacteristically at a loss for words.

"Jasper, I'd be obliged if you'd let me correct a misunderstanding, if you're willing to hear me out?"

"I was about to take a walk." His eyes searched her face. Seeming to decide something within himself, he extended his elbow, which she took gratefully, her pulse leaping at the contact.

Daisy and Jasper walked through the gardens behind the house and descended the wooden staircase to the grassy dunes, taking the footpath to the wide beach. The sea was brilliant blue, the sun a golden ball high above the horizon, gilding the stiff breeze with intermittent breaths. Waves ran hard against the sand, and farther out Daisy saw rocking turbulence flecked with whitecaps, left over from last night's storm. As she and Jasper threaded past dark, glistening heaps of seaweed, beached dusty-red crabs, and gnarled hunks of driftwood, the silence felt filled with polite distance on his side and nervousness on hers. She had no idea how to broach the topic of their last, dreadful conversation, let alone mend it. Instead, she took gulps of fresh briny air.

"Bloody hell," Jasper muttered suddenly, looking straight ahead.

Nate, once again in the wrong place at the wrong time, came striding in their direction. Daisy heard snatches of his voice on the wind, as though he were arguing with someone unseen, but she couldn't make out the words. His gold-streaked hair was wild in the breeze, and he staggered a little.

"Jasper," she said swiftly, "I must clear something up—"

But Jasper wasn't listening. He kept walking straight toward Nate.

To Daisy's horror, Nate ducked past Jasper to pull her into his arms, spinning her to stand in front him like a shield and clapping an arm around her shoulders like a vise, his other hand gripping her by the waist. "Hands off my girl, Fitzwilliam!"

"Nate, what are you . . . ? Unhand me!" she yelled.

"Winthrop," said Jasper with dangerous calm. "She's asked you to release her."

Nate's forearm was close to her mouth. Daisy stretched her neck out and sank her teeth into it as hard as she could.

"You little . . . !" Nate let Daisy go with a howl. "And you!" He circled Jasper with his fists up. "You're damned lucky I haven't done you grievous bodily harm yet, you traitorous bastard. But maybe it's come to that, at last."

Jasper stepped forward and punched Nate in the nose, hard. "Shut your bone box, Winthrop," he said. "And I'll thank you to watch your language around a lady."

Daisy gasped as Nate bent over, breathing hard. He wiped the blood on his sleeve, touching his nose gingerly. "This is war!"

"You're acting like animals," Daisy exclaimed.

Jasper glanced back just as Nate took a swing at him. Jasper shifted at the last moment, sending Nate sprawling in the sand with a hard shove. Nate sprang up and barreled headfirst into his opponent's chest. Wheezing, Jasper hunkered over, struggling to get his wind back.

Just as Daisy stepped toward him, Nate lofted a piece of driftwood like a club. As he swung it downward, she leapt up to grab the other end and hung on to it with both hands, giving Jasper a split second to sidestep the blow. The log glanced off his temple, carving a deep gash, which immediately swelled with blood.

"Stop!" Daisy shouted at them both. "This is ridiculous!"

Paying no heed, they ran at each other, punching wildly. They were so consumed with rage that they could see or hear nothing else.

Just as Daisy was about to run back toward Aunt Mary's for help, Nate shouted, "Daisy! This bastard ruined my life!"

"Is that what you've been telling her?" Jasper grunted, wrenching free of Nate's hold. "Daisy, this hornswoggler has played on your sympathies. It's a lie!"

"Then I insist you stop fighting," she said. "At least attempt to talk like civilized men, or I'll be forced to walk away and leave you to destroy each other."

Nate tried to land a blow on Jasper's sternum, but Jasper wove and caught him in a chokehold. Now Nate was pinned with his back to Jasper, with no way of hitting him. Nate made a strangled sound, but Jasper didn't loosen his grip.

"I don't trust this scoundrel not to come at me the moment I let him free. And don't worry. Despite his theatrics, your suitor can still breathe."

"He's not my suitor!" Daisy exclaimed.

"Let's start with what he told you about me," Jasper said.

"He said that you got him thrown out of Harvard by telling lies about him to Dr. Franklyn," Daisy said. "That you dashed his hopes for a medical career because you were jealous and wanted the spot for yourself. That you ruined his life."

Jasper gave Nate's head a good shake. "You lying weasel."

Nate hacked a foot backward at Jasper's shins, but Jasper evaded the boot heel.

"Not even close," Jasper said. "My life, my ruin. Our fathers were friends, and mine took Nate in when he was orphaned, raised him up alongside my sisters and me. I loved him like a brother!" Nate struggled, arms flailing, though Jasper kept him contained. "Did you hear that, Winthrop?" Then Jasper addressed Daisy again. "I protected him and shared everything I had. I even helped him get into medical school! In fact, I was the one who arranged his apprenticeship, thinking it would give him an advantage. It was his own terrible error in judgment that got him expelled. I tried to help him then, too, and how did he repay me? There's a reason I can't go home."

"Then why does he hate you so much?" Daisy asked, truly puzzled. "Why invent a story like that about you out of whole cloth?"

They were talking about Nate as if he weren't right there, hanging from Jasper's elbow, sputtering with impotent fury.

"Remember when you visited the lecture, and someone mentioned that woman from the charity wards who was killed by medical error at the hands of one of the students?"

"That was Nate," Daisy realized with a sickening thud.

"She had a fever from malnutrition," Jasper said. "He gave her arsenic, a toxic dose."

"Why did you do that?" Daisy demanded of Nate, desperately hoping he'd have an explanation that made sense.

"It was an accident!" Nate looked genuinely sorry. "I tried to help her!"

"He's reckless, sloppy," said Jasper. "And that wasn't his only mistake. I did my best to cover for him for months, begging him to stop drinking all night in taverns and concentrate on his studies. But he wouldn't—or *couldn't*—straighten up. And a patient died for it."

"I'm only human," Nate protested. "We all make mistakes!"

"Please, Jasper, you'll strangle him," Daisy cried.

"I'd like nothing better, but I won't stoop to his level," said Jasper. "Even though when it all came out, he tried to cast the blame on me."

"But why?" Daisy burst out. "Why would he blame you, if you really were his friend?"

"Because Jasper has never been my friend!" Nate croaked. "He only wanted me around to make him look better."

"That's a lie, Nate!" Jasper sounded despairing. "I've always been your friend, even in your darkest hour. I urged you to go back to my family's home so my parents could help you get yourself together, and you turned my own parents against me!"

Daisy heard a shout: Her sisters and Henry were running along the beach, their voices blurring together.

"Fitz, what the deuce?" cried Henry, as Avery yelled, "What is going on?"

"We saw the fight from the solarium," Morrigan panted.

"Hurry," Daisy called. "They won't stop!"

Taking advantage of the distraction, Nate wrenched his neck free and smashed the back of his head into Jasper's face, sending him reeling. But Jasper recovered fast, flicking the blood from his face.

A well-aimed punch sent Nate to land sprawling on the wet sand. A wave crashed in and rushed up the beach to drench Nate's head, the water covering his face. He didn't react. He was out cold. Jasper just stood there and watched, his hands clenching and unclenching.

Daisy and Henry ran to Nate and knelt together to pull him out of the surf. Cradling his head in her lap, pressing her handkerchief to his face to dry it, Daisy glared up at Jasper. "He could have drowned!"

"Let him," Jasper said, spitting blood.

"Jasper! To say such a thing! No matter what he's done, can't you see he's suffering? Is he not still your brother?" As Daisy said this, Nate's eyelids fluttered, and he tried to sit up, batting away Henry's proffered hand.

"He's no brother of mine," said Jasper. "Haven't you heard a word I've said? Or are you so besotted with this devil that you can't hear reason?"

"Besotted?" Daisy said, anger pounding in her temples. "No, I'm just *humane*, unlike you."

Jasper's face went white. "And I thought you understood," he said, his voice clipped. "I'm a fool. Nate made me into one, and now so have you." He gave Daisy a long, hard look and then turned away, marching back up the beach toward the main house, harshly wiping the blood from his face with a shirtsleeve.

Henry looked aghast. "My apologies for this ungentlemanly display."

"What on earth happened here?" asked Avery.

As Daisy recounted the fight and Jasper's story contradicting everything Nate had told them, Nate came to, managing to stagger onto his feet. He coughed a little, dazedly shaking his head.

"Nate, are you quite all right?" Morrigan eyed him warily.

He put a hand on Daisy's shoulder to steady himself. "Come with me," he exclaimed, catching Daisy's hand.

"No, Nate," Daisy cried, resisting with all her strength. "You're in a terrible state. Please come back and let us bandage you, treat your pain."

"You're breaking my heart," Nate cried, "you treacherous girl, I'm in a state because of you, can't you see . . ."

But then he dropped Daisy's hand and went staggering away along the beach at a clip, without a backward glance.

"Damned strange," Henry murmured.

Morrigan and Avery led Daisy back up the walkway, Henry trailing behind, casting apprehensive looks at Nate's retreating form. Blackwell House, that enormous brick bulwark, had never before looked so welcoming to Daisy. Then she remembered Jasper. There was no escape from her troubles. She would have to face them all head-on, just as the Judgement card presaged. She took a deep breath and steadied herself.

Entering the solarium, Daisy was surprised to see Frankie at the table, surrounded by a compass, a protractor, a ruler, two books, a box of colored pencils, and a notebook, with its sprawled sheaf of pages. Frankie was deep in conversation with a young housemaid. The maid was asking, "And what are those books?"

"Those are my *Ephemeris* and *Table of Houses*." Frankie was about to say more when the housemaid looked up and straightened her cap. Instantly, her face resumed its customary mask of professionalism.

"Finally, you're here!" Frankie exclaimed. "I've been explaining what I've just discovered." She flashed the housemaid a smile. "It's okay, Bridget, these are my mates."

Eyes downcast, Bridget bobbed her head and backed out of the solarium, Henry following her out.

Frankie leapt up, clutching her notebook, pointing to whatever she'd just been writing. "I did the calculations on the new moon ritual, and it's not at all the timing you'd think. It's not the twenty-seventh, nor what they say in the almanac, which gets closer by having it on the twenty-sixth but still mistakenly puts it at ten oh two p.m., because how could they know, not being tutored in the finer points of—"

"Frankie," Avery cut in.

Daisy smiled to herself. Her older sister had met her oratory match.

"The new moon," Frankie said. "It starts on Thursday evening, the twenty-sixth of October, but at exactly *seven* minutes past ten o'clock, not two."

They all stared at her.

Frankie flipped to another page in her weathered notebook and held it up so they could see the numbers and symbols she'd scribbled there. It looked like geometric balderdash to Daisy, but going by Frankie's wide-eyed excitement it was clearly something very important.

"There's one other thing," Frankie said, "and I don't know if this will mean anything to you, but I think your demon might be possessing an Aries."

CHAPTER XXI

The World, Part 1

"It is far from being true that all women want courage, strength, or conduct to lead an army to triumph."

—Lady Sophia Fermor Carteret, *Woman Not Inferior to Man: or, a Short and Modest Vindication of the Natural Right of the Fair-Sex to a Perfect Equality of Power, Dignity and Esteem with the Men*

Daisy fell into a chair, flabbergasted. The possessed person was an Aries? "How do you know?" she managed to ask.

Frankie gave her a quizzical look. "Not know, think. Big difference. But it's basic math."

Daisy's head was reeling. For one horrible moment, she wondered if this meant that she herself was the possessed and didn't know it.

"What's really fascinating," Frankie continued, caught up in her astrological enthusiasm, "is that there is an absolutely *unbelievable* concentration of energy in Scorpio."

"That is interesting," Avery said, clearly torn between an

awareness of Daisy's rising agitation and her own keen desire to hear Frankie's discoveries. "What does it mean?"

"Well, it's all there, isn't it? Have a look yourself." Frankie held up her notebook with its pages of circles within circles bisected by multicolored spokes radiating outward, each segment containing curious diagrams and figures. "As you can see, there are variations for each house, but across the board we've got sun, moon, Mercury, Venus, and Mars, all in Scorpio. I've never seen anything like it. They're in massive, *overwhelming* conversation with each other. And with moon itself being in strong combust with sun, and only one degree ahead? Well, that's your new moon right there!" Frankie tapped the diagram for emphasis, her eyes shining.

Daisy was listening as if from a great distance, focused on one question only. "What does any of that that have to do with the demon possessing an Aries?" She waved off Morrigan's gentle hand on her shoulder. "Frankie, please forgive my impatience, but I don't get it."

"It's simple, really: Mars rules Aries." Frankie stretched her spine to get the kinks out.

"Yes," Avery said, "but doesn't Mars also rule Scorpio?"

"Sure, that's the obvious interpretation," Frankie said, "but it's October, we're on the cusp of the Scorpio birth month, which will be well under way when the new moon rises on the twenty-sixth. That's the zodiacal energy of the season, can't be avoided. But so much Mars influence in a period of the year when the fixed Scorpio sign is *already* ruled by Mars indicates the presence of another sign. And that can only be Aries."

"I'm an Aries," Daisy said.

"Interesting," Frankie murmured, regarding Daisy as if she were a curious scientific specimen pinned to a corkboard.

"You're not the *only* Aries, though, are you?" Avery said. She frowned at Daisy.

"No," Daisy sighed, finally saying it aloud, "Nate is an Aries, too."

Nate had been troubled and reckless and even vicious at times, but the thought that this flesh-and-blood, beautiful if deeply flawed man might be possessed by the demon who had brought the Bleakness to Redcliffe filled Daisy with dread. If she had, as she'd long suspected, unleashed the demon with her flawed new moon ritual, then this, too, was her fault. Poor Nate! Then something occurred to her. "But Nate drank the elixir! I saw him do it with my own eyes."

"Well . . . if he was already possessed by a powerful demon," Avery said thoughtfully, "a simple herbal remedy may not have been strong enough." She started pacing back and forth, unable to contain her nervous excitement. "Putting aside the question of Aries and demons—just for the briefest moment, Daisy, I promise you. But I wonder, what does this reading tell us about *how* to defeat the demon, whoever it may end up being?"

"Excellent question!" Frankie said. "Think of next Thursday night as the new moon's birthday, with the, well, baby crowning at precisely ten oh seven p.m., and not a minute before. That's the seeding hour when the energy of the event is at its most potent. And it stays strong until the next day at seven p.m., though I recommend getting whatever you need done by midnight for peak effect."

"That makes sense!" Avery's eyes were electric. "Farmers use the almanac to determine the best time to plant their crops, and the new moon is when the ground is at its most receptive, when the highest amount of energy is available for things to take root and grow."

"Yes, precisely!" Frankie exclaimed, smiling at Avery before turning her gaze on Daisy. "And here's where you come in, Daisy.

You'll be the other side of the Aries coin. The other side of this fellow Nate, who's most likely been possessed."

"But how can we free him from the demon?" Daisy burst out.

"You care about him," said Frankie. She paused, considering. "That's good. It'll end up being your best weapon. As a fellow Aries, you're best positioned to destabilize Nate. He's going to be vulnerable and reactive. All that Scorpio will thrust him into the depths of acute loneliness on a truly cosmic level and trigger the worst aspects of Aries: a penchant toward corruption, selfishness, the desire for control—"

"But doesn't that make Daisy just as vulnerable?" Morrigan interrupted.

Avery gasped, a Knowing settling upon her. "It's in empathizing that Daisy retains the advantage."

Of course. Daisy realized she'd have to leverage her worst self to defeat Nate's worst self.

"Just remember," Frankie continued. "Scorpio is the only visibly dangerous sign of the zodiac. Think of the scorpion with its stinger raised and ready to strike. It's also the only sign that has a secondary avatar, the Phoenix, with the ability to rise from the dead. Not coincidentally, Scorpio rules Death and the underworld. This night's entire chart is absurdly explosive. I won't lie. There will be great danger."

"I'm not afraid of danger," Daisy said, though her heart was thudding.

"Your Aries courage," Frankie nodded. "Avery will also play an important role."

"Me, why?" Avery said.

"Because in that firestorm of energy hammering the new moon, the moon in Scorpio will be conjunct Mars in Libra. And you're a

Libra-Scorpio cusp. So you'll be the conductor. But of a battle. And from everything I see, the night will bring an unimaginable battle."

"But how am I to conduct a battle?" Avery said.

"Why, as the spellcaster, my love," Bernadette said, having wandered into the room in that eerily soundless way of hers. Daisy was struck by a rush of gratitude for her mother.

"Even so," Morrigan said, gazing at her twin with deep sympathy, "how do we get Nate there?"

"By conjuring the demon that's living inside him, of course," Bernadette said. "The same way you girls did it in the first place, by creating a new moon ritual at the clifftop. Only this time, we'll send it back from wherever it came. And we'll slam the door on it." Her smile was that of a powerful warrioress preparing to wage war.

"We have five days," Frankie said.

"And so much to do," said Avery. She stood tall and commanding in the center of the solarium, blazing with authority in the strong sunlight. "Should we get Kathryn?" She looked at Bernadette.

Bernadette replied without hesitation. "Yes. We need her expertise."

"This will be our war room," said Avery.

Morrigan mused, "We can ask to have our meals brought to us here as well; no sense keeping formalities with Aunt Mary sick in bed. Henry won't mind."

"I won't mind what?" asked Henry, coming in just behind Bridget, who carried a tray of tea things and began setting them on the table.

"Helping. We have five days to figure out how to kill a demon," said Avery.

"Sorry," Henry said, stumbling only slightly, "but did you say *demon*?"

God's teeth, they'd forgotten to tell Henry about the demon!

"We appear to have conjured one," Morrigan said a bit too gaily.

Henry paused. "As one does," he said finally, with arch solemnity.

The laughter was a welcome relief from the tension and madness.

"Tea all around," Henry said, nodding at Bridget. "Looks like we could use it! Perhaps with some more whisky? Bridget, you may want some yourself."

"I couldn't possibly, sir," she said, utterly askance, edging out of the room.

"No worries, I'll serve," Henry said, starting with Morrigan.

"Henry, you'll never believe who the demon's victim is," Daisy said.

He didn't miss a beat. "Nate, of course."

Everyone stared at him. He looked steadily and seriously back.

"How did you know?" Daisy asked, dreading the answer.

"I didn't, it was Jasper. Just before I came down, he told me he's sure that man he fought on the beach is not the same person he grew up with. And he knows Nate better than anyone. He swears Nate is overtaken by something, possibly a diagnosable illness. He didn't use the word *demon*, but—"

"That's how the scientific world categorizes behavior it doesn't understand," Daisy said.

Henry nodded. "Well, anything you need, all you have to do is ask. Can't say I know much about demons, but I and the resources of Blackwell House are at your disposal. How can I be of assistance?"

Morrigan clinked her teacup against Henry's in gratitude. "Come and play chess with me, Henry. Let's see what the configuration of the board has to add to the plan."

While Henry joined Morrigan at the table at the far end of the room, Avery and Bernadette sat side by side with the spell book. Frankie waved on her way out the door, off to fetch Kathryn.

Daisy stood moodily by the outer glass wall, feeling useless as she looked down at the beach where Jasper and Nate had fought. She pictured Jasper upstairs, bandaging the wounds inflicted by his best friend turned bitter enemy. She could almost feel his despair. And whatever he thought of her, it was surely nothing good. She had treated him with nothing but defiance, suspicion, and a lack of compassion. Worse, she had given him reason to think she loved Nate. Whatever the sad truth of their troubled history, the current situation had turned out to be so much darker.

Waiting was the worst part. But as Frankie had said, timing would be everything. As she refined the astrological template for the night of the battle, Bernadette and Avery honed the spells to be cast. Kathryn pored over every detail of the revised new moon ritual, and Morrigan used chess to verse Daisy in the moves of her dangerous dance with the demon.

Meanwhile, Henry arranged for Kathryn and Frankie to stay in the suite directly across the hall from the Wolfsons. As the days passed, and the plan took shape, he made sure that everyone kept up their strength. Like a mother hen, he herded the women out to the beach for walks in the fresh air, made them break for meals, and forcibly sent them up to bed before midnight every night. Thanks to his constant care, they managed to maintain their health despite the strain of plotting.

As Daisy sifted through the tumult of the past few days, she burned to tell Jasper how she felt. He was playing a frustrating game of cat and mouse, anticipating her moves as deftly as Morrigan did with Henry at chess. And just like Henry with Morrigan, Daisy was no match for Jasper's superior strategic evasions. Every time she approached him, the words on her lips, he evaded her, slipping off somewhere else before she could corner him. If she hadn't known better, she'd have sworn he was taking a certain malicious glee in toying with her.

After breakfast on the morning before the battle, Kathryn beckoned Daisy outside to the wide stone terrace. She was very glad of the chance to question her mentor in solitude without her sisters chiming in. She needed some straight answers. Her sleep had been fitful and full of dreams about snakes writhing at her through mist.

"Kathryn," Daisy began as they paced in the sea air, gulls swooping over the surf, "I'm not even sure how to phrase this, but how exactly does one defeat a..."

"Demon?" Kathryn finished for her and shrugged helplessly. "I can't say for certain, but I suspect it's about countering energy with energy. What are we if not energy?"

That part made sense to Daisy. She'd often wondered what gave bodies and minds the spark that was life. "But how do we do that?"

"Well, timing is essential, as Frankie illustrated so brilliantly. And the guidance of the cards. And whatever divination comes to you and your sisters. And other teachings, of course," Kathryn added, indicating Bernadette and Avery through the window, heads together over the book of spells. "But mostly it's about intention."

"Intention."

"Because if you think about it, what makes an event divine or evil or accidental but intention? Say a man dies of hunger. That's terribly sad, but is it evil? Did someone deliberately starve him, or was it caused by circumstance, perhaps famine? Was his death even providential, saving other lives by stretching thin food supplies? Nothing is without context. There are forces at work in our world that we may not ever understand. We can only strive to know our own hearts."

Daisy thought of how she'd been so drawn to Nate at first, and she was confused and unsettled all over again.

"Don't blame yourself, girl, you're just learning your own mind," Kathryn said kindly. "And body." This time, she allowed herself a cheeky grin, which only deepened Daisy's embarrassment. "And there's no shame to be had in that. Our bodies are lovely, sensual things. It's how we create life here on earth, so how can that be anything but beautiful?"

"But about this demon," Daisy said, diverting from the topic of her mortification. "What do you think its intention with Nate is?"

"From what I've seen," said Kathryn, "nothing good."

"Do you think there's any way we can we save him?"

"The answers lie in the way we approach disease, how we work with positive, healing energies to oust illness from a sick patient."

"Are you saying I'm to heal Nate of... the demon?"

"What is a demon if not diseased energy turned violent?" Kathryn said.

"And if I can't?"

"Then you must cast him out—along with the demonic energy he contains. The way we do with people who've perished from contagious illnesses, isolating their bodies from others. Except in this case, energetically. That's the banishing spell right there."

Then something horrible occurred to Daisy. "Wait! What if Nate isn't the one who's possessed after all?"

"Then he won't respond to the incantations. Whoever appears in the circle will be the one possessed."

"But our entire strategy is predicated on my feelings for Nate, and his for me," Daisy said.

"It's true," Kathryn said softly. "There are so many variables: the strength of the hold, the strength of the held."

"Is there a way to be certain?"

Kathryn didn't answer right away, instead looking out at the ocean, over which a thin mist hovered, ghostly in the sunlight. She put a warm, strong arm around Daisy's shoulders and pulled her close. "No," she said finally, and the two of them went back into the solarium together to rejoin the war room.

"Look at this, Daisy," called Morrigan, beckoning Daisy over to the table where she and Henry had set up a chess game. "What do you see?"

"The pieces are all surrounding . . . the black queen?" Daisy hazarded. Morrigan saw patterns in the arrangements of chess pieces that no one else could grasp. Their father had taught her. It had been their special language.

"On the face of it, yes," Morrigan said. "But Henry's two knights are both being very quiet at the far edge of the board, each within two moves of my king. Henry is leaving them there, letting them idle while these other pieces move my queen into a vulnerable position. And I almost fell for it."

"Too clever for me by half!" Henry chimed in.

"He's going to sacrifice a few pieces to distract me into leaving my king wide open. He'll move the two knights into position during the skirmish, making it look like he's moving them to attack my queen, not to take my king, his real aim. It's a sleight of hand. An unwary player would find herself checked in eight moves."

Henry scratched his head. "How did you see that? I barely saw it myself."

"Well, it's a clever plan," Morrigan said. "And I think we should steal it and use it against Nate. I mean, the demon."

"Who are the king and queen?" asked Bernadette from across the room.

"It's not an exact analogy," said Morrigan. "My idea is that we'll appear to make a sacrifice to lull the demon into letting go of Nate."

"Who will the lurking knights be?" Avery asked.

"Well, you're one of them, of course," said Morrigan.

"And the other?"

"Brother Terrence," said Morrigan. "If we can find him in time to enlist him."

"He won't be able to stay away," said Bernadette with a confidence Daisy didn't share.

There was so much that could go wrong. What if the demon got stuck on this side of the portal permanently? What if Brother Terrence didn't come? And worst of all, what if Nate wasn't possessed? Daisy couldn't believe she was positing that as a bad outcome. Of course she didn't want Nate to be the one possessed by the demon. Oh, it was all so confusing!

Avery peered at the chessboard. "Who are the decoys to be sacrificed?"

Morrigan hesitated, giving Daisy a look of apology. "We only need one pawn, in this case."

At once, Daisy grasped it. "Me."

"Aries is the sign of sacrifice," said Frankie.

"You will only be in danger for a very short time," said Morrigan. "And our two knights will be lurking quietly in the background, waiting for the demon to be distracted."

"How will I distract him?"

"By tapping into that extreme emotional vulnerability I was telling you about," said Frankie. "This is brilliant, Morrigan! The chess strategy dovetails with everything in the chart."

Morrigan blushed at the compliment, quietly pleased.

Daisy nodded. "But if it fails . . ."

"We won't let it," Morrigan promised.

"I'll do it," Daisy said with all the bravado she could muster, though she felt doubtful and afraid.

As the fateful meeting grew closer, Daisy lay awake at night, cold with self-blame and fear. The last time she'd performed a ritual, she'd opened the portal and let that darkness in. Her mistake had already cost lives.

How many more would be lost?

At dawn on the day of the battle, the team sat in the breakfast room, books and tools and materials all put away, the outcome hanging before them. They forced themselves to eat, drinking tea to move the lumps of food into their bellies.

Right before they left, Daisy drew a tarot card—the World: *Within a garland of wildflowers dances a figure that is male on one side and female on the other, clothed only in a sash shaped into the figure-eight symbol for infinity. It is decorated with wands, swords, cups, and coins. In each corner of the card, a water sprite, eagle, lion, and bull represent the four fixed zodiacal signs—Aquarius, Scorpio, Leo, and Taurus—as well as the four elements, the four seasons, the four suits of the tarot, and the four corners of the cosmos.*

The final card of the Major Arcana, the last step of Daisy's journey.

"This is good," Kathryn said. Bernadette nodded in agreement.

"Yes," Avery said. "It signifies overcoming hardships."

"Plus," added Morrigan, "a renewed wholeness and harmony. Oh, I think this might go well!"

"I dearly hope so." Daisy spoke as positively as she could, but she was feeling far less optimistic.

CHAPTER XXII

The World, Part 2

"Achieve enlightenment, then return to this world of humanity."

—Bashō

"Brother Terrence will meet us there," said Kathryn, and Bernadette nodded, but Daisy had no idea how they could be so sure. They filed out of Blackwell House through the front hall, to the waiting carriage, and there was Mr. Miggs again, back at his post, holding the front door open.

"Mr. Miggs," Daisy asked him, "are you feeling better?"

He gave her an odd look, as if she were being impertinent for asking such a personal question. "Better, miss?"

"I heard you had a touch of ague. . . ."

"People say all kinds of things," he snapped as he handed her into the barouche. At the touch of his hand, Daisy jumped. It was so cold it almost burned her, like dry ice. And yet he denied being ill.

The most terrible thought occurred to her: What if Mr. Miggs was the one possessed and they'd missed seeing it? Servants passed invisibly, everywhere. She recalled with a sharp foreboding his suspicion of the prevention elixir. What if his recent absence had something to do with the Bleakness? Maybe the demon had taken him away for a few days to work its mischief on the town, and he had no memory of it. That would explain his aggrieved denial just now. Well, she supposed there was only one way to find out.

As the carriage rolled down the drive, Henry waved somberly. Daisy glanced up at the large house just as a curtain was pulled aside at the window of one of the higher floors. Jasper's face stared down, unreadable from such a distance. Then the curtain swung back, and he was gone.

The hazy air smelled scorched, as if Redcliffe itself had been smoldering all this time. The few people out and about looked either listless or choleric. At the edge of the forest, the coachman handed them down from the carriage, and as the jingling and clop of hooves receded back toward town, they walked into the heart of the woods. Morrigan held Daisy's hand tightly.

When they arrived at the small moss-covered clearing deep in the trees, the six sat in a circle. Sunlight dappled their faces. The respiration of all the hidden watching creatures interlaced with theirs in a rhythmic thread. Kathryn softly began the chant, Bernadette joining her, then Frankie and Morrigan and Avery, and then finally Daisy herself. Their voices became stronger, merging with the chatter of birdsong, the light piles of fallen leaves rustling like dry tongues. They chanted as the hours passed, gathering strength, becoming one force.

And then the Bleakness was upon them.

"There they are," someone shouted, "the witches in their coven!"

The women rose as one to face the mob, tightening their circle so that they each looked out in a different direction, facing the hot press of bodies encroaching on them.

Finny Stewart led the charge, and a clot of townspeople thronged the clearing. Lizzie swore unintelligibly into Daisy's face as she screeched past. Were there fifteen people, or a hundred? Daisy couldn't tell. Kathryn had kept the chant going, and now Daisy and the others rejoined her, their voices creating a screen of pulsating waves keeping the attackers at bay, but just barely. Where was Brother Terrence? Were Kathryn and Bernadette wrong? Would he not come?

"Oh she of little faith," rang out a familiar voice, the robed figure of Brother Terrence striding through the mob as easily as wading across a shallow pond. He threw Daisy a quick wink. "I'd never miss a party!"

Daisy felt the folds of his robe whoosh past as he stalked the periphery of their circle, bits of dazzling dust swirling in his wake. In the distance, the ocean shimmered in the setting sun. Brother Terrence looked in his element in this dusk-darkened pandemonium, dancing with the provocation between the mob and the women's tight little circle.

"Terrence," Bernadette said sharply, "your love spell is partially to blame for this monster. Undo it."

"It's an odd feeling, being wrong. I don't know how you cope," sighed Brother Terrence, casually flicking his fingers in Finny's direction, then drawing Finny to him with a beckoning motion. He placed his hands on either side of Finny's head, an intangible something passing between them. "You are free, man, can't you see? Choose your life!" For a moment, all was still. Even the mob seemed frozen in place.

Then Finny suddenly reared back, arching his spine as if

electrified. He fell from Brother Terrence's grasp to the ground. A moment later, he leapt back up and shook himself, eyes darting around madly, as if waking from a nightmare.

"How did you do that?" Daisy demanded.

"It's amazing what people wish to believe," dismissed Brother Terrence.

"Wait," Avery said, "are you saying it's some form of... hypnosis? A trance?"

"Call it what you like," he shrugged.

Finny stared, his mouth open. "You," he said to Brother Terrence. To Lizzie: "You trapped me." And then to Daisy: "This is all your fault!"

He turned to the mob with his arms raised: "I was tricked! My life is ruined!" He plunged away, dashing over stones and gnarled roots into the darkening woods. With a wild cry, Lizzie pursued him, and then the ill-fated lovers were gone, leaving their followers rudderless in their wake.

Brother Terrence flapped his hands at the mob as if he were shooing a flock of errant geese. "Go on, people, go home, disperse," he called languidly. "We have work to do, and you'll just be in our way."

Muttering to themselves, the townspeople wandered off in twos and threes, disgruntled to find themselves in the middle of the woods at sunset, a long walk ahead of them.

At the clifftop above Crescent Beach, just past the border of the forest, the sky was almost completely dark now, the path lit only by fishermen's lanterns. Daisy glanced up at the trees as she passed the wide, flat altar rock at the edge of the bluffs, noticing the strange, twisted shapes they made. It suddenly made sense that such a potent location would affect the natural landscape. And yet she hadn't thought to simply look around her. How little she had known when she'd brought her sisters there to perform their first ritual. She'd been so proud, so heedless in her determination to work with powers and rituals she barely understood.

Avery caught Daisy's gaze. "Don't think you get to take all the credit for this mess," she said warmly.

"A glorious mess it is," Brother Terrence said. "This is going to be fun."

While the six of them unpacked their satchels and began the work of assembling their supplies near the altar, Brother Terrence wandered to the edge of the red-brown cliffs to peer down toward the roiling sea.

"All this has happened before," Morrigan murmured, unwinding the ball of twine and arranging the materials for the *luminaires*, the primitive French torches they'd used at their original new moon ritual, almost two months ago.

Daisy stared at her. "A Vision?"

"No," Morrigan said. "A Knowing."

Immediately, Daisy understood, her entire being flushed with a Knowing of her own. "And all this will happen again."

"But we do have choice," Avery said, holding the candlesticks in place as Morrigan secured them to the branches with twine and attached the waxed paper wind shades. "And that's not a Vision either, Daisy. I don't know if I'd call it a Knowing, but I do know it. And so do you. Have faith in yourself, baby sister. We do. We wouldn't be here otherwise. Now, does anyone have a box of bloody matches, or will poor Morrigan have to wage war with that flint and steel again?"

Daisy laughed, the dark mood almost broken. She sheepishly handed over the box of matches.

"I have some, too," Frankie called from the pile of kindling she was assembling with Bernadette and Kathryn in front of the altar rock. "Did you know these are called Lucifer matches?"

Daisy and her sisters exploded into unexpected but very welcome laughter.

Frankie looked puzzled, and Avery said, "I'll explain when this is over."

When the bonfire was built, Avery and Frankie touched their burning match tips to the kindling. Soon leaping flames formed a blazing tower in the chilly autumn darkness. The *luminaires* were anchored into the earth and looped around the bonfire. The clearing was ablaze with light.

"Okay," Daisy said, "I think we're just about ready."

Her sisters stared at her.

"Putain," Daisy cried, "the salt!"

"You wouldn't have forgotten, Daisy," Kathryn said, handing her the bag of salt with a hole already cut out of one of the corners at the bottom. "It's just nerves."

Gratefully, Daisy took the bag from Kathryn and, walking backward in a slow loop, carefully poured out an especially thick line of salt that circled the ringed *luminaires*, the bonfire, and the altar just behind it. When she was done, she paced the salt circle with one of the oil lanterns, peering closely at the protective barrier she'd drawn, determined that there be no mistakes this time.

"Good work," Bernadette said as she took the empty bag. Then she handed Augustus's pocket watch to Frankie, the time master, charged with clocking the crucial moment at precisely seven minutes past the hour. Bernadette and Avery did a last consultation of the spells as Morrigan reviewed her chess strategy with Brother

Terrence. And Daisy arranged her treasured deck of tarot cards on the smooth altar rock, weighing it down with the crystals, each connected to everyone's astrological signs and roles in the battle ahead. For her sisters and herself, she placed the same cards and crystals she'd used in the first new moon ritual: the Justice card and peridot to ignite Avery's coolly analytical Libra intellect, the Moon card and amethyst to awaken Morrigan's dreamy Piscean intuition, and the Emperor and scarlet-veined dark-green bloodstone to ground her own Aries fire.

She took a deep breath to center herself.

Frankie gave the nod. "It's time."

"Not quite," Brother Terrence said, handing Daisy, Morrigan, and Frankie each a small amulet. Daisy gasped, recognizing them as replicas of the one Bernadette had given Avery on her birthday. "Where do you think she got hers?" he said impishly. "Speaking of which, dear Bernadette, I do believe you might be needing another talisman yourself."

With a charmed smile she couldn't hide, Bernadette neatly caught the shining object he tossed to her, tucking it into a skirt pocket.

"But what about Kathryn?" Daisy blurted.

"I still have mine," Kathryn said, reaching up to touch the leather thong that hung from her neck. "I only put it on for special occasions," she explained, noting Daisy's look.

Brother Terrence slipped away into the shadows, taking the extinguished oil lanterns with him, that odd little tuneless melody wafting after him.

"He'll be back," Bernadette assured them. "He likes his grand entrances."

One by one, they stepped inside the salt circle and started their chant again, this time a slightly different tune, the incantation weaving a ring of protection. As one, they each took a *luminaire* and twined their bodies around the fire and the altar rock in a clockwise circle. The cadence of their dance became part of their breath and bone and cells, connected to that invisible force Daisy had felt the last time she'd performed the ceremony back in August. It seemed like an eon ago, and her connection to these ancient practices felt far stronger, far more grounded in hard-earned experience.

"It's time," said Frankie.

The *luminaires* all went out.

Then the fire.

Daisy's blood ran cold as she skidded to a stop, almost bumping into Morrigan.

Silence rang out in the night.

"He's here," Avery murmured.

"I know." Daisy felt him in her very marrow.

"Don't move," Bernadette whispered.

They didn't have to wait long.

Mr. Miggs ran out of the shadows, waving his arms and shouting incoherently.

Daisy didn't know whether to be horrified or relieved. Behind her, the others gasped in confusion and alarm.

But then Mr. Miggs fell to his knees, struck down by an unseen force.

That's when Nate melted out of the shadows. "Thank you, Miggs, for leading me here," he said, "and now you may go." He flicked a lazy glance at Mr. Miggs, casting his limp form back into the trees without raising a finger, his hands in his pockets as he sauntered nonchalantly into the clearing, sparking the bonfire back into life, each *luminaire* relighting itself as he passed. He paused briefly to sear Daisy with a look before he lifted a boot easily over the line of salt and stepped cleanly inside the circle.

Daisy did her best to swallow her shock, her stomach roiling with all the reversals. It was like pulling cards in a tempest.

Nate's demeanor was cool and collected for the first time in weeks, no scent of liquor on him, no hint of a stagger. He was dressed exquisitely in gleaming black leather boots, a dark gray fitted cutaway tailcoat of the finest wool, and a snow-white linen neckcloth. Straightening his jacket and shooting his cuffs, Nate cracked his neck, first to one side and then the other, clearly relishing the impact he'd made. Then he strode to where Daisy stood, stopping a few inches away, the corners of his generous mouth curved up slightly.

"Well, hullo there, Daisy," he said, the old charm rolling off him in tangible waves. "What a lovely little soirée you've created. I hope it wasn't on my account."

"What have you done with Mr. Miggs?" she demanded.

"That's what you care about?" he exploded, aggrieved. "Are you determined to spoil our fresh start?"

Feeling the collective anxiety of her team, Daisy took a deep breath. "You're right, I'm sorry," she said as calmly as she could. "You're looking . . . well."

Nate grinned wolfishly, calmer, his moods as labile as ever. "Clean up nice, don't I?"

Daisy said nothing, though she couldn't deny it even to herself, and she knew he saw this in her face. He was as handsome as she'd ever seen him, the color high on his cheekbones, his surf-blue eyes glinting in the firelight, which picked up the golden hues of his hair.

The demon is in there, she reminded herself. *The demon is in control of him.*

Nate took a step forward and grasped her hand, sending a surge of hot energy crackling up her arm and into the center of her chest. Sensing her allies surging with protectiveness, Daisy mentally willed them not to intervene. This was the plan. They'd all drilled themselves to meet this moment.

"Don't worry, pretty Daisy," Nate murmured. "I won't bite." Turning her hand over, he bent down to press a warm kiss into her palm. Her skin blazed as it had the first time, his touch continuing to melt her from the inside out. What madness was this, she wondered in the one clear part of her mind that wasn't consumed by a sudden rush of renewed attraction for him.

Daisy took a steadying breath. Outwardly, she let him see the effect his kiss had wrought upon her physical senses. She forced her gaze to meet his and smiled at him with all the affection she'd once felt, the echoes of which still reverberated, despite everything she knew. Not expecting this, his own expression softened, and she took that moment to cup his cheek in her palm, her heart flipping in her chest.

"I know, Nate," she told him, tilting her face up to brush her lips lightly against his, her pulse fluttering in her throat. By his quick intake of breath, Daisy could tell she'd connected with something unguarded within him, a sweetness. Did that mean he wasn't completely lost to the demon's power?

Behind him, Avery and Bernadette stood together just beyond the altar rock, silently intoning the spells they'd rehearsed. A muscle jumped in Nate's cheek, and Daisy hurried to say, "I've been worried about you," making sure to mean what she said, reaching into his soul with her own, hoping to connect with the pure heart she had to believe was still in there.

"Have you?" he demanded. "You've given me every reason to believe you'd thrown me over for my archenemy."

He tried to pull his hands away, but Daisy held on tightly and centered the full force of her compassion on him. "No," she said. "How could I? He almost let you drown!" Nate searched her eyes to see if she was lying. "Nate," she breathed, "I fell for you the very moment we first met." And this *was* the truth, although she now recognized those feelings for what they'd been: mere schoolgirl infatuation.

"I felt that way, too," he said, pulling Daisy into his arms and burying his face in her neck, his breath hot and fevered. "That's why I was so hurt when you got close to that cur!"

"But I'm confused, Nate," Daisy murmured, stroking his hair. "Why would Jasper say that he's done nothing but try to keep you out of harm's way?"

"Oh, Daisy." Nate laughed bitterly and tried to push her away, though she was able to hang on, her strength reinforced by the spells her sister and mother had been weaving, simultaneously binding him to her even as they banked the strength of the demon's hold on him. "That you could say that, knowing what you do! Jasper never treated me as his equal, leaving me in his shadow, even turning his parents against me, despite everything I did to help." His voice shook with rage. And something else. The confused, lonely hurt of a little boy cast out.

"And yet you didn't help them, did you?" a familiar voice said from off to the side.

Daisy was stunned to see Jasper's tall figure in the dimness just beyond the circle. Nate shoved Daisy aside, their connection broken, and she staggered backward, catching herself from falling at the last moment.

Nate shot Daisy an accusing glare. "Reinforcements, Daisy? Good thing I brought some of my own." He threw his head back to shriek unintelligibly, his face contorting itself for a split second into a monstrous mask before his features recomposed themselves as before, handsome if enraged.

He wheeled away from her to confront his foe. "I did help your parents!" he shouted at Jasper. "Even after you had me kicked out of school, ruining my credibility and prospects, I still did everything I could to save your father."

Daisy scrambled to marshal the forces of her mind.

"I see a man clutching his heart," Morrigan's clear voice rang out suddenly. "And a woman, weeping over his body."

"That would be my parents," Jasper said. "They trusted Nate's medical knowledge, believed in him as if he were their own son. But Nate poisoned and very nearly killed my father with powerful herbs he didn't understand, caused him to have an almost-fatal heart attack under the pretext of curing him."

"I did no such thing," Nate yelled. "I wept, too! I loved him, too!"

"Crocodile tears," Jasper said dismissively. "You love no one but yourself."

"You bastard!" Nate spat and lunged for Jasper, who stood just outside the salt circle. But as Nate tried to cross over, he bounced backward as though he'd hit an unseen wall. This was a good sign. It meant the protective barrier was finally working, if not exactly as intended. But at least Nate was off-balance, the entity inside him weakened by extension.

Just then, Brother Terrence materialized from the darkness, his hands tracing glowing white patterns in the air, his fingers shooting tendrils to ensnare Nate in a sticky web. Trussed by these invisible ropes, Nate fell, bound at the knees and writhing on the ground. Creeping like a gigantic tarantula, Brother Terrence fired more threads at Nate's chest, this time binding his arms.

"I was trying to heal your father," Nate shouted with impotent rage.

"You almost killed him with your shoddy doctoring," Jasper said. "Because that's what you always do, isn't it, Nate? Fake your way into everything. Including Daisy's affections."

This was her chance. Kneeling by Nate's side, Daisy murmured, "I know you meant it, Nate, I know your feelings were real." She brushed a shock of hair back from his forehead, understanding in a rush that he'd never meant to hurt anyone. He was a wounded boy, lashing out in pain, inflicting it randomly on others. "You only ever wanted to belong," she told him, remembering what Kathryn had said about evil being diseased energy that needed, ached to be healed. Had Nate been struggling with his darker side even as a boy? Was this why the demon had chosen him to inhabit, had been drawn to this fellow Redcliffe newcomer? It all made sense. The cracks in Nate's shattered sense of self had allowed the demon in; his shadow side was a hungry ghost aching for solace, so easy to manipulate.

Behind her, Daisy sensed Avery and the others moving into place. As Morrigan leapt out of the circle to pull Jasper away with her, whispering heatedly into his ear, Daisy made certain to keep Nate's attention, gazing at him with sympathy, letting the tears she'd banked up flow freely. "It's all you've ever wanted, isn't it?"

"Yes," he said, his own eyes welling. "And I thought you understood, I thought I could belong to you, and you to me."

"I did understand," Daisy told him, stroking his face. "It's what I wanted, too."

"Really?" Nate said, his voice catching.

"Yes, Nate," she murmured, forcing herself to remain utterly defenseless, letting him feel the full depth of her emotion, ignoring the hammering waves of fear.

In a flash, Daisy felt Nate's vulnerability vanish, replaced by a renewed cockiness that solidified into something powerful and hungry. She had to steel herself to not resist when he flung away Brother Terrence's invisible bonds with preternatural strength and stood upright, dragging her with him.

Though her entire body thrummed with terror, Daisy returned Nate's eerily translucent gaze. She felt the pull of the portal as it opened around them, everyone and everything else receding into the distance. With dread coiling around her spine, she understood that she wasn't looking into Nate's eyes. She was staring directly through and past his soul, down into a terrible abyss of unquenchable evil.

"Come with me, Daisy," Nate whispered, though it was the Other that shaped his words.

A cold thread of venomous energy spiraled out at her through Nate's open mouth, and, with unspeakable delicacy, it licked her lips, a grisly sensuality flaring between them, sparks glinting through the air.

Daisy fell backward through time and space, frozen and lost to everything she had known or loved, doomed never to be found again, her very anima flickering before her eyes. She hovered on a knife's edge of existence.

NATE, she shrieked soundlessly, reaching for him, for the man he'd once been, for anything of this world. As the remnants of his former self reached back for her, Nate's physical body was suddenly yanked away by a fresh web of Brother Terrence's spidery tendrils.

Daisy flailed for balance, staggering, while Nate lay in the dirt, thrashing in Brother Terrence's ethereal web.

"Daisy," Nate whispered hoarsely, "don't leave me. . . . I love you."

He looked so helpless in that moment that Daisy hesitated. But she reminded herself he wasn't alone. She sensed that Other still swirling within him, rippling with violent energy and inchoate rage.

Suddenly, Avery's voice rang out, her words a steel shield, defending Daisy: "The evil that smiteth the living, the evil that like a cloak enshroudeth the man, the evil that seizeth upon the body, that smites it with sickness, be thou *exorcised*!"

This gave Daisy the opening she needed. It was time to banish this contagion. Terror gripping every cell of her being, Daisy marshaled the most savage of her own primal impulses and unleashed a torrent of blistering hatred, forging it into a hot scythe to slash Nate in the heart of his deepest vulnerability.

"The thing is, Nate," she said with measured and deliberate cruelty, "I don't love you. I could never love something as broken and frankly ridiculous as you. Jasper's right, you are a fake. Worse, you're a coward. Everyone sees it. And no one wants you, least of all me. You're better off dead."

Nate gasped as Daisy's vitriol pierced him. Then his eyes narrowed in outrage. A guttural howl tore out of his throat.

"You lying . . . little . . . *slag*!" he thundered, loosening the hold of Brother Terrence's trap, leaping to his feet, and swiping wildly at her with a closed fist.

But Daisy was prepared. She sprang back out of his range.

His face contorted hideously, his former beauty swallowed by a wrath so incandescent it blurred the air. The malevolence of his possession was now fully visible, shimmering around him in a sheath of molten fury. Empowered, he flung the last shreds of the binding web from his body. He staggered upright, bellowing with such ferocity that Brother Terrence was hurled back against the bluff. With another roar, he swept his arm in Bernadette's direction, sending her tumbling toward the cliff's edge. Morrigan, Kathryn, and Frankie raced after her, pulling her back just in time.

With a feral snarl of her own, Avery blasted Nate with the full impact of her spellcasting, flinging intricately braided ropes of magic through the air and furiously incanting, "As the elements tear your ghastly spirit to shreds, I call on the four wraiths to banish you from this world, this life, and this man! Begone, begone, begone!" Then she shouted at him in a language Daisy couldn't understand but felt in her bones.

This mighty, primeval incantation cracked the hold the entity had on Nate's soul, and he suddenly broke free of its shackles, falling to the ground on his hands and knees. Though his entire body shook, and he was slick with sweat, Nate lifted his head and gaped around the circle. His eyes shone, once again blue as the sunniest day. Daisy could see that he had returned to himself at last.

"Daisy," he gasped, "I'm so sorry, I didn't mean to—"

Whatever else he might have said was interrupted by a clamor of shouts and footsteps. Answering the demon's earlier summons, the mob had returned.

"Die, witch!" Finny Stewart cried. He lofted the pike he carried and hurled it at Daisy with all his strength.

As she watched the steel of its sharpened spearhead tunneling directly at her, time slowed, and Daisy was immobilized by the inevitability of her imminent death.

Then Jasper flung himself into the pike's path.

"No!" Daisy cried.

But a split second before it could strike and kill Jasper, Nate launched himself across the clearing with otherworldly speed to take the full force of the spear straight in his heart, collapsing backward into Jasper's arms.

Blood erupted from his chest in hot, ropey sprays. Nate clutched at Jasper, gazing up at his old friend in remorse. "Forgive me," he sighed on a final exhalation, releasing Jasper and slithering to the ground, where his physical body slid off the remnants of the demon's energy sheath like an empty suit. Above Nate's drained body, a hissing, serpentine outline fueled with maleficent electricity flared briefly in the air before sparking out of sight.

There was a collective gasp of horror from the villagers. Brother Terrence swept back into the midst, his black robes billowing behind him. "Away with you, pestilence!"

"We must disperse!" shouted Finny, his face white with horror at the realization of what he'd done.

The townspeople fled with him into the forest, no longer under the sway of the demon. The fever of the Bleakness seemed to have broken at long last.

Daisy's sisters and mother rushed to her side, Kathryn and Frankie hot on their heels, checking her for injuries.

"I'm all right," Daisy told them weakly, though it felt like a lie.

"He's coming back!" Jasper's voice burst out.

They all watched speechlessly as Nate's shapeless body fleshed out again to resume its human form, and his eyes shot open to stare at them all. Bewilderingly, calling on incomprehensible reserves, he dragged his bleeding, broken body upright once more and swayed for a moment, regarding Daisy and Jasper with an expression of utter despondency. Then he lurched away, stumbled to the cliff, and pitched forward into the darkness.

Daisy and Jasper ran to the bluff's edge and peered down. A

strange light illuminated Nate's twisted body on the rocks below, where it thrashed violently one last time before crumbling to dust. A powerful red tide swept onto the shore and just as quickly receded, the waves carrying what remained of the man they had known out to sea. And then the light went out.

Jasper let out a harsh sob, and Daisy caught him in her arms as he fell to his knees. Everyone else stood in witness, understanding that they'd just lost someone who had once been human, who'd been loved, even in his brokenness.

"He took the spear meant for me," Daisy said. "The one you tried to take, Jasper."

"Nate saved my life," said Jasper, his eyes streaming with tears. "His final act was to protect me."

"A sacrifice," murmured Frankie, echoing what she'd foreseen in the stars.

Just then, a strange bird with a neck like a snake glided up over the rocks that ringed the clearing, rising above them on silvery wings. It hovered, then landed on the altar rock. With a look back at Daisy, it extended its long neck and dropped something from its daggerlike bill.

The snakebird lifted back up into the air, floating briefly in the black moonless sky, the underside of its fanlike tail gleaming in the light of the bonfire, and vanished.

The flat rock was empty except for two overlapping tarot cards: the World once again, and with it the Fool, both cards sizzling, their edges curled and burnt.

Daisy was struck with the force of utter clarity that all along she had been both fool and herox. The two roles were intertwined, were in fact one and the same. To be heroic, she had to be willing to be a fool, to not know. And in accepting her own foolishness, her imperfect humanity, she could find the strength to be heroic. In a crystal-clear split-second Vision, she foresaw that this knowledge would give her the courage and self-compassion to sustain herself through all the challenges that would come next. Her journey was complete. And it was also starting anew.

When she touched the cards, they crumbled away to ashes.

CHAPTER XXIII

THE FOOL REDUX

"Two hearts that are but one have shown their strength in fierce enmity."

—WOLFRAM VON ESCHENBACH, *Parzival*

Immediately after the battle, everyone returned to Blackwell House, where Mr. Miggs greeted them, inexplicably restored to his usual position at the foyer, no sign of any bodily harm or mental distress. He made no mention of the events that evening, so neither did they. It wasn't clear if he was even aware of what had happened, though Daisy did wonder momentarily if she'd imagined it when his eyes had glinted at her meaningfully. Perhaps it was just in acknowledgment that she and her family had finally allowed him to divest them of their cloaks.

But she was too exhausted and wrung out to give the subject more attention. It would have to remain a mystery for another day.

By unspoken agreement, she and the others retreated to their respective beds and slept deeply for many hours. The next day, replenishing their strength with trays of nourishing meals, they spent hours discussing the fantastical events that had taken place up on the clifftop. When Kathryn went back to the cottage she now shared with Frankie, she bid Bernadette goodbye with an embrace.

Over the next several days, the Wolfsons did their best to reacquaint themselves with the normalcies of a life they'd all once taken for granted. Bernadette worked on her needlepoint, and Morrigan and Henry played chess, while Avery met up with Frankie for long rambles through the forest to plot their future collaborations with clients when Frankie had free time from her new job at the cranberry bogs. Daisy and her family were extremely eager to be back in their own cottage. But it would take several months, perhaps even until spring, for the team of workmen to fix the roof and walls, so they were settling in for a long winter at Blackwell House. It felt churlish to complain, but all four were chafing a little at their enforced dependency on Aunt Mary, who had also generously if grumpily paid for the renovations of their cottage.

To distract herself, Daisy had begun work on the painstaking task of creating a new tarot deck to replace the one that had mysteriously vanished from the altar rock. She began by sketching the Fool. As she drew that devil-may-care figure jauntily and heedlessly sending a toe over the clifftop, she realized it was and had always been a self-portrait. There she was, at the beginning of her journey, and here she was, drawing a picture of that commencement, having reached its end. It was both the first and the last card of the Major Arcana. Unlike the warm sun she'd painted for the old Fool card, it felt fitting to now draw a darkened sky lit only by the finest sliver of the new moon, the curling sea down below.

Daisy paid frequent visits to Aunt Mary, who was improving

daily, no thanks to Jasper. He'd absented himself entirely after that awful night, a fact that unsettled her, though she'd done her level best to give him time to process the loss of the adversary who'd once been his closest friend and near-brother.

On the afternoon of the fifth day, when she was struggling to talk reason into Aunt Mary, Daisy looked up and was startled to see Jasper in the doorway. He looked as taken aback as she felt.

"Whose house is this anyway?" Aunt Mary grumbled. "I insist you open these infernal curtains at once!"

"I understand, Aunt Mary," Daisy began, "but the sunlight makes your rash so much worse—"

"I cannot live like a worm in the dark forever," she snapped. "I need sun!"

"Oh for god's sake, just open them," Jasper sighed.

"But—"

"The curtains, please, Ginny," he said to Aunt Mary's personal maid, who stood nervously by the window, never sure whose authority prevailed in here. "You heard Mrs. Blackwell."

Daisy stared at him. "Jasper, I must—"

But Ginny had already flung the heavy brocaded drapes open, and sunlight flooded the room. And then Aunt Mary shooed them all away with little flaps of her hands.

Out in the hall, Ginny vanished into the depths of the house, but before Jasper could pull another of his own disappearing acts, Daisy darted in front of him. "You can't make such an important decision without asking me what I think."

"I just did," he said.

"Ask me what I think? No, you did not!"

"Make the decision," he barked, turning on a heel and marching away down the hall in the opposite direction, pretending not to hear when Daisy called after him.

Daisy stormed back to her family's quarters and found them all in a cheerful flurry of preparation to go out. Her heart sank even further. She had forgotten it was the eve of Samhain, the annual festival the town put on to celebrate the end of autumn and the start of winter. Everyone was excited about it but her. She was already feeling out of sorts living under Aunt Mary's nose, but Jasper's behavior just now had made her positively crispy.

"But it'll be so much fun!" Morrigan enthused. "It will do us good to see the town back to itself again."

"Yes," chimed in Henry. "You must come!"

"It's an important time in the wheel of the year," Bernadette said with a glance over her needlepoint. Since when had she embraced the ancient rituals?

"Exactly," Avery piped in, "when the veil between the living and the dead is at its most translucent. That feels even more important this year than ever before."

Daisy suspected her eldest sister's desire to attend the festival had everything to do with wanting to see her new friend. "Go if you like, but don't ask me to come. I've had just about enough of peering through the veils of death to last a lifetime."

"Someone's prickly," Avery observed dryly.

"I'm not prickly!" Then Daisy flushed at her outburst. "Sorry."

Her mother and sisters exchanged glances, while Henry diplomatically vanished to fetch the carriage.

"Besides, someone has to stay behind and see to Aunt Mary," Daisy muttered.

"How is that going?" Bernadette asked mildly.

"Terrible! I mean, fine!" She took a deep breath. "Aunt Mary's condition has vastly improved. But Jasper is being absolutely impossible!" Daisy let go of any pretense of composure, telling them about that day's meeting with Aunt Mary. "Can you believe the utter gall?"

"Well," Morrigan began carefully, "perhaps it was just a misunderstanding. Why don't you take it up with him at the festival tonight?"

"Ha!" Daisy exclaimed. "Jasper, at a festival? That man is allergic to fun."

"On the contrary, Daisy," Henry said, coming back in to let them know the carriage was waiting. "Jasper told me himself that he'd meet me there for a glass of cider."

Daisy was shocked into silence.

"Good," Bernadette said, "we'll all have some merriment. We could certainly use some!"

Meeting her mother's kind but steely gaze, Daisy knew there was no sense in arguing.

It was strange to see the town restored to normalcy, as if none of the madness had ever happened. The chilly air of the village green was filled with music, drifting smoke, and the smell of warm cinnamon and cloves. Many of the revelers were dressed in orange and black, to symbolize the fading and redawning of the light, and small groups of musicians played jigs and airs, fiddlers and pipers accompanied by hand drums. Women stirred large pots of mulled wine and cider over small fires, handing out cups to anyone who wanted them. Others distributed fresh-baked soul cakes, the little spiced raisin cookies only eaten on this day. Colin Hynes the cobbler was dressed as Stingy Jack this year, the con man banned in both heaven and hell for his tricks, which struck Daisy as appropriate casting; he walked through the crowd carrying a carved pumpkin under his arm with a lit candle inside. Behind him slinked a curvaceous young woman, dressed as the deity of death in a black cape and feathered crow's head mask with a carved wooden beak.

"Look, it's the Morrigan!" she said to her twin, who was named after this Celtic goddess.

"My namesake," Morrigan sighed. They had that same exchange every year, but this time, Morrigan looked oddly stricken. With a sharp intake of breath, she clutched Daisy's arm.

Before Daisy could ask what Morrigan had seen, someone called their names. "Good day to you, Mrs. Wolfson, Misses Wolfson," called Mrs. Godwin as her husband even tipped his hat to the girls. It seemed they no longer held Daisy and her sisters accountable for Tabitha's death, or else they had simply forgotten all about the accusations against them.

In fact, everyone seemed to have forgotten everything that had happened in Redcliffe in the past two months, though Daisy hadn't entirely lost her fear of walking through the streets. Ever since that dramatic night on the cliff, the Bleakness had by all reports lifted and vanished as if it had never been. So marked was the change in all of Redcliffe, Daisy was baffled by the quotidian politeness and benevolent warmth on display at the festival. It was a newfound luxury to be able to walk among the townspeople and not be vilified, not met with whispered gossip as people shrank in horror, hurling invectives and threatening violence. Seeing everyone happily gathered together in festivity, faces once again friendly and open, pleasant hellos all around, almost felt too sudden.

"Good day to you too, Mr. and Mrs. Godwin," Daisy called when her mother nudged her.

Avery caught sight of Frankie and rushed off to greet her.

Warming herself at the blazing bonfire with Morrigan, as Henry went to fetch more hot cider, Daisy caught sight of Lizzie Cuttle, now Lizzie Stewart. Before she could avert her gaze, Lizzie noticed and came straight over, her hands protectively cradling her belly as she crossed the green.

"Daisy, Morrigan," she called. "I've been meaning to speak to you."

"Hello, Lizzie," Daisy said with as much calmness as she could muster. The image of Lizzie screeching wordlessly at her, eyes crazed with hatred, was not one she'd easily forget. But everything had changed since then. And Lizzie's behavior hadn't been her fault, after all. The Bleakness cast by the demon had taken hold of her the same as everyone else.

Lizzie's expression was hesitant. "Oh, Daisy, Morrigan." She paused, as though her planned speech had deserted her. "My word, I want to apologize, but I can't quite express it. You and your entire family have been so kind to me, even in my lowest state. And I feel I owe you some kind of..." She trailed off, confusion clouding her face.

"There's no need, Lizzie, I promise," Daisy said, realizing Lizzie couldn't recall what she was sorry for, so effectively had her memory of the events of the Bleakness been erased. "That's all behind us. We're just glad everything has worked out. It has, hasn't it?"

"How is Phineas doing?" Morrigan asked. Since the clifftop ritual, they'd heard nothing of Finny, whom they'd last seen howling off into the night after trying to kill Daisy. "Is he here tonight?"

"Dr. Wellington thinks a month of hard physical work on the Cumberlands' sheep farm will do him good, tending to those gentle animals. He'd been so exhausted from his studies, and then the shock of becoming a husband and soon-to-be father, though he is of course overjoyed." Her words tumbled out in a nervous haste.

"I'm glad to hear it," Daisy said, but privately she had grave doubts that anything good would come of their marriage.

Lizzie pressed one of Daisy's hands between both of hers. "Please call on me," she said. "Your sisters, too!"

Daisy and her twin gaped at one other, watching Lizzie vanish into the throng of merrymakers.

Then Henry was back with cider. Standing there, watching him and Morrigan laugh and chatter together, their faces bathed in the glow of the bonfire, Daisy wondered how everyone could act like this was just a normal Samhain festival. Had even Henry and her family all forgotten that the night of terror had happened only five days ago?

"I need to walk," she announced abruptly.

"But Daisy," Morrigan said anxiously, "you shouldn't—"

"I'll be only a short while," Daisy called back over her shoulder, swiftly crossing the green and continuing at a fast clip along the footpath that ran along the town's northern bluffs. Lit by a sliver of crescent moon, the darkening sea seemed to stretch to meet the violet sky, the horizon invisible in the dusk.

Yet she was overcome by a feverish tangle of thoughts and emotions. This was the same sea that had swallowed up Nate, whose death still gnawed at her conscience. The spear had been meant for her. She wondered what might have happened if she'd been able to save him from the clutches of the demon.

With a sigh, Daisy spun around, intending to return to the festival. Instead, she ran into Jasper, quite literally.

"You!" Daisy cried as he reached out to catch her from bouncing into the wooden rail.

"Sorry," Jasper said tightly, snatching his hands away. "I'll give you privacy."

"*You'll* give *me* privacy?" Daisy said, freshly reminded that she was furious with him. "That's rich."

"Are you saying I haven't given you solitude?" He sounded deeply affronted.

"You've given me solitude all right," she said. "And then some."

"I thought that's what you needed."

"Of course you did. Because you know what everyone needs, always deciding for them, never bothering to ask, just barreling ahead like an arrogant, thickheaded, imperious oaf."

"You barreled into me," Jasper exclaimed.

"You know what I mean!"

"I know many things, Daisy," he said, "but when it comes to the way your mind works, I've got nothing."

"In case you'd care for a jot of insight, let me remind you that sunlight is harmful to Aunt Mary's condition. And if we're going to treat her together, you can't act unilaterally. So in the future, please keep the curtains closed."

"That's a terrible idea," Jasper said. "The constant gloom is deleterious, and the benefits of sunlight upon her spirits vastly outweigh any potential contraindications. You heard her. She can't live like a worm underground forever."

"She's barely recovered. It's too soon."

"That's your opinion."

"Yes," Daisy cried in frustration, "it's my opinion! Which is equal to yours! In case you've forgotten, we are *both* in charge of her treatment. So you have to take it into account!"

"But you don't have to take my opinion into account?"

"I... What do you mean?" Daisy faltered.

"You said it yourself: We're both in charge of her treatment. But you don't listen to my suggestions."

"That's not true!"

"Isn't it? I want the curtains open, you want them closed, but only you can be right, because I'm— What was it? Arrogant, thickheaded, and imperious. Not to mention an oaf."

"Oh." Daisy grimaced, the truth of his words suddenly and painfully undeniable. "I hate that you're right about this."

"I suppose . . . thank you?" Jasper flung his hands in the air and strode off.

"Wait," Daisy cried, "we're not done!"

"Feels like we are," he muttered over his shoulder, continuing down the path toward the other end of the cliff walk.

Daisy followed close behind, but Jasper's strides were so much longer, she had to hurry at a stupid little trot to keep up, flapping at his coattails. The indignity of it revived her outrage. "That's right, run away! It's what you always do!"

He spun to face her. "Is this still about your aunt Mary?"

"No, it's not about my bloody aunt Mary. You can nail her curtains open forever, if that's what it takes to get you to stand still long enough to have a real conversation." They were standing close together, both breathing hard. Jasper's jaw was set, but Daisy stared right back up at him, her feet planted with equal stubbornness.

"Fine," he said through clenched teeth. "Say what you need to say."

"I'm sorry I couldn't save Nate."

He gave a startled cough. "What?"

"I said—"

"I heard you." Jasper turned to brace himself against the railing, staring out across the sea. "Nate was in the grips of a grave illness." He spoke dispassionately, as though consulting a stranger's medical chart. "I saw it come over him these past months but didn't understand the sheer scope of the damage to his brain until that horrible night. The strain of the guilt over what he'd done to that poor woman in the clinic, as well as to my own father, aggravated the pernicious symptoms of what was clearly the latter stages of brain disease, a lunacy much like Griesinger's description of 'dementia paralytica,' an unavoidable consequence of his careless lifestyle." Jasper might have been commenting on the weather, so impersonal was his tone.

"Nate was possessed by a demon," Daisy said just as evenly, "the same one that caused this town to go mad."

"That's one way to describe a sickness of the mind, though I'll have you know that modern medical science no longer believes demon possession causes insanity."

"He wasn't insane, he was— Oh, you know what? Never mind what we call Nate's ailment. What's important is you understand that I only meant to free him."

Jasper nodded, but his face remained shuttered.

"And even though Nate was possessed"—Daisy put up a hand to stop Jasper from interrupting—"whether by a malevolent entity *or* a rot of the brain, he at least broke free in the end." She pressed on, her throat tight, eyes smarting. "I'm just so very sorry that he died in the process."

"He shouldn't have," Jasper said. "When I jumped between you and that pike, I never thought Nate would take the brunt of it for both of us. Perhaps he could have been treated at a sanitarium."

Daisy opened her mouth to speak, but Jasper silenced her with a sharp look. "There's no good ending here," he said, starting back down the path again. "Just let it be. I'll be gone in the morning."

Daisy glared at his retreating back, unable to tell if she was angrier at his proud obstinacy or her inability to make herself clear.

And then it hit her. It was like Frankie's reading all over again. She had to be willing to be open and vulnerable herself to crack through his own defenses. But how to do that when he was so damnably frustrating? "You infuriating man," she yelled after him. "Why do you refuse to see what's right in front of you?"

Jasper whirled around, eyes blazing. "I only see you, Daisy!"

"Yes, exactly!"

"For the love of all that is holy," he said, stalking back over to her, "what are you talking about?"

Daisy grasped his arms to hold him in place. "What I'm talking about, Jasper, is that I care about you."

A muscle jumped in his jaw as he stood there, unyielding. "I don't need your pity, not for the brother lost, nor for the love of the woman who was never mine for the winning."

"You really think I'm a fool, don't you?" Daisy said despairingly. "You don't respect me at all."

"I tried to die for you, Daisy," Jasper cried. "I can't think how to express my respect any more directly than that."

"Then listen to me, for god's sake. I'm trying to tell you I love you, you high-handed knucklehead! I've loved you from the moment we met, just over two months ago, in High Street, when you told me you hated doughnuts, which would have ruled you out of my affections for all eternity if I hadn't assumed you were only saying that to be rude, because to not like doughnuts is the most ridiculous thing in the entire world, and also unforgiveable. In fact, for a little while I even thought *you* were the demon, if you can believe it, because that was the only explanation I could think of for how you made the skin at the back of my neck tingle!"

"Let me get this straight," Jasper said. "You thought I was a demon—a concept I don't even entirely accept as a factual possibility but will briefly entertain for the sake of argument—because I said I didn't like doughnuts and made your skin tingle, or because you think I *do* like doughnuts but lied about not liking them as a ruse to get under your skin . . . that I made tingle?" The shadow of a smile lurked in the corner of his mouth.

How *dare* he smile. Daisy glared up at him.

"By your own logic, that makes *you* the demon," he added, eyes glinting.

"Wait, what?" But now she was smiling, too.

"That, or a rake." He grinned wickedly. "Do you see how you've maneuvered me, an unmarried man, into a compromising position, unchaperoned, alone with you on a cliff overlooking the sea, with all this talk of sugared pastry and tingling skin?" As if to underscore the point, Jasper raised a hand to brush an errant strand of hair from her face, allowing his thumb to rest a moment against her cheek before withdrawing it.

But the warmth of his touch lingered, leaving Daisy suffused with heat. "There's no need to blame the doughnuts." Her insides had gone molten. "Or me."

"I do apologize," he murmured. "To you both."

The air between them seemed to shift, charged and expectant as the thrill that surged through Daisy's body. With a pounding heart, and before doubt could creep in, she reached up and pulled Jasper's head down toward her, fingers curling into the unruly dark strands of his hair, and briefly but firmly pressed her lips to his. His breath hitched, and for a heartbeat he froze, just as he had when Daisy had impulsively pecked him on the cheek that evening in the street a fortnight before. But then, straightening slightly, as if coming to a decision, he looped his hands around her waist, lifted her lightly so that her feet rested atop his, drew her closer, and claimed her mouth with a kiss of his own.

They melted together, hungrily kissing each other with primal urgency, their breath mingling, warm and uneven. The world around them faded—the crash of waves against the cliffs, the tang of sea air, the muted din of the festival—all of it dissolved into the moment. They clung together, bodies molded in a long line, insensible to anything but each other.

Voices suddenly rang out nearby, and they leapt apart just as a group of townspeople rounded the corner of the pathway.

"Nice night for a walk," said one of the ladies, giggling with her friends as they swept past.

Daisy and Jasper both opened their mouths at the same time, but whatever they were going to say was lost in the crack of fireworks suddenly exploding above them. Daisy laughed, both in delight at the display and in rueful awareness that she was living the cliched embodiment of her widowed aunt's not-so-secret collection of women's romance novels. Would she tell her sisters? Oh, probably. Chuckling to herself, she laced her fingers through Jasper's and gazed up at the multicolored sky, basking in the reflected glow of the vivid explosions. Lights painted the night with a spray of kaleidoscopic jewels that streaked through the air, trailing streamers of fire behind them, the dazzling rain of embers evaporating as they fell through the trees, dissolving like candied dreams in the darkness.

Epilogue

November 1, 1848, Redcliffe, Massachusetts. Just after midnight.

Daisy slides into the bed she shares with Morrigan, still charged with elation. The simmering cinders in the grate are like the soft, silent afterglow of the fiery explosions in the sky. There's a quiet hiss as the logs settle, a sigh of embers turning to ash and sifting through the andirons, dropping onto the tiles.

"Where did you disappear to?" Morrigan mumbles, half asleep. "You and Jasper came back to the festival looking awfully happy."

"Happy," Avery snorts from her own bed across the room. "More like radiant. Have you two finally finished arguing?"

"No," Daisy says, laughing. "I doubt we ever will."

And then the room goes silent as her sisters slip into sleep, and Daisy sinks down into slumber herself, through endless layers of joy.

Hours later, Morrigan bolts upright, her face a mask of terror.

"Aileth," she breathes.

And then with a gasp, she collapses back onto her pillow, senseless to the night, eyes wide but unseeing.

But Aileth sees Morrigan. It is such a relief to finally hear her name spoken aloud after so very long. To exist within her true self at last, if only in this slip of a girl's mind. Soon, she will stand on her own. And this time, she will not be denied her satisfaction.

Sleep now my little doves, *Aileth hisses.* **While you still can.**

Acknowledgments

WITH OVERFLOWING THANKS TO:

Melissa de la Cruz, for setting us alight with her original idea and inviting us into her amazing imprint, Melissa de la Cruz Studio. Thank you for sharing the magic!

Richard Abate at 3Arts, who put everything in motion and made it all happen. And his right-hand woman, the stellar Hannah Carande, who steadied us many times.

Our editor at Hyperion, Brittany Rubiano, whose astute edits and insights made this a far better book than it would have been otherwise.

Kaitlyn Nagler, Lara Santoro, and Kelly Buchan, for providing essential tips on astrology and helping us navigate the stars as we charted the path of our plucky heroines.

Early readers Art Hanlon, Mary Ann Troiano Hanlon, and Cheryl Noyes, for their cheerleading and whip-smart notes.

Brendan and Joe, for reading countless drafts, offering always-insightful feedback, and keeping us going with never-ending cups of coffee (Brendan) and tea (Joe).

Each other—who knew it could be so rewarding to co-write a book together! We're especially proud to have made it to the other side with minimal bloodshed and our friendship not only intact but stronger than ever. Work should not be this much fun.